HER QUIET PLACE

ROBERT W. KIRBY

(eBook): B0FGV5S956
ISBN (Paperback): 978-1-7399750-4-3
ISBN (Hardback): 978-1-7399750-5-0

Her Quiet Place is a work of fiction. People, places, events, and situations are products of the author's imagination. Any resemblance to actual persons, living or dead, is entirely coincidental.

This book contains graphic violence, strong language, drug use and disturbing scenes, including themes of suicide and self-harm.

1

PROLOGUE

Time stood still as she gazed at the crumpled body in front of her and the pretty face now broken because of her actions.

A voice in her head spoke to her as if stuck on a ceaseless loop.

What have you done? What have you done?

She stumbled and let the hammer fall from her grasp.

It's all over. Everything has been destroyed.

She gently touched the battered face. As she examined the damage she'd caused, a dreadful hysteria threatened to seize her, and she understood immediately that there could be no coming back from this. Her blood fizzed, and her entire body shuddered as a feverish ferocity took hold.

'No, please don't let this be happening!' she screamed, placing her hand over her mouth and gagging, but the realisation that she'd smeared blood all over her face made her gag some more. She wiped her face with the back of her left hand but knew she'd only spread the gore further, and this made her sob.

She stood, stumbled and dropped to her knees, grabbing at handfuls of dead grass and tugging them up. Then, throwing the grass tufts aside and screaming in a violent rage, she hammered both fists against the ground. She thumped until her knuckles were raw and bloodied.

Once again, she gazed back to view the damage. She saw the long gouge above her right eyebrow glistening white where the skull was now exposed.

She'd hit hard. Hit with all her force. She'd heard an almighty crack when that hammer had connected.

She pulled herself up but stumbled backwards and fell onto her backside. 'This is your fault!' she roared. She found her feet and retrieved the hammer.

'I'm going to hell for this. I'm going to be dragged there by the devil himself. And I'm taking you with me!'

There was no undoing it now. She'd gone too far this time. *Way too far.*

2

HANNAH WATKINS

January 2023

As the train hurtled below, the bridge vibrated underneath Hannah. She leaned on the railing and stood on tiptoes as she peered down, watching the train speed off along the tracks. The area lay between a run-down park and a derelict industrial area just outside of Edmonton, North London. A bridge to nowhere. Why he had picked this spot as the place to spend his last moments on earth sure was a mystery to her.

She viewed the discarded bottles alongside the tracks, the tatty plastic shopping bags hanging from the grime-covered bushes, and the rotting sheets of wood propped up against dreary-looking trees. This sure would be the last place she'd want to be when it all came to an end.

Hannah had told herself so many times that she'd never return here. She'd probably tell herself the same thing again after she'd left today. But she'd be lying to herself. Something kept drawing her back.

A rattling noise pulled her attention away from the tracks.

Just an empty soft drink can rolling in the breeze.

What answers did she expect to find by coming to this depressing place?

Like she always did, she tried hard to get into his muddled mindset during those last few seconds after he clambered up and stood balancing on the thin railing, listening for the distant rumble and judging how far away the train was, while estimating the short timeframe between the fall and the impact. There would have been a few hideous moments after he'd landed on the tracks before the train would've struck him. A horrifying moment to contemplate his decision before that train ploughed into him and his lights went out for good.

Would time have slowed in those few seconds? She prayed it hadn't.

She pulled her parka jacket around herself and flipped up the faux fur hood as an icy wind whipped across the bridge. Her misted, white breath swirled in front of her.

She gazed across to the industrial units that were all fenced off with high metal barriers. It appeared as though it was possible to access the road leading through the units and she decided that, for once, she'd go that way and see where it led.

Hannah took the steps down into the industrial park and headed into the disused stretch of land, and all she could think about was how badly she needed another drink.

After entering the area, she decided that this desolate corner of the world would serve as a perfect movie setting for a chilling post-apocalyptic thriller. Her hands were shaking as she stepped around some rusty oil drums and a scattering of jagged metal poles.

She didn't get far before she stopped, turned and focused on the bridge walkway. And she could picture him up there now. Wearing his crumpled, grey suit with his shirt untucked. His dishevelled hair blowing in the breeze. The image became so crystal clear in her head it made her choke down a wheezy sob.

She kept dreaming of this. Him being here. Just drifting around. Lost and confused, as if trapped at this spot. In the last drug-induced nightmare, she'd been staring down on those tracks, and he'd been on the line, gazing back up at her. She was never able to get a read on his expression. What was he trying to tell her? Every time she dreamed this, the train would speed out of the tunnel, and she'd watch as those endless carriages rumbled along. Once it had finally passed, he'd be gone, and she'd wake up gasping for air and slick with oily sweat.

Now, closing her eyes, Hannah told herself again she had to put a stop to these morbid visits. When she opened her eyes a few seconds later, she heard another train racing along the tracks, and she told herself that there was nothing for her here. She was just punishing herself.

But perhaps that was the whole point.

3

ROSIE GRIMSHAW

August 1993

Rosie watched as Chloe made the final dash to the hill's summit. She let out a shrieky laugh and waved her hands. The climb had been tough going, and it had become a fun race to the top, though she was happy to let the other girl win. She didn't want to turn this little jaunt into a competition.

The sight before them left her best friend dumbfounded, and she appeared unable to find the right words to describe the beautiful scene. Rosie had bleated on about how fabulous this place was for ages. Now, at long last, she was getting to share this amazing location with Chloe, and the moment felt rather special.

'Well?' asked Rosie.

They stood smiling as they soaked up the panoramic view, eyeing the sweeping hills and blankets of greenery that continued as far as the eye could see.

'Somewhere over there is Stonehenge. Some of the land to the east is an army training ground, so we can't venture over there,' said Rosie.

As Chloe took in a deep breath of air, Rosie decided she had never seen her friend look so alive. She wore skimpy, ripped denim shorts and a purple crop top. She had square sunglasses perched on her head that were a similar colour to her top. They were only cheap things, but as with anything she wore, they looked smart on her.

Rosie removed some strands of hair from her eyes. 'Quite something, isn't it?'

Chloe sat down and crossed her legs. 'I thought you were exaggerating about this place. Sure beats London.'

Rosie tugged down her white summer dress and knelt next to her. She cleared her throat, a little cross at Chloe's words. Did her friend think she was some kind of liar? She decided not to let that get to her, or speak her mind, concerned that it might ruin the moment.

Chloe put her hands on the grass behind her and leaned back, putting her head into the air as the breeze made her light auburn hair quiver gracefully. 'You're so lucky. I'm mega jealous.'

'You have three weeks here, so enjoy every minute.'

'I cannot believe your parents agreed to let me stay here with you guys.'

'Oh yeah, they are the best,' said Rosie with a wide grin, not wanting to reveal that getting her parents on board with her idea had been ridiculously hard work. She'd had to nag them for days before they'd agreed to let Chloe join them on their annual summer break. She'd even had a crying fit and said if her friend wasn't coming, she'd refuse to leave with them. When, after all that effort, Chloe had said she wouldn't be coming, she'd been gutted.

'Because I always get the impression that your parents are not keen on me. Especially your mum.'

'What? Are you nuts? They were super keen. They were really disappointed when I told them you weren't able to come,' lied Rosie.

'Ah, that's sweet. Although she came across a bit stunned when she answered the door just now, and it seemed like you

7

were pretty keen to get me away from that cabin as fast as possible.'

'I'm sure she was just surprised you'd managed to find us. It's not exactly the easiest of places to get to.'

'You're telling me. Had to get directions from some old farmer.'

'How did you get your dad to change his mind?' Rosie asked quickly, wanting to divert the conversation away from her parents.

'Can I be honest with you?'

'Of course you can.'

'I never asked him in the first place.'

'But—'

'Yeah, I know what I told you. But when you said I could come for real, I'd not been expecting it, so I panicked. I just told you I'd already mentioned it to him, and he'd said no.'

'Why?'

'Because he's a total killjoy arsewipe, that's why. He would have said no anyway. So I couldn't be bothered to go through all that shit with him. I wasn't prepared to beg and belittle myself, when the end result would still have been a big fat no.' Chloe put her sunglasses on and wiggled them into place. 'The night before you left, I started getting annoyed about missing out. That's why I phoned you and asked for the address. I did say I might make a surprise appearance in a couple of days.'

'Yeah, I didn't really think you'd follow through with that idea. I assumed you were...'

'Assumed what? That I was talking shit?'

'No, I assumed you were trying to make me feel better about cancelling.'

Chloe grinned. 'I don't lie to my friends.'

Rosie stood and rubbed off the grass that was clinging to her knees, still a little confused by what she was hearing. And Chloe didn't lie to her friends? That was rich, considering the whopper she'd just admitted to.

Chloe stretched out her legs and tilted her head back, basking

8

in the sun. 'Then I thought, screw it. I left him a note, swagged some of his cash, packed a bag… and here I am.'

'Chloe!'

'What?'

'Are you saying you've run away? Does he even know where you are right now?'

'I explained that I'm taking a trip for three weeks and that if he's got a problem with that, then tough titties!'

'This is so bad.'

'It's cool.'

'There's no phone at the cabin, but there's a phone box in Little Wick by the post office. How about I ask Mum to speak to him and explain everything?'

'Calm down, girl. It's fine.'

'It's not fine. You've practically run away from home!'

'Don't be so dramatic. Look, I've merely taken a holiday. I'm sixteen. I am allowed to take a break.'

'Are you hearing yourself? Your dad will go out of his mind with worry. He's probably already called the police.'

Chloe giggled. 'You're so funny when you get worked up. You should see your little face. It's all scrunched up like an angry pixie's. Rosie, you'll get wrinkle lines. Chill.'

Rosie let out a long, groaning sigh.

'Don't get yourself in a flap. I have done this before. He won't call the police. Trust me on that. A man like my dad, he doesn't get the law involved. They would likely nick him because he's always up to no good.'

'Won't he come searching for you?'

'No way. He's not that proactive, and he wouldn't be able to find me here. I will be in for the bollocking of a lifetime when I return. He'll tell me I'm grounded for months. He might even give me a good whack. Big deal. It'll be worth it.'

Rosie gazed back out at the sweeping landscape and tried to process everything. How did her friend manage to be so laid-back about all this? How could she be so callous to believe her dad wouldn't be worried sick about her?

Chloe got to her feet and joined her. 'I get you're uncomfortable about the situation. You would never do something like this. You're not that person, but you need to understand that things are different for me. The relationship I have with my dad is complex. Look, I didn't travel on that stuffy bus and come all this way out here to talk about him. Let me worry about my dad. I want to have fun. With you. So please get over this already. You're bringing the vibe down.'

'Fine, I won't mention it again.'

'Promise?'

'Yes.'

'Good. Now, what about this place you've told me about, like, a million times?'

'I'm saving that for when the time is just right.'

'Ooh, I'm thrilled that I'm finally going to get the chance to see this famous quiet spot of yours.' Chloe nudged Rosie with her shoulder. 'It better be as marvellous as you say. I have high expectations, girl.'

'You pack a swimming costume?'

'Nope. If it's as quiet as you say, then that won't matter.'

'Chloe!'

Chloe winked at her. 'Come on. Let's go into the village and get some booze for later. I spied a shop on my way through. Reckon we might be able to lift some if we play it right.'

'We will not.'

'Then we'll ask some old fart to get it for us. But, if that's how you want to play it, you're paying.'

They linked arms and started down the steep hill.

Although the circumstances of her friend's arrival were concerning, Rosie still felt so excited she could pop. She was now optimistic about this holiday. With her best friend at her side, this would be the most amazing summer break ever. And she hadn't even told her the best bit yet. In a couple of days, she had an epic surprise in store for her.

4

LOUISA HUDSON

February 2023

Where the hell did you come from? The monstrous red spot above Louisa's top lip was a serious cause for concern. Could this be the start of a spell of acute acne? Would she wake up in the morning with more of the unsightly things all over her face?

Louisa tied back her tangly hair into a ponytail using a red band and scrutinised herself in the dressing table mirror. She pouted her lips, but the spot was still noticeable. It probably would be visible from Mars, the size of it.

Her phone buzzed again for what seemed like the hundredth time that afternoon. Estelle wasn't giving up that easily. But, like all the previous calls and messages, she ignored it.

It buzzed again. Voicemail now. Her friend must be getting annoyed if she was bothering to leave voice messages.

Louisa played it.

'Lou, you better have a good reason to be ignoring me all day. I'm talking about some major life-threatening situation going down. You better have been kidnapped by an Albanian trafficking gang or something. WhatsApp me so we can organise shit. You can come to mine and get ready. Or, I dunno, maybe I'll come to yours if I'm allowed entry into the Hudson residence.' She gave a horse-like laugh. 'I won't hold my breath. Just stop pissing around already. Ash and his mate want to take us for a spin. Guess you remember Taylor? The one who we stalked online. Him! Yup, you heard me right. Tick-fucking-tock. Clock's ticking, bitch. Don't let me down and miss out on yet another decent night. Ciao for now!'

After deleting the message, Louisa puffed out her cheeks and scanned her bedroom. For a start, Estelle would *not* be setting foot in here. The girlish decor made the place look like it belonged to a ten-year-old princess. She'd never live it down if her new friend got a glimpse of this eyesore. She picked up her yellow, plush dinosaur and stared at it. 'I mean, this is what I'm talking about. Just look at you.' She let out a long, deflating sigh as she studied the toy. Its mouth was open, and with its ridiculous zipped gob, it almost appeared as though the stupid thing was laughing at her.

'We need to make some huge changes around here, you yellow loser. Yeah, I'm talking to you, Herbert Crunch.' Louisa zipped up the dinosaur's mouth and tossed it onto her bed, which was covered in even more soft toys and plump bears. And as for that lousy rainbow and butterflies quilt cover. God, she'd only asked her mum about twenty times to get her a less childish one. What did a girl have to do around here to get her parents to listen to her? Then she caught an eyeful of the real highlight in her room. That three-dimensional wall art. A garish flamingo with a crown perched upon its stupid, large pink head. The urge to right-hook the annoying bird straight off the wall became more and more tempting with each passing day. Two long years she'd had to put up with that beady-eyed creep looming over her. Her mum loved the ridiculous thing, but she hated it. She huffed and grumbled as she fingered the painful spot again. Pushing it hard, as if that might somehow help remove it. But the blemish was the least of her problems, she knew. She was unable to muster the courage to message Estelle to tell her that, once again, she was going to be the massive let-down. That, as per usual, she would not be granted permission to come out at the weekend.

Louisa whacked the palms of her hands on the dressing table and knocked over her deodorant and hairspray. Friends like Estelle wouldn't wait for long. She'd be able to replace Louisa at the drop of a hat because she had loads of decent people to hang out with.

But how on earth would she convince her parents, or more importantly her dad, to allow her to go out all night on a Saturday?

Louisa eyed her reflection in the mirror and grimaced at the pale, sullen face peering back at her. Quite simply, she wouldn't be able to convince them.

5

HANNAH

April 2023

'What did you take, Hannah?' asked a deep voice. 'Hannah? Can you hear me? Stay with me.'

Hannah's eyes flickered as the harsh lights burned into her brain. She realised she was in the back of an ambulance.

'What did you take?' repeated the voice.

A paramedic.

Her eyes adjusted to the harsh lighting. The paramedic was a stocky man with cropped grey hair and a deep scar under his left eye.

Hannah tried to sit up, but her head spun, so she stayed put. 'What happened?'

'You collapsed outside the Grape and Hops. The bartender called it in.'

'Huh, I don't recall that.'

'I want to check your blood pressure. Do you have any pain in your head? Apparently, you went down hard.'

Hannah realised she had an oxygen clip on her index finger. 'I don't think so. I'm not in any pain. Just fuzzy.'

'You sure? Let's pop this cuff on you there,' he said, placing the material around her left bicep. 'Have you been drinking?'

'I've had a few.'

'Is there a chance someone put something in your drink?'

'Not that I'm aware of. Though, I guess that would be the point. But no, I'd say that was unlikely.'

'Any medication?'

'Cipralex.'

'Anything else?'

'No,' she lied, not wanting to mention the benzos she regularly scored from the dodgy website she'd been lucky enough to find last year.

'OK, and how much would you say you've had to drink tonight?'

Hannah felt the pressure around her bicep as the cuff enclosed around her limb. 'I think... well, I'd say eight or nine vodkas.'

The paramedic let out a heavy sigh. 'Your doctor should've warned you about drinking on those meds. That's not a good idea.'

'Yeah, she may have mentioned it. This isn't the first time I've mixed those pills with alcohol,' said Hannah, almost adding, *It's actually a daily occurrence.* 'I have never encountered any issues before, save a little drowsiness from time to time.'

'You're not doing yourself any favours. Mixing the two has likely caused you to pass out. You're very lucky you were in a public place.'

The cuff's pressure eased, and he removed it.

'Working alone tonight?' asked Hannah, trying to shift the subject away from her bad habits.

'My colleague is across the road at a kebab house. Some guy almost sliced off two fingers by falling through a glass pane, so she's seeing to that.'

'Sounds like a busy night.'

'Yep.'

'I should probably let you get off and assist with that. I'm sure I'll be fine. I'm feeling better already.'

'Yes, but I'll be the judge of that. Your blood pressure is quite high, and I'd like to check your head. I want to be sure you didn't give yourself a whack.'

'Sure, knock yourself out.'

The paramedic raised his eyebrows and cracked a wide smile. 'I always get the comedians.'

'Laughter is the best medicine.'

'Can you sit up for me, please?'

Hannah did as he requested, and once she was looking away from the man, her smile faded. She was good at acting the joker in front of company. She found it easy to hide the anguish continuously burning inside her. How she hated people to see she was struggling.

Hannah didn't need anyone's help. Alcohol was her only escape from the misery of her life. OK, it only dulled the pain, but she'd take that.

The paramedic examined her head and she flinched.

'A bit tender on that spot?' he asked.

'A bit. What's the worst thing you've ever witnessed in this job?'

'You really want to know?'

Hannah shook her head and an image of her dead husband flashed in her mind. Not that she knew what he looked like afterwards.

'I have no idea how you do what you do,' said Hannah quietly.

'I often ask myself the same question.'

Hannah was unable to view her husband and identify the body. There'd been little left of him *to* view. But that didn't stop her from imagining. That didn't stop her mind from creating those terrible images. Every single day.

Almost two years ago. What had she done with herself in that time? What else, other than wallowing in a drink-fuelled sadness?

'It looks OK,' said the paramedic.

Hannah smiled her thanks.

But what else was there to do when your life felt so pointless and empty?

6

ROSIE

August 1993

Rosie was getting worried as her friend studied the small room with a disgruntled frown. Had Chloe expected more? Hadn't the cabin lived up to her expectations? Perhaps she'd exaggerated how great this place was.

Chloe sat down on the sofa bed and chewed her lower lip as she continued to scan her surroundings. It appeared as though she was trying to decide if she could bring herself to endure three weeks of this place. She coughed and bounced up and down on the sofa, making the springs squeak in protest under her weight. 'And I have to sleep here, on this thing?' she asked as she sniffed the air and crinkled her nose. 'Does it smell damp in here?'

'It doesn't look it, but, you mark my words, that sofa is surprisingly comfy once it's all pulled out.'

'I'll swap you for your single then.'

'And I have extra pillows in that cupboard. We'll make your bed super snuggly,' said Rosie in a rushed, upbeat voice. She needed to divert the discussion away from the sleeping arrangements, as she had no desire to spend the entire holiday on a lumpy sofa bed. 'Think of it like posh camping. It'll be so fun. You like camping, right? Everyone likes camping.'

'Mm,' said Chloe, looking unconvinced and ignoring her question. 'We don't have a light? Is there no power here?'

'We have gas lamps and candles. Cool, right? We have a log burner in the living area. And running water.'

Chloe laughed. 'Is that what you call it? I'd describe it more like a dingy, ramshackle shed. And I didn't see a TV. Is there a TV?'

Rosie shook her head. 'But we'll be out exploring and having fun, so we don't need a silly TV.'

'Right. No TV. OK.'

'We won't be in here much. Just for food and nap time.'

'How are we supposed to cook if the place has no electricity?'

'Oh, don't worry, we have a proper cooker that's hooked up to big gas bottles. It's fantastic. But we won't be cooking.'

'I see.'

'My dad doesn't like anyone else touching the gas cooker. He deals with that.'

'That toilet isn't so great, either. Is that flush powerful enough to tackle solids?'

Rosie nodded, not wanting to tell her friend that often a big bucket of water was required to clear most large deposits. She was feeling quite embarrassed about this place now. 'Don't you like it here, Chloe?'

'No, yeah, I mean, I do like the cabin. I think I'm just surprised. It's a bit more… basic than I'd been expecting.'

'Is it? Sorry.'

'No, I mean, it's smart. Like, rustic and a little gloomy but still smart. Nah, it's pretty cool. A little spooky, kooky den. Could still be fun.'

Rosie chewed over the words Chloe had used. *Damp. Basic. Gloomy. Spooky.* Was the cabin spooky? She'd been coming here for years, so she was used to the old place.

'I'm not so sure your parents *are* too pleased about me

coming here. I mean, shit, are you sure you even asked them? Cos they keep gawping at me like I'm a burglar.'

Rosie cringed. Chloe had spoken in her normal voice, not even bothering to be discreet. Didn't she know these walls were super thin?

'And your mum gave me a stare like I'd taken a big turd on the carpet when I used the bog. Mardy-faced old goat.'

'Like I already said. She *does* like you. They both do,' said Rosie in a fast whisper. 'They prefer to keep themselves to themselves because they are very private.'

Chloe chuckled. 'Yeah, maybe your dad likes me. I clocked him eyeing me up. Probably why your old dear was scowling at me.' She lowered her voice and said, 'She needn't worry herself because balding, middle-aged blokes with hairy beer bellies don't do it for me.' She playfully wiggled her eyebrows. 'Unless I'm mega pissed, then I do lower my standards.'

'Pillows! I'll find those pillows! Yes, let's find those pillows for you,' said Rosie, desperate to veer the conversation away from her parents.

Chloe laughed out loud. 'Your face. Oh, you make it too easy for me to tease you. They both went out five minutes ago. They can't hear me, you dozy twiglet.'

Rosie let out a relieved giggle, pleased to learn that her parents were not in earshot. But the name, *dozy twiglet*, really got under her skin. She hated being called that.

7

LOUISA

3rd May 2023

Louisa had a nosy around the room, observing that the dining table had been extended and set for a family dinner. Her mum had gone all out with the fancy tablecloth tonight. Woodland green, as she liked to call it. Not a single crease on it. The cutlery had been positioned methodically and glasses set out. She caught the whiff of freshly-baked bread, garlic, and a hint of cinnamon. Someone had been a busy bee today.

Louisa found her mum in the kitchen, perched on a tall leather stool. Her dark, shoulder-length hair looked immaculate and glossy under the bright kitchen lighting. She'd dyed it yet again. She wore a long, pale-blue dress with a single strap over one shoulder, fastened by a gold clasp. She caught the sweet smell of perfume. Paco Rabanne's Fame, if she wasn't mistaken. Her mum's absolute favourite. Anyone seeing her mum now would assume she was setting off to a fancy restaurant or to some glitzy function. They'd laugh if they knew she'd got glammed up like this for dinner with her family.

Louisa stood behind her mum, watching her. She'd not seen

her yet, and she sat dreamily staring into space, fingering her wedding ring with a lazy smile on her face.

'Hey, Mum. Bread smells awesome.'

Her mum spun the stool around, gave her a charming smile and said, 'I've made cinnamon and raisin buns.'

'Dad's favourite.'

'Well, he doesn't mind them.'

'Special occasion?' asked Louisa, referring to the dress. She guessed it wasn't.

'It's nice to glam up a bit sometimes.'

Louisa gave her a tight smile.

'It's just an old dress from the back of my wardrobe,' she said in a self-deprecating manner as she smoothed down the silky material.

'Looks like you've gone to quite the effort.'

'Why not lose those fluffy pyjamas and put on something else?'

'No, you're all right, Mum. It's six o'clock and I can't be bothered.'

'Go on. Untie your knotty hair and tidy it up a bit. I'll brush it if you like. Make you all spruce and lovely.'

'Why? What's the point?'

Her mum pulled a silly face and pinched her cheek. 'So we all look nice for your father. You can't sit at the dinner table in your scruffy pyjamas.'

'Why not? And why all the effort? I mean, isn't this all a bit much for a weekday dinner?'

'What are you talking about? A bit of glazed salmon and some homemade bread. It's hardly going over the top. You'll understand one day when you're older.'

Louisa grimaced. *God, I hope not*, she thought. She had no desire to get into these odd little rituals for anybody. Stuck in a rut and slaving over some grumpy man who would never appreciate all the effort anyway. 'Jamie doesn't eat salmon.'

'Your brother pretends he is a big fuss-bag, but he secretly isn't.'

'He sure does a brilliant job of pretending.'

Her mum flashed her a wistful smile and twisted the ring again. It was as if she had to keep checking it was still attached to her finger. As if she did this subconsciously.

Sometimes, Louisa wanted to scream at her mum for all the trouble she went to. Because she knew her dad didn't value her mum's endeavours, and it grated on her. 'Mum, why does Dad never wear his wedding ring? I mean, you never take yours off.'

'He keeps his in a safe place. Upstairs. In his bedside table.'

'But he never puts it on.'

'He does sometimes. You need to understand the world your father lives in. He's pitted against ruthless individuals who seek any weakness as a way to hurt him. It is common for police officers not to wear them.'

'That's what you are? A weakness?'

'Correction. We're all a weakness to him. Now come on, my squishy little mushroom, let's do something with that messy hair of yours. It's driving me a little bonkers here.'

'Mum, enough with the pet names. I'll be sixteen soon. I'm not a toddler.'

Her mum pressed Louisa's nose. 'Beep, beep. I'm well aware you're growing up, my little sausage roll. But no dinner until we make you look pretty.'

'Thanks a bunch.'

'You know what I mean.'

Louisa sighed. 'Fine, but I want to go out with my friends on Saturday. Cinema and some food after.'

'Perhaps. We will see what your father says about that.'

'I'll be back by eleven at the latest.'

'I'm not sure we can agree to that.'

'Mum, come on. I'm losing my friends because of my lack of social commitment. I need to interact with my peers outside of school.'

'Listen to you. What on earth are you talking about?'

'I'm never allowed to go anywhere. That's what I'm talking about.'

'You have all the time in the world to be a grown up. Why are you in such a big rush? Hey, why are you so desperate to grow up, silly socks?'

'Look... I just... Can you stop patronising me? Please.' Louisa took a moment to collect her thoughts and set her head straight before she lost her cool. 'I just want a bit more freedom. That's all. Is that so much to ask for?'

Her mum offered her a simpering smile by way of response.

'Is it?'

'My baby girl thinks she's all grown up already.' She pressed Louisa's nose again and in a silly voice said, 'It's very sweet. Yet a little scary.'

Louisa screamed inside but kept her face impassive. 'So? Can you at least think about it?'

'I can't make that call, squishy chops. I just can't,' she said and again twisted her wedding ring.

8

HANNAH

Hannah heard muffled voices and woke up. Through her blurred vision, she tried to focus and recall where she was right now. For a moment, she considered she'd nodded off in front of the television and was slumped on the sofa. She soon dismissed that idea once she spotted the rows of spirits, glass shelves that housed mixers, and several beer pumps. The voices were getting irate. Two men were arguing right by her. She rubbed her eyes and tried to focus. Her surroundings were unfamiliar.

'I saw you. Saw you with my own eyes, so don't bullshit me over this. I wasn't bloody born yesterday, mate,' said one of the men, an Australian with more than a hint of sarcasm in his tone.

'Leave off. I was just picking it up,' came another man's voice. This one was a cocky, South London accent. 'It ain't your business.'

'I'm making it my business,' replied the Australian firmly.

'I'm telling you I just picked it up from down there,' growled the other man.

Most of the day was a blur, but Hannah had a fuzzy recollection of stumbling upon this dodgy drinking den. At her local haunt, they'd started becoming a tad judgy regarding her drinking habits of late, and not wanting to be seen as the bar's resident wino, she'd started seeking pastures new.

'This drunk slag dropped it,' said the cocky man.

Hannah grasped that she was the "drunk slag" the man had referred to. Not the most affectionate term of devotion she'd ever received, yet she was way too groggy to scold him for the offensive comment.

'Sling your hook, you gobby knobhead,' said the Australian. He was a thickset man in his late forties with wiry, grey hair and an unkempt beard. Hannah realised the barman had her black handbag clutched against his chest, as if protecting it from the other man.

Hannah stole a glance at this other guy. He was tall and had a narrow, mean face. He caught her eye, and she immediately averted her gaze from his belligerent stare.

'Oi, you! Tell him you dropped it, and I was just picking it up,' the young man demanded.

Hannah said nothing and gazed around, still trying to get her head straight.

The barman snorted out a sarcastic laugh. 'Look, mate, I'm not going to keep repeating myself. I want you out. I saw you rifling through this lady's stuff, so beat it.'

'Fuck off,' retorted the man. 'I ain't leaving, bruv.'

'Is there some kind of problem here?' came another man's voice. This one sounded level and loaded with confidence and authority.

The barman stood tall, clearly emboldened by this new arrival. 'Hey, you OK there, DI Hudson? A bit of an issue here. I caught this mutt trying to pinch from this lovely lady. Now he won't leave.'

The young man glared at the barman before swigging his drink and weighing up the newcomer. It was obvious the barman had deliberately referred to the man as a DI.

'Oh, come on, Squid, you can call me Max. I'm off duty,' said the man.

Hannah glanced at the new arrival. The guy was over six feet, with wide shoulders and cropped, brownish hair that had a few flecks of grey at the sides. His chiselled face was deadpan as he stood there, eyeing the young lad with cool-blue eyes that were as hard as granite.

'I think it's time you left now,' said this Max. He spoke in a calm voice that had a strict edge. 'And if you stole anything, I suggest you hand it back.'

The young man jutted his pointy chin and eyed Max with contempt. It was clear he wanted to dispute the matter further. But it was also clear he was apprehensive of the threat from this bigger guy, who now fixed him with a flinty gaze. At this, the younger guy kept swallowing as he appeared to deliberate his next move.

Max folded his powerful-looking arms and nodded at a nearby table. 'See those blokes? They might look like a bunch of scruffy losers, but they are some of the toughest coppers in the Met. They eat goofy lads like you for breakfast and still have room for a full English with extra bacon and fried mushrooms.'

The young man glanced at the table of middle-aged men drinking and chatting in muted tones. Hannah did too; she didn't think the men looked at all like police detectives.

Max grinned. 'You've come into the wrong gaff tonight. You're surrounded by plod.'

The barman leaned closer to the young man. 'What's up, kangaroo got your tongue there, mate?'

The young man necked his pint and zipped up his puffer jacket. He made to leave.

Max's hand shot out like lightning, grabbing the lad's wrist. 'Put it on the bar,' he ordered in a harsh whisper.

The young man's eyes blazed in defiance. He bared his teeth. Then slowly he fished out a mobile phone from his faded jeans and threw it onto the bar. With that, Max released his grip and the young man scurried out, muttering something Hannah didn't catch. She gazed at the device and saw the case with a printed cartoon bear wearing huge glasses. She winced. *Her phone.*

'Cheers, Max, you're a bloody legend,' said the barman.

Hannah didn't know where to look. She wanted out of here pronto.

The barman handed Hannah the bag and gave her an apologetic smile. 'Here you go.'

'I'm so sorry for causing a fuss. I feel like such an idiot,' said Hannah, accepting the bag. She went to thank the guy called Max, but he'd already gone.

The barman shook his head. 'Hey, you don't need to be sorry.'

'But again, sorry. Long few days. I shouldn't have nodded off,' said Hannah as the paramedic's words from the previous month echoed in her head. *Your doctor should've warned you about drinking on those meds.*

What was going on with her lately? First, she flaked out and whacked her head, and now she was crashing out in strange bars and forgetting where she'd been all afternoon.

The barman waved goodbye to a couple of guys. 'See you around, Freddy. Say hello to the missus.' He focused back on Hannah. 'I didn't want to wake you, love. When you came in earlier, you looked dog tired. Three sherbets later and you were sound asleep and seemed so content. There was no way I could bring myself to disturb you.'

Hannah grimaced. 'Agh.'

'Some fella said he could hear you snoring in the loos. Said he thought the mirror was gonna fall right off the wall.'

She winced again and chuckled. 'Oh, come on.'

The barman grinned and winked at her. 'I'm only messing with you.'

'Where am I?'

'The Sailor's Arms.'

'Where's that?'

'Outskirts of Tottenham. Good night?'

'I can't say I remember.'

'Fancy another vodka to jog your memory?'

Hannah smiled. 'Guess a small one won't hurt. Thanks so much for saving my bag.'

'While I'm the manager here, I won't allow cockroaches like that to take the Mick. No way I will.' He set about making her drink. 'The name's Bob, by the way. Everyone here calls me Squid.'

'Maybe make that a double. Where in Oz you from?'

'That sunny old metropolis they call Melbourne. I moved here six years back to be with the love of my life. That old boot binned me off. But I like London, so I decided to hang around.'

'Um, I'm Hannah.'

'Good to meet you, Hannah,' he said, sliding over the drink.

Hannah accepted the vodka and searched her bag for her purse. 'Please, have a drink yourself.'

When Hannah located her purse, she found Max had returned to the bar and was holding up his empty glass. 'Chuck a fresh one in here, Squid.' He glanced at Hannah then stared at her drink. 'Thought you would have gone home to bed.'

Hannah gave the man a wry grin. 'Wide awake now. Best snooze I've had in weeks. Let me buy your drink as a thank you. I'm lucky you guys were here. Otherwise, that lad would have pinched all my stuff.'

Max held her gaze. His blue eyes were mesmerising. Yet, something about them also evoked a sense of nervousness in her. He was, indeed, quite an imposing figure, but it was more than that. Maybe it was because he was a police detective, so this inherently put her on the defensive.

Max gave her a cheeky smile. 'Go on then. Why not?'

Hannah smiled warmly as she paid Squid, and he gave her the thumbs up.

Max had drifted away from the bar, so, drinks in hand, Hannah sought him out. She found him leaning against a fruit machine, scanning his phone. 'Pint of crude oil for you.'

Max accepted the drink with a wide grin. 'Perhaps I should play the hero more often.' He took a sip. 'Yum, the best in the city.' He lowered his voice and said, 'In truth, it's the only reason I come here.'

Hannah scanned the pub. It was a dreary old place with

decor that could have done with updating a good three decades ago. 'Anyway, I'll leave you in peace. Thanks again.'

'You don't seem the type.'

'Sorry?'

'To fall asleep in random bars. Especially on a Wednesday.'

'Well, I tend to keep my pub-napping to the weekends,' she said with an embarrassed grin.

'Is your own bed *that* uncomfortable?'

Hannah grinned again. Her bed was comfortable. But also, the most solitary place in the world. She could never find peace there. In fact, she could apply this to every room in their house. No… *her* house.

'Something like that,' she said.

Max took a seat at a nearby table. 'Care to join me?'

Hannah sat and they sipped their drinks for a while. Max seemed relaxed. She felt anything but. Her eyes darted around as if they wanted to fix on anything other than this man opposite her. OK, she'd bought the guy a drink to say thanks, but that didn't mean she had any desire to spark up an amiable chat with him.

'Are you OK? You seem a little jittery?' he asked.

'I can't believe I did that.'

He gave her a polite smile. After a momentary pause, he said, 'I fell asleep fixing my car once. Right underneath it. I woke up to my neighbour prodding my thigh. I'd been under there for so long he thought I was trapped. He scared the life out of me, and I bashed my head on the exhaust. Needed ten stitches.'

Hannah chuckled. 'Sorry, shouldn't laugh. That must have hurt.'

'Yeah, it did. But don't worry, I found it hilarious. Well, I did once I regained consciousness.'

'Oh dear.'

Another pause. Hannah cleared her throat and sipped her vodka. 'Are you really in the police?'

Max nodded. 'Sure am.'

She gestured to the other table. 'And all those guys are too?'

'As hard as it is to believe, yep, those scoundrels as well.'

Hannah sipped her drink again. 'So you're CID?'

'Drugs.'

'You're in the drugs squad?' she blurted, feeling her cheeks flare with anxious heat.

'They don't call it that these days. I work in a... specialised unit.'

'Are you meant to be telling me this?'

He sucked in some air. 'No way.'

'What do they call it now?'

'Hm, we'll just call it a drug action team and leave it at that.'

'Mysterious. So do you spy on people and get into car chases and stuff?'

'Oh, yeah. Sure do. My life makes James Bond's look like a blissful stroll in the park. And what about you? What do you do for work?'

'I... I don't. I mean, I did. I'm having a break. After I lost my husband, I needed some time to get my head straight. I quit my job.'

'Sorry to hear about that. You look way too young to be a widow.'

She flashed him a bashful smile and wondered why on earth she'd told a total stranger about her business. It was unlike her to be so forthcoming with this type of information.

'What did you do? Before your bereavement?' he asked.

'Mortgage adviser. I just couldn't function. They allowed me some leave, but I wasn't able to go back.'

'I can only imagine how hard that must have been. Do you live alone now?'

Hannah nodded.

Max sipped his pint. He appeared a little uneasy now, and Hannah wondered if he felt awkward about opening that door.

'Must be real tough,' he said with a stiff, half smile.

'My mum has tried countless times to get me to move away and join her in Grenada. She lives over there with her sister. In Grenville.'

'You didn't fancy that? Might have been a pleasant change and a good way to repair. Not to mention the decent weather.'

'My dad was a Londoner. Camden born. His heart-and-soul belonged to the city, but when I was twenty, he passed away, and Mum decided to take some time away. She went back to her island roots and never came back to the UK.'

'You must really miss her.'

'Yeah, I do. Mum helped my aunty set up a boutique clothes store. It does pretty well these days and they would love for me to get involved. Sometimes, I wonder if I should give it a shot.'

'You're worried the same would happen to you? That you'd go there and never return. Would that really be a bad thing?'

'I have given the idea serious consideration. Many times. It's a beautiful place. But it's not my home. And I haven't been back since...' *Since my husband killed himself,* she almost said but stopped herself. 'Also, I'm not much of a flyer. I actually detest planes, and I can't travel alone because I have major panic attacks.'

'Hey, if you are looking for someone to hold your hand on the plane, look no further.' He sipped his drink and grinned. 'Oo, yeah, what I wouldn't do for a few weeks sipping white rum on a glorious Caribbean beach. I can almost smell the coconut suntan lotion now.'

Hannah smiled and sipped her drink. She liked this guy. He seemed pretty laid-back.

'Do you have other family or people around you?' he asked.

Hannah hesitated and considered her reply for a few moments. She nodded. 'I have a son called Ollie. He's in Berlin right now. With his partner. They are touring Europe. I think Prague is next on their list.'

'He's in a band, is he?'

'Not a band. A symphony orchestra. He's a violinist.'

'No way. Cool. You must be so proud.'

'I am. He got obsessed with the instrument when he was five. Turned out he was a natural and progressed really fast.'

'Seriously? Aged five? That's insane.'

'There are some world class musicians in his group. They do film and TV soundtracks sometimes.' She took a big gulp from her drink. She was talking fast now, and the strong drink was easing her anxiousness. 'They did a dramatic piece for this historical fiction epic. It will be on Netflix next year, but I can't recall what it's called off the top of my head.'

'Did you teach him to play?'

Hannah shook her head. 'Oh no. I don't have a musical bone in my body.'

'How old is he now?'

'Twenty-two.'

Max studied her face as he tapped his chin. 'Righto. I'm trying to do the maths.'

Hannah was tempted to divulge her age but kept quiet. 'Anyway, I should probably get going.'

'Don't leave me alone with those boring sods. They'll be talking shop all night.' He faked a big yawn. 'Come on, let's grab another drink.'

Hannah nodded. 'OK. I guess one more won't hurt.'

Famous last words.

'Great. And if you experience a pressing need to take a nap, you go right ahead. Your belongings will be safe with me. Trust me, I'm a cop.'

'Mm, sure. If you say so,' she said with a wily smile.

9

ROSIE

August 1993

Chloe sat in the wild grass and pulled her knees up to her chin. 'This is the famous spot, then?' she asked, sounding indifferent.

Rosie shot her friend a look of confusion, astounded by her lukewarm response. This hadn't been the reaction she'd been anticipating. Why was she so unmoved?

Chloe yawned. 'Well?'

'Are you for real?'

'I mean, by the way you waffle on about this place...' Chloe scanned the lake with an apathetic expression fixed on her face.

Rosie's mouth fell open. Now she was speechless. Did her friend *not* see what she did? Rosie had even waited until right before sundown to make the moment extra special. In truth, the spot was even more magical now than ever. The large lake's blue-green water was serene and inviting. Lush greenery surrounded them. On the low banks of the lake grew heaps of common brush, thick and high, with cigar-like heads. There were blankets of milk-coloured reeds and purple water mint that you could smell in the air every time a faint breeze hit. On the further banks sat bright yellow daffodils that looked sublime with the sun dipping behind the pretty flowers. That enormous sun which had now dropped so low its blazing rays speared the hills on the horizon. Only a few wispy clouds dotted the sky, and they were glowing a magnificent fiery orange.

Two big swans glided majestically past, giving them a cursory glance as they drifted by. They moved with such elegance that they hardly disturbed the water. Six grey, fluffy cygnets followed the two large birds.

Rosie gazed at the regal birds and sobbed. She guessed the cygnets were only about a month old.

'Are you upset? What's the matter?' asked Chloe.

'I… I thought… I always thought this was the most captivating place in the world.'

Chloe shuffled up close to her. 'Rosie, my little sweet lamb, I absolutely love this spot.'

'But you said… you—'

'I was pulling your leg. I'm blown away.'

Rosie laughed through her tears and smiled. 'You mean it?'

'Are you kidding? Look at this place! Who wouldn't fall in love? Sorry, I shouldn't have teased you.'

Rosie wiped her eyes, feeling ridiculous now. 'Oh, Chloe, now I've made myself look like a complete dick.'

'Yeah, but I won't tell.' Chloe bumped shoulders with her. 'You're so lucky. Coming here every summer must be so amazing. No wonder you've talked about this lake so much.'

'I would stay here forever if I could. I tried to draw this lake for an art project.'

'Was it good?'

'No, it was utter rubbish. You can't capture what's here in a drawing. Well, I can't anyway.'

'Can you imagine if this spot was back home? Beer bottles would be scattered all over the place. You'd see Jonnies floating in the water and loads of dog muck in the grass.'

'It's unspoilt because there is no public access.'

'Are you saying we're trespassing, Rosie? Naughty, naughty.'

'No, I'd never do that. There's a stunning old manor house a mile north of here. This is part of the grounds. My parents know the owners, and they kindly let us use this spot when we stay at our holiday cabin. Cool, hey?'

Chloe nodded and stretched out her legs. 'That'll be why the place is so nice and clean, then.'

'Yes. This spot is untouched. Immaculate. My parents don't come down here because they are too lazy to get back up the steep hill, so it seems like it's all mine.' Rosie let out a little giggle. 'I pretend it is sometimes. I pretend I own all this, and it will always be my special spot. I want my ashes scattered here when I die.'

'That's a bit bleak.'

Rosie chuckled. 'I wouldn't say that. It's comforting.'

'If you say so. Can we drink my booze now?'

'No. Wait for a little while. Wait until the sun has gone right down.'

Chloe gave her a questioning stare. 'You trying to keep me sober or something? Can I at least have one sip, Mummy?'

'In a minute.'

Rosie wanted her best friend to embrace the occasion with a clear perspective on things. She wanted the moment to be experienced in a pure, unimpeded state. Not blunted and ruined by alcohol. She wanted her to understand the true allure of her quiet place.

'Don't talk. Just stay silent and soak it up. Watch as this perfect day ebbs away and draws to a close. There's nothing quite like it. I promise you, Chloe.'

'Um, sure.'

'Remember that this day is almost over, and we can never get it back. It'll be gone. Forever.'

'You just dived a little deep there, girl. But I get it. I do get why this place is so special. It's idyllic.'

Rosie turned and took Chloe's hand in hers. Her friend giggled as she did this.

'Watch this perfect day end with me. We can always

remember this moment,' whispered Rosie. 'Here, I made you this.' She offered Chloe a friendship bracelet that she'd hand-crafted with beads a few weeks back in art class.

Chloe took the bracelet and examined the piece with a sunny smile as she ran her finger across the colourful beads, which spelled out their names. 'Aw, my little rose petal. That's the sweetest thing ever.'

Chloe rested her head on Rosie's shoulder, and they sat in total, enchanted silence as the last of the spellbinding sun gradually disappeared in front of them.

10

LOUISA

It was pure torture watching her mum trying to put on a brave and cheerful face as the three of them sat at the table, picking at the food. She saw the hopeful smile fall from her face each time there was a noise outside that turned out to be a false alarm.

Jamie shoved the food around his plate and pouted. 'Can I go upstairs now? I have stuff to do.'

'Like what? Playing *Tomb Raider* all night?' said Louisa.

'I'm playing *The Last of Us*, actually. The remastered version,' said Jamie.

'Just eat all your salmon, like a good boy,' said Louisa, mocking him with a goofy smirk.

'I don't like fish,' he complained. 'And we've been sitting here for an hour.' He picked up a chunk of bread and chewed it like it was the worst thing in the world.

Their mum took a delicate bite of fish and pointed at a ramekin filled with oil. 'Dip your bread in the oil. It's good for you. Extra virgin is a superfood. That's why the Italians like it so much. And why they live such long, healthy lives and have glowing skin. *Deliziosa!*'

Jamie grimaced. 'I'm good. I don't want that greasy muck all over my food. It's a no from me. Dad's obviously not coming, so why do we have to sit here like a bunch of twats?'

Valid point, Louisa was tempted to add but decided not to, as siding with her twelve-year-old brother wasn't a good look.

'Can we not use that language, Jamie?' She expelled a defeated sigh. 'Fine, but when your father comes home, I want you to come down for cinnamon buns. Deal?'

'Sure, Mum,' he said, shoving his plate aside and bolting out of the room.

Louisa shared an awkward glance with her mum. She studied her closely for the first time in a long while. Her mum's skin was the colour of milk, and although she wouldn't say she was unattractive, there was something about how she looked these days that made her appear very plain. Somehow, the nice clothes and extra effort made this even more noticeable. She thought this odd, as she'd always perceived her mum as a beautiful and bubbly woman. Nowadays, the words dowdy, dull and doormat came to mind. Louisa wondered if this had always been the case, and her perception of the woman was changing as she grew old enough to notice her imperfections and obvious flaws.

The door slammed and Louisa saw her mum tense and her eyes widened with excited delight.

How Louisa pitied the deluded woman. Her desperate need to please *him* was so pathetic.

'Your dad's home,' she said gleefully.

'And only a mere two hours later than he said,' said Louisa to herself. Then she spoke loudly and said, 'Yay! Let's all dance a merry jig and cheer in euphoria because Papa is home for dinner now.'

'Will you be quiet, Louisa?' Her mum stood and adjusted her dress as she fixed an upbeat smile on her face.

When her dad breezed into the room, Louisa caught the whiff of booze on him straight away. She also caught the disdainful expression on his hard face as he looked his wife up and down.

'What are you wearing?' he asked with zero emotion in his voice.

Her mum gave him a bashful grin. 'Oh, nothing. Just chucked on an old dress. Sit down. I'll get your starter prepared.'

'I'm not hungry,' he said.

Louisa's eyes flicked between her parents.

Her dad appeared indifferent now.

But her mum had a hearty grin slapped on her face. 'Long day? Shall I run you a nice hot bath and bring you up a drink?'

He gave a shrug and a grunt. 'Started a big case.'

Louisa noticed the muscles under her mum's left eye twitch as she smiled at her dad and said, 'OK, lovey.'

Then he left the room without another word.

Louisa watched her mum in utter despair as the woman eagerly set about tidying up.

11

HANNAH

Hannah was surprised when she awoke to find the first thing that popped into her head was *him*. She shifted herself upright and stretched out her arms. No headache. No aches or lethargy. She felt well-rested. Had she slept, uninterrupted, the entire night? In her own bed? She fell back against the plump pillow and snuggled her head against it as she cast her mind back to the previous night. The nap in the bar, the Australian bartender, the thief… the detective called Max.

What a strange evening, she decided.

Hannah rolled onto her side, and a sudden stab of guilt hit her. Even thinking about this Max character made her feel like she was already being unfaithful to Archie, and she'd not yet decided if she would even see him again. Yes, there'd been something about him she'd been drawn to. She'd found him easy company, and their conversation had flowed without any effort. It hadn't been stilted or forced. After just a short while with the man, she'd found herself wondering if she could move on. If there might be another life for her. Another companion to settle down with. OK, this didn't necessarily mean Max was the one. However, it had given her a glimmer of hope; a faint sign that, perhaps, there might be more to life than this solitary exis-tence she'd confined herself to.

Was two years long enough?

How long did grief last?

Are you supposed to consider moving on so quickly? If ever?

Hannah sat up ramrod straight, her jolly mood already fading away, and grabbed her phone from her bedside table, which was nestled between a glass of water and her strawberry lip balm. Then she received the second surprise of the day. A text message. From Max. Nervous, yet also thrilled, she opened her message feed.

Get a grip, Hannah, you're not sixteen, she rebuked herself, though at the same time grinning at her immature behaviour.

> Hey, Hannah. Great to meet you last night.
> Enjoyed our little chat and I hope to catch up
> with you in the bar again soon. Hope you slept
> well. Max.

He finished the message with three snoozing emojis.

Hannah was about to thumb a reply but hesitated. She didn't want to appear too keen. No, she'd shower, make coffee and contemplate how she'd respond. But she had to admit, she did rather fancy him.

12

ROSIE

August 1993

'Can't you just tell me where we're going, Rosie?' said Chloe, clambering over a lopsided stile. 'I need to eat. My stomach needs eggs and bacon.'

Rosie giggled. 'Why are you always hungry? You had a massive bowl of cereal before we left.'

'Yeah, with no sugar. I had to force them down. Why is there no sugar in that old cabin?'

'Dad won't allow it.'

'No wonder you're so skinny.'

'You eat like a hippo and never put on any weight. Lucky thing.'

'Sure, have you not seen my chunky arse, Rosie?'

'You serious? You have a very nice-sized bum. If you ask me.'

'Oo, are you hitting on me, rose petal?'

'Very funny.'

They walked through a tunnel of trees that blotted out the morning sun.

After a five-minute walk, Rosie gestured at an overgrown

pathway down some rickety wooden steps. Rosie stepped down them, deftly avoiding the tangle of nettles and brambles as she went. She felt giddy with excitement now as she anticipated this encounter. Her hands were trembling at the thought of seeing him.

With a reluctant groan, Chloe followed her onto the uneven steps. 'Ouch, these bloody stinging nettles! Are these super-strength things or something?'

'You're not much of an outdoorsy person, are you?'

'Not sober. Is it much further? I've just been pricked straight up the arse! Some bloody shortcut this is.'

Rosie chuckled. 'Almost there. Along this track.'

'What's next? Are you going to make me swim across a leech-infested swamp? I'm not a country bumpkin, Rosie. I'm a city slicker, so I'm not used to cow shit and knife-sized thorns.'

'I think we should get you some lovely green wellington boots and a straw hat. Make you really look the part.'

'Super sexy, I'm sure.'

'Here we go. Over there,' said Rosie, pointing ahead at some static caravans in the near distance.

'Yay, civilisation.'

'It's Deer Meadows. It's a camping holiday park.'

'I can see that. Why are we here?'

'You'll see. Come on.'

Rosie led her friend through a swing gate that had a sign stating – *Deer Meadows. Please close the gate.* They headed along through a line of big white static caravans that had nice little gardens attached. On one decking area, sat two rotund elderly women drinking tea and reading books. They paid them no attention.

'Is this place full of old fogies or what?' asked Chloe, none too quietly.

'Definitely not. Come on. This way.'

They made their way into the centre of the site, where there were lots of tents of various sizes set up, rows of VW camper vans and tons of smaller caravans on hard pitches. The place was a hub of activity. Families eating their breakfast under awnings, kids whizzing about on bikes, people walking about with their dishes stacked in washing-up bowls.

Rosie smiled at everybody they crossed paths with. She even gave a little wave here and there after spotting a few friendly faces. She'd always enjoyed coming to Deer Meadows. It was a charming place with a chilled vibe. However, she'd never fancied staying here on her holidays. It wasn't private enough for her. The pitches were too closely placed for her liking. She preferred fewer people. More of a quiet space. Though she'd guess this setup would be more up Chloe's street.

'I wish we were staying here, Rosie. Looks way more fun, and I bet there will be some lads our age hanging about.'

Rosie tried and failed to contain a giggle.

'Rosie Grimshaw, you total minx. Are we meeting lads?'

Rosie giggled again. 'Maybe. Maybe not.'

'You dark horse. You act the shy little sausage at school, but I bet deep down you're a right home wrecker. Come on then, you floozie, where have you been hiding all these fit boys?'

Rosie opened her mouth to speak but snapped it shut. She'd seen him. He was waving at her.

13

LOUISA

Louisa poured the milk until her Frosties were swimming in the stuff. Out of the corner of her eye, she saw her mum preparing the espresso machine, causing the potent smell of roasted coffee beans to fill the kitchen space. She eyed Louisa's breakfast and pulled her usual: *Don't you dare spill that* glower. She'd perfected that expression of disapproval to a tee. Her mum had other looks, too. A special reproachful scowl used when anyone dared to step onto her carpets wearing shoes, and Louisa's favourite, her intense, scolding glare saved for those few occasions when Louisa had the audacity to wear a skirt or shorts, which she deemed inappropriate.

Louisa picked up the bowl and slurped back the milk.

Her dad strolled in.

'Morning, snugs,' he said to Louisa, eyes scanning his phone. 'I'll take a cup of brain juice.'

Louisa assumed this request was aimed at her mum, even though he'd not even bothered to acknowledge her presence.

'Hey, Dad,' mumbled Louisa through a mouthful of milk.

'You drink more milk than a baby giraffe,' he said, a wide smile spreading across his face.

Louisa lowered the bowl and wiped her mouth. 'Do giraffes drink a lot of milk, then?' she asked, thinking that her dad looked quite menacing when he smiled. Like a sly jackal about to pounce on a helpless, baby antelope.

He shrugged, eyes on his phone, the smile already long gone. Whatever he was reading made him grunt. Louisa noticed this action caught her mum's attention, and she stiffened, a phoney, light-hearted grin stuck on her face.

'Sure they do. I saw a documentary about giraffes the other night. The calves are reliant on their mother's milk until they are a year old,' he said, still scanning the screen. 'Some even steal milk from other female giraffes.' He stuffed his phone into his trouser pocket.

Louisa's mum pitched in and cheerfully said, 'Some people drink giraffe milk. Apparently, it's something of a superfood. Lots of vitamins. Here's your coffee, love.'

He snatched the cup with a bitter grin. 'What a load of nonsense. How would you even milk the damn thing? On stilts?' He left the room and muttered something about superfoods to himself.

'He's in an upbeat mood today,' said Louisa, leaning over a stool and now using a spoon to eat the dregs in her bowl. 'It's proper creepy when he's happy, don't you think?'

'Stop slurping your food. It's unladylike.'

'Why's he in such good spirits?'

'Is he?'

'Mum? He was grinning stupidly and talking rubbish about giraffes stealing milk.'

'So?'

'So… he called me snugs. Red flag alert. Sound the alarm. Time to panic.'

'Isn't he allowed to be chirpy and nice to you?'

'I'm just pointing out that he's acting odd. Did he bust a load of bad dudes yesterday? Take a ton of gear off the streets? Would that make him all perky?'

Louisa kept a close eye on her mum while she scraped out the rest of her cereal from her bowl. Her mum was acting a little strange herself. She seemed tense and distracted. Once again, fiddling with that wedding ring.

'Is everything OK, Mum?'

'Of course.'

Before Louisa could reply, her mum picked up her cup of coffee and left the kitchen.

Louisa grunted and dumped her bowl into the sink. 'Why can't I have normal parents?' she grumbled to herself.

14

HANNAH

13th May 2023

'Nice place,' said Max, giving Hannah's house the once-over as he squeezed one of her chunky, gold sofa cushions with two fingers. 'Colourful... no, funky and retro, I think is a better description.'

Hannah smiled, considering if the phrase he was searching for was actually *cluttered shithole*. 'Thanks. Can I offer you a drink? A beer?'

'Sure, what do you have?' asked Max, taking a seat on the sofa and crossing his legs. He was dressed in blue jeans and a tight, navy-blue sports hoodie with Los Angeles emblazoned across the chest.

'I have Guinness. Extra cold.'

Max laughed. 'You get some in especially for me?'

'Nah,' she lied, heading off into the kitchen and opening the fridge. She chuckled at the well-organised shelves inside. She'd spent the entire weekend tidying up and rearranging every room in the house. The place hadn't been this spruce for a very long time.

'Smells fresh in here. Citrusy,' he said.

Hannah grabbed a can of Guinness and cracked it open. 'I do burn a lot of fruit-scented candles.' This wasn't a lie as such. She did burn a lot of candles. But she didn't want to admit to the fact she'd scrubbed the house like a possessed person in the hope Max would pop by, and what he could now smell was the new citrus-burst cleaner she'd liberally applied to every inch of her house. She'd been living like a layabout, and with no visitors dropping in, she'd stop bothering. In a way, his visit had been the big kick up the backside she'd needed to stop living like a dirty slob. OK, it would still likely be considered a messy home by many people's standards. She had let things slide since... since a long time ago.

As she took out a tall glass with the Heineken beer emblem printed across it and rinsed it, a stab of guilt hit her. This had been one of her husband's glasses, and it felt wrong to let Max drink from it. She shook her head and poured the dark liquid from the can. She didn't own many glasses; Archie would've used all of them at some point, so it was stupid to think along those lines. Using that logic, she'd need to tell Max not to sit on the sofa, watch the TV or even piss in their toilet. In *her* toilet.

Hannah stared at the Guinness swirling in the glass, entranced by it. She placed her hands on the kitchen counter and closed her eyes. 'I'm not ready, I'm not ready,' she told herself in a cracked whisper.

'You need a hand with those drinks, Hannah?'

Hannah ignored his question and cast her mind back over the last couple of weeks. Her frequent trips to Max's local. Her third 'chance' encounter with him. Their fun little chats that always cheered her up. Their friendship which seemed to grow stronger with every meeting, due to a connection they shared. A connection which she just couldn't fathom. It was just there.

Was she obsessed with this man? This man she'd hooked up with in a shady boozer.

Hannah opened her eyes and jumped when she saw Max standing there, grinning.

'OK?' he asked.

She gave him a timid nod.

'Hannah, I get it. If you want me to leave, I will.'

'I don't want that.'

'I will completely understand.'

'It's just tough. This is the first time…'

'Let's go out somewhere. I'll take you out for dinner instead. Have you eaten?'

'We can stay. We can.'

Max took her hand. 'I don't want to rush you.'

'Sorry. I'm being ridiculous. I invited you over.'

'After I separated from my wife, I didn't think I'd ever be able to move on. I was certain that was me done. So your situation… I can't even begin to comprehend what it must be like for you. How about we enjoy a couple of drinks, stick on a movie and talk? I'll just stay for two hours, tops.'

Hannah smiled and nodded. 'Sure. Sounds good.'

15

ROSIE

August 1993

Take a big, deep breath, Rosie. Don't go all silly now, she warned herself.

'We have come to Deer Meadows because I would like to introduce you to my boyfriend,' Rosie explained to Chloe.

Chloe spat out a horsy laugh. 'Your what? Since when did you have a boyfriend?'

Rosie set her eyes on Max. He was standing by the water tap, filling a silver canister. He wore tight blue shorts, a green Reebok vest and was barefooted. His biceps appeared more muscular than ever. And his calves were huge and shapely.

Rosie flashed him a shy smile.

Chloe caught the exchange. 'Ha, yeah. In your dreams, banana brain.'

'That's Max Hudson.'

'You've got the hots for him, I see. His muscles have muscles.'

Max strolled over in their direction, flashing a huge, confident grin as he came.

Chloe nudged Rosie with her elbow. 'Ah, the hunk is strutting over. Don't say anything stupid. Let me do the talking. OK, don't mess this up.'

Max arrived and said nothing. He just planted a long kiss on Rosie's lips. She took a step back and gazed at his round, handsome face. Those big, mysterious yet mischievous, cool blue eyes.

'Max, I want you to meet my best friend, Chloe. The one I told you about,' said Rosie, feeling her cheeks redden.

Max gave Chloe an amiable smile. 'Hey, how's it going?' He took hold of Rosie and pulled her close to him.

Her friend's cocky demeanour sizzled away. Her bold grin was replaced with a rather confused half smile. 'Should I leave you two lovebirds to it?'

Rosie reluctantly peeled away from Max's firm embrace. The last thing she wanted to do was to make things uncomfortable for her friend. And public displays of affection always embarrassed her.

'Max, where is your cousin? Didn't you say he'd be here?' asked Rosie, raising her eyebrows.

Max scratched the side of his head. 'Ah, yeah. There was a last-minute change of plan. There was some rave he wanted to go to in Staffordshire. A big event called the Eclipse Laserdome. He blew me out to wave glow sticks in a muddy field, the sad prick.'

Rosie tensed. 'Are you serious?'

Max shrugged. 'What can I say? Jay is a total loser.'

No, no, no. Rosie wanted to scream. Why did everything have to go wrong? She glimpsed at her friend. She looked bored, scanning the park's little fenced-in play area.

'Max, is the camp café open?' Rosie asked.

Max nodded. 'You want some brekkie? Trust me, they do the best ham omelettes in there.'

'They do?' said Chloe, now snapping her attention back to them. 'I'm starving.'

Max winked at her. 'Tell the guy serving you're a friend of mine. He'll whack in extra cheese and eggs.'

Chloe rubbed her hands together. 'Now you're talking. I'll let you two play catch up. Meet you over there?'

'Thanks, Chloe. Give me a minute,' said Rosie.

'Oh, can you sub me some cash? Left my purse back at the cabin like a dick,' said Chloe.

'Sure. Here,' said Rosie, grabbing a ten-pound note from her denim shoulder bag.

'Awesome, sister,' said Chloe, snatching the note and strutting off with purpose.

'So, why exactly did you bring the freeloader?' asked Max.

'Hey, that's my best friend. And you know why.'

'It's not my fault Jay changed his mind.'

'Now it's going to be mega weird. Two's company and three's a crowd. How can I spend time alone with you if she's not occupied? I only invited her because I thought this was all arranged.'

Max grinned. 'I have another lad in mind. I think he's arriving in two days. Deano. That lad from Hull.'

'Are you serious right now? She won't like that idiot. He acts like a thicko hillbilly.'

'Yeah, but he's like a dog with six dicks.'

'Max! I want her to find a decent lad. Someone who will treat her nicely. Not some sex-crazed user.'

'She seems like the type who might enjoy his company.'

'Don't be horrible. You don't even know her.'

Max kissed her on the lips. 'Shall we go to our spot?'

'Later. I can't just leave Chloe.'

'Come find me when you have ditched her.' With that, he strolled off across the grounds, whistling as he walked, tossing the canister from one hand to the other.

Rosie groaned. Why was nothing ever simple?

Max glanced back at her, offering her a flirty smile before turning away again.

Rosie's heart thudded and beat a little faster. How she'd missed that big idiot. Missed him like crazy.

16

LOUISA

Louisa strolled into the kitchen and yawned. She'd expected to find her mum preparing breakfast, so she was a little surprised to find the room empty. No coffee prepared. No crumpets popping from the toaster. Her mum hadn't even set the bowls and butter out along the breakfast bar. Very odd.

'Mum?'

Louisa placed her hand against the glass bowl of the coffee machine. Stone cold. She did the same with the kettle. Also cold. 'Mm. Where are you?' She took her phone out of her dressing gown pocket and called her mum's mobile. Straight to voicemail. Where would her mum have gone at eight in the morning? She was such a creature of habit. She'd always be in this kitchen from seven until nine.

Louisa stood on tiptoe and gazed out of the window, and she eventually spotted her mum right at the bottom of the garden.

'What on earth are you up to, woman?'

Louisa walked into the laundry room, kicked off her slippers and stuck on her dad's huge garden sliders. She shuffled down the garden path to the patio area, tightening her dressing gown toggle as she walked. When she got down there, she noticed the grey porcelain slabs were wet and gleaming, and her mum appeared to be stroking the leaves on one of her tall bay trees.

'Mum?'

No reply.

'Hey?'

Still nothing.

'Mother!'

Her mum jolted, turned, flashed a faint smile. 'Hello, missy.' She turned her attention back to the plant.

'You all right?'

'Uh-huh.'

'Did you clean the patio this morning?'

'Uh-huh.'

'Couldn't you sleep or something?'

'I slept just fine.'

Louisa became aware that her mum had something clutched in her left hand. A set of beads? A bracelet? It was hard to tell. 'What have you got there? In your hand?'

'Oh, nothing,' she said, sounding distracted. She closed her hand into a tight fist, hiding the item.

'Let me see.'

'Sorry? What's that, love bear?'

'In your hand? What's that you have?'

'A keepsake.'

'Can I see it? Is it a friendship bracelet?'

'My red robin is being stubborn this year. I think she wants to stay evergreen like the rest of the gang down here. She should be blooming by now.' She brushed a hand over the plant's long leaves. 'But I really don't mind. She's still beautiful.'

'Yeah, sure,' said Louisa, trying to get another gawp at the bracelet, but her mum tucked it away into her black trousers and patted the side of her leg.

She stopped stroking the leaves and turned to Louisa. 'It's nice to have a place like this. A little spot where you can... reflect. Where you can—'

'Did Dad come home last night?'

'You know, I'm going to order some spotlights to go inside my pots. That'll be a pleasant touch, won't it? Warm white, I think. Yes, I'll find some today and get them delivered tomorrow.' She gave Louisa a quick, unassuming smile. 'No, he's busy with work stuff. Did you have breakfast yet?'

'Not yet. The stuff isn't out. Are you OK?'

She squeezed the tip of Louisa's nose and said, '*Boop, boop.*' Then she turned back to one of her bay trees. 'I'm sure you can manage.'

Louisa pulled her dressing gown tighter about herself. Her mum's behaviour was doing her head in. She was acting super weird, even for her.

'Do you want *me* to make the coffee, then?' asked Louisa.

She gave the plant a cheerful grin. 'That would be super. If you don't mind.'

Louisa trudged back up the path, the giant sliders slapping the ground and hampering her movement. 'I'll get on with that straight away. Like I can't make some coffee.'

'Mummy won't be around forever, my little cream puff.'

17

HANNAH

Hannah snapped her eyes open. Bright white walls. An abstract image of a white terrier racing across a beach with a smudgy red sun in the background.

My room.

She sat up, rubbed her eyes, and smiled.

A knock on the door.

Then she remembered Max. Had he stayed last night? Was he still here?

Who else if not him?

'Are you decent, Hannah? Can I come in?'

Hannah pulled the quilt a little higher to cover herself. 'Yes.'

The door opened and Max peered in. 'I have made us both a coffee. Hope I'm not taking liberties helping myself.'

'No way. Not at all. I'll be right out.'

'See you in a tick.'

Once Max left, Hannah got out of bed, threw on some clothes, tied back her hair with a ribbed scrunchie and checked herself in the mirror. Just to verify she didn't appear too bedraggled. She didn't. She looked perky. The photo of her and Archie caught her eye. In the shot, they were both pulling silly faces and pretending to bite the medals they'd received after doing a charity bike ride. That shot of them always made her smile. A different time when they were different people. Young and carefree.

Hannah left the bedroom and headed downstairs, where she found Max drinking coffee in the kitchen and scanning his phone.

'Sleep OK?' he asked, flashing her a playful smile.

'Like a log. I don't even remember taking myself off to bed.'

'You can probably put that down to the two bottles of red. I flaked out myself.'

'Wasn't sure if you'd stayed. I hope you got *some* sleep. I know from lots of experience it's not all that comfy on my sofa.'

'It was fine. I drifted off straight away.'

Max offered her a black coffee. She accepted it and took a sip. They stayed silent for a while as they drank.

It was strange having another man in their house. In *her* house. So very strange.

As if sensing this, Max gave her a reassuring grin and said, 'I get it, Hannah. I do. I'll just be a friend who stays over when you need company. We don't need to rush into things. I enjoy your company. That's enough for me.'

Hannah nodded. She'd had fun with Max last night. They'd laughed a lot. She couldn't even recall the film they'd stuck on because the pair had been so preoccupied with talking nonsense and jesting around.

Had that been why she'd crashed out and enjoyed such a pleasant night's rest? Had she been content? Had the thought of not being alone somehow helped her to relax and settle for once?

Hannah gestured for them to go into the lounge.

Once there, she was pleasantly surprised to see the room was spotless. The glasses and bottles were gone. The sofa had been tidied up, with throws and cushions neatly in place.

'You didn't need to tidy up, Max. But thanks.'

'I need to come clean about something,' said Max. His eyes flicked to a photo on the wall.

Hannah's eyes also moved to the photo. Archie and Hannah on

their honeymoon. The shot taken on a beach in Cala Fornells, Mallorca. They had been so happy during that entire trip, and now those days seemed like a lifetime ago. Archie had his arm wrapped around her as they both beamed at the camera. A local fisherman had offered to take the photo. He'd been an absolute gent and he'd told them in his smooth Spanish accent, 'You two will be together for all time. I can tell. You are made for each other.'

Max cleared his throat. 'He was a handsome man. Where was it taken?'

'Spain,' said Hannah. She didn't want to go into any more details than that. She liked Max, but as far as Archie and her memories of her husband were concerned… they were off-limits. To everybody except her.

'What is it you need to come clean about?' she asked, keeping her tone breezy.

'I told you about my separation. My current situation with my wife.'

'You did,' said Hannah.

Here we go. I should've bloody known, she thought.

Max put his coffee mug down on the table and raised both hands. 'I like you, Hannah. I mean, I really, really like you. So I want to be totally transparent about my marriage situation. If, after I have explained, you run for the hills, I will understand.'

Hannah's hands clasped about the mug. She sat down. 'This sounds serious.'

Max took a seat next to her. 'I still live at home, and I haven't moved out like I said. This is temporary. Only until I sort out what I'm going to do.' His words were rushed, and he appeared worried.

Hannah laughed without humour and shook her head. 'What you mean is, you're not separated, are you?'

'It's complicated.'

'Isn't it always?'

'I can't leave. I can't leave my two kids. Not with her.'

'What does that even mean?'

Max shifted closer to her. 'It means… it means my wife… my soon to be ex-wife, isn't well. She's unstable. She can be—'

'This is a bad idea.' Hannah slid away from him. 'Us, I mean. You should go home to your family, Max. You shouldn't be here.'

'Please hear me out.'

'Does she know where you are right now?'

Max sighed. 'We don't even talk. I can't stand to be in the same room as her. She drives me insane.'

'Does she know?' Hannah repeated.

'I have tried to get her help—'

Hannah cut him off. 'Is she going to flip out and come after me? Am I going to find her at my door armed with a meat cleaver one morning?'

'God, no. No way. She's not violent. Plus, she doesn't like leaving the house. She's just a little unbalanced.'

'That doesn't make it sound any less worrying.'

Max scratched the top of his head. 'I'm not explaining this all that well.'

'No, I think you are.'

'She's sick. An anxious, troubled woman. She's impossible to live with. I have shared an unhealthy relationship with her for years. I can't take it any longer.'

Hannah gulped down some coffee. 'OK.'

'She's a basket case. There. I said it. I don't like to speak about her this way, yet it's true, and if we are to continue to see each other, then it's only fair that you have all the facts.'

'You should've told me the truth before you came here.'

'Yes. I can leave.'

'You should.'

Max stood up and smoothed down his jeans. 'I'm sorry I wasn't straight with you.' He bowed his head. 'Now I have ruined it.'

Hannah stared at Max and tried to read his face. His sadness was sincere. She felt sure of that. She decided that perhaps she'd been a little hard on him. It's not like he'd waited until after they'd been intimate before dropping this delicate news on her.

They had shared nothing more than a friendly kiss. If he'd told her this after they'd slept together, then she'd have been far more annoyed with him. No, she'd have been furious. As she processed this information, it helped to calm her down and put everything into perspective. He could have easily kept this from her.

Max gave her a shy smile. 'I enjoyed last night. Spending time with you always makes me forget my problems. When I'm with you, I'm in a wonderful bubble. I don't worry about all the stuff going on at work. I forget all that drama with her. I'm at peace.'

Hannah averted her eyes. Set them on that beach photo and her chest tightened.

'All right, that sounded a bit corny, but I get the sense our time together is helping your situation. Tell me if I'm wrong,' he said.

Her eyes still on that photo.

A sudden image of that train thundering towards her husband came crashing into her thoughts and washed everything else away.

Hannah flinched. Fingers snaking about her mug. The damn thing would break if she applied any more pressure.

'If you ever need to talk, Hannah. I'm here. I'll always be here.' Max made to leave. 'Maybe catch you in the pub. I'll let myself out.'

'You need to tell her!'

Max stopped and turned.

'Tell your wife. Sort out your situation. Leave her properly because I won't be some bit on the side. That's not going to happen.'

Max eyed her with big, expressive eyes. He appeared somewhat startled by her words.

Hannah, shocked that she'd even said those things, struggled to find her tongue to add anything else to this.

Max's features softened. 'I promise you I'm working on that. I'd better make a move.'

After he'd left, Hannah let out a heavy sigh and was frustrated with herself for blurting out those demands. Now, she felt bad for Max's wife. The mere thought of him turning his back on the poor woman tied her stomach in knots. Could she be that person? One of those people who ended a marriage. Albeit a marriage that had long since fallen to pieces by the sounds of things.

Something inside of her was screaming at her to stay away from Max. To turn her back on the entire sorry affair. But something else was overriding that emotion. A selfish urge. A profound longing for a chance to change her sorry existence at long last. Because it didn't matter how much she tried to deny it, this man had given her a much-needed purpose. A reason to wake up in the morning. For the first time since losing her husband, she experienced something other than sorrow.

'Life's too short,' she whispered to herself. 'It's way too short.'

18

ROSIE

August 1993

Rosie tried to tickle Max's stomach, but he shoved her away and gave her a gloomy look.

'What's up with you?'

'Your friend will be waiting, won't she?'

'Chloe's gone into town for a mooch around. She'll be OK for a short while.'

'You told her you'd catch her up. I heard you.'

Rosie snuggled her head against Max's chest. 'Yeah, once *we* have done some catching up. Perhaps we should hurry in case your dad comes back.' She tried to kiss his neck, but his body language was all wrong. He was tense and offish.

'Did I do something?' asked Rosie.

'Dunno, did you?'

Rosie shuffled away from him and crossed her arms. 'Can you spit it out, already?'

'I overheard you two. While you were eating your breakfast.'

'You were spying on us?'

'I was just standing there. Not my fault if you didn't notice me. I guess you were too preoccupied making plans with her.'

'What did we say that's got your back up?'

'I heard her talking about how you were going to get pissed and find lads. She sounds like a right slag if you ask me.'

'Chloe can be loud and crass. She's always like that. But she is really sweet once you get to know her.'

He stood up. 'She's well annoying.'

'Max, please try to get on with her. For me. It will be so difficult if you two don't click.'

Max went into the small kitchen and rummaged around, appearing a moment later with two cans of Coke. 'Here. Sorry, fan is up the creek, that's why it's so stuffy in here.'

Rosie cracked open the can. 'I thought you'd left it off, so we get hot and need to strip.'

He opened his Coke and shrugged. 'No, my dad's getting a new one later. Wish he would piss off home, he's being a right moody prick.'

She swigged the cold drink and wiped her mouth. 'I won't be out finding lads. Why would I when I have you?' she said with a deliberate note of irritation in her tone.

He studied her with his blue, penetrating eyes. Kept them fixed on her until she felt her cheeks flush and stomach flutter. He kissed her on the cheek.

'How much have you missed me?' she asked softly. 'Because I have been pining for you every day, Max. Can we meet tomorrow? At the lake? Say nine? We could have a swim if it's nice and warm.'

He stroked her cheek and kissed her again. He let his lips linger on her skin and then in her ear he whispered, 'Fine. Now you better find your friend.'

19

LOUISA

Louisa found her mum in the lounge, using a handheld Shark to hoover down the sides of the sofa. She stepped over the chunky, blue seat cushions and searched the table for her phone.

'Mum, don't suppose you've spotted my phone knocking about?'

Her mum used the Shark to vacuum the deep recesses of the sofa. 'If you've lost another phone, you'll be in big trouble, missy.'

'It's just misplaced, not lost.'

She turned off the mini hoover and held it against her shoulder like a vigilant hunter propping a rifle. 'I've heard that before.'

Louisa picked up one of the sausage-shaped scatter cushions. 'Remember when I hit my brother with one of these and he whacked his ice cream into his face?'

'That was mean.'

'His face. That was hilarious.'

'Jamie bit his tongue and couldn't eat hot food for three days.'

'Yeah, sure. He was playing on that.'

Her mum placed one of the seat cushions back and moulded it by using her free hand to slap it down.

'Mum, why do you rarely leave the house?'

'I like staying home.'

'Are you one of those people that are frightened of going outside? I can't remember what it's called.'

'You are referring to the anxiety disorder called agoraphobia.'

'That's the one. Do you suffer from that?'

'No. I just don't have much cause to go out.'

Louisa spun the sausage-shaped cushion and placed her chin on the top. 'It is a bit sad. You don't have any friends, do you?'

'Don't be mean to Mummy.'

'But it's true.'

'I've got you, my little snuggle monkey.'

'Mum, I'm not your friend.'

Her mum slotted the second seat cushion into place and gave her an offended scowl as she ran her hand over the fabric. 'Oh, well, that is rather a horrible thing to say.'

'Don't give me that look. I'm just saying that our relationship is not the same thing. It's not like having proper friends. Like older buddies your own age.'

'No, it's not. It's far, far better and one day I hope you will find that out.'

'But why don't you have any friends? You should join a club. Yoga, perhaps.'

'Friends are… overrated.'

Louisa considered if her mum had a point. She thought about her own selfish friend and sometimes wondered why she was so obsessed with being seen as Estelle's friend. At times, she questioned if she even really liked the surly girl and why she tried so hard to be liked by her. Status, she supposed.

'Besides, I've got your dad. He's my best friend.'

'Yeah, Mum, but aren't friends meant to be, you know, friendly?'

'What's that supposed to mean?'

'It means, in my honest opinion, Dad treats you like shit.'

'That's not a nice thing to say, Louisa. Not nice at all,' she said, tugging the fabric sleeve from the sofa's arm and giving it an aggressive shake.

'If you really viewed me as a friend, then you should maybe take my advice,' said Louisa, in a tone way sharper than she'd intended.

'You don't have any idea what you're saying. You don't understand how marriages work.'

'I understand more than you realise. I have eyes. Ears, too,' said Louisa in a petulant tone.

'You don't get it. I'd like you to stop talking about this now. You're being a total grump-zilla and I don't like it.'

'Mum, do you want me to point out the many, many red flags I'm seeing on a regular basis? I mean, do you not see them? Because they are flying high enough for them to be spotted in space by a bloody blind astronaut. Just lately he's—'

'I don't much care for your tone. Now, I said, drop it.'

Louisa locked eyes with her. Although her mum's tone had been cheery, her eyes were now hard and challenging.

'I'm just looking out for you, Mum.'

'I'm not sure what you're implying here, but there are things you don't see. Things *I* don't see. But we must accept the situation. He has an obligation to do his job. Regardless of the impact on his personal life, he must follow it to the end. Sometimes this warrants unorthodox methods.'

'Oh, sure.'

'He has no choice but to stay away.'

'You believe that?'

'Go find your phone.' Her mum's eyes narrowed. 'Go find it now, my prickly porcupine. Go on, off you trot.'

Louisa let out a long, frustrated sigh. 'Ah, there it is. Over by the Sky box. Silly me.'

Her mum thumbed the Shark's power button and made a start on the armchair, shaking her head.

20

HANNAH

Hannah was in a daze as she sipped her first coffee of the day and watched the Monday morning cars trundle by. All of these people were off to start their day. Busying themselves. Living their lives. She pictured Archie standing there next to the cooker as he gobbled down his breakfast, complaining that he'd be late. His hair had been untidy, tie askew. 'I need to set my alarm fifteen minutes earlier.'

'You say that almost every morning, but you never do. You've got a jam splodge on your shirt,' she'd teased.

'I'm not falling for that one again. It gets busier out there every morning. Do you ever wish we could move to a nice deserted island?'

'Nah. The Wi-Fi would be terrible. And I'm not sure if there'd be much need for an insurance salesman on an island. Or mortgage advisors, for that matter.'

'We'd get new jobs. I'd live my dream of becoming a dolphin trainer. Hey, do they have dolphins in Grenada?'

Hannah had laughed. 'We're not moving to Grenada. Mum and my Aunty Grace would drive you bonkers with their henpecking ways.'

Archie had gulped down a glass of cranberry juice. 'But what a place for Ollie to grow up.'

'He'll make do with yearly visits.'

'OK, off I go. I'm heading into the madness out there. See you at six.'

'Bye. Take care.'

He'd left, only to return a minute later wearing his bike helmet, the straps hanging down his face. 'Bugger. My bike has a flat. I'll have to take the car. Keys, keys, keys. Where are the keys?'

'Lounge. Middle shelf of the bookcase.'

He'd raced off again.

'Hannah? Earth to Hannah.'

Max's deep voice pulled her out of the hazy, distant memory.

'Hey,' she said.

Max had been staying over twice a week, yet she still struggled to get used to having another person in her house in the mornings.

'You OK? You're staring out of that window like you've been frozen in time,' he said.

Hannah snapped out of her trance and turned to him. 'This isn't fair on your wife.'

'It's been on the cards for a long time.'

'That doesn't make me feel any less guilty.'

Max leaned against the fridge and crossed his arms. 'You have no reason to feel guilty. None whatsoever.'

'Come on, I have taken you away from your family. I had no right to do that.'

Max smiled broadly. 'We've been over this.'

She gazed back out of the window and watched the stream of traffic again. Was she even ready for this? She'd told herself she was. Now things were moving way too fast, and she couldn't make up her mind.

'I wanted to bring some things over tonight. If I'm spending more time here, I'm going to need some more supplies. Mainly clothes for work.'

Hannah nodded. 'Does she know my address?'

'No.'

'Does she even know my name?'

'No.'

'What have you told your kids?'

'Nothing. Not yet.'

Hannah sighed. 'You should explain the situation to them. It's the least you can do. How old are they?'

'My daughter is fifteen going on thirty. My son is twelve.' Max stepped over to her. She didn't turn to face him as he wrapped his arms around her, pulling her close. 'We deserve to be happy, don't we?'

'But our happiness comes at a cost, doesn't it?'

Max held her tighter.

'What's her name, Max? Your wife. Tell me her name.'

'It doesn't matter. Forget about her.'

Hannah closed her eyes as the guilt washed over her. She was tempted to pull away from this man. Tempted to tell him that this couldn't happen. That it wouldn't be fair for them to continue down this path. Only she was unable to move. Once again, her own selfish needs had defeated those bubbling feelings of guilt and regret. It didn't matter. She needed Max right now. She'd been drowning in her own miserable loneliness. This was a light at the end of a bleak tunnel she'd been wading through for two years. A light she never thought she'd ever see, let alone reach.

If she didn't take this chance now, she might never leave the darkness.

Yet once again, that niggling voice returned and said, *This is a big mistake, Hannah. The biggest mistake you'll ever make.*

But she knew that couldn't be possible. Because she'd already made the biggest mistake of her life.

21

ROSIE

August 1993

Rosie raised her arms in the air and spun around and around. She could hear Chloe's laughter and her shouts of encouragement from somewhere in the vast meadow. The enormous moon cast an incredible bluish glow over them, and Rosie watched it blur as she whirled and became dizzy.

'Mind out for the cow poo,' laughed Chloe.

Rosie shouted at the moon. 'I love him, I love him, I love Max!'

'Ah, shut up. You're drunk.'

Rosie fell backwards, her world still spinning. 'It's true.'

'Mind you don't stick your hair in cow crud.'

Rosie laughed and sang, 'I was dancing through the field without a single care, a sparkle in my eyes, wind blowing through my hair. Looked up to see a cow with mischief in its big round eyes… But I don't care, I really don't care about a little cow poo in my hair.'

Chloe belly laughed. 'You are nuts, girl.'

Rosie continued with her silly song. 'So if you see me with a smelly poo stain or two, just know I'm happy, and you should be too… Because I don't care, no, I really don't care… about a little cow poo clinging to my hair!'

Chloe was in stitches now. 'Ah, you're killing me. You might just have a smash hit with that one.'

Rosie howled at the moon and shouted, 'I love you, Max!'

She really meant it. The alcohol had made her realise, even more so, that he was the one for her, and she couldn't be without him.

Not ever.

22

LOUISA

Sounds of rapid gunfire reverberated around her brother's bedroom. Louisa stepped inside and scooped up his school tie from the floor where his bag and blazer also lay. Jamie, far too engrossed in his PlayStation game, didn't notice her as she snuck up behind his gaming chair. She took a peek at his screen. The graphics looked stunning. She'd often considered getting into gaming herself. Unfortunately, she'd spent so long ridiculing her brother for spending his days thumbing away at those controllers and calling him a lame nerd that she couldn't possibly consider gaming herself. Plus, who wanted to invest all their time running around shooting pretend zombies? What a waste of time. Yet, as she continued watching the screen and saw the teenage character duck behind a wall, and then sneak out and batter an armed ruffian with her spiked baseball bat, she had to admit to herself that this game did have some appeal.

Louisa undid the knot in his tie, stretched it out and stuck it across her brother's eyes like a blindfold.

'What are you doing? Get off!'

Louisa laughed and pulled the tie tighter. 'Guess who, butt face?'

Jamie tugged the tie free and tried to pause his game, but

groaned as his character got set upon by several assailants and was beaten to death outside a dilapidated building.

'Why would you do that? Just why?' he whined.

'I'm saving you from a bollocking.'

'You got me killed!'

'Tidy up your stuff. Mum doesn't spend all day cleaning up so you can come home and dump your crap everywhere. Does she even know how violent your game is? One word from me and she'll make you delete it.'

Jamie pulled a sour face. 'Whatever, I'd just download it again. Ah, I have to start again now. I hadn't reached my checkpoint.'

Louisa put a hand to her mouth and fake gasped. 'Oh my.'

'Go away.'

'We need to talk about Mum and Dad.'

'What about them?'

'Something weird is going on. Don't you see it?'

'No.'

'Try dragging yourself out of your game and concentrate on the real world for once in a while.'

'Why?'

Louisa slapped him around the shoulder with his tie. 'Because it's important.'

'Leave me alone.'

'Don't you care?'

He shrugged, his attention back on the game now.

'Jamie, listen to me. I think Dad's screwing around.'

'What's that got to do with us?'

'So you don't care?'

'No. It's nothing to do with me. Or you. If they split up, they split up. Big deal.'

Louisa slapped the tie against his right ear, making him flinch.

'Ouch! That really hurt. I'm telling Mum.'

'It was meant to, you little turd. Don't bother concerning yourself then. Leave everything to me.'

'Stop sticking your beak into their business. Get a life. Wait, I get what's happening here. Dad keeps stopping you from doing what you want to do, so this is your way of getting revenge.'

Louisa pouted in disbelief. The nerve on this insolent little brat. She once again wrapped the tie around his head, tied it in a tight knot behind his head and spun his gaming chair as hard as she could.

'Louisa, you idiot!' he cried out as he spun, desperate fingers fumbling with his controller buttons.

'Your lack of consideration is pissing me off,' said Louisa. She stopped the chair from spinning using her foot and snatched the controller from his hands.

'Why are you being such an arsewipe about this?'

As she stomped along the hallway, she shouted, 'You can have this back when you decide to stop being so selfish. Keep your bloody ears open and help me.'

'Take it. I have a spare,' he yelled.

Jamie's door slammed shut.

Louisa stormed into the bathroom and hid the controller on top of the bathroom cabinet behind a stack of girly products. A place where she knew the little twerp wouldn't search. Then she strutted into her room and sat heavily on her bed, slapping an assortment of fluffy animals aside. She already felt a bit silly for overreacting and losing her cool. For a second back there, she'd almost tossed his controller down the toilet. She was glad she hadn't, or her parents would have forced her to pay for a new one.

The situation with her dad was making her cranky. How come she was getting frustrated with the situation, but her mum appeared happy to let him get on with things while she floated about the house like a flaky airhead?

So many red flags, it was painful. His change in attitude. Those silly smiles as he viewed his phone, skulking off into the front office to make secret phone calls and leaving the house with packed bags, those random overnight stays... somewhere. And then, the worst part of all: his blatant disregard for her mum. He spoke to her like rubbish. Every question answered with a short, curt reply. Whatever she did, he threw it back in her face.

If her mum wasn't prepared to do something about the situation, she would. How could any adult be so gullible? Surely she didn't believe this was all connected to some type of police business? Did she?

23

HANNAH

23rd May 2023

Hannah stared at the table and viewed the huge bouquet of roses propped up against the empty fruit bowl with a confused frown. This wasn't a cheap bunch grabbed from a local supermarket, but a lavish assortment of gorgeous pink, white, and orange roses with a lilac ribbon tied around the stems.

Max appeared behind her and pulled her into an embrace. She caught the hint of a nice fragrance on him, mixed with alcohol. He spun her around to face him. He wore a white, crumpled shirt with the two top buttons undone.

He kissed her neck. 'Do you like the flowers?'

'Max, please…'

He held her tighter, kissing her cheek. 'There's a bottle of Moet in the fridge. Want to take it into the bedroom?'

Hannah pulled away from his embrace. 'I thought we agreed that we weren't going to meet tonight. And I told you I'm trying to ease off the booze.'

He gently tugged her back to him and resumed kissing her neck. 'I changed my mind.'

Again, she pulled away. 'I can't. Not tonight.' She glanced at the bouquet and frowned again. Under normal circumstances, she would've been happy to receive them. But not today. Today, they were extremely inappropriate.

'I'm sorry, Max. I can't see you today. I need to be alone.'

He stared at her for a moment, then took a step back. 'Did I do something?'

'It's nothing to do with you.'

Max walked over to the dining table and plucked a white rose from the bouquet.

'I… just… not tonight. OK?'

He sniffed the rose and muttered, 'Yes, you said.'

'But they are lovely.'

'How many years would it have been?' he asked before tossing the rose down onto the table.

'Sorry?'

Max picked up another rose, this one pink. 'How many?'

'You know? But… I don't understand.'

Max plucked a petal free and studied it. 'It's a simple enough question.'

'If you knew about our anniversary, can I ask why you deemed it appropriate to buy flowers and champagne?'

Max tossed down the pink rose and stared at her. 'Archie can hardly buy them for you, can he?'

Hannah's mouth dropped open as she processed Max's words.

'So, I got them,' he said as he delicately slid an orange rose free and studied it. 'You're welcome.'

Hannah snatched the rose from his hand. 'I never told you.' She stepped away from him. 'Have you been going through my personal records?'

'I'll pour us some fizz.'

'No.'

Max headed for the kitchen.

She stomped after him, her anger boiling to the surface now. 'I said no.'

He rummaged around in one of her cupboards and pulled out two tall wine glasses. 'These will do. I'll just give them a rinse.' He gazed around. 'This place needs modernising. Is this the original kitchen? Those doors are warped.'

'I'm not celebrating my dead husband's wedding anniversary with you. What the hell?'

Max rinsed the glasses under the cold tap. 'You want to mope about alone?'

'Yes! I need this day to reflect. To remember.'

Max placed down the glasses. 'Of course you do.'

'Then you should go. This isn't fair.'

Max approached her and placed a hand on her cheek. 'Grief looks so good on you.'

Hannah froze, taken aback by his words. Had she misheard him? 'What did you just say to me?'

He stroked her cheek with one finger. 'You look so hot when you're upset.'

The rose dropped from Hannah's fingers. 'You're making me feel uncomfortable.'

'Cry for me.'

'What?'

Max continued to stroke her face, but with his other hand, he took hold of her wrist. He put his face close to hers and whispered, 'Do you want me to *make* you cry? Is that what you want?'

Did she hear him right?

Max squeezed tighter. 'Well?'

'Let go of my arm and get out. Now!'

'You don't want me to go.'

His cold, blue eyes looked both wild and full of amusement now.

Was he enjoying seeing her this way?

'Let go,' she demanded through gritted teeth.

'Fine. OK. Fine, be like that,' he relented as he let go and took a step back. He adjusted his shirt and appeared ashamed by his actions. He picked up one of the glasses and stuck it back into the cupboard. 'This all went much differently in my head.'

He left the kitchen.

Hannah emitted an audible gasp and placed her hand against her chest.

Max came back in, buttoning up a blue, quilted Barbour jacket. 'Weather looks shit today. Feel free to enjoy the bubbly. I'll make a move. Get those flowers in some water; they cost me loads.' He smiled and fished his car keys out of his trouser pocket.

Hannah gaped at him. He'd spoken like everything was normal and he hadn't just said those things to her mere minutes ago. She wanted to tell him to leave and never come back, but instead, she just watched him dumbly, willing for him to turn around and get out of her house.

'See you later,' he said as he strolled out.

Once she heard the door close, she raced to the window. She watched him get into his black BMW and speed off the driveway. He drove away so erratically, another driver had to slam on their brakes to avoid a collision with Max's vehicle.

Do you want me to make you cry?

His words made her shudder. Why would he say such a thing?

24

ROSIE

August 1993

Rosie opened her eyes and her head spun. It took a few moments before she could shift herself upright.

'Ah, God, my head,' she mumbled, slumping back down. Pain radiated behind her eyeballs and even thinking caused waves of sickening aches throughout her entire body. 'This is why I don't drink, Chloe.'

No reply.

'Chloe? You awake?' After getting no response, she moved over onto her side and shifted a plump pillow that was blocking her view. The sofa bed was empty save some crumpled blankets and a discarded pink bra. 'Chloe?'

Still no reply.

Rosie forced herself upright again, wondering just how drinking alcohol could possibly make you feel so rubbish. Had she been poisoned? Had her liver rotted and turned to jelly during the night?

Head spinning, she took the plunge and slipped out of bed. Searched the floor. Mess everywhere. Clothes strewn about, wet towels, an empty bottle of Thunderbird... 'Oh, no.' She held her stomach and dry heaved as she caught the sickly-sweet smell of the drink. She saw a trickle had soaked into the beige rug. Why had she let Chloe talk her into drinking that stuff? In retrospect, as she recalled Chloe telling her to down the pale, sour liquid, she wished she'd guzzled toilet cleaner instead. She caught the slogan on the label: *The American Classic.* She doubted that. The stuff should be outlawed. It truly was a crime to sell this stuff to teenagers. She kicked the bottle under the bed, the sight of it making her stomach bubble and cramp.

'This stuff is epic, Rosie. Gets you pissed so fast,' she remembered Chloe saying before she took a massive swig.

She had a vague recollection of a walk back through a meadow with livestock in. Had they been singing about cow shit? Where the hell was her friend now?

Rosie heard muffled voices and noises outside the room. Her parents talking and clanking about in the kitchen. She grabbed her wristwatch from the bedside, surprised she'd taken it off before bed. By the shockingly vile taste in her mouth, she sure hadn't brushed her teeth before crashing out. It was gone nine. She chucked on her jean shorts and baggy white sweatshirt. Sun rays were streaming in through a small gap in the window, confirming that the day was set to be a glorious one. Not that she'd enjoy it in this state.

Rosie slunk out of her room and darted into the toilet before her parents noticed her. She just made it before she vomited, though not before flushing the chain to hide the noise of her retching. Now at least a stone lighter, she brushed her teeth and guzzled some cold water from the tap. Did she feel better? Maybe for about two seconds before another bout of sickness hit her, and she dropped to her knees, coughing out more lumpy puke.

As she yanked the chain again and gazed at the swirling water in the loo, it came to her. *Swimming.* That's what she'd been talking about on their inebriated walk back from the village. Chloe, very drunk, had wanted to go to her lake for a moonlight swim. Rosie had talked her out of that dumb idea and promised to take her there first thing this morning.

Had she gone without her?

After a big swig of mouthwash, Rosie slipped out of the bathroom. She moved deftly, careful not to alert her parents to her presence. She grabbed her green flip-flops from the hallway and tiptoed barefoot out of the cabin, clutching them to her chest. She squinted as the harsh sun rays burned her eyeballs. Rosie was tempted to nip back in and hunt for her shades but decided not to risk it. There was no way on earth she could face her parents in this sorry state. Her dad would cotton on straight away and she'd be punished. Probably confine her to the cabin for the rest of the holiday and send her friend packing.

She slipped through the row of tall oaks on the border of the cabin, sidestepped through the gap in the fence and took the path down the steep hill and headed for the lake.

25

LOUISA

Louisa sensed somebody was in her room and plucked out her AirPods. She found Jamie standing at her door, holding something to his chest.

Louisa sat up. 'What are you doing in here?'

Jamie held out his hand. There was a small camera device nestled in his palm. It was white with a black screen and was about the size of a snooker ball. The camera sat inside a white plastic base.

'What the hell is that?'

'A camera. Well, a pet monitor.'

'I can see it's a camera, dummy. Why are you giving it to me?'

'You could put it to use. To find out stuff. To get proof.'

'To spy on Dad? You serious? Where did you even get this from?'

'Borrowed it from my friend at school. He has two of my games as collateral so please don't break it.'

'Doesn't he need that for his pet?'

'No. He doesn't use the camera for his pet. He got it for his stepsister.'

Louisa swung her legs off the bed and jumped to her feet. 'Sorry, what? Why?'

'She steals his things. To sell for booze and cigarettes.'

'Right.'

'Why did you pull that face? What else would he use it for?'

Louisa snatched up the device. 'Um, something… else. Doesn't matter.'

'But what?' he asked with a perplexed frown marking his forehead.

Louisa studied the device and ran her thumb over the small lens. 'Never mind about your dorky mate. Show me how this works.'

'Here's the power lead. It has an SD card slot in the back. Put the app on your phone and sync the device using Wi-Fi. Then hide it. You can even pan the device via your phone.'

Louisa gave him a questioning glare. 'Why the change of heart? You suddenly care about the situation?'

He shrugged. 'A peace offering. Can I have my controller back now?'

'Thought you had a spare.'

'It doesn't always hold a charge, and I have an online gaming session tonight.'

'Aw, and for a second there, I thought you cared.'

'I do.'

'Yeah, right.'

'I really do.'

'Can your mate get us a device to track Dad's car?'

'Can't you buy one on Amazon?'

'On Mum's account? Well, that won't look suspicious. And you know she gets all the deliveries. Trade some more gear with your nerd-friend and see if he'll get you one.'

'No way.'

'Go on and then I'll think about letting you have the controller back.'

'I could just tell Dad what's going on. Maybe he'll just buy me a new one.'

'Sure. How many chores would that take?'

'Let's find out.'

'Don't you dare, or I'll make your pitiful life a living hell.'

'Louisa!'

'I mean it. I need your help.' She wiggled the camera. 'This is a good start. It's not enough, though. We need to find out where he goes when he stays away.'

Jamie's shoulders slumped. 'Why is nothing ever good enough for you? You're such a bitch.' He shuffled out of her room.

'Two days. Or I'll smash the thing to bits with Dad's hammer.' She threw her legs back up onto the bed and considered where best to stash her new spy cam.

26

HANNAH

Even wearing her eye mask, Hannah saw streaks of blue flashing through the gap in her curtains. She'd forgotten to drop the blackout blind, she knew. She pulled the sleep mask up onto her forehead and slipped out of bed.

Instead of closing the blind, Hannah put her elbows on the windowsill and viewed the vivid purple-blue lightning brighten the world outside in sporadic, angry bursts. She anticipated the ominous sound of thunder, yet it didn't come. Just silent, dramatic flashes. She'd always enjoyed a good storm. So had Archie. She cast her mind back to those times when he'd nudge her awake during the early hours like an excited kid, exclaiming that there was a storm starting. When they'd been in their early twenties, living in a Camden flat, watching storms had become something of a hobby for them. Up on the eighteenth floor, they'd had a decent view. She now recalled one memorable occasion when the pair had stayed up until three in the morning and enjoyed an amazing spectacle from their balcony. Both sipping cheap beer as they observed the unrelenting storm light up the empty streets below and illuminate the distant tower blocks and structures of central London.

Max's face popped into her head.

Hannah rested her chin on her fist and couldn't help but

wonder what he was up to right now. Had he gone home? Crawled back to his wife and made things right with her? Was he with his wife now or out in the city somewhere? She pictured him giving a pep talk to a group of hard-faced police officers dressed in black attire. Doling out orders as they prepared a dawn raid on some drug dealer in a shady part of North London. Some dodgy backstreet where no sane person would venture. Yet, for Max and his team, heading into such a threatening place was all part of their daily business. Kicking down the doors of London's most feared criminals and rushing inside some dingy basement flat to face the unknown dangers awaiting them. Did he even do this? Did Max get his hands dirty? Or did he issue the orders, then stand back and let his underlings do all the high-risk stuff? She didn't know. Didn't have a clue what his job really entailed because he wouldn't discuss even the minor details with her.

Hannah thought about his strange behaviour the other day. It didn't matter what she told herself, or how many times he apologised for the way he'd behaved because the simple fact was this: it had been uncalled for and malicious. So she'd refused to meet him for drinks and responded to all his lame, heartfelt messages with curt, perfunctory replies.

He'd tried to blame the drink, pressure at work and his wife's crankiness, but at the end of the day, as far as she was concerned, those reasons didn't excuse his actions.

So why then did she keep thinking about him? Why did she keep checking her damn phone in the hope she'd have another message from him? Another apology. A genuine reason for his actions. What a sad idiot she was being.

To take her mind away from Max, Hannah got back into bed and grabbed her phone from the bedside table. She clicked on the YouTube clip she'd saved the other night. *The London Virtuosi Orchestra in Budapest.* She popped in her wireless headphones, keen to catch every moment clearly.

The clip started with a shot of the entire orchestra, so silent and still as they waited for him to start. Then the camera zoomed in, and she spotted a faint, keen grin playing on his lips. No tension. No anxiety. Not a worry in the world as he started to play with delicate strokes. Just pure concentration now, as he did what he loved to do. As he played his heart out to the watching crowd. His solo rendition of Schubert's "Ave Maria" melted Hannah's heart. How she'd love to be there in person among that attentive crowd. That large, engrossed audience holding onto his every movement. His every magical bow stroke.

The music, so deep and haunting, almost moved her to tears.

His solo ended and the tall, male pianist took over without preamble. Slow, sombre, yet melodic notes that shifted in speed and intensity. The entire violin family suddenly burst into action and there was an immediate change in emotions as the performance switched to an uplifting vibe. There was a note of a lively Irish jig to this one. It got faster and more intense as additional instruments joined in the medley to give it a jazzy edge. Within a minute, the entire ensemble was involved in the exhilarating piece.

Still that tiny smile on his face. He was where he should be.

Where he belonged.

Hannah fought down the urge to cry. She got back out of bed and grabbed her duvet. She knocked over the gold photo frame on her bedside table and quickly flipped it back up. She momentarily gazed at the photo of Archie and Ollie, then she left the room, dragging her duvet downstairs.

27

ROSIE

August 1993

As Rosie approached her lake, she heard distant giggling and splashing. With her delicate stomach in knots, she made her way through the spongy grass towards the noise. She was going to give Chloe a major earbashing for making her drink that vile booze last night. Never again would she be talked into something so foolish.

More giggles. A big splash, followed by a boy's silly laughter. Rosie stopped in her tracks and froze.

That hadn't been just any boy's laugh. It had been Max's.

Rosie put her hands on her hips and took a deep breath. 'Right,' she grumbled to herself as she forced herself on, kicking off her flip-flops as she went.

Then she heard Max shout, 'Oi, leave off. You splashed me first!' He laughed idiotically and more frantic splashing and silly laughter followed.

Rosie moved nimbly, making sure she made no sound. Her hangover wasn't helping. Her head was killing her, and the harsh morning sun was making her dizzy and even more annoyed that she'd abandoned the idea of returning for her shades. Once close enough, she crouched in the long grass and gazed at the water. What she saw made her emit a shrill gasp that stung her dry throat. She couldn't believe her eyes. Her best friend and her boyfriend were both in the water. Together. The pair were messing around, blissfully unaware of her presence.

So shocked to find the pair here together, Rosie hadn't registered the fact that Chloe, like Max, was topless. But now she'd noticed the girl's breasts were on full display, she was beyond livid.

Rosie stood and proceeded down the hill. She gave up sneaking and stomped with purpose. Yet, they still did not notice her, so engrossed in the frolicking fun they appeared to be having. When she reached the dry, muddy bank leading to the water, she spotted Max's crumpled blue T-shirt and Nike Air Max trainers. She did a double take when she spied Chloe's clothes. Because the girl's red knickers were tucked into one of her chunky white Reeboks. Her purple top was further down by the water. Rosie visualised the girl tugging it free of her body as she ran for the lake, flinging it aside as she laughed and charged into the water.

Rosie's eyes shot back up and she glared at the pair. She felt sick again as she watched them both. She saw them cease the splashing and giggling so they could talk. Chloe put a hand on Max's chest, and he made no attempt to push her away. Max's eyes moved down to her friend's breasts, before shifting his gaze away from them as he flashed a boyish grin.

Max noticed Rosie. He muttered something to Chloe, who smiled and waved at her without even a hint of embarrassment or shame.

Rosie did not return the wave. Instead, she issued them a silent, icy scowl.

Chloe pushed Max and he fell backwards. She slapped the water, bombarding him with a volley of small waves. 'Come on, Rosie. The water is lovely.'

Rosie did not say a word. Kept glaring.

Chloe, now obviously grasping how annoyed Rosie was, waded through the water and headed her way.

Rosie told herself to stay calm and not flip out. Her heart was racing, and her hands were shaking so much she had to clench them into tight balls.

'Hey. Why the mopey face, my little rose petal?' asked Chloe.

Rosie swallowed hard and didn't know where to direct her gaze when her friend stepped out of the water.

Chloe turned and caught Max's eye. The pair shared a look and both of them grinned. A grin that suggested a private joke that Rosie wasn't privy to.

Rosie's blood boiled, yet she couldn't help but gawp at her friend's naked form. Her buxom body was stunning. Perfect, even. Perfect tits with tiny pink nipples. A curvy bum and rounded hips. Flawless, glowing skin. And the girl oozed confidence. She was comfortable in her own skin. There could be no doubting that. Rosie felt a surge of intense jealousy that she had never experienced before.

'Come on, girl. Come swim with us,' said Chloe.

'I didn't bring my swimwear,' said Rosie, her tone sharp and unfriendly.

'Who cares? Didn't stop me.'

'I can see that.'

Chloe waved Max out with her hand. 'You staying in there all day? Why aren't you coming out to say hi to your girlfriend?' she said with a slutty smirk.

'I'm swimming,' said Max, letting out a nervy laugh and wading out into deeper water.

Chloe picked up her purple top and shook the dry mud from it. 'Come out. Don't be shy. What are you hiding?'

'In a minute,' yelled Max, still laughing.

Rosie crossed her arms. 'Yes, come out, Max,' she said, throwing him her best death stare.

'I'm swimming,' repeated Max, before diving into the deeper water.

'You look rough, Rosie. I take it you've got a massive hangover.'

'That vile stuff made me vomit.'

Chloe stretched up her arms and basked in the morning sun. 'Lightweight. Don't suppose you brought any towels?'

'No.'

Max resurfaced and shook his hair.

Rosie took a deep breath. She'd assumed Max wouldn't come out to face her because he'd taken off his shorts in the water, but then he stood and waded through the lake, adjusting his grey shorts as he came. Rosie's mood darkened even more as she came to understand why Max had been so reluctant to come out of the water just now.

Chloe plucked her knickers out of her trainer and ungracefully pulled them on, wiggling her bum and hips as she struggled to get them over her wet bottom. 'Oops, excuse me.'

It took all of Rosie's self-control to refrain from viciously clawing at the other girl's face.

28

LOUISA

30th May 2023

Louisa was regretting answering her phone. Now she'd need to come up with more excuses for why she wouldn't be able to do whatever it was Estelle had planned for her this weekend. Once again, she'd have to be the big, lame sad case who was unable to go out and have fun. She'd even gained the nickname Louisa Let-down, though nobody had yet said this to her face. But she'd heard the rumours.

'And don't even get me started on that vibe-killer, Stella Avon. You see her latest Insta post, Lou? What the fuck is that? Do you know what she said to me the other day? She only went and said…'

Louisa lay on her bed and tried to switch off as her friend spouted the latest mundane gossip, waffling on and on about her life and her problems. Her exam worries. Her problematic love life. The name of the latest boy who'd had the audacity to ghost her. She couldn't get a word in edgeways. As per usual, it was the Estelle show. Never mind about what she thought. Never mind about her hassles or dilemmas. Her endless battle with her parents to give her the freedom she so desired. Her messed up parents who were likely on the verge of a divorce. Her mission to catch her dad in the act of cheating. Her migraines and the pressure she faced at school, with everyone expecting her to do so well, but she was crumbling beneath the weight of it all. Never mind that all she wanted was a little escape. A little fun to distract herself from it all.

On Estelle waffled and moaned. Still, Louisa zoned out, barely listening.

'I've got you some ket.'

Estelle's words grabbed Louisa's full attention.

'I'll bring it into school for you, Lou.'

Louisa sat up and double-checked her door was still closed.

'You still there?' asked Estelle.

'Yep, sure I am.'

'You hear what I said? I'll bring you the stuff.'

'Sorry, I don't have the money for that right now,' she lied.

'No charge. I didn't pay for it. Ash's mate gave me some last weekend. I remembered you said you were desperate to try it. So, like the decent friend I am, I saved you some.'

A wave of panic washed over Louisa. 'Did I say that?' She had; she knew she had. But that had just been nonsense talk. She'd been trying to show off and sound cool in front of a big group of her peers. Trying to salvage her shattered reputation. She'd have probably said she was well up for injecting smack into her eyeball if the others had been bragging about doing it that weekend.

'If you don't want it, Lou, then just say.'

'Shut up. What are you saying? Of course I want it.'

29

HANNAH

Hannah spotted Max through the window as he got out of his car and headed for her front door with a confident swagger. She inhaled and marched to the front door to face him. It had been a week since he'd last been to her house. A long week in which all she'd done was think about him.

Hannah fixed her face into an unreadable, blank mask. Then she yanked open the door. 'Morning, Max.'

He was wearing a well-pressed suit and carrying a white bag. He flashed her a lopsided smile. 'I come bearing gifts.' He held up the bag. 'These are some of the best pastries you'll ever try.'

'I thought you'd come to collect your clothes.'

'Come on, it's only a spot of breakfast.'

'You can't win me over with a few croissants, Max. Those things you said were pretty messed up.'

'How many times can I apologise? Can we not just enjoy a coffee and a chat?'

'I don't think so.'

'Come on. One quick drink. Afterwards, I'll grab my gear and get going. I need to be in Muswell Hill for a briefing soon.'

Hannah crossed her arms and shook her head.

'I'll be stuck talking shop with a bunch of dreary senior officers all morning. Talking to you for a mere five minutes would be the highlight of my day. My week, in fact.'

Hannah let out a long, annoyed sigh. 'One coffee.'

They went through to the kitchen and Hannah filled the kettle up with water.

'I do think you're hot when you're sad, but I think you're super sexy when you're happy. Please forgive me.'

Hannah slammed the kettle down. 'You grabbed my arm and asked if I wanted you to make me cry. Who would say something like that?'

'I'd been drinking brandy with some old work buddies. It makes me cranky.'

'That's no excuse.'

'I'm kicking the booze. I had a health check the other day and my cholesterol is shockingly bad. I'm looking at a heart attack for my fiftieth birthday at this rate.'

'Well... I've been cutting back myself. I'm sleeping a little better, too.'

Max put down the bakery bag on the worktop. 'That's good to hear. We could kick the booze together, hey? Have a dry June. Screw it, a dry year. What do you say?'

Hannah grabbed two mugs and shrugged. 'Do whatever you like.'

'I'm going to get back into running again. I've let myself go these days. Do you run?'

'Did you know?'

'Sorry?'

'Did you know it was our anniversary?'

Max fumbled with the wrapper and looked as though he was considering his response. He shook his head and said, 'No. No, of course I didn't. It was a coincidence. Look, Hannah, about what I said... about Archie not being able to buy you flowers...'

Hannah's chest tightened and she glared at him.

'I... I shouldn't have...'

'No, you shouldn't have!'

'It just came out. I guess, in my drunken, muddled mind, it was meant as a joke.'

'Oh, I see. That's what it was. I'm glad you've explained that.' Max cleared his throat and continued to fumble with the bag. 'I see now that it was in bad taste. Extremely bad.'

'Not at all. Now I know it was "a joke," I totally get it. Ha, ha. That's all fine,' said Hannah, keeping her face expressionless.

'Shall I get some plates?' asked Max.

'Did you ever see that movie *Split*?'

'Doesn't ring any bells.'

'You were like a different person, Max. You stood in my kitchen, and you weren't *you*. And you scared me.'

Max tried to take her hand, but she yanked it away.

Hannah turned away from him. 'I like you. I think about you all the time.'

'Same. I mean, I think about *you* all the time, not myself.'

'Shut up and let me talk.'

Max nodded. 'Sure.'

'I'm not ready. I can't do this.'

'Hannah, she knows now. I've told her it's over. Are you saying that I did all that for no reason?'

'Don't make out I'm the only reason. You already said that you needed to get away from her. It can't be me you run to. Not now.' She grabbed the coffee jar from the cupboard. 'I need more time.'

'How much time?'

'I can't say. I'm sorry, I just can't.'

Max nodded. 'I can wait. I promise I will wait. The truth is, I need you in my life.'

Hannah stared him directly in the eye. 'You can't say that unless you mean it. You… can't.'

'I mean it. I hope you believe me.'

Max's words came to her again. *Do you want me to make you cry?*

The sentence kept playing over and over and over in her head.

Again, that niggling, creeping feeling.

Do the right thing and stay well away, Hannah, she told herself.

30

ROSIE

August 1993

Rosie spotted Max fiddling with his shorts as he left the lake and approached. His cheeks flushed as his eyes flicked between Rosie and Chloe.

'Here he comes,' said Chloe, eyeing Max with a dirty, lopsided grin. She ran her hand over her arm and shoulder and wiped off the drips of water with little flicks.

'Where were you?' Max asked Rosie in an accusatory voice.

Rosie glared at him. 'What do you mean?'

'You told me to meet you here at nine in the morning for a swim. Remember?' said Max.

'I overslept,' said Rosie.

Max shrugged. 'I heard you were pissed and singing about cow shit all night. Guess you forgot.'

Chloe poked Rosie on the arm. 'Whoops, you double booked yourself, Rosie. Last night, you also agreed to swim with me this morning. What a surprise I got to find this big lump down here waiting and looking all grumpy cos you'd stood him up.'

Rosie grimaced, vowing never to drink again.

Chloe gave her vest another shake and pulled it over her head, jerking it on and making her breasts jiggle as she did. 'OK, I'm going back for a shower. I'll leave you two lovebirds here alone.' She gave Max a long, brassy smile. 'Nice chatting with you.'

Max returned her smile. 'Yeah, cool. See you about, Chloe.'

Chloe winked at Rosie. 'See you back up there. Don't do anything I wouldn't.' With that, she scooped up her Reeboks and skipped away, adjusting her knickers as she went.

Max tried to kiss Rosie on the cheek.

'Don't you touch me.'

'What are you all grouchy for?'

'Don't even talk to me.'

'You're acting like a child.'

'Are you for real?'

'A grownup wouldn't have acted that way. A grownup would've got into the water and not even acknowledged that the other girl was swimming naked.'

'Oh, is that what a "grownup" would do?'

'If she wants to swim in the buff, that's her choice.'

'I agree. But not with my boyfriend she can't.'

'Don't be such a prude. In the South of France, they have nude beaches.'

'I bet. I'm sure you've been to plenty of them, haven't you, Max? You perve!'

'I never knew you were such a jealous person. You need to relax.'

'Are you seriously going to turn this all around and make it sound like I'm in the wrong here?'

Max shrugged and grabbed his Nike trainers. 'I just think you're overreacting.'

'I'm speechless. I really am.'

Max slid on his trainers and snatched up his T-shirt. 'Screw this. I'm going back for a shower. That water looks inviting, but it stinks.'

'It does not stink! Why would you say that?' she snapped with such vehemence it shocked the pair of them.

'What's got into you? Calm down.'

'Why couldn't you get out of the water, Max? Why?'

'I was swimming.'

'Liar!'

'I'm going.'

'Admit why. Go on, admit that you didn't want me to see how excited you were. Go on.'

Max smirked and shook his head. 'You want me to get excited now? Is that what you want? Just say, Rosie. Tell me what you really want.'

'Oh, just… just piss off!' With that, Rosie spun on her heel and marched off.

'You're acting mental right now. You're going to ruin your holiday at this rate. And mine.'

Rosie kept going, sticking up her middle finger as she walked.

'You invited her here.'

Once Rosie got out of his sight, she let the tears she'd been suppressing come tumbling out.

31

LOUISA

'Don't laugh at me. Don't you dare,' Louisa warned Herbert Crunch with a prod of her finger. As quickly as possible, she removed the packet of powder hidden behind her phone case and shoved it inside the dinosaur's mouth. She zipped it up and put him back in his position next to her pillow. She sat on her dressing table chair and felt so guilty she almost sobbed. Was this her? Had she become that person? Hiding drugs inside her favourite childhood stuffed toy. She looked at Herbert Crunch and shook her head. He almost appeared upset now, with his mouth zipped shut and head tilted sideways.

Estelle's words came to her then, and she pictured the moment she'd gingerly accepted the wrap of drugs from the girl in the school toilets. 'What would daddy say if he could see you now, Lou?'

Louisa had just given her a nervy grin.

What *would* he say?

Could he get in trouble at work if this came out? Would he march her off to the nearest police station and have her tested for drugs? Would he arrest her himself?

The urge to remove the ketamine and flush it down the toilet was so strong that she went over to Herbert Crunch and picked him up.

'This weekend. No excuses. It's party time,' Estelle had said with a feral glint in her eye.

But Louisa Let-down would no doubt strike again. Her parents would see to that.

32

HANNAH

Hannah had studied Max's message several times, yet she was still unsure about how she would reply. A reality love show she was only half watching droned on in the background. The contestants were irritating and driving her mad. Everything was a drama. She didn't switch off, though. She needed the distraction. The noise. Anything to break the punishing silence. She checked his message again.

> It's a big ask, but could I stay with you for a few days? Things at home are so bad. I need to get away.

Necking her fourth glass of wine, Hannah finally caved in and typed a reply.

> I don't think that's a good idea. Sorry.

> Please, please, please. Five days tops. I'm going to be renting my mate's flat soon. Just need to sort out the final arrangements.

Hannah sighed, then typed a fast reply.

> Sorry. No.

However, she didn't press send. She couldn't seem to bring herself to. She put her phone on the sofa and drew her knees up to her chin. It was as if she needed to stop holding the phone now. She didn't trust herself with the device. Didn't trust herself not to say *yes*. But deep down, she knew she'd already decided she'd let him back in, and she hated herself for being so weak and desperate. She closed her eyes and let her head slump forward.

33

ROSIE

August 1993

Rosie found Chloe asleep on the sofa bed, entangled in a thin sheet with one leg hanging off the side. She eyed the girl with contempt. She'd left wet towels and crumpled clothes all over the floor. She was such a slob. It riled her so much.

Rosie opened the bedside drawer and slammed it shut. Chloe didn't stir, so she did it again. Harder this time. So hard, the gas lamp toppled.

Chloe moaned and sleepily said, 'Rosie? What are you doing?'

Rosie sat on her bed and crossed her arms.

Chloe sat up and yawned. 'That swimming made me so tired this morning.'

'Did it?'

Chloe rubbed her eyes and grinned. 'What's that look for? You could open up a safe inside a bank's vault with that laser-beam stare you're giving me.'

Rosie let out a huffing sigh and continued to glare at her.

Chloe yawned again. 'I take it you've got the grumps because

I went swimming with Max.' She stretched up her arms and let out a contented groan. 'Please don't go all weird on me. It's not like we did anything, and I was in the water first, by the way.' She sat up, letting the sheet drop away, leaving her breasts on full display.

'Jesus, will you cover yourself up!' snapped Rosie. 'My parents might come in.'

Chloe stretched again and wiggled her breasts from side to side. 'Your dad would like that.'

Rosie jutted her bottom lip and tried to suppress her anger. She was in danger of saying something awful. Something she might truly regret.

Chloe shook her head. 'It's just a pair of tits, girl. Take it easy.'

'Yeah, well, not everyone is comfortable seeing naked bodies. It's not the done thing to parade yourself about.'

Chloe giggled and pulled the sheet up to her chin. 'Happy now, you delicate flower?'

'Can you please tidy up all your things? My parents will go mad if they see the state of this place.'

'How often do you see him? Max, I mean?'

Rosie sat up straight and let her arms drop to her sides. 'Two or three times a year.'

'Is that all?'

'His dad owns the pitch, so Max can come whenever he likes. I just tell him when I'm due to come down to the cabin and he makes sure he's around. And we speak on the phone at least twice a week. Once he can drive, things will be much different.'

'Ooh, right. I see.'

'What does that mean?'

'He's not really a proper boyfriend then, is he?'

Rosie's jaw tightened. 'Yes. He *is*. We have known each other for four years.'

Chloe pulled a face. 'Since you were, what, twelve? Bit weird.'

'Not like that. We've just been hanging out. We didn't become an actual couple until last year.'

'Still weird.'

'Why are you so interested in him?'

'You never mentioned him before.'

'I have.'

'I don't remember.'

Rosie shrugged. 'I have talked about him plenty. I told you I've got a boyfriend and he lives in Cheltenham. Maybe you just don't listen to me.'

'Look, I hate to be the bearer of bad news, but I have to say it.'

Rosie crossed her arms again and lifted her chin. 'Say what?'

'I mean, do I *have* to say it?'

'Yeah, I guess you do.'

Chloe pulled the sheet tighter about herself. 'I think he's using you. I think he just leads you on, so he has a little shag-friend when he's at the caravan site.'

'Why would you say such a thing?'

'Come on, Rosie, don't be so stupid. You think a boy like Max would stay faithful to you? I know his type.'

'You know nothing about him.'

Chloe's face shifted into a smug sneer. 'Um, you'd be surprised. I learned a lot from our little chat this morning. A helluva lot, actually.'

'I would like you to change the subject now.'

'I'm saving you from total humiliation. From the heartbreak that I am certain will come. What sort of best friend would I be if I let this slide? Hey? I'm looking out for you. I don't want you to get hurt.'

'I'm going for a walk.'

'Rosie, Rosie, Rosie... my grumpy little possum. Don't be like this. I can help you.'

'Oh yeah, how's that then?'

'I say we give Max a little test. To see if he passes. To learn if he really is the boy you believe him to be. What do you say? Interested?'

'I'm not sure I follow.'

'I say we go fishing. I'll be the bait and we'll find out if he bites. Then we can determine whether or not he can be trusted.'

'You want me to let you try it on with my boyfriend? Are you serious right now?'

'I bet you fifty quid he'll take the bait. Not only take it, but snatch it like a greedy, horny shark.'

Rosie stood and stomped over to Chloe. 'I get what you're doing, and I'm telling you now, it won't work.'

Chloe flicked some hair out of her eyes and blinked as she pulled an innocent expression. 'What are you trying to say about me?'

'You don't understand, Chloe. We have something special that can't be broken. Not by you. Not by anyone.'

'Then prove me wrong. Let's put it to the test. Because I promise you, given the chance, he'd do the dirty. One gawp at my tits earlier, and he was practically drooling. He couldn't keep his eyes off me. Sorry to have to break it to you like this, but it's for your own good. I couldn't bear the idea of him stringing you along and…'

Rosie didn't hear any more of Chloe's words. She jammed her hands against her ears and raced out of the room.

34

LOUISA

As Louisa climbed onto her bed and opened the camera app, her heart started racing. Bingo. A live feed in her dad's study. A crystal-clear picture and a wonderful view of the entire study. Louisa let out an excited giggle. She'd been shitting herself when she'd used her dad's leather swivel chair to gain access to the top shelf of his tall bookcase. She'd been shaking all over as she hid the small device between a fat, dusty book about angling and a small photo frame containing a family photo of all of them in Paris. The cluttered shelves made an ideal spot to hide the device. Unless you knew where to look, you'd never spot it. Or, at least, that's what she was banking on. If he found the spy cam and discovered she'd hidden it, she dreaded to think how he'd react.

Jamie popped his head around the door. 'Did you do it?'

Louisa spun her phone and showed him the screen. 'Camera one is live.'

'Is the wire hidden properly?'

'Yeah, I dropped it behind the bookcase and plugged it into the socket hidden behind.'

'If he finds this, he'll likely blame Mum for spying.'

'I'm sure he won't notice it.'

'If he does, you better come clean.'

'Yeah, yeah. What about something for the car?'

'My friend said he'd sell me his key finding device.'

'But will that work in a car, Jamie?'

'He said it should do. It's like a knockoff Airtag and it works by bouncing off Bluetooth and phones using iOS.'

'OK, that might just work.'

Jamie shrugged. 'He said it's a bit glitchy but should easily flag up all the main stopping points.'

'Make sure he resets it. We don't want your mate's mum banging on Dad's car window looking for her son's lost door key.'

'He's not a complete idiot. He isn't—'

Noise from Louisa's phone stopped Jamie mid-sentence.

First, a door opening and then a cough. They exchanged a wide-eyed stare.

Jamie slumped next to her, and the pair eyed her phone.

'We can see him,' whispered Louisa, not too sure why she pointed this out to her brother.

'Why are you whispering? Unless you click the microphone, he can't hear us. And don't click it by mistake!'

'What's he doing?'

'Not sure.'

The pair watched as their dad sat heavily in his swivel chair and checked his phone. He grinned and typed something on the device.

'Shame we couldn't zoom in and see what he's typing,' said Louisa.

'It does zoom. But it wouldn't work. You should've put the camera on the other side. So it would've been behind him.'

'There wasn't a suitable place on that side. Not where I could hide it properly.'

Their dad finished on his phone. He scanned a letter on his desk and grunted, as if unimpressed with what he'd read. Then he got up and left the room.

Jamie got off the bed. 'Riveting stuff. So, what did you learn today, detective?'

'These things take time.'

'Whatever,' he said, sounding bored.

'You get me that key tracker from your mate. Understand?'

Jamie rolled his eyes. 'When I next see him, I'll mention it and see if we can make a deal.'

'You'd better.'

35

HANNAH

4th June 2023

Hannah snuggled up next to Max on the sofa. She'd enjoyed the lazy Sunday morning spent with him, and she had to admit to herself that she was pleased she'd succumbed and let him back into her life. Things had been going well and having him stay over for the last few days had been fun.

Max stroked her cheek with one finger. 'This year is flying by. Can't believe we're over halfway through it.'

'Yes,' said Hannah, even though she didn't agree with his statement. For her, the year had dragged by. A hazy, depressing blur of days that blended into a series of events that she could barely recall. Like the previous year. Just like every day since Archie had left her on her own.

She'd tell herself there must be a light at the end of the black hole she'd been stuck in. The endless swamp of misery she'd been wading through all this time. That there had to be more to her existence than continuous pain, regret and heartache. There had to be a reason to keep going.

Now, at last, things were changing.

'And the weather is improving,' he said.

'Is it? I hadn't noticed.'

'We could go somewhere for a long weekend. Somewhere nice and quiet, so we can get away from the city.'

'I'm listening.'

'How about Hampshire?'

Hannah tensed and swallowed hard.

'No? What's up with Hampshire?'

'We went on regular jaunts to the New Forest. Burley was the last trip we took together before... well, before I lost him.'

'Sorry, I had no idea.'

'Archie bought me a crystal with a horse inside. He got it from one of the mystic gift shops in the village.'

'I saw that somewhere.'

'In the downstairs loo.'

'Yeah, that's right.' Max kissed her on the cheek. 'You say the place and I'll book us somewhere.'

Hannah rolled onto her side. 'I like Dorset, especially along the Jurassic Coast. My parents used to take me there for camping trips.'

'OK, Dorset it is. I'll arrange something for next weekend. My treat for you letting me stay.'

Hannah pouted at him. 'Oh yeah? Got any more treats for me?'

Max kissed her on the lips and whispered, 'You bet I have.'

Archie's face suddenly popped into Hannah's head, and she recoiled from Max.

They'd argued on that New Forest trip, hadn't they? Archie had tried to be nice to her the entire weekend, and she'd thrown it back in his face.

'Hey, what is it?' he asked.

Hannah sat up and struggled to get air into her lungs. 'I'm OK. I... I'll be OK.'

'You sure? You need a glass of water?'

Hannah sat up and pulled the tangled hair out of her face.

The bridge… The train… The haunted look on her husband's face.

'Now, this might sound like I'm losing my mind, but…' Hannah shook her head. 'It doesn't matter.'

Max rubbed her arm. 'You can tell me?'

'I don't know if I want to discuss it.'

'You can tell me anything.'

'Well, OK… I keep dreaming about Archie. I keep seeing him at the place…'

'The place?'

'The place he killed himself. Messed up, right?'

Max didn't appear shocked. He gave her a sympathetic smile and took her hand in his. 'I guess that's why you don't talk about this. I… shit, sorry. I didn't realise that's how he…'

'Yep, threw himself in front of a speeding train. I don't normally talk about any of this.'

'It's no wonder you're having nightmares.'

'Oh, I have nightmares, too. But this thing with my husband isn't a nightmare. It's something else entirely. It's so clear… so real, it blows my mind. It's like I actually see him. He never talks and neither do I. Yet it's like he's trying to tell me something. He stares at me with this woeful look and…'

'Trauma can screw with the mind. Trust me, I get it.'

'I mean, I know it's not real, yet I still feel bad for ignoring him. How silly is that? I wake up…' She stopped talking and decided she didn't wish to voice all of her thoughts. Didn't wish to tell Max that after waking up, all she could think about was rushing straight to the place where her husband took his life.

'How often is this happening?' he asked.

'When I first lost him… I guess, three or four times a week. I'd be upset if I didn't have the dream. Now, don't tell me that's not a bit mental.'

'And now?'

'Only once every week or so. I can smell him sometimes when I wake up. I'll catch a whiff of his deodorant or the scent of his clothes.'

'Hannah, this is part of the healing process. You're discussing all this with somebody, so I'd say that has to be a step in the right direction.'

'Maybe.'

'Definitely.' Max held her hand a little tighter. 'Has this happened while I have been here?' he asked.

'Not so often. I think I told myself…'

'What?'

'It's silly.'

'Go on.'

'I told myself it's bonkers, yet a tiny part of me must believe he's stuck in limbo. You read about these cases where people are convinced their loved ones can't move on until certain things are resolved. But I don't believe any of that paranormal bullshit. I never have, so it drives me mad when I let those ridiculous ideas sneak into my head.'

Max put his arm around her. 'Whatever you need, I'm here. Just say, OK?'

'Thanks.'

'I'll need to pop back home a bit later. Check on the kids.'

'OK.' Hannah rested her head against his shoulder and closed her eyes, trying to block out the images of her late husband's woeful expression as he watched her from that railway line. She knew what those dreams were really about.

She was punishing herself for what happened to him.

Because it had been all her fault.

36

ROSIE

August 1993

The cramped store shed smelled of harsh petrol and rotten wood. Rosie closed the creaky door and propped a lump of timber up against it. The single plastic window was cracked in several places, and shafts of sunlight speared through and lit up an old workbench that dominated the messy space. She stepped over some rusty garden tools and a neglected, red lawnmower that had a puddle of liquid around it. Cobwebs attacked her face, and she wiped them away, grimacing as they clung to her fingers. The wooden floorboards groaned underfoot, and she felt something scrape against her arm.

Rosie used her foot to push away some wood-stain containers and studied the bench. It was covered in oil stains and housed a chunky, blue vice which was bolted to the front. She examined the array of old tools scattered on it and opted for a long screwdriver, its handle sticky with dark, tacky oil. Max and Chloe popped into her head as she raised the screwdriver. She closed her eyes, seeing Chloe's hands on Max's naked chest, and then she visualised the pair kissing. Full-on French kissing as their hands grappled and explored.

Stop it, stop it, stop it, she ordered herself as she brought down the screwdriver and slammed the sharp end into the wood.

'Stupid, Rosie. Stupid, stupid, stupid, Rosie!' She raised the screwdriver again. She'd invited the girl here. This was all her fault. All because she wanted to be "Miss bloody popular." Now it had backfired. It had all gone wrong, and she hated herself.

Rosie slapped her left hand down onto the bench and splayed her fingers. Her right hand and arm trembled as she gripped the tool and willed herself to bring it down once more. Her breathing was going wild now and more images came to her. Max kissing Chloe's neck as he seductively made his way down towards her naked chest. The details were so vivid in her mind. Like it was happening right here in front of her. Their intimate behaviour was impossible to endure.

'No, no, no,' she sobbed, hurling the tool blindly into the corner of the shed. It landed somewhere with a clang that made her flinch and open her eyes. She kept shaking her head, as if doing so would erase the flood of disgusting images. It made things worse. She pictured Chloe undoing the toggle on Max's shorts. The image hit her like a hard punch to the stomach, causing her to take a sharp intake of air that made her chest burn.

Then she saw the claw hammer sitting there among a scattering of rusty nails. She snatched it up.

You did this to yourself, Rosie, she told herself.

Rosie placed her hand on top of the vice. It felt hard and cold.

You need to be punished.

She raised the hammer and prepared to strike.

It's the only way you'll learn.

Using all the angry force she could muster, she smashed the hammer straight across her knuckles.

The cracking sound the hammer had made as it slammed against her hand was hideous. The sickening pain was diabolical.

Rosie cried as the hammer slipped from her grasp and landed on the bench with a clunk. Then she fell to her knees, catching a stronger waft of petrol and rot down there. She shrieked in agony, pressing her battered hand to her chest.

'You did this to yourself, Rosie. Stop being such a fucking cry baby,' she said through gritted teeth. As she tried to move her fingers, the overwhelming pain almost made her vomit for the second time that day, but somehow, she fought down the bile in her throat and struggled to her feet. Then she decided that she hadn't been punished enough and grabbed the hammer again. Left hand shaking and dripping with dark blood, she placed it back onto the vice and inspected her damaged knuckles with morbid fascination.

'Stupid, stupid, Rosie!'

She gnashed her teeth and prepared the hammer for a second strike.

37

LOUISA

The sun felt warm on Louisa's face as she soaked up the Sunday afternoon rays in the garden. She stretched out on the reclining sun lounger and yawned. Her mind kept drifting to those drugs she still had hidden in her bedroom, and this was ruining her chilled vibe. She kept telling herself to ditch the stuff. However, the powder was still stashed inside Herbert's mouth. Why did she seem unable to flush the drug away when having it in the house worried her so much?

Today. I should just do it today, she told herself.

'Hey, you.'

Louisa shielded her eyes from the harsh sunshine and squinted at the blurry figure at the foot of the lounger.

'Dad, you're home.'

He'd finally remembered where he lived.

'Lovely day, right?' he said with a lopsided smile. He was wearing black sports shorts and a silver, long-sleeved running top that had a half-zip design. It lay open, revealing a small shock of dark chest hair.

She shifted herself up. 'They had you working all day? On a Sunday?'

'Afraid so. I've also been to the gym for a stint on the treadmill.'

'Are you staying home tonight?'

He gave her a long, questioning stare, his eyes full of mistrust. Then his face softened, and he said, 'Not tonight.'

'Mum was hoping you'd be home for Mexican Monday. She mentioned churros were on the menu for dessert.'

'I might be here for dinner tomorrow. We'll see.'

Louisa pulled up one leg and hugged her knee. 'Do you ever pretend to be someone you're not?'

His face darkened. 'Sorry?'

Louisa had let the words rolling around inside her head spill out without engaging her brain. 'For work, I mean,' she hastily added.

'I can't talk about that stuff. You shouldn't ask me about my work.'

'I'm not asking for specifics. Surely you can tell me something, can't you?'

'No, Louisa. I can't.'

'Not even a simple yes or no?'

He crossed his arms, offering no reply.

'All I want to know is if sometimes you need to change who you are. If you have ever pretended to play another character.'

'You want to know if I've ever worked undercover?'

'Have you? Are you?'

'Come on, Louisa.'

'I'm interested.'

'Yes, I have. But that's as much as I can tell you.'

'And you've had to do things? Like say, stuff that—'

'What did I just say?' His eyes flicked down to her feet. 'What's this?'

Louisa wiggled the toes on her right foot. 'It's called a foot. I have two of them and you use them to walk. They are incredibly useful.'

'Don't be glib. Take that white nail varnish off. Today. You hear me?'

'Why?'

'Because you're only fifteen. So do it!' he demanded aggressively.

Louisa bit her bottom lip and grumbled a curse under her breath. Her dad's fiery outburst made her stomach lurch.

'Did you say something?'

Louisa turned away from him and lifted her chin. 'Nope.'

'Look at me.'

Louisa grunted and turned back to him.

He uncrossed his arms and let them fall to his side. 'I'd rather not turn this into a massive debate. Just *do* it. I won't ask nicely again.'

Louisa smiled sarcastically. 'God, it's white varnish, not a skimpy mini—'

He interrupted her with a sharp, 'Enough with the smart-arse comments! This cocky attitude of yours will land you in major strife one day. It's not becoming, Louisa, it really isn't. The world is a vile place.'

His blue eyes bulged with intense fury, and Louisa struggled to keep eye contact. He scared her when he got like this.

He shook his head, then relaxed a little. 'You have no idea. No clue what's out there. No idea how sick some people can be.'

Here we go again.

He turned and started back to the house. As he walked, he said, 'And don't lay in the sun too long. You'll burn to a crisp.'

Louisa jumped to her feet. 'Are you and Mum going to get a divorce?'

He stopped in his tracks and gazed up into the sky.

'I have the right to know,' she said.

He let out a long, annoyed sigh. 'Not everything is as it seems, and you'd do well to remember that. It's a good thing you've got a smart head on your shoulders, but you still need to wise up and learn respect. Engage your brain before you open your mouth. Understand?' With that, he went inside the house.

Louisa flopped back down on the lounger. 'What the hell is that supposed to mean?' She let out a frustrated groan. Sometimes, she really disliked that man. Maybe her brother had been right, and she was just trying to blacken his name for no other reason than that she wanted *him* to suffer for once. She couldn't help fantasising about the day her mum finally came to her senses and threw him out. She'd watch from the window, giving him a coy wave as he loaded his suitcases in the car. Perhaps then she might be able to live her own life. She gazed at her white toes and groaned again.

38

HANNAH

10th June 2023

The dazzling sun dropped behind a mass of sugary-white clouds as Hannah stepped off the mountain bike and took in the stunning scenery. Miles and miles of dramatic, curving coastline stretched out in both directions. The corkscrew pathways rose and fell through hilly peaks, spotted with yellow flowers, weaving right along the side of limestone drops. The high-tide waves rolled in, crashing into the rocks below with an intense, foamy explosion. She caught the sound of screeching brakes and Max came to a jerky stop next to her, sweat beads glistening on his forehead.

Hannah offered him a playful grin. 'What kept you?'

Max unbuckled his helmet and tugged it free. 'You sped off like a lunatic down that last hill. I take it you're no novice?'

Hannah smiled. 'I used to ride a bit,' she said. That was an understatement. She'd had a spell of doing regular charity rides and once rode 120 miles in one day, but she didn't want to brag. 'These are not bad machines for rentals. Gears are a tad sticky for my liking.'

Max raised his eyebrows and pulled a silly face. 'Exactly, right? That's what's holding me back.' He wiped his brow with the back of his hand. 'Quite the view here. This looks like a decent picnic spot.'

'I was thinking over there looks ideal,' said Hannah, gesturing at a prominent, craggy spit of land covered in patches of verdant grass and dark, reddish rock.

'Seriously, you're really going to make me work for my lunch today. Should I worry that my balls are going numb?'

'Ah, you poor thing. You need a ten-minute breather?'

'Yeah, but something tells me I'm not going to get one.'

The sun edged out from behind the clouds, and Hannah adjusted her wraparound shades. 'Just another two miles and we'll be over there.' She remounted the bike. 'Let's go.'

Max laughed and scanned the land with one hand shading his eyes. 'Two miles? I like your optimism, but that looks more like a good four miles to me.'

Hannah started off with a push and raced down the trail. 'Guess there's only one way to find out,' she yelled.

'Right behind you.'

Hannah hit a steep downhill section and really went for it. With the wind smashing into her face and the fresh sea air in her lungs, she felt more alive than she had for ages. The weekend had been fantastic so far. Max had been a fun companion and a change of scenery had done her the world of good. She stood up and pedalled harder as the dry, snaking path inclined, bringing her close to a sheer drop. Hannah peered over the edge and glimpsed aggressive waves swirling around a collection of boulders in a small inlet bay.

The bike's chunky tyres flung up small rocks and dust as she crunched through the gears. One false move here and she'd lose control of the bike and plunge over the edge.

But she wasn't worried. Today, she was in total control.

39

ROSIE

August 1993

Rosie's eyes were becoming heavy, and she let the magazine slip from her fingers. The painkillers the nurse had given her were making her drowsy, and she felt like she'd been glued to the bed. The sound of footsteps jolted her awake.

'Hey, sleepy pants.'

Rosie stared at her friend, offering no greeting. Chloe was wearing her purple crop top with no bra underneath and ripped denim shorts that could almost be described as knickers. Her hair was up in a high ponytail, and she looked tired. It was clear she'd not packed enough clothing for their trip. She even smelled musty and dirty now.

'What happened, Rosie?'

'I shut my hand in a door.'

'Ouch. How the hell did you manage that, you clumsy tit?'

'Just a stupid accident.'

Chloe sat on the end of the bed and offered her a droopy-lipped smile. 'Well, this is shit. Your dad said you had a funny turn in the night, and you need to stay in for observation. He's in the shops, by the way.'

'I fainted. But I'm OK.'

'So what am I meant to do now?'

'Look, I'm so sorry, Chloe, but it might be for the best if you went back home in the morning.'

'I can't. I'm too skint to get the bus home. I was assuming I'd come home with you and your parents.'

'Sorry, but with all this… it's probably for the best. I'll get my parents to lend you the bus fare. I'll explain about your dad and everything. Say you need to get back because you're in big trouble back home.'

'No.'

'What? You have to. Who knows how long I'll be stuck in here?'

'I said no. I'm not going home.'

'But… you have to. You will have to go home tomorrow. I'm sorry, but that's final, so you'll need to leave our cabin first thing.'

Chloe slid off the bed and came closer to her. 'Lucky it's your left hand.' She smiled and took hold of her hand, making her wince.

'That hurts. Don't touch it.'

'I see what you're doing here, Rosie,' said Chloe in a sing-song voice. 'I know what you're up to.'

Rosie sat up and let out a whimper of pain. 'Stop acting weird.'

'You don't trust me around your boyfriend, do you?' Chloe stepped away from her and let out an exaggerated sigh. She walked over to the bulky TV parked on a stand in the corner of the room and switched it on. 'Isn't it nice they took you off the ward and gave you this special room all to yourself?'

'The TV doesn't work,' said Rosie.

'So, what are you going to do? Hey? Lie there like a grumpy chump feeling sorry for yourself?'

'I'll cope.'

Chloe put her hands on her hips and flashed her a wide, nasty smile. 'If I wanted to fuck Max, I'd fuck him!' She raised one hand and clicked her fingers. 'It would be as easy as that.'

Rosie, so shocked by her friend's words, was speechless.

'You are seriously grating on my nerves now. Just who do you think you are? Trying to pack me off home because you're a jealous little bitch who has trust issues.' Chloe rubbed her hand over her forehead and groaned. 'Every person in school thinks you're a sap. A flaky, annoying sap. But me, I decided to give you some slack and risk my reputation by being your friend. And this is the thanks I get.' She sneered. 'Though, if I'm honest, me coming here isn't public knowledge. I mean, I need to keep some dignity, right? I do have my street cred to consider.'

'I would like you to leave. I'd like you to go now,' Rosie managed to mutter.

'I was prepared to help you. To help mould you into... into something.' She flicked her fingers at Rosie. 'Something that isn't *this*. Something that isn't a saddo loser who's got a fondness for self-harm.'

'What? No. This was an accident. I already said.'

'Gossips talk, Rosie. Are you that thick? You reckon it's such a *big* secret?'

Rosie felt the tears forming behind her eyes as she bit back a gasp.

Chloe smirked. 'You're angry at yourself for inviting me here, aren't you? Angry because things didn't turn out like you'd planned.'

Rosie tried to hide her surprise but guessed she'd failed. She wiped away a few tears from the corners of her eyes.

Chloe came back over and put her elbows on the bed and rested her chin on her knuckles. 'You wanted to punish yourself, didn't you?'

Rosie shook her head over and over. 'No, stop saying such things.'

'Yeah, you did. Admit it. Admit that you hurt yourself when things don't go your way? Do you hate yourself that much?'

'Leave me alone.'

'You need help, and sorry if this sounds mean, but you need pills to sort out your messed up head.'

'What I need is for you to go away. What will that take?'

Chloe flashed her a lazy smile and nodded. 'Fine… fine… fine… If that's what you want. I'll leave you to wallow in your own miserable self-pity. I tried to be nice. Don't say I didn't try. I certainly won't bother again.'

'You don't know me, Chloe.'

'Oh, but I do. I see you for what you are.'

'I thought you were different from the others.'

'You're pathetic. I know it, you know it, everybody knows it,' whispered Chloe. 'So does the wonderful Max. See you around.'

Once Chloe had left the room, Rosie grabbed her damaged hand and squeezed it until she hissed in pain. How stupid had she been to believe that she could have been genuine friends with this vile girl?

She'd got it all wrong. Why did she always get it so wrong?

40

LOUISA

Louisa raced to the lounge window and flung the curtains aside. Her dad had come home, and it was time to put her plan into action. But now it was time to act; her confidence had dwindled. She watched him get out of the car and stretch out his arms.

'He's come home,' said Jamie.

Louisa turned to find her brother standing in the doorway, smiling deviously. He was wearing his blue cotton dressing gown, his hair wet from the shower.

'Do you have it?' he asked.

Louisa nodded and tapped her floral pyjama shorts. She wanted to moan at him again for taking so long to get the damn key tracker from his nerdy mate, but decided now was not the time. 'Where's Mum? I'm surprised she's not sprinting up the drive to welcome him with open arms and a goofy smile.'

'She's tidying up the bathroom. Apparently, I made a massive mess.' He shrugged. 'But it's best she's out of the way for ten minutes.'

Louisa heard the door open and close. She shared a nervous smile with her brother, and they both shuffled into the hallway to greet their dad.

'All right, Dad,' said Jamie.

Their dad was wearing a blue Adidas tracksuit and had a black sports holdall slung over his shoulder. 'Hey. You two OK?'

'How was the bike riding trip with your friends?' asked Louisa, doing her best to keep the barbed tone out of her voice.

'Tough going. Really tough.' He dropped the bag at his side. 'I might start going a couple of times a month.'

'Great, maybe we could all go,' said Louisa with a smile. 'Where did you say you went again?'

'I didn't,' he said. 'What's with the welcoming committee? You two need something?' he asked as he strutted past them and made for the stairs.

Louisa lifted her chin. 'Dad, I—'

Jamie cut in. 'Can you grab something from your car for me, Dad? My phone charger isn't working. I think I left my spare in the back somewhere.'

Their dad fished a set of keys out of his tracksuit pocket and threw them at Jamie. 'I'm not your personal assistant and don't forget to lock it.'

Jamie pulled a face that suggested this would all be a massive effort. 'I won't,' he grumbled.

'What did you want to say, Louisa?' her dad asked her.

'Oh, I… Mum said there's some leftover sausage pasta in the fridge. She made loads.'

'I ate with my buddies, so I'm good,' he said, then continued up the stairs.

As Jamie walked past Louisa, he held out his hand, and she slipped the key tracking device, which wasn't much bigger than a two-pound coin, into it.

Louisa had to stifle a laugh as Jamie strolled through the front door with zero apprehension. Her heart was beating a million times a minute, and she'd been worried sick at the thought of asking her dad for his keys. That little turd had carried out the task so easily that it made her feel ridiculous. She had to hand it to her brother; he'd handled that well. Perhaps he wasn't a completely useless loser after all. Now, thanks to Jamie and his geeky mate who'd let them borrow the device, she might get some answers.

41

HANNAH

Hannah woke up and stretched out her legs. They still ached from the weekend's cycling trip. When she checked her phone, she was surprised to learn it was almost ten. She pushed herself upright and rolled her head to ease the tension in her neck. She sat for a while, listening for any sound that might suggest Max was still here. He'd not even mentioned his friend's flat again. Neither had she. They'd behaved like a proper couple during their weekend getaway. What was she thinking? They *were* a proper couple now. Weren't they?

Hannah slipped out of bed, threw on her dressing gown and stared down at her bedside table. She frowned. Her small gold photo frame was missing. She dropped to her knees and rummaged around her things, tossing make-up wipes and books aside in her frantic search for it. Not finding it, she lifted the small unit and checked behind to determine if it had been knocked down the back. But there was still no sign of it. She stood up and immediately noticed that the photo of her and Archie biting their medals was also gone.

Hannah left her bedroom and discovered that the wedding portrait photo of her and Archie was missing from the top of the stairs. All she saw now was a single picture hook. It hung by a thread, suggesting the missing frame had been torn down.

'What the hell?' she grumbled to herself as she stomped down the stairs. 'Max? Max, where are you?' she called as she stormed into the lounge. Somehow, she knew. She just knew that her beloved holiday photo would also be missing. Yet, confirming this caused her to let out a nervous shriek.

Hannah spotted Max in the adjoining room, sitting at her dining table, drinking coffee. She swallowed her rage and charged into the room. She stopped dead when she saw what was on the table. The glass ball with the silver horse inside it. And next to it, Archie's old claw hammer that he kept under the sink.

Max offered her a calm smile and said, 'Hey you. Good morning. Sleep well? My calves are still burning from the weekend. How are yours?'

Hannah put her hands on her hips. 'What's going on?'

'Coffee? You look like you need it.'

'Max, where the hell are all my photos?'

'Gone,' he said in a carefree tone.

Hannah slapped her hand onto the table. 'Where are they?'

'I took them.'

'I want them back. Right this second.'

'What can I tell you? I can't get them back. I took them to the tip in Islington first thing.'

Hannah took a deep breath and a step back as she tried to gather her thoughts and keep it together.

'OK, I'm going to need you to pick up this hammer, Hannah. I'm going to need you to smash this crystal orb into pieces.'

'I want those photos. You haven't binned them. So don't lie to me.'

'Take the hammer. It's for your own good. Trust me, it will help.'

'I want them back. Now. Do you understand me? Right now, Max!'

Max let out a tired huff. 'I told you. They are long gone. It's time to let go of the past and move on. And think about me for a minute. I mean, come on, you can't expect me to stay here with your dead husband's face gawping at me everywhere I go.' He laughed dryly. 'No wonder you're having dreams about him, so will I at this rate.'

'You get them back. I mean it. Get them right now!'

Max gave her a callous smirk. His eyes were different. He was different. This was reminiscent of the way he'd acted when he took hold of her wrist and instructed her to cry for him. He rubbed his hands together. 'OK, here's the thing. We need to make some changes around here. *You* need to make changes. Understand?'

Hannah's breathing had grown so ragged her nostrils were flaring and she was wheezing and shaking.

Max drummed his finger on the table. 'Now, I'm also going to need you to try harder. With this place. Frankly, you live like a slob and it's unacceptable. What do you do all day? It's not like you have a job now, is it? You're lazy. My wife might be a total fruitcake, but at least she's a tidy fruitcake. She's a very clean person and that—'

'Then I suggest you fuck off back home to her!' hissed Hannah.

Max tutted and shook his head. 'Don't interrupt me.' He picked up the hammer and offered the handle to her. 'Come on, take this. It's time. You'll feel so much better afterwards.'

Hannah stepped over to the table, battered the hammer aside and made a grab for the glass ball. Max had clearly foreseen the move and snatched it first. He slammed the hammer down onto the table, causing Hannah to jump back as the coffee cup bounced and tipped over. He stood up, sending the chair crashing backwards.

'Give it to me and get out of my house!' she demanded. 'Get out before I call the police.'

Max laughed out loud. 'Oh, Hannah, have you any idea how badly that would end for you?'

'You think I won't call them? I will! What are you up to, you vindictive bastard?'

'Go ahead. Go on. I won't stop you. We'll show them the

illicit drugs you keep in your bathroom cupboard. For a start, those Diazepam you buy on the black market because, I assume, the doctor won't prescribe them any longer. And that's only the start. You really want to open that door? What else would they find?'

'I don't give a shit what they find.'

'I can get my hands on all kinds. Copious amounts of all the good stuff.'

'What is that meant to mean?'

'I'm not so sure you'd cope so well inside. Prison would break a woman like you.'

'What's this all about? What are you doing?'

'How much coke did you have on you? When you got arrested outside that club in central London? Four grams, wasn't it? Then there's the drink driving charge last year. Four times over the limit, right?' He let the hammer fall to his side and held out the crystal, giving it an intense stare. 'Mm, I foresee a very bleak future for you. Unless you make some big lifestyle choices.' He tossed the ball into the air and batted it with the hammer. The ornament exploded into a shower of tiny pieces which clattered down onto the dining table and floor.

Hannah gawped at the shimmering fragments and couldn't even work out where the little horse had gone.

Max studied the mess he'd made with a listless smile. 'It would have been better for you to have done that.'

Hannah placed both hands on her head and dug her fingers into her skin. She wanted to scream in frustration. Who was this man?

Max tossed the hammer down onto the table. 'You should stop going to that bridge. Would you do that for me?'

She gave him an incredulous glare but was stunned into silence and couldn't respond.

'I know lots of things, Hannah. In my world, it's essential to have all the information. All the important facts. If I decided to, I could make your life even more miserable than it already is. Do you believe me?' His features darkened and his eyes narrowed. 'Do you believe me?' he asked again, more forcefully.

Hannah swallowed hard and nodded. She did believe him. Even though she had no idea why this man was treating her so badly. It made no sense. What had she done to warrant this malicious behaviour from him?

'Anyway, I have things to attend to. You fancy a takeout from that Vietnamese place tonight? Get some of that fantastic spicy crab dish?'

Hannah couldn't get her head around this. Now he was talking to her like nothing had happened and looking at her as if he expected an answer about the damn crab dish. As if everything was suddenly back to normal.

'Drop me a text and let me know what you fancy eating. I need to pop back to mine to grab some bits later. See you around… say six-ish. Does that work for you?'

Hannah could only stare at him, flabbergasted, as he gave her a friendly smile and sauntered off like everything was all fine. She gazed down at the broken fragments. If she hadn't seen them, she'd have sworn she'd imagined the whole episode and was losing the plot.

Then she thought about those missing photos and her heart sank.

Another wave of panic hit her. Ollie's room. She bolted upstairs to her son's bedroom door. Tried the handle. Locked.

She breathed a tiny sigh of relief that Max, at least, hadn't been in there. That would have completely destroyed her. She touched the wooden name plaque on the door and silently cried as she pressed her forehead against it.

If Max was telling the truth and he'd binned her cherished memories, she'd make him pay.

42

ROSIE

August 1993

Rosie awoke and her first thought was of Max and Chloe. Together. She'd even dreamed about them. Dreamed about them being intimate. She'd seen the pair blatantly making out in front of her. They'd been touching each other, despite knowing she was standing there witnessing their sickening betrayal. Both of them had been enjoying her discomfort. Revelling in her suffering and the devastating heartbreak and torment they were subjecting her to.

Rosie shook her head, desperate to shake away the graphic images. When this didn't work, she grabbed her bad hand and pressed her fingers into the bruised knuckles. The wave of sudden pain made her hiss out a silent scream. She jumped out of bed and paced the room.

Why was she like this? Why didn't her mind switch off? Even when she slept, it just never, ever switched off. She'd do anything to be able to find a way to empty her head. Remove all her thoughts. To turn her brain into a barren place. So it would become a blank canvas. So she no longer cared. About the past, the future, or even right now. So she could just exist. Be happy and enjoy life. Carefree and normal.

Chloe's words echoed through her broken mind: *Do you hate yourself that much?*

She did hate herself, but not nearly as much as she hated that bitch. Not nearly as much as she hated the entire world right now.

The question was, would Chloe really go after Max? Would she steal her boy?

Rosie pictured the pair at her quiet place. Pictured Max kissing the other girl. Pictured Chloe wrapping her arms around his big shoulders. This was enough to spur her into action, and she hunted the room for her clothes.

43

LOUISA

Louisa had a beast of a migraine and decided she must've looked pretty rough for her remorseless maths teacher to have suggested she went home early that afternoon. She'd refused to go at first, but the grinding ache in her temples had made it nigh on impossible to concentrate, so she'd folded and called it a day. She hated getting these strange headaches. They came on so suddenly and sometimes they'd make her feel lightheaded, and she'd get flashing dots behind her eyes. Each time one hit, she'd convince herself it was something other than a migraine. She'd convince herself that it had to be something worse. Something life-threatening. The doctor had told her they were likely acute tension migraines, but she wasn't so sure. She hadn't been impressed by how quick he'd been to dismiss her. Her parents were just as bad, and they thought she was a total hypochondriac and, according to them, her obsessive online researching and the constant need to find reassurance was clear proof of this. Louisa couldn't help it. So many things could go wrong with the fragile human body. You ignored the signs of ill health at your own stupid peril. She'd read enough scary stories online to know that much. So being ignorant was plain foolish.

Louisa stuck her key in the front door and let herself inside. She emitted a long groan in response to the loud music blaring out from the kitchen. 'Ah, turn that down,' she mumbled, too whacked to even manage to raise her voice over the noise. She let her school bag drop to the floor and kicked off her shoes, leaving them where they landed. 'Mum,' she moaned as she shuffled along the hallway. The kitchen door was open a crack. She put her hand against it, but instead of shoving it open, she froze. The scene that greeted Louisa caused her jaw to drop, and then the impulse to erupt into a fit of hysterical giggles hit her so hard she had to slap both hands over her gaping mouth.

Her mum was dancing. Not merely dancing but bouncing around like a lunatic and wearing nothing but her underwear. A black frilly set which Louisa couldn't imagine her mum even owning, let alone wearing while parading about the house like a mad person.

Louisa wanted to bash open the door and ask her what in the world she was up to. Yet, she couldn't move. She was glued to the spot, so entranced by this weird little display in front of her. The music seemed to get louder as the track intensified. She knew that song. She'd heard her mum play it before. "The Sun Always Shines on TV" by A-ha.

Now her mum's energy soared. Arms pumping the air as she jumped on the spot like she was at the front of a wild music festival, surrounded by an uplifted crowd leaping around her. As the tempo of the music changed, she stretched out her arms to the side and wiggled her hips.

For a moment, Louisa considered snatching out her phone to film the funny dance routine but dismissed that idea. Then something caught her attention. Her mum was clutching something in her right hand.

It was that friendship bracelet she'd been holding in the garden.

Louisa strained her eyes to see the name on the small, coloured cubes, but her mum was too far back, and her arms were moving fast again as she pranced and gyrated about in a circle.

As the song ended, her mum held the bracelet to her chest

and gazed up to the ceiling. She let out a thrilled chuckle, appearing as though she'd just had the time of her life. With a bright smile on her face, she trotted over to the kitchen table and picked up a glass of water. As she sipped the drink, she appeared to tense and listen. It was as if she'd become aware she was no longer alone in the house.

Louisa slunk away from the door and edged backwards to her stuff. She slipped on her shoes and grabbed her bag. As she silently left the house and scurried off along the driveway, she realised her migraine had cleared at least.

44

HANNAH

Hannah's eyes flicked open and she blinked several times. Her heart was racing, and she was drenched in cold, sticky sweat. She rolled over, sending several sofa cushions tumbling. She noticed the three empty wine bottles on the lounge table and winced. Now, she recalled that she'd not even bothered with a glass last night and had made do with chugging the booze straight out of the bottles. *How classy.* Not her best move, she now decided as a wave of head-pounding pain radiated around her skull. She'd passed out and fallen into a deep, disturbing fever dream, leaving several candles burning.

Hannah stood and walked into the dining room. The strewn crystal shards over the floor and table were evidence enough that this morning's events hadn't been part of that diabolical dream. She leaned on the table, her head spinning as the sequences from the dream came to her. It had been a visceral, torturously realistic nightmare that had assaulted and over-whelmed every one of her senses.

She'd been stepping through an inky black tunnel that had been reminiscent of an abandoned Tube line. Every now and then, the dull yellow lights would flicker, revealing patchy, grey walls, twisted pipes and scurrying rats. Inside the small, cramped tunnel, there were doors. Lots of steel doors.

There had been a memory behind each door. A glimpse at the bad times. A vivid depiction of the things she detested, feared, or had lost. Not just a glimpse. She hadn't simply seen those memories. She'd relived them.

A series of intense flashbacks came to her as if she was opening those doors all over again.

Hannah had seen a bike twisted in the road, one wheel spinning ominously. The bike crash she'd witnessed as a young girl in Hackney, she knew. Her dad had told her not to look at the aftermath, yet she'd stared at the startling damage caused, regardless.

Upon opening another door, Hannah had found herself inside her little Renault Clio as it spun across the motorway, and she'd experienced the terror before the moment of impact. The near-fatal crash she'd been involved in at the age of nineteen. The lorry she'd seen hurtling towards her. It had veered away and missed her car by mere feet.

Another door had led to Hannah standing in the hospital's accident and emergency area, where she witnessed her eight-year-old son being moved from the ambulance with frightening swiftness. Seen his small body laid upon that moving stretcher. He'd looked so helpless as he passed under those blinding, fluorescent lights, and they'd taken him into the isolated intensive care area in the depths of the massive complex. And she'd felt so useless as she'd run after the staff, calling for them to bring him back to her.

Hannah crouched down and placed her hand on the broken pieces of glass. She closed her eyes and grimaced as more snippets of the dream came to her.

A train thundering along a rubbish-strewn track.

Everything bad she'd ever experienced had come back to haunt her.

Those suffocating memories.

The deep sense of sorrow. Depression. Fear. Hate. An all-consuming, harrowing sensation that was enough to make her hunt for more alcohol to numb her overactive brain.

She'd found herself in a disgusting toilet cubicle, sniffing a long line of white powder and tilting her head to snort it right back down her throat.

Shoving pills into her greedy mouth and washing them down with strong booze.

Another scene developed in Hannah's head of that po-faced police officer who'd been wearing a bright yellow jacket... wet from the heavy shower. A breathalyser unit gripped in his hand as he gestured her over with a stiff wave.

Then she remembered the snow, and recalled putting on shoes and racing outside, full of excitement. The field she found herself in was vast and blanketed in wintry white. A hefty white horse stood in the distance. Every time she moved closer, it drifted away as though it didn't want her getting near. She tried to capture it on her phone, but the image came out as a ghostly blur.

Was it even a memory? She wasn't sure. It stirred something heavy in her gut, though she couldn't say why.

'I want to guide you off this path. This path towards total self-destruction,' came a soft voice that broke her from her moment of remembrance.

Hannah peered up to find Max looking down at her with an expression on his face that suggested genuine concern and despair.

Hannah closed her eyes and didn't even push him away as he stroked her cheek.

'I'm not mad at you. I know how hard it is, Hannah. Trust me, I do.'

She wanted to tell him to get out. To leave and never come back. But she didn't possess the energy. She was weak, shaky, broken, useless, pathetic.

'Did you take any pills?' he asked, his voice gentle. 'Can you remember if you took anything today?'

'No.'

'No, you can't remember? Or, no you didn't?'

Hannah rubbed her clammy forehead and ignored him. She needed more sleep. Even if that would lead to more dark places.

'The food is in the kitchen. You should eat. Then I'll help you tidy up all this mess. We'll put everything straight. I promise.'

'Where are those photos? I want them,' she said, frustrated by how feeble she sounded. 'I must have them back.'

'Come on, we've been over all this. I want to make you better, and I want to pull you out of this pit of misery you're wallowing in. I want to give you the fresh start you need. Can't you see that? Can't you see what I'm trying to achieve here? If I had known you were this bad, I would never have encouraged you to drink. Why didn't you tell me?'

Hannah opened her eyes and blinked. 'You shouldn't have taken my stuff. You shouldn't have done that.'

'I see things, Hannah. In my world, I see things. I see what addiction can do to a person. How it changes them. Ruins them. I can tell you right now that this path you're on leads to a grim place. A downward spiral that will destroy all that you have. Do you want to lose everything?'

Hannah fingered the broken crystal pieces under her hand and just stared at him. She already *had* lost everything.

'Now, please tell me, did you take any pills today?' he asked.

Hannah shrugged. 'Probably.'

He watched her for a moment, as if weighing up how best to respond to her flippant reply. Then he said, 'I want to help you. But you need to try. You need to put in the effort. Come on, grab some plates. Let's eat up before it gets cold.' With that, he left the room.

Hannah stood up and eyed the hammer on the table. She brushed her fingers over the handle yet decided not to pick it up. Because if she did, she'd follow Max into the kitchen and smash it over his head. Not that she had the strength in her to carry out the task in that moment if someone had offered her a million pounds to do it.

45

ROSIE

August 1993

When Rosie caught the distant sound of electronic dance music, she knew straight away the noise was coming from her lake. The eagerness to learn why music was playing in her spot spurred her on, despite the darkness hampering her footsteps.

As Rosie descended the last section of the hill, the intensity of the music increased to the point she felt the beat inside her chest, and she became aware of more noises intermixing with the booming tune. Laughter, high-pitched yelling, whooping, shrieking.

There were people down there. Lots of them. This idea made her head spin. It couldn't be. It just wasn't possible.

For a moment, all Rosie could do was stand there gazing dumbly at the darkness ahead as she caught the sounds of excited youngsters echoing through the blackness. The idea of heading down there to see what lay in wait for her made her go weak at the knees, but she pushed herself on and went down the grassy hillside.

What she saw when she reached the clearing made her heart shatter into a thousand pieces.

There were bodies moving everywhere.

Teenagers swimming, dancing, drinking, smoking, making out. One lad was unashamedly urinating into the water, even though some of the group were bathing in the lake. Nobody even appeared outraged by his disgusting behaviour, nor did they attempt to get out of the water.

Yellow lights spun and flashed. For a moment, Rosie couldn't for the life of her grasp where the source of the lights was coming from, but then she realised that several roadwork lights had been dotted around the edges of the clearing.

The music blasted out from a black, beefy boombox which sat upon a green beer crate. A bunch of cassettes bounced on the top. The pounding dance track faded to a stop, and another track kicked in. Haddaway's "What is Love" came on, and this generated a roar of whoops and cheers as the rowdy bunch danced harder and waved their hands.

More bodies pranced about a makeshift fire that spewed unhealthy-smelling smoke.

Rosie, flabbergasted, edged into the madness and tried to process what was happening right in front of her. Tried to discern why a boisterous, uncivilised bunch of teens had taken over her spot. She recognised a few faces from the Deer Meadows caravan site, and she also spotted some of the young, unruly soldiers she'd seen loitering around the village.

One skinny teenager, wearing just green boxer shorts, necked a beer, smashed the can over his head and set off at a sprint. He charged into the lake, making a sound like a crazy chimpanzee.

Rosie witnessed a teenage girl in a black bikini flick her cigarette butt to the ground, which was littered with bottles, beer cans and other rubbish.

Rosie tried to find her voice. She wanted to scream at these trespassers. Order them to leave and never come back. Yet, she couldn't speak. The words wouldn't come. The intense emotions left her disoriented, and all she could manage was a feeble, 'No, no. Stop.' The lyrics of the noisy song pulsated in her throbbing head. 'You must leave.'

Now the partygoers noticed her presence. Reproachful eyes started following her every move. Amused smiles. Big, nasty grins and arrogant sneers. Some pointed at her. They glared at her as if she were the encroacher. As if she was the one in the wrong here because she'd turned up to spoil their riotous party.

Rosie's eyes scanned those faces. Swept the lake.

Searched for *her*. Hunted for *him*.

A skinny boy with a ponytail started gyrating in front of Rosie. He wore a baggy, unbuttoned chequered shirt and Hawaiian-style swim shorts. She sidestepped past the annoying boy and moved closer to the water. Stepping into a pile of smashed glass was the final straw. Her blood boiled. Her heart pounded, echoing behind her ears. They were wrecking her spot. It felt like they'd ripped out her broken heart and were stamping the organ into mulch. This gathering of vile people wanted to ruin her special place. They'd defiled her cherished lake.

These dire sensations were too much. She detested these teenagers. All of them. She wished they would all drop dead right there and then.

'You can't be here!' she managed to shout over the music. 'You all need to leave! Come on, out of here, the lot of you.'

A few of the teens acknowledged her words with a sneer or a snigger, but most of the group ignored her or likely hadn't even heard her.

Rosie spotted a topless yob with a mop of wiry hair finish his beer and lob his empty bottle into the centre of the lake. He pumped his fist as if he believed the mindless act had been so clever.

Rosie couldn't take it any longer. Storming over to the boombox, she let out a hideous, high-pitched scream as she stamped on the stereo, killing the music and casting an instant, tense silence around her.

The silence lasted for a good ten seconds before a stocky lad with a shaved head came wading out of the lake and made a beeline for her. On his arrival, he stared down at the broken boombox with a furious scowl before his eyes locked onto Rosie. Eyes that blazed with a smouldering hatred. 'What did you do, you mad bitch?' he asked through gritted teeth. 'My new Sony.' He touched his broken gadget as though it was a dying puppy lying at his feet. 'My Sony!'

Rosie lifted her chin and gave the big lad a defiant stare. He was an intimidating character with a round face and thick, rubbery lips.

'You can fucking pay for that, you skinny little slag! You hear me?' spat the lad. 'It's brand new that.'

'You are not supposed to be down here,' stated Rosie, crossing her arms as she tried to stand taller in the hope this would gain her some authority over the older teens.

The group gathered around, clearly eager to watch the angry exchange unfold.

The big lad got in Rosie's face and snarled, 'Why? You own the entire lake, do you? Who the fuck do you think you are?'

'Chuck her in the water, Griff,' shouted a girl standing with the group who was wearing a pink baseball cap and a skimpy white bikini. 'Stupid bitch has shagged the music box.'

'For fuck's sake, she's totally killed the mood,' chipped in another girl who had wet ginger hair stuck to her face. She was dressed in an oversized, soaking wet T-shirt and super-tight hot pants. 'She's ruined the party now.'

Rosie, although scared, did not back down. This place belonged to her, and she'd fight for it. 'I know the owners, and I will tell them what you're doing here, so you need to go before they call the police, and you all get into trouble.'

The group erupted into spiteful laughter. The spinning road lights made their faces appear ethereal and mean.

'That's Hudson's bird,' yelled a lad standing in the shadows.

'Where is Max? Is he here? I need to see him!' exclaimed Rosie.

More laughter and sniggering.

'Yeah, he's here all right,' said the girl in the baseball cap. She offered Rosie a dirty sneer. 'He's definitely here!'

'Over the other side of the lake,' said another lad.

'Maybe you should go and spoil his party, too,' suggested the ginger-haired girl, before whispering something to another catty-faced girl standing next to her.

The boy, Griff, now down on his knees, studied his damaged boombox, his face a mask of pure fury.

But all Rosie cared about now was finding Max.

'Talk of the devil,' said the boy with the ponytail. He nodded down to the water's edge, where two figures strolled along, hand in hand. The pair chatted away, lost in each other's company, blissfully unaware of the commotion that had unfolded in the clearing.

Rosie stepped out of the group and made for the pair, who were now heading for the fire circle.

As the pair came into the light, Rosie's stomach lurched. Max, topless, a wide, delighted grin plastered on his face. And Chloe, in her jean shorts, which were unbuttoned, and her crop top with no bra. Both of them had a sheen of sweat on their foreheads.

It felt like icy splinters were slamming right into the very centre of Rosie's crushed heart. It couldn't have been more obvious what the pair had been up to. It was written all over their gleeful faces for the entire group to see. She wanted the ground to open up and swallow her. To plunge her into a pit deep enough to send her to her death. Anything would be preferable to enduring this utter torment.

Max noticed her standing there, and the smile dropped from his face and morphed into a confused wince. Yet he did not let go of the other girl's hand as he stared at Rosie.

Chloe noticed her then. Her smile was brief and unapolo-getic. No, she looked pleased as punch that Rosie had caught them together. She even tilted her head and rested it on Max's shoulder. She'd claimed him, Rosie knew. Her so-called friend had stolen her boy.

Then Rosie sensed movement behind her. The enraged Griff steamed towards her, his eyes burning with explosive hatred. Before Rosie had the chance to act, the muscular lad grabbed her by the arm and spun her around to face him.

46

LOUISA

16th June 2023

Concealed between two parked vans, Louisa studied the key icon on her phone's screen, which confirmed her dad's BMW had left the property in Finsbury. The device didn't do real-time route tracking, so she had to keep waiting for it to update its current position. Even though the icon had moved a couple of miles away now, she stayed hidden and kept updating the app every twenty seconds so she could monitor his route. She wanted to make sure the car was heading well away from here and her dad wasn't just nipping five minutes up the road.

After a few more updates, Louisa concluded he would likely be heading home or back to work after the tracker showed his position was Seven Sisters Road, and he appeared to be heading north in the direction of Tottenham. With her heart thudding and her hands shaking, Louisa took a slow walk to the house. The building, a dull, yellow-bricked semi-detached home, brought about a sense of gloom. She guessed it was a two-bedroom and couldn't help noticing how grimy the windows were and how tatty the blinds and curtains looked.

Louisa scanned the unkempt, weed-covered driveway. If she hadn't spied her dad's shiny BMW parked here earlier, she might have doubted she was standing outside the correct property. And calling this a driveway was being kind. You could barely call it a parking space. Though, she guessed any off-road parking was a sought-after luxury in these parts.

Now, standing here, gazing at the scruffy house and contemplating what she needed to do, she struggled to find her backbone. She forced herself across onto the road and strode, with a confidence she did not feel, up the small driveway and knocked on the red, paint-peeled door.

No reply. She knocked again.

Still no reply. Another knock, harder this time.

Louisa heard a click and rummaged in her pockets for the piece of paper she'd shoved in her school blazer earlier.

The door opened and a woman stood there, staring at her with clear mistrust in her eyes.

'Can I help you?' asked the woman with a guarded frown.

The first thing that hit Louisa was the smell. The woman carried a definite boozy odour, and it wasn't just her. The house itself had an iffy whiff about it. A stale, heavy pong, like the windows hadn't been cracked open in many days, drifted out and this almost caused Louisa to take a big step back.

Louisa forced a smile and tried to work out what exactly her dad was up to here. She deduced this lady must have been in her mid to late forties. She was of mixed race and had coffee-coloured hair, frizzy locks styled in a messy bun, with a few loose strands framing her face. Her glazed, acorn-coloured eyes were accusing and weary. The skin under those eyes was puffy. She wore white jogging bottoms with the toggles undone and a faded, green New Balance T-shirt.

'Can I help you?' the woman repeated.

Louisa decided the woman's face was beautiful and her well-defined cheekbones demanded attention, but she got the distinct impression she hadn't been taking care of herself. She was, as her mum would say, a bit rough around the edges.

Louisa wanted to ask this woman why her dad's car had just left her driveway and why he'd stayed here this week. Because she knew he had. She'd been continuously monitoring his whereabouts with the key tracker. Instead, she nodded and showed the woman the crumpled piece of paper. 'I lost my cat. This is her. She went missing from Oakdale Road,' lied Louisa. She then spied all the wine bottles and beer cans piled high in a recycling box nestled between two wheelie bins. A couple of vodka bottles as well.

The woman gave the piece of paper a cursory glance and shook her head. 'Sorry, can't say I've seen your cat around here.'

'Oh,' said Louisa, as she desperately tried to think of something else to say to this stranger. Her mind went blank.

'I hope you find her,' said the woman, preparing to close the door.

'Her name is Beatrice,' blurted Louisa. 'She's fond of chicken. If you see her, leave some on your driveway and she'll be your best friend.'

'Sure. Can I take that picture of her?'

Louisa handed the woman the random cat poster she'd printed from a lost pets website. 'Of course. Here.'

The woman studied the poster, then set her eyes back on Louisa. 'How will I contact you if I see Beatrice? You don't have a number on here.'

'Oh, some of the posters didn't print the number at the bottom. My printer is rubbish.'

'Do you have another poster?'

'Um, no. That's the last one. I'll write my phone number on the back.' Louisa pretended to search her pockets. 'Now, what did I do with my pen?' Then she pretended to rummage in her school bag. 'I'm so disorganised.'

'I'll go get you one.'

'Thanks. Sorry.'

As the woman shuffled back inside the house, Louisa darted off the driveway and dashed up the road. She didn't stop running until she was several streets away from the woman's house.

Louisa made her way to the train station and wondered if running off like that had been a sensible move. But she had to get out of there and she'd just panicked. She'd only set out to see what the other woman looked like. Only now she had more questions than answers. And then a thought struck her like a thunderbolt, and she slapped her hand over her mouth.

What if this was connected to her dad's work, and she'd just gone wading in like a total idiot?

47

HANNAH

The vodka on the kitchen worktop was calling Hannah's name, yet she resisted the desperate urge to go to it. She would soon, but she had things to do before collapsing into another booze-fuelled stupor. That could wait. First, she had to do something about Max. She flipped up her laptop's lid and typed in *"Corrupt Met detective"* in the search bar. One of the first hits was a BBC news report. She clicked on one that read: *Meet the police officers investigating the Met.*

The Met recently launched a hotline for reporting officers suspected of misconduct. Anyone can contact the Police Corruption and Misconduct Reporting Service to raise concerns about officers, staff or volunteers believed to be abusing their authority, whether for financial gain, sexual exploitation, or prejudice. Trained call handlers have promised confidentiality, taking statements anonymously and passing the information to internal investigators.

Hannah closed this page and typed *"detective Max Hudson."* She scrolled through the results.

One headline instantly caught her eye: *Detective Sergeant Max Hudson cleared of all charges.*

She clicked on the link and scanned the report.

A detective constable has been found not guilty of sexually assaulting a vulnerable young woman. The incident allegedly occurred when he attended her property in Cheltenham in May 2008 to take a statement after a reported burglary and aggravated assault. DC Max Hudson, who at the time was part of Gloucestershire Constabulary CID unit, claimed the woman was hell-bent on destroying his career, and she was doing it for no other reason than that she was severely unhinged and looking for someone to punish for all her pains. DC Hudson professed that it was his belief that the young woman had intended to blackmail him for a substantial sum of money, though he was unable to offer any evidence to support this claim. He said that the incident, and the subsequent court case, left him greatly distressed and pushed his wife into a deep depression.

Hannah unscrewed the lid off the vodka, typed: *Max Hudson Gloucestershire Constabulary* and hit the search button. This flagged up several more news stories about the alleged sexual assault but, after skimming through these, Hannah wasn't able to find any further helpful information. Nothing on the woman's name, or Max's wife, or his role in the Met.

Hannah swigged the neat vodka and considered calling the Met's hotline. But what would she say?

I let Max into my world, and I think he's manipulating me.

He threw away my memories and likes to see me suffer.

He continues to visit my house, even after I asked him to stay well away.

Hannah took another deep swig from the bottle and tilted her head back. She closed her eyes and enjoyed the warm burn as the spirit moved down her throat.

He threatened to plant drugs on me and told me he can make my life hell. So he is abusing his power.

Hannah opened her eyes and wondered just how much power Max had. Was he an integral part of an important division? A major player in a large-scale case? Was he a high-priority officer who had the backing of the top brass? He'd implied these things. Plus, once she opened that door, there could be serious consequences that she would not be able to control. They would delve into everything. Dig into her life. Air all her dirty laundry. Did she really want that?

And why would they believe her? She wasn't important. She was a nobody. A drunk loser who lived in the past.

Hannah took the small silver horse out of her pocket and studied it. She'd found the little figure under the dining table two days after Max had smashed the glass ball it had been set in. She clenched it in her fist and recalled her son, aged five, telling her and Archie how much he'd like a giant, white shire horse for his sixth birthday. Archie had laughed and told Ollie that he might have to improvise and make do with a rabbit or a cat. This made her think about the schoolgirl who'd knocked on her door that afternoon, and she picked up the poster of Beatrice the cat. That girl had been acting strange. Very nervous. She'd not recognised that school uniform either. It wasn't like the ones the kids around here wore. The girl had no doubt panicked when she realised she'd knocked on a pisshead's door. How this thought depressed her. She'd let herself really fall off the wagon this week after what Max had done to her. Yet, he'd still kept coming here throughout the week, acting like nothing had happened and telling her he'd help her to get better. He'd even slept over, though she'd downright refused to be intimate with him. Plus, she'd deliberately been making the place as messy and uninviting as possible. The more unliveable her home was, the better. She'd continue to neglect her chores, in the vain hope he'd get sick of the mess and stay well away.

Hannah screwed up the poster and took another swig of vodka, letting the strong booze fog her aching mind. She needed more. She needed to learn much more about Max and what she was up against. If he was prepared to play dirty, then so would she.

48

ROSIE

August 1993

Rosie faced the shaven-headed Griff and tried not to waver under his menacing shadow. 'You let go of me. Right now,' she demanded.

'I want paying for my stereo. You hear me, you crow-faced bitch?' snarled Griff, getting right in her face. 'You think I can afford another one? Well, do you?'

Rosie tried to retreat as the group circled. They chanted and whistled as they enclosed her, closing off any escape route.

For a moment, Rosie thought this lot expected her to fight this big lump, but then, out of the corner of her eye, she spotted Max wading through the jeering crowd.

'It's all kicking off!' one lad announced, his booming voice punctuating the noisy chaos.

Max shoved Griff hard in the chest and bellowed, 'You touch her and I'll knock out your teeth, you squaddie prick!'

There were a few woos and sniggers, but the crowd soon died to a hush as they waited with excited stares.

Griff's eyes hardened as he studied the new threat.

'Well? You want to do this or what?' asked Max, closing the gap between them.

Griff held up his hands and shook his head. 'I'm just pissed about my new Sony. That's all, Hudson. I'm not gonna hurt her.'

'You got that right,' confirmed Max with total confidence.

Griff turned to Rosie and raised his palms. 'Look, I shouldn't have grabbed you like that. I wasn't going to hit you. I don't hit girls.'

Max continued to stare at Griff, fists bunched, appearing to weigh up whether to let the matter drop or steam right into the big lad.

A sudden cold hit Rosie, and she shivered so much her teeth hammered together. She wrapped her arms around herself and dropped to her haunches. The very idea that most of the group were semi-naked made her even chillier, and she couldn't move from the spot because she was so frozen.

Max crouched beside her. 'Rosie? What's up?'

'Nothing. Go… away. I'm just… cold,' she said through a series of uncontrollable shivers and whimpers.

'Aren't you meant to still be in the hospital?' asked Max.

'Leave me alone,' said Rosie.

Max shook his head. 'You're shaking all over. Come on. Over here.' He wrapped his chunky arm around her and led her to the fire. 'Come and warm up.'

Rosie allowed him to take her with no reluctance, the allure of the heat too much of an enticement now. The need to find warmth and stop the icy chills encouraging her to get there fast. Teeth clacking together wildly, she welcomed the heat from the rank-smelling fire and held her palms close to the dancing flames. Her battered hand throbbed, and she guessed the last batch of painkillers had long since worn off.

The group of youths began to disperse, and some were muttering and complaining that it was cold now and the party atmosphere had fizzled out.

Max rubbed Rosie's shoulders and told her she'd be fine in a few minutes, but all she wanted to do was cry. She felt so stupid. So utterly foolish. She caught Chloe watching her through the flames. Her face was unreadable, and her eyes were fixed on her. Rosie struggled to hold her gaze. Struggled to even look at her. Because all she could envision was Chloe and Max together. All she could visualise now was the pair fervently making love and it sickened her to the very core. If she'd eaten anything in the last twenty-four hours, she'd have puked.

Chloe stood up and walked around the fire. 'I'll leave you two to have a little chat so you can clear the air.' She gave Max a wide, dirty grin. 'Am I still good to stay at your caravan?'

Chloe's words caused Rosie to go rigid before another wave of icy shudders attacked her entire body.

'Yeah, like I told you, Dad said you can crash on the sofa,' said Max as he continued to rub Rosie's shoulder. He at least had the good grace to sound embarrassed.

Chloe strutted off to where Griff stood, still messing around with his boombox and scowling at the broken plastic.

Rosie pushed Max's hand away. 'So, that's it then. We're done, are we? You picked her over me?'

'It's… it's complicated,' said Max.

Rosie snorted, 'It really isn't.' She wiped away a few tears and shifted closer to the flames. 'You said you'd never hurt me. You lied.'

'Rosie, you mean a lot to me. I don't want to see you hurting,' whispered Max.

'You've crushed my world. You have ripped out my heart and torn it to shreds. I have nothing now.'

'I'm sorry.'

Rosie closed her eyes and relished the heat against her cheeks. The shivers were becoming less frequent, and the welcome warmth was returning to her blood. Once she'd recovered from her cold spell, she'd leave this place, and she'd never be able to return. Her lake had been tarnished. She'd never be able to enjoy the tranquillity of this magical spot ever again. Because now, she'd always associate this lake with them. She'd always remember their betrayal and what they did here. It was one thing to discover that Max and Chloe had been having sex... but doing it here... in her special place.

That was just unforgivable.

49

LOUISA

Even though she knew for sure it would be there because she'd checked the app, when Louisa glimpsed her dad's BMW on the drive, her anxiety levels still shot through the roof. Her delicate stomach was in knots, and her face became so hot she needed to fan herself with her hand. She went inside, slipped upstairs unnoticed and shut herself inside her room. She'd barely had time to collect her thoughts when a knock on the door made her jump on the spot.

He knows where I've been. He's sussed out what I'm up to, she thought. Her cheeks were on fire. If she spoke to her dad now, she'd fall to bits like a soggy banana in a blender set to full speed.

Louisa used an old swimming certificate to fan her burning face. Her temples pounded. Another migraine was coming.

'It's me,' said Jamie.

'Come in. Quick.'

Jamie let himself in and closed the door behind him. 'Did you see her? What was she like? Do you reckon he's moving for good? Is she pretty? Did she suss you? What did you say?'

'Enough with all the questions. This was a mistake. A massive mistake.'

'Why?'

'I might have stumbled into one of Dad's jobs. I'm sure of it.'
She perched herself on the edge of the bed. 'He can't be seeing
that woman. He just... can't.'

'Why? Is she ugly?'

'No... no, she wasn't. I think she was like... like an alkie.
Possibly even a junkie.'

'How do you know that?'

'I could see it. Her eyes. They were crazy! Wild and glassy.
And the smell. She stank of booze. Even the house reeked of it.
There is no way on this earth he'd be able to stomach living with
somebody like that. He throws a mental one when you don't
flush the loo after a wee or leave your dirty socks in the hallway.
That house was neglected and dirty.'

'Perhaps you simply don't know him like you think you do.'

Louisa grunted at this. 'He likes order and neatness. No, this
is something else.'

'Like a drugs operation? Hey, could it be a safe house? Is
there a chance that she might be a witness or something?
Perhaps Dad's watching over her because some criminals want
to kill her.'

'I dunno, Jamie. But if it is, we'd be in serious trouble. If we
have jeopardised a big case, then we'd be screwed. Can you
imagine how pissed off he'd be?'

Jamie sat down next to her. 'What did *I* do? I didn't go. Why
will I be in trouble?'

'Really? You going to dump this all on me? The camera was
your idea!'

'But tracking the car wasn't.'

'You hid the thing down the back seat.'

'But... but...'

'We should take it out. The camera too.'

'Dad's in his study now. Are you sure you're not overreacting? Did the other woman get suspicious? What even
happened?'

The pair shared a look. Louisa stood up and paced her

bedroom. 'She asked for a number. About the missing cat. I panicked and legged it.'

'Why didn't you give her a fake number?'

'Don't, OK. I thought the same on the train journey home. I lost my head and I had to get out of there. God, I'm such a massive tit.'

Jamie let out a long, theatrical sigh. 'I should have gone.'

'Don't be ridiculous, you would have got lost in the city.'

'I mean, I should have gone with you and done the talking.'

Louisa opened up her phone and clicked on the camera app. 'Too late for should haves.' She sat down next to her brother. 'It's all fine. I'm just freaking out. We don't need to panic. I was having a minor moment. A mini meltdown. Did Mum suspect anything?'

'She believed your lie about homework club. But any longer and she would have been phoning you and asking questions.'

The pair gazed at the camera feed, seeing their dad slumped at his desk reading a paper.

'He doesn't seem annoyed. I'm sure you're fine,' said Jamie.

Louisa heard the study door open. The pair moved closer to the phone's screen and spied their mum as she entered the study and padded over to the desk. 'Hello, Max. How has your day been?' she asked with a sassy smile.

'What do you want?' he replied stiffly.

She placed her palms on the table and smiled again. 'I can't stop thinking about Sark. It's the only thing on my mind and it's driving me a little nuts, if you must know.'

He eyed their mum with a disdainful glare. 'What is this? What the hell are you playing at?'

She sat on the desk and flashed him a flirtatious smirk. 'How long are you gonna keep me waiting? Hm? A woman could go insane waiting this long.' She flicked back her hair.

Louisa and Jamie both shifted around, and it was clear by the squirming discomfort on Jamie's face that her brother was finding this spying session as uncomfortable as she was.

Their dad folded the paper in half. He gave a contemptuous snort. 'We have talked about this.'

'Talked. When do we ever talk?'

'I'm busy.'

'I want to talk now, Max. Or… maybe… we don't need to talk. We—'

He slapped his paper on the desk. 'No, no, no. What's going on? Are you trying to ruin everything? Well, are you?'

She laughed. A silly, nervy laugh.

'Get a grip. Please, just get a grip,' he grumbled.

Jamie stood up. 'This is making me feel uncomfortable. Turn it off. Now, Louisa. Switch it off.'

Louisa did want to switch off, yet she couldn't avert her eyes.

Her mum slid off the desk. She stretched out her arms and placed her hands on the back of her neck. The action looked deliberate, so her chest stuck right out. She flashed a smug grin and sauntered out of his study. He shot up and locked the door behind her.

And Louisa caught a tiny, smarmy smile playing on her dad's lips.

Louisa decided to remove the hidden camera before her dad found it and hit the roof. She told herself she was so done with all this spying business. It was doing her head in.

50

HANNAH

20th June 2023

Hannah felt self-conscious as she stepped foot into the shabby drinking den. The place was quiet, with a couple of old guys savouring a lunchtime beer and a middle-aged bald man with a thick neck sat at the bar flicking through a paper. The emptiness did not ease her rattled nerves as she made her way to the bar area. She put her bag on the counter and rested both hands on it, remembering her first encounter in this sleazy place when the young lad had tried to steal from her.

The Australian barman appeared from out the back, and she was glad when he gave her a peppy grin and a nod that suggested he recognised her. 'Hey, two secs and I'll be right with you,' he said before disappearing into the back room again.

Hannah continued to scan the bar, focusing on both the entrance and the bald guy, who continued to flick the pages with a massive, tattooed hand, eyes skimming as if uninterested in every article featured.

The barman came strolling back out. 'How are you, Hannah? The world treating you all right, I hope.'

Hannah smiled, a little surprised he'd remembered her name. 'Hey... Squid,' she said, unable to recall his actual name and feeling silly using his nickname.

'What's your poison, darl?'

'Um, water. Please.'

'Water?' he said as if he'd misheard her.

Hannah nodded.

'You want ice and a slice with that?'

'If you like.'

'No worries. On your own today?'

'Yep,' she said.

'Righto.'

As Squid used a scoop to pour ice into a glass, Hannah said, 'I don't suppose you've seen Max around today, have you?'

Squid used metal tongs to pop a lemon wedge into the glass. 'Nah, not seen him in here since... let me see... must have been quite a few weeks back. When you came in here with him.'

Hannah did have a hazy memory of coming here with Max one night after they'd been out for dinner at a nearby restaurant, but she struggled to recall much about her visit.

'I thought this was a regular spot for him,' said Hannah, trying to sound breezy and incurious.

'He'll come in for long stints, then vanish again. After he buggers off, I don't see him and his band of merry detectives for weeks at a time. They also drink regularly at a place in Crouch End. No idea what the bar is called.' He poured water from the tap and handed it to her. 'No charge for water.'

Hannah smiled her thanks.

'Can't you just call him? I got the impression you two were an item,' he said.

'Not exactly. I don't know him that well.'

'Oh.'

'Do you?'

'Do I what?'

'Know him well?'

Squid gave her a toothy grin. It was a somewhat psychotic

smile that made her uneasy, and she now wondered if it was sensible to snoop around here.

'Nah, not really. I mean, I know him. But I don't "know" him. If you catch my drift,' he said after a momentary pause.

She sipped the water. 'Any idea what his wife's called?'

Squid laughed. 'He's married? Seriously? News to me. He doesn't wear a ring. I do notice these things.'

Hannah was tempted to point out that Max was heading for a divorce but stopped herself. After all, she didn't believe anything the man had told her. In fact, she had no way of knowing if he even had a wife and two kids. Could that have all been lies?

'You sure everything's OK? You look a little shaken up,' he said.

Hannah gazed at the melting ice rolling around her water. 'I'm fine.'

'Are you staying dry? Hard, right?'

Hannah's eyes shot from the ice to the Australian. He gave her a knowing half grin.

She shrugged and couldn't help but smile at the man's directness. She opted for a candid reply and said, 'I manage a few short periods... but never for very long.'

'My older brother had issues with the old booze. I'm familiar with all the signs,' he said, as if he needed to clarify how he'd clocked on to Hannah's dependence on alcohol. 'Coming in here and just ordering water is no easy task. I wouldn't be far off the mark if I said you've pushed yourself to come inside for a good reason, would I?'

Hannah nodded. 'You got me.'

'You're fishing for info, right? And what better place to start looking, hey? Us bar staff hear and see a lot of things.' He winked and gave her that toothy smile again. He cleared his throat and checked around the bar.

Hannah did the same. The bald guy was now engrossed in a page which he'd folded over. He scanned the text with his finger and didn't appear to be paying them any heed.

Squid edged further up the bar, out of earshot of the bald guy, and gestured with his finger that Hannah should follow. She took several sidesteps until she was facing the barman again. She flashed him a questioning grin.

He lowered his voice and said, 'Look, you seem like a nice lady, so can I give you some advice, darl?'

Hannah sipped her water again. 'Advice?'

'You should stay away from Hudson. The guy is bad news.'

'What do you mean by that?'

'I like to think I'm a pretty good judge of character. But it's not just that. There's more to it. Has he hurt you?'

'I've let him into my life. Into my home. Now I need him gone.'

'That night you two were in here, Hudson was feeding you shots of tequila like it was going out of fashion. I told him you'd had enough, but he kept ordering more and more until you could barely hold your head up.'

'I don't recall that.'

'Now I'm guessing he knows you have a problem with booze, so I ask myself why he'd do that?'

'It all started off as a bit of fun. Now... now I'm not sure what's going on. I'm afraid of him. Of what he'll do to me.'

Squid lowered his voice even more and said, 'What if I told you that you weren't the first person to come in here asking about Hudson and searching for answers?'

'Who? Who else has been here?'

'Another copper came asking questions a few years back.'

Hannah sat up straight. 'Are you serious? Why?'

'She was trying to dig up some dirt on him, I reckon. She was asking all sorts of questions about Hudson and some missing woman. Some young copper. At the time, I didn't want to Jack on the fella, but the more I've learned about the guy, the less I like him. There's no smoke without fire. I reckon the guy's as dodgy as they come.'

'What was she asking?'

'If Hudson ever brought this other woman to the bar. Oh,

now what was her name? Tara, I think. The detective said she was a fresh-faced PC. Sounded to me like Hudson was trying to take advantage of her.'

'And did this Tara come here with Max?'

'Not that I could recall. But the whole thing was super fishy. The detective was cagey and didn't give much away. Maybe you should chat with her. She could probably give you some advice and help you figure stuff out. I'm betting you're reluctant to go complaining to the regular coppers, so at least you can rest assured that this detective isn't Hudson's number one fan.'

'Do you remember the detective's name?'

'Better than that. She gave me her card.'

'You kept it?'

'Nope, I binned it. But not before I snapped a pic on my phone. Must be buried in my photos somewhere. Give me a minute to grab my blower,' he said, heading out the back.

Hannah gulped down the water and eyed the many bottles of spirits lined up behind the bar. The water hadn't quenched her thirst or eased her insanely dry mouth. She had to keep a clear head. Just for now. Just for today.

She put the lemon wedge into her mouth and sucked it as she eyed the door once again.

Squid came back and discreetly slipped her a piece of paper. 'Detective Constable Meera Kapoor. I've jotted down her number for you,' he said quietly, eyes darting about the room.

Hannah took the paper and smiled her thanks.

'She came across as a bit of a hard arse. But I tell you now, that detective had a massive axe to grind with your guy.'

'I really appreciate you helping me.'

'Men like Hudson are bullies. I've seen enough of them in my time. You stay safe and it goes without saying…' His frantic eyes scanned the bar. 'If he asks, we didn't have this chat. OK? I don't need that arsehole creating problems for me.'

'I promise he won't hear anything from me. Thanks so much for this.'

'Take it easy.'

Hannah left the bar, clutching her bag and Meera's number to her chest. She was tempted to call the detective there and then. She decided to wait and get her head together and work out how best to approach the situation. But at least she had another path to take now. Someone who might be able to help her get Max out of her life. For good.

51

ROSIE

August 1993

Rosie had warmed up enough to consider walking back to the cabin, but it saddened her deeply to think that she'd never be coming back to her wonderful lake. She'd never again watch the sun setting beyond the picturesque horizon here. Never witness the regal swan family gliding past her. That's if the poor creatures ever returned and hadn't been scared away permanently by the noise and commotion those unruly teenagers had brought about earlier that night.

Rosie stared at the white-hot embers in the dying fire and struggled to fight off the tears collecting behind her eyes. It was silent now. Save the tiny crackle of the wood spitting and hissing. Max had moved away from her, at her request, and now sat a few feet away, also staring into the fire. He looked forlorn, and she had the urge to shuffle over and put her arms around him but stopped herself. Partly because she would never forgive him and partly because she feared he'd reject her. Feared he'd tell her they were over and that he wanted to be with Chloe now.

Then Chloe's giggle broke the silence.

Chloe and Griff were sitting down by the water's edge. Rosie could make out their silhouettes and hear them talking in hushed voices. Chloe kept giggling and throwing her head back. Max was watching them now.

'I'm going back,' said Rosie.

'Shall I walk you?' asked Max, with no enthusiasm in his voice.

'No.'

Max shrugged and kept his attention on Chloe and Griff.

Rosie got to her feet and dusted herself off. 'I guess this is it then.'

'What do you mean?' he asked, sounding distracted and keeping his eyes fixed on the pair at the lake's edge.

'This is the last time you'll ever see me and yet you're more interested in her! Nice. Really bloody nice, Max.' She wiped her eyes and glared at Chloe.

'Don't be so dramatic,' said Max, pulling himself up.

Chloe laughed out loud and playfully slapped Griff on the arm.

Rosie studied Max's face. Even in the bad lighting, she noticed that his frustration was growing. She wiped her eyes again and gave him a sad goodbye smile. Max, too engrossed with the other two, didn't even notice the gesture.

'Bye, Max. Have a nice life.'

'What did he call you?'

'Hey?'

'When you smashed his stupid stereo. What did he call you?'

'It doesn't matter about all that.'

'A "crow-faced bitch", right?' muttered Max, bunching his fists. 'You OK with that, Rosie?'

Rosie didn't answer.

'Fucking ugly skinhead prick needs a smack in the face!'

Max charged down the bank, muttering curses to himself.

'Max!' called Rosie.

Rosie chased after Max and could only watch in disbelief as

he stormed down towards the pair and, without warning, let loose a flurry of hard punches onto the back of Griff's head.

Chloe screamed and shouted.

Griff tried to hold up his hands to defend himself, but Max attacked with such ferocity, he punched through the feeble defence and slammed his fists against the big lad's head and body, knocking him to the ground.

Rosie and Chloe bellowed at Max to stop, but he continued the merciless beating and each thump seemed to echo round the serene lake.

'I'll teach you some manners, you ugly fuck!' roared Max as he attempted to grab the downed lad. With no hair to snatch, he made do with seizing Griff's neck, and he dragged the defeated lad into the water.

'Max! You have to stop!' screeched Chloe.

Griff, comprehending what was happening, tried to fight back again. The pair ended up wrestling in the lake, sending water splashing everywhere. Max soon got the upper hand and threw Griff forwards, punching him several times. Then he held the beaten boy's head down in the lake.

'Stop it! Max, you're gonna kill him!' screamed Chloe.

Griff fought back. His arms and legs were thrashing around.

Max let out a booming laugh. 'You like that? Hey, you fucking like that?'

Chloe waded into the water and tried to stop the fight, but Max wasn't letting go. She tried to pull him away but was unable to budge him.

Rosie stepped right down to the water's edge and shouted, 'Max Hudson, you let that boy go! Right now!'

Max's frenzied eyes afforded Rosie a quick glare. He held Griff down for a few more seconds, then released him. 'Pussy,' he snarled as he marched out of the water.

Chloe helped Griff, who was choking and coughing, out of the lake.

'What the hell was that, Max?' shouted Chloe, patting Griff's back.

Max continued to march off, his face a mask of pure rage.

Rosie followed his movements until he vanished into the darkness. She turned back to the others. Griff was down on his knees, heaving and spluttering.

Chloe caught Rosie's eye and gave her a confused scowl.

And Rosie, despite the shock of the ordeal, couldn't help but give her so-called best friend a tiny, smug grin. Then she noticed that Chloe was still wearing the friendship bracelet she'd given her, and the smile slipped from her face. She'd been wearing the thing during her time with Max. This riled Rosie. It almost riled her as much as the act of betrayal itself.

Rosie detested her. She wished there was a way to wipe the image of her horrible face out of her memories forever.

52

LOUISA

Louisa swore under her breath when she found the door to her dad's study wouldn't open. He'd never locked it in the past. She gave the handle a hefty tug and nudged the door with her shoulder in order to confirm it wasn't jammed.

'Um, Louisa, what are you up to?'

Louisa froze mid-nudge. She turned to her mum and gave her a wide smile. 'Hey there.'

'Well? Can I ask why you're trying to break into your father's study, my little chocolate sprinkle?' Her mum was offering up a bright grin, but her eyes were burning with accusation. 'Are you trying to get yourself grounded for the entire summer? Well?'

'I'm getting too old to get grounded all the time.'

'Tell that to your father.'

'Maybe I will.'

Her mum stepped closer to her. 'What is it you expect to find in there, little miss nosy pants?'

'Nothing. I wanted to see if Dad has any good crime novels. I need one for a piece I'm doing for an English project. Ideally, a murder mystery.'

'Is that right?'

'Yep.'

'Aren't all the exams finished by the twenty-first of June? A little late to start new projects, isn't it?'

'This isn't exam related. More of a fun exercise.'

Her mum raised one eyebrow and regarded her with a suspicious stare. 'He doesn't read crime novels. Why would he? Why on earth would he possibly need more depravity in his life? He hardly needs crime fiction for entertainment when he lives it.'

'Yeah, course. Silly me. He won't even allow a police procedural drama on the TV, will he?'

'No, he won't. And with good reason. The world is obsessed with needless violence. It is rather tedious.'

'Not if they are just stories. A good mystery can be interesting.'

'You should be concentrating on your final exam tomorrow and not worrying about stupid stories and pointless mysteries. We're expecting fantastic grades, young lady. We're—'

'Yeah, yeah, straight eights or nines. No pressure. God, all I wanted was a decent crime book. Not a lecture.'

'Your father puts his life on the line when he goes out into that sleazy city every damn day. It sucks him dry. Your blood would run cold if you found out the kind of things he's had to deal with. You have no clue what it's like out there. It's dark. It's… inhospitable. Deadly. He faces these dangers, so we don't have to. So we can be safe.'

'Oh, please stop with this already and change the record. You sound like him now. It's not that bad out there. And how did we go from me borrowing a book to Dad's bloody job again?'

'Because you don't get it.'

'Dad's not a bloody superhero, and, come on, he chose that profession. He understood the dangers. And it's not like he's kicking doors down these days. I bet he spends most of his time with his feet stuck on his desk.'

Louisa could tell by her mum's face that she'd overstepped the mark now.

She drew in her thin lips until they were the colour of chalk and raised both eyebrows impossibly high. 'You know, sometimes, your flippancy infuriates me to no end. It drives me so nuts, Louisa.' She stepped closer and slapped her hands together, rubbing them in an aggressive motion. 'Oo, sometimes…' Her mum's face was all screwed up, her lips now pushed out like an angry duck about to snap. 'What am I going to do with you?' She pressed Louisa's nose. 'I'm at my wit's end.'

'Please don't boop my nose. I got the impression that we were engaging in an adult discussion here so stop treating me like a five-year-old kid.'

'We are, indeed, having a grown-up chat.'

'Then don't go all weird and boop my nose and call me jelly pants or some weird shit.'

'Well, OK,' said her mum tersely. 'Fine. Fine.'

'You might be suckered in by all Dad's nonsense, but it doesn't mean I have to be. It's like you're brainwashed by all his crap. What's with that? And why don't you ever stand up to him?'

Her mum's nostrils flared, and she slammed her palm against the door. 'Right, end of grown-up chit chat. You stay out of your father's study!' With that, she spun and marched into the kitchen, bare feet squeaking on the oak flooring.

Louisa was tempted to march after her mum and tell her about the woman she'd gone to visit in the city. The house her dad had been frequently going to. Where he'd been spending entire nights. Entire days. She pictured the woman once again. Her pretty face and dishevelled locks of hair that had escaped and fallen over the sides of her face. Was she connected to a case, or could her dad be taking advantage of her? Was she vulnerable? A victim of some terrible crime? Was there a chance he'd been using his position to exploit the woman somehow? Was he manipulating her into doing things for him?

Louisa shook the thoughts out of her head. Why did her imagination run wild like this? She felt like she was going around in circles, and the more she considered the facts, the less sense they made.

She wondered if her mum knew what was going on and he'd sworn her to secrecy. Yet, that didn't ring true because lately he spoke to her mum like shit. If he spoke to her at all.

Louisa understood that mentioning the other woman was not an option. Not until she had all her facts straight.

Then she thought about her parents' strange exchange in the study.

I can't stop thinking about Sark.

Louisa went into the kitchen and yanked open the fridge. Her mum, now busy loading the dishwasher, ignored her stroppy entrance.

Louisa and Jamie had searched the internet for Sark after their spying session. It was a small island nestled between Guernsey and the north-west of France. One of the few places in the world where cars were banned. To the best of Louisa's memory, they had never taken a holiday there. Not as a family. She was tempted to ask her mum if they'd visited the small island when she and Jamie had been little, but she quickly booted aside that idea. If she mentioned Sark to her mum now, it would be blatantly obvious she'd overheard their odd little chat the previous day and alarm bells would ring.

No matter how hard she tried not to, Louisa just couldn't stop thinking about all this stuff. She took out a carton of apple juice and scolded herself for being so sad and getting obsessed with all this nonsense with her parents. She'd told herself she was done with all this. Didn't she have her own life to worry about? Her own dramas?

Evidently not.

Because she couldn't stop dwelling on that other woman with the glassy, vacant eyes.

What happened in Sark? And was this somehow connected to the woman in that house? She was so desperate to find out.

53

HANNAH

'Yes, can I help?' answered the woman on the other end of the phone. Her tone had been curt, and it sounded like she'd been interrupted and wasn't best pleased about that.

Hannah peered out of the window just to make sure Max hadn't pulled up in the last few minutes. 'Um, hi. Is this Detective Constable Meera Kapoor?'

'No, it's Detective *Sergeant* Meera Kapoor,' she replied in a brisk tone. 'Who is this, please?'

'My name's Hannah Watkins. I was hoping to talk to you about something. About someone.'

'Have we spoken before?'

'No.'

Silence on the other end.

Hannah unscrewed the lid to a bottle of vodka that sat on the kitchen counter. 'I need help. I...' Hannah's mind went blank as she rolled the lid around her fingers. She considered ending the call. She was getting bad vibes from this woman. What if she'd got this wrong and Max found out she was snooping into his affairs?

'Are you going to tell me what, or whom, this is about?' asked Meera, sounding cagey.

'I need help,' repeated Hannah.

'Are you in danger? Is there an imminent threat to your life?'

'I'm calling about Max Hudson.'

'OK. Can you give me a little more information?' she asked, her tone inquisitive but less surly now. 'How are you connected to DI Hudson?'

'Could we meet? I don't want to discuss this over the phone.'

After a brief pause, Meera said, 'It would really help me if you could give me some idea as to what this is about. Can you do that?'

Hannah studied the lid and continued rolling it around her fingers. 'You asked me if I'm in danger... I think I am. Not right this moment, but I'm in trouble and I don't know who to turn to.'

After another pause, Meera said, 'Can you get to Camden Town on Saturday morning? I can't get free until then with the schedule I have. Will that work?'

'Yes,' said Hannah, a little disappointed she couldn't meet her sooner.

'There's a small café that's tucked out of the way. I'll ping you the address. Is ten OK?'

'I'll be there. Thank you.' Hannah ended the call and let out a long sigh of relief. For a moment, she was certain the detective was going to refuse to talk to her. Clearly, Hannah had sparked her interest by mentioning Max.

Hannah took a deep breath and somehow forced herself to put the lid back on the vodka. She gazed out of the window again. There'd been no sign of Max since the previous Friday. Not one call or a single message. Somehow, this worried her even more.

Just what was his game?

54

ROSIE

August 1993

Rosie eyed Chloe with open hostility after she'd dared to let herself into her room and strolled in as though she didn't have a single care in the world.

'Your folks let me in. I told them I needed to get some stuff and that I'm going home tonight.'

'Are you? How nice for you.'

'I'm not. I'll be crashing in Max's caravan.' Chloe scanned the floor and scooped up a bra and a pair of socks from under the sofa bed. 'Why are you being such a dick about this? Grow up. Did you honestly believe you and Max were going to be together long term? I mean, seriously, did you?'

'You ruined everything we had. You were jealous, so you stole him.'

'Yeah, sure, I mean, blame me if it makes you feel better.'

'You forced him. You… you…'

Chloe laughed. 'Yeah, sure. Right. I totally forced him to bury his face right in my snatch last night for twenty minutes.'

Rosie saw red and reacted impulsively. Her lousy slap failed to strike Chloe because she caught her by the wrist. 'I'll let you have that attempt for free, Rosie Grimshaw. But that's the only one. If you try to strike me again, I'll claw out your eyes, you mental slag. You hear me?' She squeezed Rosie's wrist hard, digging her fingers right into the flesh.

Rosie tried to pull her arm away. Chloe just glared at her.

'Let go. You're hurting me. Chloe! Let me go.'

'What's the matter? You like pain, don't you? Oh, that's right… only when it's self-inflicted.' Chloe let go and stepped so close to her they were nose to nose. 'If you really knew me, you'd watch your step. And when we get back home, I strongly suggest you stay the fuck out of my way, or you'll see a side to me you won't like.'

'I've already seen plenty I don't like,' said Rosie quietly.

'I am warning you. Don't push me, or I'll break every bone in your lanky, brittle body.'

'I want you to leave.'

'You keep away from Max. Understand? Far away. We have something good. And if you mess it up, I'll mess you up. Keep yourself locked up in this freaky, dark cabin where you belong.' With that, she left, slamming the door behind her.

Rosie sat down on the bed and silently screamed as she punched herself over and over and over in both legs. She wanted to rip that girl's face off with her own bare hands.

55

LOUISA

Louisa nibbled on a slice of Marmite on toast while her mum busied herself making scrambled eggs. Neither of them had spoken one word since their little tiff, and the stilted silence created an uncomfortable atmosphere, yet she didn't want to be the one to yield.

Jamie shuffled into the kitchen, ripping his school tie free. He dragged a chair back and plonked down at the table.

Her mum beamed at him. 'Hey, pickles. Good day at school? I've made you some eggs. Would you like a sprinkling of cheddar cheese melted into them?'

'Please,' said Jamie.

As her mum grated a wedge of cheese into the saucepan of eggs, Louisa tried to see if she had that friendship bracelet on her wrist. She was wearing a white, baggy cardigan, so her arms were covered, and she kept pulling the sleeves back that were hampering her effort to stir the eggs.

Jamie cleared his throat and scrutinised Louisa with his eyes narrowed and his lips downturned. She guessed he was none too pleased with her because the camera device was now stuck in that room, and they had no way of retrieving it. They both knew their dad would find it at some point. It was only a matter of time and then there'd be explosive trouble. For them to have the audacity to pull something like this... well, she dreaded to think how mad he'd be. His ego would be well and truly smashed to bits. An astute police detective allowing his own children to spy on him would not be a great look. Maybe if he did catch them out, she'd turn it into a joke and say she'd been testing him. Tell him he shouldn't be so careless and that someone in his position should feel humiliated that his clueless kids had got the better of him. *This is a stark lesson to learn, Daddy, but it's for the greater good because, believe me, you won't be so careless in the future now, will you? You're welcome.*

Louisa pictured her dad's enraged face and had to smile to herself.

'I'm working on it,' Louisa whispered to her brother.

'Shut up,' he mouthed back.

Louisa turned her attention back to her mum, who was using the wooden spoon to serve Jamie's eggs. 'Whoops, I forgot to put the toast in. Your mother would forget her head if it wasn't screwed on.'

'Eggs will be fine on their own, Mum,' said Jamie.

As her mum scraped out the last of the eggs, she pulled her cardigan sleeve back again.

No bracelet today, then.

So, where had she put it? Louisa mused as the temptation to say, hey, Alexa, play "The Sun Always Shines on TV" became almost impossible to resist.

56

HANNAH

24th June 2023

At ten o'clock on the dot, Hannah stepped into the café. The place had a Caribbean theme and was bursting with colour. Red and yellow tables and chairs, vibrant artwork on imitation brick walls, and decorative streams of bunting showcasing the flags of Jamaica, Barbados and Puerto Rico, alongside a few others. The detective had advised Hannah to head into the back of the building, where she'd find her sitting under a picture of a tropical beach hut. She walked quickly and tried to avoid eye contact with any of the patrons already seated. Nobody manned the counter, which sat under a tiki-style beach umbrella with white lights woven into the thatch.

Hannah made her way to the rear quarter of the café, and a woman seated in the corner clocked her. They eyed each other for a few seconds before the suited woman gave Hannah a stiff nod. She was sitting in front of an image of three green and yellow beach huts overlooked by a line of lush palm trees.

Hannah walked over to the table but didn't sit. 'Detective Kapoor?'

Meera had a long, serious face. Her jet-black hair was shiny and neck length. Her small, shrewd eyes looked like they belonged to a no-nonsense predator. And those eyes stayed focused on Hannah, making her feel very uneasy.

'Sit,' said Meera, gazing at Hannah as if assessing whether she was trustworthy. 'I took the liberty of ordering you a coffee and some banana fritters. Service in here is shockingly slow, but these things taste like heaven. And the jerk bean patties... oh, don't even get me started on those delicious bad boys. I'm addicted.'

Hannah dragged a chair back and winced at the sound it made. She was so nervous she couldn't find her tongue, and she had no stomach for food, no matter how delicious it sounded.

Meera interlocked her fingers and sat up straight. 'I need to ask you one question before we have this conversation. If I'm not happy with your answer, there will be *no* such conversation. Is that OK?'

Hannah nodded in response.

Meera's face didn't change. No hint of emotion at all. 'I would like to know how you came by my number.'

'I got it from an Australian barman called Squid. He works at—'

The detective put up her hand to silence Hannah. 'Say no more. I remember that Aussie. Makes sense now. The guy is a total bloody motormouth.' She cracked a smile that lit up her face. She appeared prettier with a touch of amusement brightening her features. However, the smile faded fast, and the composed sternness returned once again.

Hannah did a quick scan of the room. They were alone back here. She focused on a flashy art piece capturing a smiling Caribbean woman wearing light-pink lipstick and sporting a floral head wrap. She stood amid a backdrop of tropical flowers and a perfectly serene blue sea. The piece, set inside two weather-worn shutters, gave the appearance of a window to the outside world. A beautiful place far removed from London. It made her think about her mum and Aunty Grace in Grenada. That pair lived for the ocean.

'You're safe here. Don't look so worried, Hannah.'

Hannah turned back to Meera and nodded.

Meera nibbled on a fritter. 'Can you tell me why you think you are in danger?'

'I misjudged him.' Hannah shook her head. Something inside of her had been screaming out that dating Max would invite problems into her life, yet she'd ignored her own warnings because she'd been desperate for change. She had convinced herself that being a married police detective, Max would possess some undesirable qualities and carry emotional baggage. Nevertheless, she could never have predicted any of this. 'I'm afraid of what he'll do next. I'm alone and don't know who to turn to.'

The detective exhaled through her nose, but her face stayed free of emotion. 'Start at the beginning and tell me the entire story.'

57

ROSIE

August 1993

The mess left behind in the wake of the party was a depressing sight to behold. Far worse than Rosie had been expecting. Those disgusting teenagers had treated the lake with zero respect.

Despite promising herself she'd never come back here, she had not been able to stop herself. It was almost as if her legs had been on autopilot. She tried to justify this by telling herself she had no choice but to venture down here. No choice because those swans needed checking on for a start. Glass and rubbish needed collecting for the sake of all the wildlife living down here. Yet in truth, where else did she have to go? Nowhere.

Unable to start the soul-destroying task of clearing away the mess, Rosie sat on the hill and drew her knees up to her chin. The fire had destroyed a large patch of grass which would take months, if not years, to recover. The patch of scorched earth stood as a stark reminder of the grim night she'd endured here. A hideous reminder that she'd always associate with the time Max cheated on her, and the moment Chloe stabbed her in the back in such an atrocious fashion.

Her quiet place would never be the same again. It would be ruined for all time.

Rosie scanned the motionless lake, desperate to lay her eyes on the family of swans. She'd once read that most swans mated for life; if they lost their partner, it wasn't unheard of for them to die of a broken heart. This thought filled her with a sudden raw sadness. She willed those birds to materialise. She needed to see them because the idea that they'd left this spot made her already shredded heart ache. It was as if seeing them would bring back some of the magic and give her some hope that all was not lost. A flicker of hope that maybe, in time, things could go back to how they'd been before she'd led Chloe here to her sacred space.

Yet, the lake remained unusually silent.

No swans.

No birds singing their carefree songs.

No hope. Above all else, there was no hope for her any longer.

It was all ruined. All because she wanted to change things at school. All because she was desperate to be Chloe's best friend and longed to be seen as a somebody and not perceived as a total loser who was the butt of everyone's jokes. Now, she'd lost the one thing that truly mattered to her. The one place she'd ever felt safe was gone. Just like everything else.

58

LOUISA

The moody sky promised rain at any moment, and Louisa decided that when she was older and had her own money, she'd move somewhere with a warmer climate. How could the weather be so rubbish in the middle of June? Where had the sun gone? With a sigh, she settled on the bottom of the sun lounger. She sighed again when she spotted her mum heading down to the patio. She smiled at Louisa and said, 'You won't be working on that tan this morning, my little peach surprise.'

Louisa peered up at her mum, shocked that she'd relented and decided to communicate with her in a civil tone.

'Just getting some air to clear my migraine. Could we go somewhere nice later this year, Mum? Like a holiday in the Mediterranean?'

'I don't think so.'

'Can you at least get me some fake tan? I'm so pale, I hate it.'

'Your father won't allow that.' Her mum pulled up a chair and sat facing her. 'We need to talk, don't we? About your funny mood swings.'

'My what?'

'Louisa, I don't want us to keep falling out. I don't like it when you're mean to me.'

Louisa was tempted to say, *You don't like it when I speak the truth, more like.* Instead, Louisa considered her words as she studied her mum. She appeared so innocent and downcast it was hard not to feel a little sorry for her. 'I guess we are just very different people, Mum. That's all.'

'You see me as a sad, downtrodden housewife, don't you? Some kind of miserable loser who doesn't have the ability to form my own opinions or have my own aspirations.' She focused her attention on her plants down the bottom of the garden. 'You can be honest.'

'It's going to rain. We should go inside,' said Louisa.

'I said, you can be honest.'

'Don't you ever stop and think to yourself, is this it? Is this what I get up in the morning for? Two self-centred kids and a husband who can't even treat me with the respect I deserve.'

'You admit you're self-centred, then?'

'Yeah, of course, I admit it. So don't you sometimes think… screw it, life is too short, and I'm going to do what makes *me* happy? And don't you dare say that looking after all of us makes you happy. That's just a cop-out.'

Her mum flashed her a mischievous smile but didn't make eye contact with her.

'What? What's that smile for?'

'It doesn't matter. I know it's a little early, but would you like some ice cream? I made it myself yesterday.'

'You are evading my question.'

'Creamy lemon and honey. Interested now, I bet? I have waffle cones. The nice, thick ones you like. Let's go mad and have ice cream before lunch.'

Louisa let out a pained groan. 'I have been super focused on myself lately. On what I'm missing out on with my own friends. But, you know, I really want you to have a life, too. I want you to stop being a doormat. Stand up to him. Will you just please find some backbone and stand up to him?'

'Oh, my chocolate swirl, you are so cute. It's nice you care about me, but you have this all wrong.' She put a hand over her mouth as if suppressing a giggle. 'We're very happy. You don't understand.'

'He's trapping you as much as he is me. It's time we both made a stand.'

'Oh, Louisa, stop with all the drama already.'

'OK, fine. You carry on living in your bubble. You carry on showing Jamie how to fawn over a husband who mistreats you, and, you never know, once he's married with his own kids, he'll mimic what he sees and treat his own wife like a shitty slave.'

'You make it sound like your father routinely beats me up and chains me to the kitchen sink.'

'Some of the worst bullying is mental, not physical.'

'You're the expert on that, are you?'

Louisa cast her mind back to what she'd seen the other day. Her mum's frantic dance around the kitchen. What was that? A sign the cracks were forming. Was this woman on a downward spiral and heading straight into crazy town? She wondered if they'd let them visit her mum in the loony bin. God, she was mad enough now, so what would she be like if they doped her up on nutty pills?

'No, I'm not an expert,' said Louisa with a glum shrug. 'But... forget it.'

A patter of rain fell, small spots dotting the surrounding slabs. Louisa watched the patterns form and decided not to move as the drops got bigger.

'Can we be friends again, Louisa? Please?'

Seeing the needy desperation etched on her mum's face made Louisa's heart sink. She wanted to grab her by the shoulders and shake this pathetic behaviour right out of her. But she couldn't. Instead, she smiled and said, 'I'll have some ice cream later. I might go back to bed for an hour. My head's still a little fuzzy.'

59

HANNAH

After unloading about Max, Hannah took a sip on her velvety-smooth latte and waited for a reply. She'd told the detective everything. About Max's strange behaviour, the cherished photos he'd taken, his threats to get her arrested, and his refusal to stay out of her life and out of her home.

Meera coughed into her fist. 'DI Max Hudson has been involved in making some serious arrests. Thanks to him, some big players have been taken out of the game, so the top brass reckon the sun shines out of his arse. You were right not to make a formal complaint. He'd have turned things around on you. It is what he does. What he's good at.'

'I got the sense I'd be making things worse if I went down that route. But I need to do something about him.'

'Seems like you are, and you're clued up enough to have been careful.'

Hannah nodded, not convinced she was being careful by coming here to meet this woman. What if she was now on good terms with Max and this was all a pretence? Meera could be playing her. 'Do you still work with Max?'

Meera shook her head. 'Nope. I worked under him for a while, but I requested a transfer from his unit after we clashed.'

'Why?'

'A difference of opinions, for a start. We have very different work ethics. He came out smelling of roses and I looked like the agitator. It became common knowledge that Max and I did not see eye to eye. That's why PC Tara Wordsworth came to me about him.'

'She's the one you were asking questions about?'

'Correct. She had a drunken fling with Max. This must have been in 2019. But he started getting weird with her and he tried to take Tara under his wing. Tara was pretty insecure and certainly not cut out for a career in the Met. She called it quits, but Max still didn't let up. She called me one night, scared out of her wits. Got it into her head that Max was going to hurt her. Then she vanished. No one knew anything about her where-abouts, so I spent weeks and weeks searching the city for her. Hence speaking with the Australian.'

'Did you find her? What happened?'

'I took a call out of the blue. One of her family members I'd spoken to managed to get in touch with Tara. Turns out she'd fled overseas and has no intention of returning.'

'Because of Max?'

'She refused to go into specifics, but yeah, she fled because of him. Travelled to France and never returned.'

Hannah felt goosebumps prick her skin and the sudden urge for a real drink hit her. She searched for the waitress.

'Sorry, they don't serve booze here for another twenty minutes,' said Meera, as if reading her mind.

Hannah stared at her and didn't bother to deny her intentions.

Meera leaned in closer to Hannah and quietly said, 'As far as abusing his position is concerned, this is just the beginning. Word is, Max is in line for promotion in the near future. Once he makes DCI… I dread to think.'

'So he's dodgy? He's like a corrupt cop? Can't we try to prove this?'

'Put it this way, when I tried digging the dirt on Max, bad things happened to me and my family.' Meera pulled a fritter apart and fumbled with the pieces as she considered her words. 'I'm only going to tell you this so you can truly understand what you're up against. OK?'

Hannah nodded and swallowed hard in her parched throat.

'First, my husband left his office and had a white van follow him. These two guys inside made it abundantly clear what they were doing. A few days later, we had more men watching the house, trying to intimidate us. There were dubious phone calls, strange emails, and then I had a delivery left on my doorstep. An unmarked box with a bulletproof vest stuffed inside.' Meera tossed down the shredded pieces of food. 'The next day, my two daughters were walking home from school when a couple of young thugs approached them, and each of my girls had a bullet tossed at their feet.'

'Shit! What did you do?'

'I managed to get one guy arrested outside my house, but he denied everything, of course. Refused to admit someone had put them up to it. So I backed off. Max played it cool, but I understood the score. If I kept pushing, or went behind his back to his superiors… well, I'd been warned off, hadn't I?'

'But who were these people? Other police officers?'

'No, I doubt that. Max has made a lot of connections during his time working drugs. It was probably one of his informers or criminal contacts who helped him organise the harassment plot against me.'

Hannah checked the room again before she said, 'You're clearly rattled, so why are you helping me now?'

Meera raised her eyebrows. 'I believe you have misconstrued the purpose of our meeting, Hannah. I'm not planning to help you.'

'What? I don't understand. Then why—'

The detective silenced her with a frantic wave of her hand. 'OK, hold up, that's not technically true. I will give you some information that might help you. But after that, I'm done. OK? Once we are finished here, you don't contact me again. Is that clear?'

'But…'

'Is that clear? If you don't agree to that, we're done here right now.'

Hannah nodded. 'Yes, I agree.'

'OK then. I'll tell you why I was really searching.' Meera took out her phone and thumbed the screen. 'I am going to show you a photo of a woman called Bailey Lloyd.' She showed Hannah her phone screen, which displayed a woman in her late twenties. 'She went missing in 2008.'

Hannah studied the woman's face. She was attractive with messy, brown hair. Perhaps cute might have been a more accurate description, Hannah decided. On closer inspection, she could see how drawn and colourless her face was. How a deep sadness swam in her round, hazel-coloured eyes.

'She doesn't look very old,' said Hannah, mesmerised by the photo.

The detective put her phone away. 'Twenty-seven at the time of her disappearance. She looks a lot younger, doesn't she?'

Hannah sipped her latte and glanced about the café once more. The drink seemed to have lost its flavour now.

'Max transferred from Gloucestershire Constabulary to the Met, and the gossips say he left the county under a dubious shadow.'

'When?'

'Around six months after Bailey vanished off the face of the earth.'

'You're saying he's involved somehow?'

'Although nobody knows for certain what happened, it's a fact that Max, a DC at the time, was involved with Bailey Lloyd.'

'Have you spoken to his ex-work colleagues?'

'I tried. Obviously, I had to tread carefully. I gleaned from one of them that Max definitely was 'involved' with a young woman in his hometown of Cheltenham. They wouldn't name Lloyd, but they didn't have to. Once I knew I was on the right path, I spoke to a local journalist and Lloyd's family. Lloyd was a widow. She'd only been married a few months when her fella died in a fatal collision. He had some sort of altercation with another driver and lost his temper. There was a huge fight, and this culminated in a bit of a car chase. And Lloyd's fella flipped his car and died at the scene.' Meera interlocked her fingers and bunched her hands. 'Max was the investigating officer on the case. I guess this is how he wormed his way into Bailey's life. Some people say they were romantically involved, yet I was also told that Max just became infatuated with her, and these feelings were not reciprocated.'

'I saw an online article about this. Seems weird he didn't get into trouble over that, doesn't it?'

'These claims were never proven, and Max said these were just unsubstantiated rumours being spread by one of his colleagues. An officer who had it in for him after a falling out over a case. As you say, the papers printed something about it, but they never named Bailey Lloyd. Soon after these allegations, she went missing.'

'And then Max left?'

'Around six months after, yes. He claims he always had his sights set on the Met.'

'Do you honestly think he had something to do with her going missing?'

'Yeah, I do, and I'm certain she's not the only one.'

60

ROSIE

August 1993

Instead of tidying up like she'd planned, Rosie lay on her side and gazed at the water. She'd been there a long time, and the sun had started to burn her left arm and cheek. Let it cook her. It could melt her away like a candle for all she cared.

'Rosie? Is that you?'

Her heart skipped a beat at the sound of Max's voice, but she didn't respond or move a muscle.

'I guessed you'd be down here,' he said, sitting down in front of her. 'Are you OK?'

Rosie continued to stay fixed on the lake, not giving Max even a tiny hint that she'd registered his arrival.

'I know you said we would never see each other again, but I didn't want to leave things like that. Rosie? Are you hearing me or what?' He rolled onto his side and faced her, blocking her view of the lake. 'I know what this place means to you. I wanted to explain that I had no idea so many people would show. Chloe said she'd asked a couple of girls she'd met to come down here for a bit of a laugh. Word spread and soon loads of idiots were flocking here. Blame those army lads. They were the trou-blemakers.'

Rosie rolled over and turned her back on him. She had no intention of talking to this boy ever again.

'I still care about you. Honest, I haven't stopped worrying about you since what happened here. I'll help you tidy up this mess. I'll grab some rubbish sacks from the site later.' He placed a hand on her shoulder and caressed her. 'Can't you even look at me? Hey, come on, give me a little shy smile at least.'

Rosie didn't reply. Didn't move or even shove him away.

'I can't help the way I feel about her. I'm sorry, I truly am. Rosie, I think I love her. I never set out to hurt you. That's the truth. She's pretty messed up herself. Her mum walked out on her when she was little, and her dad's a total loser and he doesn't treat her good. I guess our situations are similar. With our mums, I mean. That's why we have that connection.'

Rosie closed her eyes and fought back the tears that were trying to burst from her eyes. He didn't have a clue about rubbish parents. Not like she did.

'If I had a way to switch off my feelings, I would. I swear I would. Because I love you too. I always have. Guess I always will.'

She clamped her eyes tighter now, desperate to not let the explosion of sadness flow out. She would not cry in front of him. No way.

'Chloe feels the same way. She never set out to fall for me like this. She just wanted a bit of a laugh. Funny how things turn out.'

Rosie bit her tongue until it hurt. She wanted to shout at Max. Wanted to tell him what a complete idiot he was by being taken in by Chloe. How did he not see she was using him? How could he be so blind? Was sex with her so wonderful that he couldn't see past that? The pressure behind her eyes built so much, it became impossible to keep the gates closed, and a few hot tears escaped and rolled down her burning cheeks. She didn't move to wipe them.

'This is the real thing. We want to stay together. Like a proper couple.' He let out a little chuckle. 'She even wants to have kids. She said that. Can you imagine? Me as a dad. Crazy, right? Not right now. No, we want to travel around first. See a bit of the world and then settle down and have babies in our early twenties. We want a boy and a girl, ideally. She likes the name Louisa. I like Jamie for a boy. Think I told you that before, right?'

More tears fell from Rosie's eyes, although a fierce fury was building inside her now, and that raw emotion was racing to overtake the sorrowful angst she'd been suffering.

How many times can your heart break like this before it's beyond repair?

'You can cry. Let it all out,' he said.

'Go away.'

'Cry for me. I mean, really cry, Rosie.'

'No!'

'I like it when you cry,' he said softly, stroking her arm. 'You're so pretty when you're sad.'

She flashed him an icy glare.

He stopped stroking her and let his arm drop. 'I'm still considering the police force as a career option. I'd say that was my calling. Chloe reckons I'll make a good copper. Especially after she saw me deal with that twat Griff last night. Yeah, things are looking good. She's going to be a stay-at-home mum. Keep the house in order. Good dinners on the table. Sounds like I have it all to look forward to.'

'Over my fucking dead body,' said Rosie in a cold, hateful whisper. Her voice had been loaded with so much venom, she freaked herself out.

Max chuckled again and pinched her arm. 'Ooh, there she is. Hello, Rosie. It's good to hear from you again.'

61

LOUISA

Louisa's eyes snapped open when a knock on the door broke her out of her drowsy sleep.

'What?' she grumbled.

'It's me,' said Jamie.

Louisa rubbed her eyes and sat up. 'Come in.'

Jamie let himself in and closed the door behind him. 'Thought you were up?'

'I was. Felt my migraine creeping back, so I went back to sleep.'

Jamie held up the pet camera. 'Job done.'

'How did you get that?'

'Waited for Dad to use the loo and darted in there. He was hardly going to lock the study door while he went to have a pee. I almost fell off his swivel chair trying to reach it.'

'Why didn't I come up with that idea?'

Jamie shrugged. 'Can we quit with all this spying stuff now?'

'You need to get the key finder back from his car.'

'He won't find that. It's wedged right in between the back seats. I can just grab it next time Dad takes me to my sailing club. I'll just sneak it out then.'

'Are you still a member of that lame-arse club?'

'Beats moping about complaining that I have a headache all weekend.'

Louisa ignored his snarky comment and swung her legs off the bed.

'I don't know why you quit gymnastics. At least it got you out of the house three times a week and gave you something to focus on,' he said.

'As you are well aware, I broke my foot, and my coach was a total hag. Besides, the sessions were repetitive and boring.'

'Your obsession with our parents has become repetitive and boring. You should get a new hobby.'

'Piss off. Like I need life advice from a nerd like you. Is Dad still home now? Unlike him to be here on a Saturday these days.'

'He was. He went back out.'

'Oh.'

'Why not go ahead and check where he's going? I'm guessing you will anyway.'

'I already said I'm done with all that now.'

'So, you deleted the key finding app?'

'I will. I'm going to,' she said, using a defensive, huffy tone.

'It's for the best. It really isn't our place to get involved.'

'No, it's only the future of our family, after all. Why should we give two shits, hey?'

'Louisa, do you want Dad to be having an affair? Would you be pleased if he got caught out?'

'Sorry?'

'You don't like him much, do you?'

'Like him? What's to like? What's me not liking him got to do with anything?'

'You hardly go without.'

'What is that supposed to mean? I'm not materialistic like you. I care about respect, Jamie. I care about having genuine support and sincere affection from my parents. I care about being valued as a person. I wouldn't expect you to understand.'

'I think you enjoy proving yourself right and making Mum look like a complete failure.'

'Utter dick. You don't have a clue… I want Mum to have a life. I told her as much. Is that seriously what you think?'

'Sometimes, yeah. Let me ask you this. If we could definitely prove, right this moment, that Dad was messing around with that drunk lady, then what would you do?'

Louisa stood up and placed her hands on her hips. 'Are you asking me if I'd run off and blab to Mum straight away?'

'Would you?'

'Um, yeah.'

'Why?'

'Because it's the right thing to do. Wouldn't you?'

Jamie shrugged and said, 'She still wouldn't leave him, so what would be the point? Apart from hurting her, it wouldn't help.'

Louisa opened her mouth to respond to this yet decided against voicing her thoughts. Because she concluded her little brother had hit the nail on the head, the clever little git. Whatever their dad did, or however badly he treated her, their mum would never divorce him. She'd never cope without him. She was way too fragile.

Louisa thought about their conversation in the garden. She'd tried to tell her mum, hadn't she? Tried to explain that she needed to do something and stand up to the man. She didn't want to listen.

Jamie grinned smugly. 'I hate to say it, but Mum is a pushover. It's that simple. There is nothing either of us can do to change that. We should stop playing private investigators now.'

Louisa, for once, didn't bother to argue with him. But then she thought about that bracelet again. Why was she so desperate to get a good look at that stupid thing? Why did she care about it so much?

She knew the answer. It was simply because her mum didn't want her to see it. Didn't even want to talk about it. Not only that, but Louisa kept seeing that moment in the kitchen and the look on her mum's face during that dance. The way she held that bracelet like it meant everything.

But why?

62

HANNAH

Meera fumbled with a piece of squashed fritter and stared at Hannah with unblinking eyes. 'I have a file on missing women in the Gloucestershire area. Individuals I believe Max might've...' Meera stopped and deliberated on her words. 'Let's just say they are all young widows or women grieving after losing their partners. Women with no close family to speak of.'

'Are you saying Max might be responsible for what... killing these women? You think he's a bloody serial killer or something?' asked Hannah, her voice so loud she immediately scanned the room to make sure her words hadn't been overheard.

'There are two others that fit the same criteria as Bailey Lloyd. Susan Gains and Michelle Wynn sit on top of my list. Similar age and from the Gloucestershire area. No kids. Links to crime or drugs. Both had connections to Max Hudson.'

'But if Max is targeting a specific type, why go after Tara Wordsworth? Surely, she doesn't tick all those boxes.'

'Maybe he never intended to go after her. She might've been something else. A quick fling and he had no intention of taking things further.'

'And me?'

Meera raised her hands and spread her palms. 'I hate to say it, but you fit the profile perfectly.'

'Fabulous.'

'Moving away from the Gloucestershire area would've been the best move for Max. It would only have been a matter of time before he was fully exposed. Here, in the city, it's much easier for him to hide in plain sight. He understood London would make the perfect playground. Countless lost souls for him to prey upon and working drugs would be the ideal placement to find such lost individuals.' Meera winced. 'Sorry if that sounded insensitive.'

'I had a chance encounter with Max. I told you that. He didn't select me.'

'Perhaps. Perhaps not.'

'What does that mean?'

'You said you fell asleep in a bar.'

'A bar I had never frequented before.'

Meera pulled a face. 'I guess it's possible you were unlucky.'

'And his wife?'

'What about her?'

'Does he even have one?'

Meera nodded. 'Yeah, he does. Married for years. She moved to London with him. They've got two kids. A boy and a girl.'

'Do you reckon she has any inkling about what he's into?'

'Honestly, I doubt it. I met her once years back. Weak, nervous, jumpy. Max dominates that relationship. Treats her like rubbish from what I've heard over the years. Talks about her like she's some neurotic, agoraphobic servant. He keeps her away from his life in the Met nowadays. Has for most of his career.'

'I need to talk to her.'

'Forget about his browbeaten wife. You need to look into those missing women. They are the key to bringing Max down. If you send me your email, I will forward you the file tonight. Then we're done.'

Hannah leaned forward and whispered, 'What the hell do you expect me to do? I wouldn't even know where to start.'

'You dig. And you keep digging until you find some mud to stick to that dodgy bastard. Speak to everyone connected to those cases. There must be something that got missed. It's clear I was onto something big. Why else would he take such extreme measures to prevent me from searching?' Meera checked her watch. 'I need to go now. I have plans today.'

'What… and that's it? You dump all this at my feet and expect me to be able to magically find a solution and prove he's a killer. Jesus, you're supposed to be the detective. What can I do?'

These words drew a petulant glare from the detective. 'I took a massive risk meeting you, Hannah. I have my daughters to worry about. One of them is away at university now, so I can't protect her. He can't discover that I've crossed him again. Is that clear?'

'While I appreciate that you're worried, you can't possibly just leave this all to me. I don't have it in me to deal with this.'

Meera's eyes narrowed, and she gave the room a sweeping scan. 'I can't get involved. So please, can you take what I'm giving you now and be grateful I stepped out of the shadows today. Trust me, I very nearly didn't.'

Hannah could see by the detective's resolute expression it would be pointless to press this further, and as much as it frustrated her, she understood the woman's concerns. Any mother would put the safety of their children first.

'I do appreciate you telling me all this,' said Hannah. 'But are you sure there's nothing else… I feel you're not telling me everything. How can you be so sure about this?'

Meera frowned. 'Max can be charming. He can come across as sincere, warm, protective. This is all an act. When I tried to expose him, I faced the real Max and that man is none of those things. The real Max is warped and dangerous. He likes to see you suffer, and he will do whatever it takes to protect his reputation. I know what he is, OK. I can see what he is.'

'I *have* seen him.'

Meera gave a humourless laugh and stood up. 'No, I doubt it. Not yet, you haven't. Pray you don't. Either get out of his way or do something to stop him.' With that, Meera walked away from their table. 'Take care.'

'Wait... Max's wife. Can you remember her first name? He won't tell me it.'

Meera hesitated as if trying to recall this and then she nodded. 'Yes... I do know.'

63

ROSIE

August 1993

At her father's request, Rosie spent the afternoon washing up and cleaning the cabin's kitchen. She worked at a leisurely pace, putting in minimal effort. Not that she could manage much with only one good hand. Even so, her lacklustre attempts wouldn't go unnoticed, and she'd no doubt be made to do it all again. Though this would beat sulking in her room and wallowing in her own misery, at least.

Rosie wiped down the sink with a well-used dishcloth and caught a waft of gas in the air. She investigated the cooker and peeked in the cupboard underneath, where the two propane gas tanks were hooked up. The odour was stronger down there and she wondered if one of them was leaking. A sudden, funny headache materialised, and she wasn't sure if the leak had caused this, or the idea of breathing in the nasty odour had subconsciously triggered the dull pain in her head. She checked the tanks, and both were hooked up as they should be, but she tightened the taps anyway. Just to make certain.

Nevertheless, the smell endured. If anything, it had become harsher.

Rosie stepped back from the cooker and placed her hands on her hips. She wondered if Max's caravan had a similar setup. Despite her headache, the idea of her ex-boyfriend and Chloe huddled together asleep while inhaling poisonous fumes made her smile.

How long did it take for propane gas to choke you out?

64

LOUISA

The morning's rain had passed, and the sun had slipped out from behind patchy clouds. Louisa tapped her index finger against her chin as she peered out of her window and spied her mum hanging washing on the line. The basket was loaded to the top, so she guessed she'd be out there a while.

Louisa, barefoot, walked out into the hallway and tiptoed past Jamie's room. She stopped outside her parents' bedroom door. She considered her actions for around five seconds before she slipped inside and gently closed the door behind her.

Her parents' room was immaculate. Bright white walls and white glossy furniture to match. Not a sock out of place. Not a single crease on the bedspread.

Louisa crept over to her mum's bedside table and crouched. She listened. Then she grabbed the baby-pink jewellery box, sat on the bed, and brushed her fingers over the soft fabric and the embroidered flowers decorating the top. She listened again. Silence. She unzipped the box and sifted through the contents. No friendship bracelet. She removed the top compartment and found more rings and earrings underneath. Still no bracelet.

Louisa put the box back where she found it and searched all three bedside drawers. Behind her lamp. She even checked under her pillow. No sign of it.

Louisa put everything back as it was and tapped her chin as she contemplated where her mum might have stashed it.

65

HANNAH

The vodka and Coke looked appealing. The big chunks of ice clunked as Hannah raised the glass. She inhaled the zesty scent from the wedge of strong-smelling lime as the chilled liquid met her dry lips. She closed her eyes and enjoyed the sensation of her first drink of the day. The first of many, she decided.

Hannah had been sitting in the Caribbean café for quite some time, contemplating the morning's events and how she'd proceed from here. The young waitress had been giving her a few cagey glances since the detective's departure. Though she couldn't rule out paranoia.

Within seconds, the drink disappeared, and she tilted the glass, determined to drain every drop.

Now wasn't the time to stay sober. Or perhaps it was exactly the time to stay dry and keep a clear head. Either way, it was too late. She'd opened that door now.

66

ROSIE

August 1993

Rosie placed her hand on the red valve switch. She guessed there might be a dodgy connection between the bottle and the cooker because, surely, the smell shouldn't be that noticeable. She'd overheard her parents saying that you had to turn the gas on a certain way and only her dad was allowed to touch the bottles.

Rosie turned the valve on full. She fumbled with the bendy tubing and wiggled it about. The tube would be easy enough to pull right out if she'd wanted to.

Rosie coughed into her hand. The kitchen quickly became filled with the unpleasant fumes. She knew she should turn off the valve and open a window.

So why wasn't she? Why did she find herself standing there with her arms crossed and a big smile on her face?

How long would it take to do the job?

She coughed again.

Ten minutes?

She coughed once again, hard enough to make her chest hurt.

Five minutes?

Still, she waited, counting in her head.

At least two minutes had passed.

More coughing. Then she emitted a bout of throat burning, barking coughs.

Maybe less than five minutes, she considered.

Rosie shook her head to ease the intense sensation in her brain.

Time to turn it off, she told herself. Yet, still, she did not make a move for that red valve.

Now she was conflicted. Part of her wanted to hang on and see how long she could endure the gas. Another part of her started screaming at her to switch off and run for the door to grab some fresh air.

She came over a little dizzy and her head felt like it weighed a ton.

You're pushing your luck, Rosie.

The thick odour was becoming choking and awful now. An eggy, sulphuric stench that made her want to spew.

Turn the valve off before you go to sleep and never wake up.

Her heart was beating irregularly, and she was feeling strange and woolly-headed.

You can't really put it to the test. Turn the thing off.

Her arms and legs were like well-cooked spaghetti. It was like her limbs didn't even belong to her body now.

Turn it off.

Rosie, coughing and spluttering, shut off the gas supply. She came to her senses and scolded herself for her stupidity. She'd need to open the windows and clear the air before her parents returned from the village store and went ballistic.

67

LOUISA

As Louisa rifled through her mum's make-up collection, she knew she was taking too long and pushing her luck, yet she didn't stop the search.

After more frantic rummaging, and unable to find what she was hunting for, she relented and gave up. She repositioned all the bits she'd fiddled with and made to leave, but as she did, something in the room snatched her attention. On a corner shelf, stood a tall candle in a glass jar. The candle was made of layers of white, pink and purple wax. It appeared to be unused. She went over and checked it out. It still retained its cardboard seal, which sat on top. It read: *Burn me, baby. Peach and peony fragrance candle.* The untouched wick poked through a circle in the seal, evidence that the candle had never been lit. Yet, to Louisa's eyes, that piece of cardboard looked crumpled at the edges, as though it had been removed more than once.

Louisa used her fingernail to prise back the thin card and bingo. The friendship bracelet lay hidden inside the wax itself. A channel had been dug out in the candle's top, leaving a circle-shaped nook. A perfect hole, which housed the bracelet and made it easy to hide underneath the card.

The ideal hiding place, because real candles were used for display purposes only in this house. Her mum would never allow candles to be lit, as she said they posed a massive fire hazard.

As carefully as possible, Louisa plucked out the black bracelet with the coloured block lettering and examined the piece. She assumed it had been handcrafted, but by whom?

Louisa turned the little blocks so she could read them all.

The letters spelled out Chloe on one side, Rosie on the other.

The question was, who the hell was Rosie?

68

HANNAH

After the morning spent discussing Max with DS Kapoor, all Hannah could think about was getting another drink. She wanted to avoid bars now. Avoid people. Avoid any interaction. She'd made her way to the first off licence in the area and purchased two cheap bottles of vodka. Small ones that were easy to swig without drawing too much attention and would also tuck away nicely in her handbag.

Then she'd made her way to Edmonton and walked out to that disused industrial area once more.

Back to the bridge. Back to the spot.

By the time she was leaning over the railings and gazing down to the train line, she'd already started hitting bottle number two.

Hannah checked her phone. She'd had another missed call from Max. Her phone had been on silent while she'd been with the detective, and she hadn't noticed that he'd called her twice during her time spent with Meera.

Did he know or suspect what she'd been up to?

Could he have somehow worked out she was in cahoots with his old work rival, and they'd discussed his dubious past and how she might bring him down?

Hannah shook away these thoughts. The very idea that he

was already on to her made her go weak at the knees. Meera Kapoor was obviously no pushover, and the fact that somebody like her was too afraid to go up against Max…

Heavy footsteps broke Hannah from her train of thought.

'I have been worried about you.'

Max's cold voice made Hannah clamp the bottle in both hands. She tried to compose herself. Tried to fix her face and remove all traces of the worry she now felt. She didn't turn to him, instead kept her eyes firmly focused on the track below.

'It's way past time you stopped coming here. Wouldn't you agree? Look at me, Hannah.'

She ignored him.

'Look at me,' he demanded.

'I need you to go.'

'I have been trying to get hold of you all morning.' He came up to her and snatched the vodka from her hands. 'It seems I had good reason to be concerned. I can't say I'm not disappointed. You were making good progress.'

'Give that back.'

'You've had more than enough for today. Come on, I'll take you home to sleep it off.'

'Go away.'

Hannah turned to him then. Even though Max's suit looked neat, he appeared tired, and his hair was uncharacteristically messy. Had she rattled him? Had *they* rattled him?

Max threw the bottle over the side of the bridge. Then he exhaled a sharp breath and shook his head as if dealing with a stubborn child who'd refused to follow instructions. 'Car. Now. I mean it.'

'No!'

'Hannah, I'm trying my best to help you. Can't you see I care? I don't want you to go the same way as Archie. You have a life to live. Why waste it like this?' He spoke as though he had genuine concerns for her wellbeing.

'I didn't ask for your help. I will get the Tube back home, thanks.'

Max put his mouth close to her ear and whispered, 'If you don't get yourself off this fucking bridge this second and get into that car...' He put a hand on the back of Hannah's neck and pressed his fingers against her skin as he quickly glanced over railings. 'Pretty please. For me? I'm having a bad day already. Don't force my hand and make me ruin it even more.'

He let go of her neck and cracked a deadly smile that made Hannah want to claw at his face and scream. Instead, she yielded and meekly left the bridge.

69

ROSIE

August 1993

It had been two days since she'd seen Max at the quiet spot. Two days of complete, excruciating agony. She hadn't been able to eat, focus during the day, or sleep at night. The night was the worst. Never-ending despair.

Chloe's face plagued her thoughts, and nothing would change that. Jealous rage burned through her entire body, and now that rage threatened to take full control. Time would not heal her wounds. Nothing would. Like an elephant, she would not forget. Never. Until her dying days, she'd carry a profound, bitter hatred in her heart for that nasty girl she'd once considered her best friend. Even if World War Three erupted tomorrow and destroyed the entire population, leaving only her and Chloe standing, she'd still refuse to be civil to her. She'd still want to harm her. Or worse.

Never in her life had Rosie had such grim, morbid thoughts. Yet, in the days following the party at the lake, she found herself pondering over evil-minded things. Found herself concocting spiteful plans and vicious acts of delicious revenge. Weirdly, it helped somewhat. Not much, but a touch. Because during those moments of darkness where she imagined hurting Chloe, it lessened the pain in her heart for a few fleeting heartbeats.

But it was not enough.

Revenge wasn't something that Rosie just wanted to fantasise about. No, revenge was something she wanted to experience first-hand. So, if the mere thought of revenge took away the sting of her betrayal, how would following through with one of her warped ideas feel?

Would it eradicate some of the searing heartache?

Rosie decided it just might.

But if she was going to go after Chloe, she'd first need to work out how best to deal with Max.

70

LOUISA

Louisa poured a glass of water and took a long sip as she reflected on the bracelet she'd found and why her mum felt the need to stash it away like that. What plausible reason could she have to hide it? Who was she hiding it from?

Jamie shuffled into the kitchen and opened the fridge. 'Don't,' he grumbled, snatching out a Müller Corner and slamming the door shut.

'Don't what?'

'I can tell by your face you're going to start going on about *them*,' he said, sitting down at the breakfast bar and ripping the yoghurt lid free. 'Even though you said you were done sticking your beak into their affairs.'

'Unless you want to end up wearing that on your fat head, I suggest you change your attitude, you little butt-brain.'

'What is it now, then?' he asked, licking the lid. 'Toss me a spoon.'

'You ever heard Mum talk about a friend called Rosie?'

'No, why?'

Louisa lowered her voice as she grabbed a spoon from the cutlery drawer and said, 'She's hiding a friendship bracelet in her room.'

'Wow, call MI5, we've got a major conspiracy on our hands.'

She handed him the spoon. 'Don't be a dick. And don't tell me something's not off with our parents. They're both acting weirder than ever.'

'You said you were done with all this, Louisa!'

'A girl can change her mind.'

'You know why you don't really have many friends? Well, I hate to tell you, but this might be why. Did I mention this already?'

'Did I mention you're an utter twat already? And I've got friends. One of them is the most popular girl in my year, if you must know.'

Jamie gave her a sarcastic nod as he dumped his fruit out of the corner of the pot and stirred it into the yoghurt. 'Do tell me. Who do you think this Rosie is? What's your big theory?'

Louisa watched him stir the yoghurt into a pinky mix as she contemplated what exactly her theory was. Then she tapped her chin and said, 'It's obvious this Rosie must've been Mum's friend at some point in her life. I mean, you don't gift someone a friendship bracelet unless they are super special, right? Like a bestie.'

Jamie continued stirring the yoghurt and nodded in agreement. 'I guess.'

'Are you ever going to actually eat that? You're not mixing cement.'

Jamie lifted a spoonful of yoghurt and inspected it. 'OK, so if this Rosie is, or was, or whatever, Mum's best friend, then why has she never spoken about her to us? Why has she never once mentioned her?'

Louisa let out a long, annoyed sigh. 'This is what I'm trying to say. Mum, or this Rosie handcrafted that bracelet, and it must be super important for her to keep it hidden in her room. It's inside her candle. She's even cut out a channel in the wax where it sits.'

Jamie, as if deciding the yoghurt wasn't to his liking, plunged the spoon back in and resumed stirring. 'Perhaps something happened to her.'

'Like an accident?'

'Or... perhaps she died.'

'But why would she never speak about her?'

'Maybe it's too painful for her to talk about what happened, and the bracelet is her way of secretly remembering her best friend.'

Louisa thought about her mum's frantic dance in the kitchen and wondered if this was linked to this mysterious Rosie. She had to learn who she was. Or it would drive her nuts.

71

HANNAH

They had driven for a good twenty minutes, and Hannah had lost her bearings but guessed they were somewhere around the Tottenham area. They'd driven through a sketchy estate, passed through the back of some grimy industrial buildings that were chugging out white smoke, under a low railway tunnel, and then he navigated a maze of side streets and roads chock full of parked cars. Max was clearly familiar with the backstreets of North London. She'd certainly never been to this part of the city. She glanced around the filthy interior. The car, a neglected Vauxhall, wasn't a vehicle she'd seen Max drive before.

Max caught her checking out the car and said, 'It's a pool motor in case you're wondering why I'm driving around in a clapped-out shit heap. Honestly, it's a crime how messy my lot can be.' He gestured at several crumpled takeaway wrappers jammed inside a compartment above the glovebox. 'Pigs, the lot of them.' He smiled at this.

'You're taking me along on a job?'

Max gave her a side glance and changed gear, a sly smile playing on his lips.

As they entered another estate dominated by several red and white dilapidated tower blocks, Hannah's anxiety levels increased even more. They drove past wall after wall covered in crude graffiti before turning down a narrow street just wide enough for a car to drive down.

'Are you going to tell me where we are going?' she asked, trying to keep her voice level. 'I have things to do.'

Max gave her a fleeting glance, then smiled to himself. The same deadly smile he'd used on the bridge. Sinister and full of both amusement and more than a little threat.

It was a smile that belonged to a maniac, she decided.

'Is this a magical mystery tour? Where are we going? Answer me, Max.'

That smile again.

'Stop the car and let me out.'

Max increased the speed as they flew across a junction without slowing. Hannah glimpsed a gang of youths watching them from outside a corner shop. Saw the glares of animosity thrown in their direction.

'Slow down. I want to get out,' she said.

'You really don't. And we stop when I say.'

They came to a fierce stop at a set of lights and Hannah tried the door. 'I want to get out. Open this.'

'No can do,' he said with a wicked sneer. 'Almost there.'

Almost where?

He hit the accelerator the second the lights changed. A car was heading their way and Max floored it, forcing the other driver to move out of his path and jam his vehicle between two parked cars. Hannah braced for impact, but Max sped past with mere millimetres to spare.

The driver of the other car shouted abuse, and Hannah caught the man's livid face as he snarled and hurled curses.

Max drove with one hand, clenching and unclenching his left fist as he did.

'I want you to tell me where you're taking me,' said Hannah, her voice cracking. 'Stop with all the bullshit and tell me what's going on?'

Max laughed again as they left the backstreet and stopped at another set of lights on the junction of a busy main road that

Hannah did not recognise. There were lots of people here. Plus, shops, buses and restaurants, but they were soon across the road and heading down another street, away from the hustle and bustle of the main area, into more narrow lanes and tightly packed roads.

They passed a wall that had the words: *It's time for acceptance* written on it in a bulky orange font.

Max slowed to a crawl and opened his window as they moved past a big gang of twenty-somethings milling around a car that had no wheels and was positioned on bricks. Hannah could hear music thumping from a nearby black Audi parked outside a block of flats covered in scaffolding. More young men were hanging around the Audi, and Hannah caught the stench of strong cannabis as it wafted into Max's car. The music pouring from the Audi had a deep, low, rolling bass that shook the seat underneath Hannah because it was so heavy.

Max brought the car to a stop and gestured to the young lads with a mock salute. Most of them ignored him, but one stocky youngster got out of the Audi and strode over to Max's car with sizzling confidence. He was a squat, black lad with short, bleached, platinum-blond hair and several gold front teeth. He wore baggy sportswear and sliders with white socks pulled up way past his calves. He grinned at Max like he was truly pleased to see him. 'Hey, my man Maximus. How's life treating you?' he said in an upbeat tone.

'Ah, you know, hanging in there and just about surviving,' said Max.

The man let out a high-pitched laugh and smoothed down Max's shirt collar. 'This man could survive a nuclear blast and still come out with his shirt looking immaculate. Get what I'm saying? Bruv, you stink well-good, man. What shit is that?'

Max grinned. 'Oh, it's called Shady Swindler by Amoral.'

'Ha, ha. Sick. Must get me some of that class stuff,' said the man with a slash-like smile. 'Smells like… pure success.' He nodded to the beat of the music and peered into the car, giving Hannah the once over. He leered at her for a moment and then set his eyes back on Max. 'What are you doing cruising the streets on a Saturday? Don't you have any paperwork to be catching up on?'

'I get bored easily. How's things doing? Are the N17-Yard-Boys keeping things in order?' asked Max.

The man winked. 'Always. So, who do we have here? You got a new partner, DI Maximus?'

'Come on, don't be stupid. This is Hannah. You've met her tons of times,' said Max in a breezy voice. 'Isn't that right?'

The man nodded in agreement and slapped his forehead. 'Yeah, yeah, course. Hey, Hannah. Didn't realise it was *you*. You need something? Just say.'

'I think you're mistaken. We don't know each other,' protested Hannah. She wondered if this was one of the men Max had used to intimidate Meera and her family. She wouldn't be surprised if it was.

Max and the man shared a sly look and the man spat over his shoulder. 'Like that, is it?' He leaned into the car again. 'If I say you know me, then you fucking *know* me! Got that?' He cracked a crooked smile, yet a smouldering malice burned in his small, menacing eyes. Hannah noticed the other men hanging around the Audi were all openly watching the car now with contemptuous glares. One tall lad in a white beanie hat and combat jacket took a pull on his beer and blew her a kiss, although his severe face stayed deadpan.

Hannah said nothing, but her silence only infuriated the man at Max's side even more. He walked with purpose around to the passenger side, and before she could react, Max hit the button to open her window.

'Now then, don't be rude to my good friend Creeper, Hannah,' said Max.

Hannah tensed as this Creeper character rested his beefy forearms on the doorframe and eyed her with disdain. 'You going to disrespect me like that?'

Hannah caught a stench of garlic and cigarettes from the man's breath as she did her best to hold his gaze. 'I'm not.'

'Then tell me, what do you need? Don't be shy, I can hit you up.' He grinned, showing several gold teeth. 'Like always.' He put a finger to his nose and sniffed.

'Nothing,' said Hannah.

'Nah? Nothing? You always want something.' He winked at her. 'I'm just a phone call away. You call, I'll get one of my delivery boys to drop whatever you need. OK? We good, princess?'

Max put a hand on Hannah's shoulder. 'She's going straight, but she appreciates the offer. She's grateful for all the drops you've arranged for her in the past. Isn't that right, Hannah?'

Hannah looked forward and gave a reluctant nod as the bass from the music got deeper and more aggressive. The music had a dub edge to it now. It seemed to shake the entire car under her. Still, the eyes of those men were on her, gazing like brooding, hungry vultures who were waiting for a signal to launch their attack.

Max revved his engine and Creeper took a step back, grinning.

'Yeah right, bruv, she ain't never going straight. Right, Hannah-girl?' said Creeper, followed by a deep, ominous laugh. 'My best customer.'

'I fear you're right,' agreed Max. 'We can but try. And, Creeper... you stay out of trouble. I don't want to hear about any more machete attacks against that crew over in Islington. Understand? You told me all that business had been dealt with.'

'Nothing to do with us. Wouldn't even waste my efforts with those useless pussios,' said Creeper.

'You know I hate that word,' groaned Max. 'Keep things in order. I mean it.'

Creeper smiled. 'Always.' He lunged back towards the car and with a violent sneer, said, 'Don't you be a stranger, Hannah-girl.' He edged closer to her. 'And remember, we have your address.' He laughed again and swaggered back to the Audi.

Max sped off.

Hannah waited until they were several streets away before she said, 'Lovely friends you've got there.'

Max changed gear and clicked his tongue. 'Yep. Great bunch.'

'What the hell was that?'

Max gave her a confused look. 'What was what? Just mingling with the good people of the community. Not sure why you felt the need to be so rude. He's a good guy. You should know that.'

'Am I supposed to be impressed by your little gangster friends?'

'Those guys? Trust me, they are nobodies.'

'I get it. You don't need to show me the power you hold. I already got the message.'

'You said some things to me. You made threats.'

'You threw away my stuff, so I was angry at you.'

'I'd say you still *are* angry at me. You won't even let me get near you at home.' He gave a tut and shook his head.

'It's my house and I told you that you're no longer welcome.'

'OK, I'm not so sure you're taking me seriously here. I'm not convinced you understand the gravity of the situation.'

Max took a sharp right and sent the car down a bumpy track overlooked by scruffy, graffiti-covered panels. He didn't slow up and the car bounced around like crazy.

'We'll just fuck up the car's suspension with a little shortcut,' said Max with a big grin.

The car emerged onto a patch of wasteland enclosed by high metal fences, and Max skidded to a smoke-spewing stop. He got out of the car and walked to the passenger side.

Hannah's heart was racing, but she tried not to panic. This little jaunt had been an act of intimidation and nothing more. Or that's what she kept telling herself.

Max opened the door and gestured her to get out. 'Come on.'

If he'd intended to harm her, then why bother with all the theatrics? She got out and immediately regretted her decision when he snatched her by the arm and frogmarched her across the wasteland.

Hannah searched the ground for something she might use to defend herself, but she saw nothing but a tangle of weeds and an assortment of crushed cans and wrappers. In the distance, sat a tatty old floral sofa and a stack of tyres. Beyond that, a high mesh-wire fence and a skyline filled with tower blocks and several cranes. 'If you'd said we were heading to such a lovely spot, I'd have packed us a nice picnic hamper.' She forced out a nervy laugh. 'I would've put a punnet of fresh strawberries in the fridge and everything.'

Max squeezed her arm harder. 'You think I wouldn't find out? Hey? Do you genuinely consider yourself to be smarter than me? I find that funny.'

Hannah tried and failed to pull free.

Did he know? Had he found out about her meeting with Meera? She searched her muddled brain to think of how he could've possibly found out about her speaking with the other detective so quickly.

'You've been asking questions about me, haven't you?' he asked.

Max stopped walking and pushed Hannah ahead of him. Her gaze fell upon a pit in front of her. It looked eight feet long and maybe six foot deep. Similar to the size of a grave, she suddenly thought. The inside was filled with empty bottles, takeaway boxes and a shredded tyre.

'I don't... I didn't... Max, what the hell are you doing?'

'What, no more silly comments?'

'Don't you dare!'

'You spoke to Squid about me, didn't you?' He flashed a dark, feral grin. 'Don't tell fibs.'

'What? No. You've lost your mind.'

'You were seen in the bar talking to that Aussie prick. You were overheard mentioning my name, so don't lie to me.'

The bald guy with tattooed hands. Had to have been him, she decided. Just how much did that guy overhear?

Hannah shook her head. 'I was out looking for you. You

didn't reply to my messages, so I decided to take a look in there. I'd not seen you.'

'I was busy, and the only messages I received were drunken rants where you told me to stay away from your house. You wanted me to reply to those?'

'I started getting a little worried about you,' she lied. It had sounded like complete bullcrap as well.

'Don't talk nonsense. You were digging. Tell the truth.'

'I am. I asked him how often you came in and where else I might find you. That's it. I wanted to find out what was happening with us. Get a grip, Max!'

'Who else have you been speaking to?'

Hannah swallowed and eyed the dirty pit at her feet. 'No one. You've got this all wrong.'

'Whatever it is you're trying to achieve, you need to stop. Otherwise, I might be forced to get...' He shoved her and sent her plummeting into the pit.

The fall knocked the wind out of Hannah's lungs, and she felt a searing pain in her left elbow. She gasped for breath and writhed in the filth. She tried to calm herself and rolled onto her back. She could still see Max above her, watching with a domineering grin.

'I own you now. You belong to me. Forget yourself again and next time I throw you down there, I'll fill the hole in. I'll do it slowly so I can savour every moment. Are we clear on that?'

Hannah lost her head and screamed at him. A long, piercing shriek that echoed around the small space and fuzzed her ears.

'Great, I'm so glad we understand each other now,' he said, then he vanished from her sight.

'Max! You fucking piece of shit! What did I ever do to you?' she cried as she kicked out with her legs and flailed her arms, causing mud to spill from the sides, showering her face and eyes. 'What did I do?'

She took some calming breaths and sat up. The pit didn't appear as deep as she first suspected. Perhaps four or five feet deep. She'd be able to climb out once she'd managed to get her head together.

Max appeared once again, holding a bottle of vodka. 'Here, have one on me. Open wide.' He unscrewed the lid and poured the entire bottle over her. Then he dropped the bottle at her feet, causing it to shatter, then left.

Hannah screamed again and sobbed in the dingy, piss-smelling ditch he'd dumped her in. She hated him. Hated him so much, she wanted to explode with fury. 'I'll kill you, Max! I swear I will!'

72

ROSIE

August 1993

Rosie watched from a distance as Max and Chloe walked hand in hand across the meadow. Chloe said something to Max, and he burst out laughing. Soon after, she gave him a long kiss on his cheek, prompting both of them to quicken their pace.

Rosie kept following, though she had no real plan of action.

A long, idyllic, blissful summer's day. Two lovers hand in hand playfully skipping through a lush field dotted with red clover and pink orchids. Nothing else in the world mattered. Nobody else mattered. The sheer happiness of spending this warm, wonderful day with someone you adore more than life itself. Rosie had experienced exactly this with Max the previous year.

On this very spot. On a day just like today. Now, she was a mere spectator, forced to watch as this other girl enjoyed what she once had. The other girl who'd all but stolen her life from her. Or, at least, stolen all that mattered.

The pair stopped ahead of her and kissed passionately.

Rosie crouched low and kept her eyes fixed on the lovers. As hands groped and tongues entwined, she almost cried out loud and demanded they stop.

The pain of witnessing the lust this pair shared broke her all over again, and as Chloe tore Max's shirt free and pushed him down into the grass, Rosie grabbed her left wrist and dug her nails into the flesh. She kept digging until she drew blood. When Chloe straddled Max and she understood what was about to happen, right in front of her, she dug harder.

Upon hearing the first moans of pleasure from the pair, Rosie willed herself to get out of there. What did she expect to achieve by staying put and torturing herself? But it was too late now. What she'd witnessed could not be unseen. Now, she no longer needed to imagine the pair together because she had real images to plague her every waking moment.

Stupid, stupid, stupid, Rosie, she scolded herself. *Just sit here and do nothing. Like always.*

It had to be time for a change. Yes, it was time for her to be more hands-on. Time to stop fantasising and plot her revenge properly. Time to do something terrible so that the pair of them wished they'd never dared to mess with her.

As Chloe's body moved faster, her moans of pleasure intensified, and Rosie forced herself to turn her back on the scene. She instead focused on the blood spilling from the claw marks she'd made and tried to imagine that Chloe's moans were those of pure pain instead of sexual gratification. She tried to visualise herself pouring petrol over the pair of them and saw their panicked faces as they concluded their fates were sealed.

Rosie then pictured herself dropping a match and the pair going up in a whoosh of deadly flames. Her bitter smile would be the last thing they would see before their lights went out for good.

73

LOUISA

The four of them ate in an intense, dreadful silence. Louisa kept shooting her brother withering looks across the table as she pushed her lasagne around the plate, unable to stomach another bite. Jamie kept avoiding her stare, scoffing down his food so he could no doubt remove himself from the table and escape the awkward atmosphere as soon as possible.

Her mum nibbled a piece of garlic bread and smiled at her dad. 'It's nice to have us all together for dinner as a family. It's been such a long time. I can't even remember when we did.'

Her dad stared at her mum for a moment. Then he sniffed and continued to shovel the food into his mouth.

Louisa caught her dad's eyes darting in her direction. They narrowed as he focused back on his plate. 'Why don't you grab a bottle of bubbly, love?'

Her mum smiled like a giddy school kid. 'Bubbly? Are we celebrating, Max?' She giggled. 'Are we celebrating tonight?' Her eyes sparkled. 'Are we? Really?'

Louisa stopped pushing her food around and waited for her dad's response.

Jamie had also stopped mopping up his sauce with a wedge of garlic bread and was waiting.

Louisa's dad cracked a slow, lopsided grin. 'Yeah, a little project of mine is almost done and dusted.'

'Oh, what great news,' gushed her mum.

'Care to elaborate?' asked Louisa.

Her mum wiggled a finger at her. 'Don't pester your father about his work stuff, sugar-puff. Now, let me go grab a nice bottle of the good stuff and a bucket of ice.' With that, she scurried off with a jubilant grin plastered on her face, humming as she went.

Louisa and Jamie shared a gawp that conveyed their total confusion.

'What's with you two and the conspiratorial glances?' asked her dad with a suspicious frown. 'Something you want to say?'

Louisa shrugged. 'Don't know what you mean.'

'Can I have a glass of fizz, Dad?' asked Jamie.

'Small one,' he said. 'Come on, Louisa, out with it. What's with all this arrogant nonsense these days? You going to continue with your rebellious and confrontational phase until you hit twenty?'

Louisa sat up straighter and put down her cutlery. 'Nope.'

Her dad sneered. 'Yeah, why am I not convinced?'

'You want us to celebrate with you, yet you can't tell us what we're actually celebrating. Mm, that's a little strange, if you ask me,' said Louisa.

Her dad put down his fork and scratched his chin thoughtfully. 'What would *you* like to celebrate, Louisa? How about getting to the end of your exams?'

'But I have nothing to celebrate yet,' she said in a curt tone. She heard a clunk, clunk, clunk as her mum filled the bucket from the freezer's ice dispenser in the kitchen. 'Not until I get my results back.'

Her dad laughed and shook his head. Then the amusement fell from his face. 'You might walk out that door tomorrow and get ploughed down by a speeding car. You should celebrate life. It's short. Sometimes, it can be shorter than you expect. Maybe you should appreciate what you have and what people do for you. Perhaps you should remove that self-important smirk you like to slap on your face every damn day and concentrate on what's important.'

'And what is important, Dad?' she asked with a sarcastic grin. 'What's really important to you?'

Before he could respond, her mum came prancing into the room with a bottle of champagne wedged inside a silver bucket loaded with chunks of ice. 'Bubbly is here! Should be nicely chilled by the time we have pud-puds,' she sang. 'Key-lime pie and pecan ice cream. I bet there'll be no complaints from any of you about that.'

'No complaints here,' said her dad.

'Defo not from me,' said Jamie.

Louisa winced as her dad stood up and planted a long kiss on her mum's cheek. 'Sounds good to me.'

Jesus, these two are just the weirdest parents in the world, thought Louisa as she offered her mum an over-the-top smile and said, 'Ooh, yummy.'

74

HANNAH

27th June 2023

Hannah opened the door to find a woman in her late forties standing on her doorstep. She wore shapeless, baggy trousers pulled up high and an unflattering beige cardigan that had serious granny vibes.

'Hello, can I help you?' asked Hannah.

The woman did not speak. She appeared to be busily scanning her house.

Hannah put herself in a position where she could slam the door shut if need be. 'I take it you're here to see me. Mrs Hudson, I assume?'

The woman's lips twitched and she nodded. 'How did you guess?'

'I don't get many visitors. How did you find me? Did he give you my address?'

'Why would he do that?' she asked, as if the very idea would be completely ridiculous.

'How then?'

Max's wife lifted her chin and shrugged. 'I have my ways. I'm not as useless as he thinks I am. Yet I do play the part rather well. With Oscar-worthy performances.'

Hannah stared at the other woman and took in her features. She had a plain, pale face with a tiny, sharp nose. Her small eyes were hard to see, as she appeared to be constantly squinting. Her hair was dark and shoulder-length, flat and streaked with a few greys. She wasn't unattractive, but there was something odd about her face that made it impossible to forget. Hannah couldn't, for the life of her, picture this woman with Max.

Hannah put up her palm. 'If you're here for an argument—'

'I'm not here for that.'

'Your husband is not welcome here, and neither are you.'

'Hannah, I want to talk. Can I please come inside?'

'Why?'

'I have something to tell you. You're going to want to hear it.'

'We can talk here.'

'I'd rather not. For five minutes. Please, lovey.'

Hannah pulled the door open and gestured for her to come in. Max's wife followed her into the kitchen. She considered asking the woman if she wanted a drink but decided not to bother. Instead, she leaned back against the kitchen counter and crossed her arms defensively. She could see the other woman scrutinising her house with a superior scowl. To be fair, this wasn't surprising, as the place was a complete tip.

'Your arm looks very sore. What happened to you?'

Hannah turned her arm to give Max's wife a better look at the gash running from her elbow to her wrist. 'I cut it on some glass.'

'Ooh, ouch. Very nasty.'

Hannah almost added, thanks to your husband who, last time I was with him, slung me into a disgusting pit and left me stranded on the outskirts of a shady, North London housing estate.

'Did you get that seen to, lovey?'

'What was it you wanted to say?'

'It's a lovely day.'

'You came all this way to tell me that?'

'I do love the summer. Do you have kids, Hannah?'

Hannah cleared her throat. 'A son in his early twenties, but why does that matter?'

'What's his name?'

'Look, I don't want to be rude...'

'My husband told you we're heading for a divorce, didn't he?'

Hannah nodded.

'I'm here to tell you... that is not the case. He lied to you. OK? That is not true and, with all due respect, I'm going to ask you to keep well away from my husband.' The woman spoke in a calm, soft tone and there hadn't been a hint of threat or aggression in her voice.

Hannah rubbed her forehead and shook her head. 'OK, right. Wasn't expecting... this.'

'You assumed I'd come here ranting and raving? No. I understand your situation. Max told me you're a widow. You're searching for happiness. Looking for a reason to get up in the morning. He felt sorry for you, but that's all. This has to stop now. I can't let you have him. I'm sorry, I feel for you. But he belongs to me. Please don't be bitter about this. You poor lady, I bet you've been having such a hard time of it, haven't you?'

Hannah, taken aback, gaped at her. She appeared to be genuinely concerned for her and although what she'd said had been incredibly patronising, somehow, she didn't think she'd meant it that way.

'Hannah, you are such a sweet, sweet thing. So beautiful. There are plenty more men out there who'd give their right arm to date somebody like you. But Max isn't on the market. He's taken. He's mine.' She flashed a sympathetic smile. 'I can be a shoulder to cry on. I really can. If that's what you need. I'm a good listener if you need a friend.'

Hannah unfolded her arms and dropped them to her side. 'What is this? What do you want?'

'Where's your kettle? Shall I make us a nice cuppa?'

'No.'

'I wouldn't mind one myself.'

'Do you have any idea what your husband has done to me, Mrs Hudson?'

'You can call me Chloe,' she said with a shy smile. She scanned the kitchen with a pitying frown. 'You are sinking into a despairing hole, aren't you? You poor sausage.' She put her hand against her own chest. 'My heart aches for you. I don't want us to be enemies, and I can't hold a grudge against you. I'm not that kind of person. I like to see the good in people.'

'What? I slept with your husband. Why would your heart ache for me?'

'You're not the first. Won't be the last,' she said with a sad smile.

'Then I'm sorry, but you're a total mug to put up with him. Who does that? Who lets someone treat them that way?'

'Relationships are complicated things. There'll always be a few bumps in the road if you're in it for the long haul.'

'Is that what Bailey Lloyd was? A bump in the road?'

For a moment Chloe's face darkened a touch, before she flashed an upbeat grin and said, 'Max wasn't interested in her. Max didn't go near her. Blatant lies to sully his name. Plus, that's ancient news, sweetheart. Who even told you about that silly nonsense?'

'What about Susan Gains and Michelle Wynn? More bumps in the road? Those women are still missing. Are you aware of that?'

Chloe chuckled and gave Hannah a quick grin. 'Who?'

'Chloe, your husband—'

'You need to be careful and think before you voice unsubstantiated lies. My husband won't like that. He really won't.'

'If we're going to become friends, I can't see why you'd need to tell him anything about what we discuss here.'

'I have to. He's my husband. My best friend.'

'What the hell is wrong with you? He's not your best friend. He's a piece of work, is what he is.'

'I get it. You feel used.'

Hannah shook her head and couldn't help but laugh. The

laughter soon turned into a sobbing fit, as she slid down the cupboard door and sat with a thud. 'What the hell is wrong with you?' she repeated as her head fell into her hands and the tears came.

'Oh, no. Don't cry, my sweet thing; please don't cry. It'll all be fine, you'll see. He... he breaks hearts. He's broken yours, hasn't he? Looks like he's really done a number on you.' She crouched down to Hannah and placed a hand on her shoulder. 'Please don't cry.'

'You're clueless.'

'Come on, up you get.'

'Tell him to stay away from me. I don't want him to come back here.'

'He doesn't want to come back here, my little lamb. You need to stop chasing him now. Let go and move on. Can you do that? Please, can you let him go now and step away?'

With the hot tears streaming down her face, Hannah glared incredulously at the other woman. 'You're as mad as he is!'

Chloe continued to rub her shoulder. 'Love can make you do crazy things, right?'

'What did Max do to Bailey Lloyd? Did he hurt her?'

Chloe stood up and took a step back. 'You can't say things like that.'

Hannah wiped the tears away. 'I think he wants to hurt me. Possibly even kill me. Don't pretend that you don't know what he's really like. Pull your head out of the bloody clouds, woman!'

Chloe shook her head and waved her hands as if she couldn't hear this. 'No, no, no.' She waggled her finger and smiled again, though this smile crackled with nervous tension. 'You can't say that. He's a good man. He's going to make DCI soon. People trust him. He's taken countless drug dealers off the streets. He makes this city a safer place.'

'What happened to Bailey Lloyd? She's the reason you moved away from Cheltenham, right? The reason you had to leave and come to London.'

'You have no clue about this.'

'Did Max kill her?'

'What a totally stupid thing to say.'

'Susan Gains, wife of a small-time drug dealer who plied his trade in Tredworth in Gloucester. She became a young widow after her fella was stabbed outside a pub following an argument with a group of rowdy men... Max had been seen with her on more than one occasion before she vanished. One of his team had been the investigating officer on that case.'

'There was no proof that Max had anything to do with her. More baseless lies.'

'And what about Michelle Wynn? Not married, but she also lost her partner, didn't she? Another criminal who lived in Cheltenham who made his money by robbing other dealers in the area. Came to a sticky end when a rival clobbered him with a cricket bat as he approached his car.'

'Michelle's boyfriend was known to Max. He was helping him with an enquiry, but he had nothing to do with that horrible girlfriend of his.'

'So where is she now?'

'Who told you about these people? Who have you been talking to?'

Hannah got to her feet and wiped her eyes. She wasn't going to divulge to Chloe anything about Meera or the email the detective had sent her. She'd received a ton of files containing old newspaper reports and useful information relating to each of the missing women. There could be no doubting that Meera had been onto something big. Max was also connected to other missing women and, although the links were tenuous, they still might prove useful. 'I did some internet research.'

Chloe pulled a face like she wasn't buying that answer. 'Did you now?'

'If you let him keep getting away with it, then you are as guilty as he is,' said Hannah.

Chloe's cheeks reddened, and she sucked in her lips, making her face twisted and ugly. 'He's my husband.'

'He's a warped headcase! Stop protecting him, you stupid, bloody bitch!' bellowed Hannah with such raw vehemence, Chloe flinched and held up her hands as if expecting a thump.

Hannah took a deep, calming breath and pulled the locks of hair from her face.

Chloe appeared both scared and mortified. Hannah decided the woman was very childlike. Deluded, oppressed, meek. She reminded her of a fragile doll, she decided.

'Why stay loyal to a man like that?' said Hannah, now using a much softer voice. 'Are you going to play the obedient house-wife for the rest of your life? How could you let him treat you like this? Don't you have any self-respect?'

'He's given me everything I have,' whispered Chloe. 'How can I just turn my back on him now? We've been through so much. You can't possibly understand.'

'Does he know you're here?'

Chloe pulled a face like a sulky child and stuck her head in the air.

'Does he?'

'I want you to apologise to me. For calling me a bitch just now.'

'Fine, I'm sorry I called you a bitch. Now, does he know?'

'No.'

'How did you find me?'

'I used his iPad to trace his phone's location a while back.'

'He wouldn't be happy about that, would he?'

Chloe jutted her lower lip and shook her head. 'No, he wouldn't like that. Not at all.'

'Hand on heart, he won't hear anything from me. I promise.'

'He scares me, too. On occasions, I do worry if he might...' Chloe shook her little fists and gave an annoyed wince. 'Shut up, Chloe. Stop talking, you silly, silly woman.'

'You can tell me.'

'I shouldn't. I really, really shouldn't.'

'It's clear you want to get this off your chest. If not now... when?'

Chloe gazed up at the ceiling and let out a great, long-suffering sigh. 'Why did I come here? I'm so foolish.'

'To find out if it's happening again. Or perhaps, deep down, you wanted to warn me.'

'I should go.'

'Take my number.'

'I'm not so sure that will be a sensible idea. Why would I need to contact you again? I have said all that needs to be said.'

'That isn't true.'

'Surely you don't expect me to help you incriminate my husband. Is that what you're planning?'

Hannah went to the fridge and took out a chilled bottle of vodka.

'Or do you have something else in mind, Hannah?'

Hannah unscrewed the lid and took a long drink. 'Like what?' She offered the drink to Chloe.

'I have never drunk neat vodka before. What's it like?'

'Well, I like it.'

Chloe raised her eyebrows and took a swig. 'Christ, that's awful,' she spluttered. Yet she went in for a second hit. 'It sure burns on the way down.' She took three more sips and handed the bottle back. 'Whoa. Crikey.'

Hannah raised the bottle. 'To the summer.' She took a long drink.

Chloe nodded and coughed.

An agonising silence engulfed them until Chloe's throaty chuckle broke it. 'Perhaps… we could team up and kill him,' she said, then burst out into a fit of silly giggles. 'I mean, it would solve a lot of problems, right? He wouldn't see that coming.' She sniggered and put her hand over her mouth.

'Are you being serious right now?'

Chloe coughed again and held her hand to her chest. 'I'm kidding, I'm kidding,' she laughed.

'You've changed your tune.'

Chloe struggled to suppress a fit of wild giggles. 'I'm sorry,

I'm teasing. I have a very silly sense of humour, and that vodka has gone straight to my head.'

Hannah nodded and decided this little meeting with Max's wife had not gone as she'd expected.

The woman was bonkers. Mad as they come. Like Max had told her she was.

But maybe, just maybe, this woman might be able to help deal with the whole Max situation once and for all.

75

ROSIE

August 1993

Rosie opened the shed door and jumped back in shock when she found Chloe standing in the doorway with an inscrutable expression on her face. She was wearing a short, summery dress, a yellow V-neck style with a red and white floral pattern. It didn't suit her at all.

'Nice dress,' said Rosie, not bothering to hide her smirk.

'Max got it for me.'

'From the local charity shop, right? It's been stuck in the window for about two years now.' She grinned. 'Makes you look very... cute.'

'Cut the shit. I know it makes me look like a sap, but I've no other clean clothes with me, so don't be a bitch about it. What are you up to in there? Are you hammering nails into your eyeballs or something?'

Rosie stepped out of the shed and shut the door. She ignored the girl's distasteful remark. 'What do you want?'

'I saw you the other day. When you were spying on us like some whack-job creep.'

'Nope, not me.'

'Rosie, I spied you. Stop following us. I've only got three days left of my holiday. Can't you let me enjoy my last few days with Max in peace? Is that too much to ask for?'

Rosie struggled to find a reply to this. The girl had some front on her, she had to give that to her. *Her* holiday? Was she for real? Her eyes flicked around the shed. Where had she put that hammer?

Chloe pulled at the waistline of her dress. 'Stupid thing is so uncomfortable.'

'Not sure it's the right size.'

'No shit. I look like I'm about to audition for a spot in a children's clothes catalogue. Does he think I'm ten or something?'

Rosie laughed, although she promptly tried to mask her amusement with her hand.

Chloe joined in with a tiny snigger. 'It's not funny.'

'It is a bit.'

Chloe pulled the strands of hair out of her face. 'I've missed our silly chats and shenanigans.'

'Really?'

'I get it, I'm a self-centred troll. Always have been. I treated you like dirt. If I'm honest, I regret what I did.'

'You do? Honest?'

'But you've got to admit, I was right. I said if we put Max to the test, he'd fold.' She scrunched up her face. 'I guess, in a way, I've kind of done you a huge favour. At least you found out he's a cheating prick now and not a few years down the line.'

Rosie nodded. 'Obviously, I'm super pissed off, yet this fact crossed my mind the other day.'

'I get I said some bad things. I wish I hadn't.'

Rosie nodded glumly. 'You did. Awfully hurtful things.'

'Sometimes I lose my head and lash out.'

'That doesn't make it all right.'

'It is a bit naff to let a boy come between us. I mean, when we get back home, we don't want to stay enemies, do we? You don't have any friends as it is, so without me, where would that leave you? Without me to vouch for you, Laura Wells and her cronies will make your life a living hell. Just like before. Before I stepped in and put them straight.'

Rosie found herself nodding in agreement.

Chloe continued. 'I guess you could even say that you allowing me to be with Max is, I dunno, like a way of saying thanks for all the times I've stood up for you. All the times I've risked my reputation, to protect you from all the arsewipes trying to make your life a living nightmare.'

'You are going back then? After your break?'

'Yeah, of course. Why wouldn't I?'

'Max said you two had plans. Kids and a proper life together.'

Chloe grimaced. 'That's just pillow talk.'

'You don't want to have kids with him?'

'No. Well, yeah. I mean, I might. One day. Who knows? I'm going to sixth form and maybe college first. I think he needs to slow down a little.'

'And what about all the travelling you're both going to do?'

'Oh, had a good old chat, have you? Sounds like you've been having a proper gossip about me.'

'He said he loves you. I need to accept that. I *am* accepting that.'

'By following us around and spying on us like some little perv?'

Rosie looked at the ground and felt her cheeks burn hot. 'I didn't realise you were going to do it in the middle of the meadow.' The idea that Chloe knew she'd been watching, and yet she still chose to straddle Max and make love to him made Rosie's stomach churn.

'Whatever, it's done now. Just stop with all the stalking already.'

'I will.'

Chloe nodded and smiled thinly. 'OK, good. That's good.' She smiled again. 'I keep thinking about that poo song of yours. It always makes me chuckle. Think we should get blind drunk and come up with an entire album... I guess this means I actually miss my dozy twiglet.'

Rosie's jaw tightened. 'Are you OK?'

'Why wouldn't I be?'

'You seem a bit... strange. No, you seem on edge. Are you concerned your dad is getting worried now?'

'Like he gives a toss. And I'm fine. I should go. Maybe see you around.' Chloe made to leave, then stopped. 'Max can be a bit much, can't he? A bit... demanding. Not sure we're a brilliant match after all. Take this friggin' dress. I said no, but he liked it so much he just had to get his way. I won't even go into details why, the dirty monkey.'

'He can be quite stubborn.'

'Too right he can. It's his way or the highway. Gets a little frustrating. It's like he wants to change me. Like, make me into something I'm not. I'm certain he's trying to turn me into... you.'

Rosie's jaw tightened even more. 'Why would he do that?'

Chloe chuckled and shrugged. 'Is it too late to give him back, Rosie?' She toyed with the bracelet on her wrist. 'And do I still get to keep this?'

Rosie gave a noncommittal shrug. 'Do you want to keep it on?'

'Yes. Why not? We are, after all, still mates, right?'

'Sure, still mates,' Rosie lied with a big, fake smile playing on her lips as she imagined one of those propane gas bottles exploding so violently in Chloe's face, it shredded her skin and melted her deceitful eyes.

76

LOUISA

Upon hearing her mum's car pull onto the drive, Louisa ran down into the lounge and pretended to busy herself with the contents of her schoolbag.

As predicted, her mum breezed into the lounge and immediately took an interest in the mess strewn all over her precious rug. 'Lost something, Louisa?'

'Some geometry homework. I must've left it at school.'

'Please don't leave all your stuff over my rug. Ooh, you've got pencil-sharpener bits all over it.'

'You drove today?'

'Yes, I do own a licence. I am allowed to drive.'

'Where'd you go?' asked Louisa, in the most uninterested tone she could muster. She started scooping up her gear and wedging it inside her bag.

'Just out.'

'You never just go out. You hate going out. Have you been drinking?'

'If you must know, I met a friend.'

Louisa made a wheezing sound with her throat and pulled a face. 'What friend?'

'Just a friend.'

'Does this 'friend' have a name?'

'Um, yeah.'

'What is her name?'

'Who said it was a woman? Mm, Little Miss Presumptuous Pants, aren't we?'

Louisa zipped up her bag and stood up straight. 'You went out to meet another man? Are you serious?'

'I didn't say that.'

'You implied it.'

'I'm merely saying don't presume. Anyway, what if I had?'

'Dad would hit the roof for a start.'

'Yes, that would be a given.'

Louisa sighed. 'Are you two splitting up? I mean, you are both...'

'Both what?'

'I'm no expert, but I get the sense your relationship isn't exactly normal. You say he's your best friend, but he treats this house like a hotel, and when he is home, you both act so weird with each other. I mean, he barely says one word to you, and the other night he's cracking open the fizz and telling us we need to celebrate. You're both doing my head in.'

Her mum giggled and squeezed her right cheek. 'My funny little grump-a-lump. Look at that grouchy face. You've always been a prickly little sausage. I remember when you were two, and I swear this is true, I don't think you gave us a single smile for at least six months. Nothing would cheer you up. Your father and I were worried we had a proper gloomy goblin on our hands.'

'Stop changing the subject. You always do that. Why can't you give me a straight answer for once in your life?'

'You want me to tell you if our marriage is heading for the rocks?'

'Yes, I've got every right to be told. This will have a massive impact on my life.'

'Fine, fine. OK then, drama llama, the truth is we are experiencing a tiny rough patch. A... a tiny *bump* in the road. Nothing more. Nothing we can't resolve. Our divorce is not in the post. So relax.'

'I don't care if you leave him and, if I'm honest, he deserves it, but I'd like to have all the facts, so I can be ready to deal with my life once my parents are separated.'

Her mum pressed her on the nose with her finger. 'No danger of that. Happy now? Would you like a cheese-and-pickle sandwich?'

'No thanks. Wait. This friend. Is it the person who gave you that bracelet you had in the garden a while back?'

Her mum smiled as if the question had been ridiculous. 'What? No, of course not. No one gave me anything. Is the Spanish Inquisition over now?'

Louisa shrugged and went back to tidying up her stuff. She hoped, for her mum's sake, she wasn't playing her dad at his own game and had started her own fling. Louisa got the sense her dad would never let her get away with it. She dreaded to think what he'd do if he caught her mum cheating. Though she'd never seen her dad commit an act of violence, she knew him well enough to understand he had an incredibly nasty and vindictive side to him. In the last few years, she'd seen him in a different light. If she was honest with herself, she couldn't put her finger on what it was exactly, but she sensed there was a darkness inside that man's soul. Some kind of sixth sense or gut feeling was perhaps warning her.

Whatever it was, she was worried about her clueless mum.

77

HANNAH

Hannah answered her phone with a sleepy, 'Hello.'

'So, looks like I've acquired quite the taste for chilled, neat vodka now.'

'Chloe?'

There was a long pause. Chloe cleared her throat and said, 'I'm alone. I can talk freely.'

'OK. About what?'

Another pause. This one longer. Hannah checked the phone was still connected. 'Hello? You still there?'

'Can I trust you with some delicate information?' said Chloe in a conspiratorial whisper.

Hannah flopped onto the sofa as she considered the question. 'Well, can I?'

'Yeah, sure,' said Hannah.

'Next week I'm going to talk to a woman called Kathy Gibson.'

'Who is she?'

'She's Bailey Lloyd's half-sister.'

'Go on.'

'To cut a long story short, I kept in touch with an old friend back in Cheltenham, just on social media and stuff. And it turns out this friend knows Kathy quite well. Her younger sister was best friends with Kathy at school. Anyway, Kathy, while very drunk, told my friend a few juicy secrets. She let slip some rather interesting things.'

Chloe had spoken so rapidly, Hannah struggled to digest the information. 'About Max?'

'Kathy all but told my friend that Max was besotted with Bailey. That he practically stalked the poor thing. She also said she could prove Max was doing "bad things" to the girl. Whatever the hell that's meant to mean.'

'What sort of things?'

'My friend pressed her and tried to get her to clarify what she meant, but she clammed up and changed the subject.'

'You think she'll talk to you now?'

'My friend has been in touch with her again recently. Turns out she *really* does have something to get off her chest. Some secret she's been holding onto, and she's more than willing to chat with me.'

'I want to come with you.'

Silence on the other end.

'Chloe, I want to come with you,' she repeated more boldly.

'I'm not sure that would be sensible.'

'Please, let me come. It will be safer if we stick together.'

'Right. May I remind you that you've been bonking my husband on a regular basis. I'm not so sure I'd be super inclined to let you join me on a road trip.'

'May I remind *you* we are talking about a man who blatantly lied to my face. A man who told me you were unstable and that he was intending to divorce you! I'm sorry, but I won't be painted as the villain here. Do you have any idea how scared I am right now?'

'Fine, fine, you can come. But we must be very careful. I'm not picking you up from your house in case Max is watching. You'll need to meet me somewhere discreet. Agreed?'

'Fair enough. Just say when.'

'Max is away this Friday to Sunday. Some fishing trip in Kent with his work buddies. Or so he says. Unless he just said that and he's going off with some woman.'

'He sure hasn't made plans with me.'

'Then we must use this opportunity to act. I'll find out if Kathy can see us at short notice.'

Hannah heard the door open and close. 'Shit, shit, shit. He's here.'

'What? Max is there now?'

'I need to go. He's just let himself in.' Hannah ended the call and pretended she was asleep, so she didn't have to face him straight away.

A few minutes passed by when she felt air blowing on her right cheek and knew it was Max. She opened her eyes and gazed about with a sleepy frown. 'What are you doing here?' she muttered.

Max gave her a wry, bitter smile. 'Nice nap? Sorry, did I wake you?'

Hannah fake yawned. 'I told you that I want my key back. Stop waltzing in like you own the place.'

'How much of a pay-out did you get from the insurance when Archie topped himself?'

'Get lost.'

'No need to be rude, I was just asking. I'm a little worried about your spending. That money won't last if you keep wasting it like this. Perhaps I should take over your finances.'

'I have arranged to get the locks changed.'

'That won't stop me. Oh, by the way, you have a delivery coming tonight. One of Creeper's runners will drop you three grams of Peruvian flake.'

'No, they won't.'

'You're in for a treat. I hear this stuff is class. And don't worry. On the house. My treat, but I will need something in return.'

'Did you not hear me? I don't want any damn drugs!'

'Do you think I could borrow your spare room?' he asked, as if she'd not even spoken.

'It is not spare. It's my son's.'

Max laughed. 'Yeah, don't need it though, does he?'

'Go fuck yourself!'

'You don't need to lift a finger. I'll arrange for somebody to come round and clear all the old shit out so we can use it.'

'You will not.'

'Yeah, we'll do away with the junk you have stashed up in there and make it a usable space.'

Hannah glared at Max. 'You go into that room, and you'll be very sorry.'

'Does he have some violins stored in there? I might learn to play myself.' He pretended to play with an imaginary instrument. 'I could serenade you with a sombre piece when you're mooching around this shithole with a face like a slapped arse.'

'Stay out of there and leave his stuff alone!'

'Come on, Hannah, do we need to go for another little drive? Do I need to show you what I'm capable of? Trust me, I have been playing nicely thus far. Don't make me change things up a gear.'

'Does making my life a misery make you feel better about yourself? Do you get off on this weird shit?'

Max made to turn away, then spun and grabbed her by the hair. He took hold of a handful of locks and pulled her to her feet, so she was face to face with him. 'I'm going to level with you. I'm in a tight spot. No, correction, somebody else is in a tight spot and, as usual, muggins here needs to clean up their mess. I'm going to need to hide this certain someone in that room for a few weeks. One month tops. Just until I can put a few things right.'

'If you expect me to have some criminal take over my home, you can forget it. Not going to happen. I won't be party to your corrupt bullshit.'

'Come on, Hannah, you're making it sound like I'm cuck-ooing your home. I'm asking for a favour.'

'Doesn't sound like you're asking.'

Max let go of her locks. 'No, you're right. I'm not asking.

Think of it like you're just offering up your place to be used as a police safe house. Fancy a brew? Something stronger? I'll go see what I can rustle up.' He left the room and said, 'Smells awful in here. When did the bins last go out, you dirty pig?'

Hannah tried to compose herself. She thought about this Kathy and what Max's wife had told her. Was this a glimmer of hope? Could Meera be persuaded to get on board and stand with Hannah if they could find others to speak out against this crooked detective? If his own wife was prepared to start digging up the dirt on him, then yes, there had to be a chance Meera would come back out of the shadows and fight him again.

Hannah calmed her ragged breathing. She needed to keep it together and play it smart. Once Max had gone, she'd message the female detective and update her on the situation.

'Two months. No longer,' said Hannah in a surly tone as she walked into the kitchen. 'But if he's a pervert or a crackhead, he's out. But he can take my room, and I'll sleep on the sofa.'

Max, head in the fridge, said, 'You certainly don't want anyone in your son's room, do you?'

'Are we in agreement?'

Hannah would board up her windows and fit fifty bolts on every door before she'd let anyone else into her home, but she decided it would be better if she pretended to accommodate Max's demands. For now.

Max closed the fridge. 'Sure. You need to go shopping. Would you like me to grab some bits for you on my travels later? It's no hassle. Text me what you need.'

Hannah stared at him, speechless. He'd spoken like all was fine and dandy and he hadn't just snatched her by the hair and told her he intended to hide a criminal in her house. Not to mention organising some dealer to deliver her drugs, which she had no intention of taking, to her doorstep later.

The man was unhinged.

78

ROSIE

August 1993

The moody clouds dispersed to reveal the glorious morning sunshine and patches of pale blue sky. Rosie felt the heat on her face, pleased that the weather had perked up and the day looked set to be a brighter one. It lifted her spirits, and she knew it would help her focus on the task ahead. Her parents were still fast asleep. They'd gone out into the village the night before and had both staggered back here, drunk as lords, which was quite unusual for them, as they weren't exactly renowned for being night owls or big drinkers.

Rosie shifted about on the wooden garden chair and sipped on her chilled orange juice. It was watery and tasteless. She put the glass down onto a rickety garden table and once again visualised Chloe in that floral dress. Every time she thought about her in that awful attire, it made her snigger to herself. She wondered if they sold disposable cameras in the village because it would be priceless if she got a few good shots of the girl, which she could then pass around Chloe's friends back home.

Goodbye street cred and hello red-faced embarrassment. Then she slapped her forehead and giggled at the stupidity of the idea.

Chloe wouldn't be going back home ever again, so there would be little point in obtaining humiliating photos of her. But the idea cheered her up a little.

79

LOUISA

Louisa's mum was driving her up the wall. The woman had been so sprightly and chirpy in the last few days; it had become a tad aggravating, to say the least. Skipping about, singing, making stupid jokes. Even more stupid than normal. But there was also a glint in her eye that Louisa had never seen before. A giddy excitement. Like a child gearing up for a magical holiday. A child who could barely contain their glee and might pop if they didn't bounce about like an ecstatic kangaroo.

Was she overcompensating for something? Perhaps she was super nervous, and this behaviour was her way of dealing with the acute stress and anxiety of a situation Louisa wasn't aware of.

Louisa heard her mum humming in the hallway, and she poked her head out from behind her bedroom door. 'You feeling OK, Mum?'

Her mum clapped her hands together and did a little wiggle. 'Two words: chilled, neat vodka.'

'That's three words. Are you drunk? It's Thursday. Who drinks vodka on a Thursday afternoon? Oh yeah, that's right, alkies and dossers do!'

'Ooo, who has un-pickled your gherkin today?'

'My gherkin? What? Are you losing the plot, you mad, drunken cow?'

Her mum put her hands on her hips and let out a big, long moooo. Then she laughed and pinched Louisa's right cheek. 'Don't give Mummy that scathing glare, you prickly old pear. You will have the frown lines of a sixty-year-old by the time you hit twenty.'

'Is this a mid-life crisis? Is that what this is?'

'Yes, my funny fuss pot. Exactly that. Mummy is having a major crisis.' She went cross-eyed for a few seconds and started giggling. 'Now, I need to talk to you about this weekend.'

'What about it?'

'On Friday, your dad is away fishing on the Kent coast and won't be home until Sunday, and I'm going away for two days myself.'

'On your own? Without Dad?'

Her mum hiccupped. 'Oops. Yes, I'm meeting a friend and, like I said, he's away fishing. He can't be in two places at once, can he?'

'The same friend you saw the other day?'

'Nope. This is an old friend from Cheltenham. Sooo, I'm going to make a weekend of it.'

'You're going to Cheltenham? On your own?'

'She lives in Bath now. It's a wonderful place. Amazing architecture.'

Louisa was instantly suspicious about this, but she didn't react. 'So I've been told.'

'You're the one who said I needed to stop being such a sad case and get out more.'

'I didn't say anything. No, I'm super pleased. This is great. I hope you have a wicked weekend. It's just... well, this is awkward, cos I kind of made plans for this weekend myself, so I can't watch Jamie for you. Sorry.'

Her mum stifled a laugh and hiccupped again. 'You are a comedian. Obviously, I'm not leaving *you* in charge. I have sorted a babysitter. Marian's daughter from across the road.'

'Please tell me you're kidding. Not bloody pretentious Bernadette.'

'You can't expect me to leave you two alone. My God, no way. You'd burn the house down within the first hour.'

'I have been invited to a sleepover at my friend's place. And no, we wouldn't burn the house down.'

'Sorry, your dad won't allow that. You know he won't, so why even bother?'

'Then don't tell him! Oh, please, Mum. I never get the chance to go out. It's at Estelle's and she's like the coolest. Please, please, please say yes.'

'He'd be so mad.'

'I will love you for all time. Just this once, I'm begging you. I need this. It's so, so, so important to me. A treat for finishing my exams. It's been super stressful for me.'

'What if something went wrong and I wasn't here? I can't say yes. I can't, lovey.'

'Her mum will be there. I'll get her to message you. Please, don't leave me with Bernadette. That would be the lamest thing ever. She smells like old feet and acts like she's forty, even though she's only a few years older than me, and she thinks she is so much better than us because her pompous dad owns a huge, ugly Bentley.'

'Wow, this does mean a lot to you, doesn't it?'

'Yes! They call me Louisa Let-down at school, Mum. I'm fed up with it.'

'Do they? How mean.'

'I'm not a baby any longer.'

'Your dad can't find out. That means you might have to bribe your brother to keep his trap shut.'

'That's not an issue. So, I can tell her yes?'

'Agh, I need my head tested… but yes, go on then. Only if her mum sends me a message. But I want the address and confirmation that she's staying home with you girls the entire night.'

'Sure, as good as done.'

Louisa couldn't believe it. She'd finally convinced her mum, albeit in a drunken state, to afford her a little taste of freedom. She raced upstairs to phone her friend before her mum sobered up and changed her mind.

80

HANNAH

Hannah put the bag of powder on the kitchen counter, stepped back from it and placed her hands on the back of her head. The runner who'd delivered the drugs to her door five minutes earlier had only looked about fourteen. He'd arrived on a clapped-out moped and said, 'Delivery,' as he'd tossed the small packet into her hallway before remounting his bike and whizzing off.

A fast remix of Eurythmics' "Sweet Dreams" was playing on the radio.

Hannah felt a sudden urge to sample the drugs.

Just a small hit. To get that buzz that she missed so much. She went to the fridge and snatched out the cold vodka. Mere mouthfuls left.

When did I drink all this?

She knew this was what Max wanted. Her caving in. Falling back into that familiar trap.

Hannah opened the vodka and drained the bottle. Maybe she just needed one small line to give her that push. Then she could march down to the off licence to re-stock.

No, you can't go down this road.

She didn't wish to play into his hands. She was weak but not as weak as he suspected she was.

A message came through on her phone. It was from Meera Kapoor.

> I told you already, I can't be involved in this. I hope you find the answers you need when you speak with this Kathy. But please keep my name out of this.

Hannah threw the phone onto the counter and grabbed the cocaine.

Yes, the temptation was there now. Stronger and more intense than ever.

Would one little blast hurt? she thought as she opened the top and dabbed her finger inside. If she even had a tiny taste, it would be game over. Because one taste would lead to one line… one line would lead to her taking the entire bag…

This would lead to… euphoric oblivion.

Yes… exactly.

Hannah ripped open the bag and quickly threw it into the sink as if she'd been holding a piece of red-hot coal in her hand. Before she had a chance to change her mind and snatch it out again, she whacked on the hot tap and watched the powder wash away. As it vanished, she felt pleased, yet also quite depressed. She'd done the right thing. So why did it feel like losing?

81

ROSIE

August 1993

Rosie edged inside the doorway to the females' toilet block as Max approached, wearing swimming shorts and carrying a fluffy towel under his arm. He didn't notice her and strolled right past before heading into the men's shower area.

Rosie waited for about twenty seconds, then slunk out of the toilets and tiptoed into the men's shower area. It wasn't yet eight in the morning, but people were already awake and milling around the holiday site, so she assumed there'd be a good chance others would soon head into the block for a morning scrub. She guessed Max would come here because he liked his early morning showers and never used the one in the caravan, as it had little power to it and was tiny.

Two cubicles were in use and so she had to decide which one to knock on. She opted for the one that had less steam pouring from it. She rapped her knuckles on the door.

'This one is occupied,' snapped Max.

She knocked again.

'Use a different shower. This one's in use.'

'It's me. It's Rosie.'

A clank and the door swung open. Max, soaking wet and butt naked save for his flip-flops, smirked at her.

'Can we talk?' she asked, trying not to acknowledge his nakedness.

He waved her in, seemingly unbothered by her intrusion. 'Shut the door.'

Rosie stepped inside the clammy cubicle and tried to avoid the jet of water. 'Turn that off and wrap that towel around yourself, please.'

Max stood under the shower and started washing his hair. 'I've only just got in. What are you doing in here?'

'I need to talk to you.'

Max's hair was covered in suds now, and he smiled as he foamed up his hair.

'I take it Chloe's still staying with you.'

'Yeah. Dad had to shoot off home, so we have the place to ourselves.'

'That's nice for you both. I bet she's still fast asleep. Lazy beast, isn't she?'

'We had a late night. But you know me, early riser.'

'That's right, I *do* know you.'

'OK, so why are you creeping about the men's showers, Rosie? Are you trying to get a peek at a few meaty cocks?' He laughed out loud and rinsed his hair.

'Don't be so crude. You should be aware of something. Chloe came to see me yesterday.'

'You two making up already? You bloody girls, you're all crazy. One minute it's "rip her eyes out," next you're plaiting each other's hair.'

'She said she hates that dress you got her. Like, really, really hates it.'

'Did she?'

'Oh yeah.'

'Who gives a crap anyway?'

'Just... the things she said. The way she spoke about you—'

Max cut in. 'I know what your game is, Rosie. OK? You can stop now.'

'Look, the thing is, I just want you to know that she might not be as serious about your relationship as she's led you to believe.'

The smile dropped from Max's face. 'Is that so?' He turned off the taps and grabbed his towel from a hook on the door. He came so close to Rosie it gave her butterflies in her stomach.

'I'll level with you. I'm pretty fucking mad about this,' said Rosie.

'Thought you'd be pleased.'

'No. It's one thing for Chloe to ruin our relationship if what you two have is the real deal. But not this. Not if she's only using you for a bit of holiday fun. I mean, how would you feel if she'd split us up and it's all for nothing? All for a few meaningless shags?'

Max dried his hair with short, savage rubs, eyes narrowed.

Rosie tried to keep her face unreadable. 'You said you loved me.'

'I did... I do.'

'But you destroyed what we had... for *her*.'

'How can I believe you? I can't trust you. I mean, I get *why* I can't trust you, but all the same, I can't.'

'She called your little chats about your future a bunch of stupid pillow talk, and she said you are way too demanding and stubborn for her to consider you to be the father of her kids. Not to mention that she has no desire to even have kids until she's like thirty or maybe forty.'

'Why are you telling me this? You want me back? Is that why?'

Rosie shrugged. 'You treated me like shit. Yet, despite myself, I can't hate you, Max. I want to. I so badly want to hate you.' Rosie forced out a few tears. In fairness, they'd been pretty easy to produce because her emotions were still raw. 'I just... can't. I care about you and don't want her to treat you this way. She's such a vile bitch.'

'Have I made a huge mistake?' he whispered as he tried to hold her.

Rosie pushed him away. 'It's too late to change your mind. You made your choice.'

'But I want you. I need you!'

Rosie crossed her arms. 'Well, you can't have us both.'

'It's you. It's always going to be you. I realise that now. I messed up, didn't I?'

'Then one of us needs to go.'

82

LOUISA

30th June 2023

Louisa was feeling bad for the lies she'd fed her mum, and the paranoia of the situation had already started creeping in. She didn't do stuff like this. It just wasn't her. She wanted it to be. However, the reality was, she didn't have it in her.

Estelle was perched at her dressing table, applying berry-red lipstick. Her new bleached-blonde, wavy hair looked amazing. It made her appear so much older. Possibly eighteen or nineteen.

Louisa sat on a plump armchair covered in fluffy throws. 'Are you certain your mum messaged mine? I'm freaking out a bit here.'

'Chill, Lou. It's all sorted.'

'But she said we are staying home, right? She didn't mention your pal Ashton is taking us for a drive later.'

'No! Stop having a meltdown. We'll smoke some more of that joint in a bit. Try to loosen you up, girl.'

Louisa smiled and nodded. She'd only had one puff on the way home from school, and her heart was still racing and her rubbery legs didn't feel like they belonged to her.

'Your mum is such a freak, Lou. She must drive you mental.'

'Yeah, a bit,' said Louisa, not sure if she was too impressed with this girl referring to her mum as a freak.

'You remember when she turned up at our sports event that time?'

'How could I forget?'

'When everyone got an eyeful of that massive banner with your face printed on... ah, so cringe. I bet you wanted to curl up and—'

'Yep, I'd rather forget that day if it's all the same.'

Estelle pouted like a model and admired her reflection. 'Fair enough. Was funny as fuck, though. Oh, you are welcome to check out my wardrobe. We're about the same size.'

'It's fine. I packed some clothes.'

Estelle pulled a sour face. 'I can only imagine what you've brought along. Pick something lush. A nice going-out top. Ashton might take us out for a few drinks tonight.'

'What? Seriously? We won't get served.'

'Yeah, he's just turned eighteen. Taylor can't make it. He got with someone else, so you missed your chance.'

Louisa's face became hot, and she was on the brink of panicking. 'I'm not so sure about going to the pub, Estelle. If my dad found out...'

'Forget about him,' Estelle groaned.

'He's a top Met detective. He's got eyes and ears everywhere!'

Estelle laughed. 'Oh, Lou, you so need to stop him from dictating how you live your life. Bollocks to him. He only tells you all that shit to keep you on a short leash. How long before you realise that he's mugging you off? Stop getting worked up. The world is not as dangerous as he paints it to be.'

'Easy for you to say with your incredibly laid-back parents. Anyway, you said a few drinks and a movie.'

'I changed my mind. You can always go home. If you're too afraid of the big, wide world.'

'I'm not.'

'You'll turn out like your mental mother if you're not careful.'

'I will not.'

'You so will. You're already starting to sound like her, Lou.'

'Oi, shut up!'

'You are!'

'If you must know, I think my mum is seeing another man.'

'Fuck off is she?'

'It's true.'

'*Your* mum? Playing away? No way. Not in a billion years.'

'Dad is away fishing and Mum's gone off to see a "friend" in Bath.'

Estelle laughed. 'Stop making shit up.'

'I'm telling you now, my mum is up to something.'

Estelle went back to examine herself in the mirror. 'Well, well, well, what a dark horse Mrs Chloe Hudson is.'

'I know, right?'

'Perhaps there's hope for you, after all. Now grab those drinks from under the chair and toss me a Cosmopolitan already.'

Louisa grabbed the bag of cocktail cans and took a couple out. 'Oh, they are not very cold.'

'Like I care. Come on, drink up and one more word about your irritating parents, and I will be forced to use physical violence on you. You get me?'

Louisa tossed her a cocktail. 'Sure.' She opened her own can and sipped the sweet drink. It tasted lovely, but, for some reason, all she could picture was the other woman at the house she'd gone to. She could almost smell the stale booze now and it put her right off the drink in her hand.

'You going to drink that or what?' asked Estelle.

Louisa forced a smile and necked the drink.

83

HANNAH

Hannah got into the passenger seat of the parked metallic-blue Seat Ibiza and briefly thought she'd climbed into the wrong vehicle. The other woman was wearing a cream-coloured Panama-style hat with a wide brim and a pair of huge, almost comical sunglasses. She was dressed in a rather nice, blue-and-white striped summer frock, tied at the waist with a long toggle. But, somehow, Chloe, if this *was* Chloe, still managed to make the attire look frumpy.

'That is you under that hat, I take it, Chloe?' asked Hannah, tugging on her seatbelt.

Chloe pulled down her shades a touch, revealing her alert eyes. 'Can't be too careful. Max is a crafty man. Did you tell anybody about our little trip?'

'Who would I tell?'

'So you didn't?'

'No,' lied Hannah. 'Stop being paranoid and drive.'

Chloe set off and they left the quiet side street where Hannah had agreed to meet her near Stamford Hill.

'It doesn't hurt to be careful. We are playing with fire here, after all,' said Chloe.

'I do grasp that.'

'And this is my marriage on the line.'

'Yeah, but it's *my* life. Your shitbag of a husband would kill me if he found out I'd coaxed you into this. Are you OK? You look hot under that hat.'

'I'm nervous and I'm not a fan of driving if you must know. We have to take things slow.'

'What time have you arranged to meet this Kathy?'

'Eight o'clock Saturday morning. Near Bath.'

'I thought we were going to meet her in Cheltenham tonight?'

'I didn't say that. She doesn't live there now. She's moved away.'

'And why are we leaving this evening? It can't be more than a three-hour drive. It would make more sense to leave in the morning. I didn't pack any stuff.'

'Oh, you'll survive one night. I don't enjoy rushing; I like to take my time.'

'What the hell are we going to do all night?'

'Don't worry, we'll stop at a hotel once we pass Swindon.'

Hannah sighed and gazed out of the window. The idea of spending a night in a hotel with this woman did not fill her with joy. A motorbike shot past the window and made her jump. The situation was putting her on edge, and she couldn't wait to leave the city.

'It will be nice, won't it? We can have a good chat and get properly acquainted.'

'The light is red. It's red!'

Chloe slammed on the brakes. 'I'm not blind. I can see.'

Hannah shifted, her unease growing by the second. 'Jesus, are you sure you've even driven this car before?'

'Can you just stop all the griping? I'm a nervous driver and you're making me worse.'

'I'm suddenly a very nervous passenger.'

Chloe chuckled. 'This is going to be quite a hoot, isn't it?' She slammed the protesting gearstick into position.

'Right,' said Hannah, now wondering if it was too late to change her mind about going with this batty woman.

84

ROSIE

August 1993

Max wrapped the towel around his lower half. 'No problem. OK, Rosie. Then Chloe can go. I'll tell her to do one right now. I'll go back and wake her up and tell her to sling her hook.'

Rosie puffed out her cheeks and shook her head. 'No, you won't. That's not what I mean.'

'Hey?'

'I mean go. As in *go*. For good!'

Max gaped at her incredulously. 'What?' He let out a hissing laugh.

'I'm not joking. If you want me back, then I want her gone. I'll do it myself. I'm deadly serious here.'

'Say it a little louder. I'm not sure the old fella in the other shower room heard you,' he laughed.

'You don't believe me, do you? You don't think I've got it in me.'

'You'd really do that, would you? You could actually bring yourself to do that?' he said in an excited whisper.

'It's all I've been thinking about. The truth is, until she's

gone, I can't be with you. If you want me back like you say...
you need to help me. It's quite simple.'

Max took a moment and seemed to weigh all this up. 'OK.
Just so we're crystal clear and singing the same song. We're talking...' He ran a finger across his throat and stuck out his tongue,
mimicking a dying person. 'Right?'

'I cannot be with you until she's gone. End of.'

'Shit, you're so sexy when you're crazy.'

'You haven't seen crazy yet. Mark my words.'

Max stepped closer to her. 'No?'

'Bring her to my quiet place tomorrow morning.'

Max let out a hoarse chuckle. 'Fuck me, you mean this, don't
you?' He went to touch her face. She pulled away. 'You love me
so much you'd kill for me, Rosie,' he said softly. 'That's super
mental. It's super fucking hot.'

'I can't... I won't let you touch me again. Not all the time that
bitch is breathing the same air as me. Once she's gone, we can
work on things. Make a fresh start. I'll even try to put on some
weight for you. I know you'd like that.'

'Hey, come on.'

'I have mirrors and I see myself. I'm a skeletal freak.'

'Now, stop that. I don't see you that way. You're my girl.'

'Yet, you were quick to ditch me for her.'

'I was testing you. I needed to find out just how much you
wanted me.'

'You almost ruined everything.'

'I'm going to help put that right now. I screwed up. I'm sorry,
Rosie. I went too far with this.'

'You can show me *how* sorry you are tomorrow.'

'How will you do it? Maybe we could make it look like a
swimming accident?'

'You get her to the lake. I'll do the rest.'

'We'll be there,' he said with a wicked glint in his eye.

85

LOUISA

The cocktails, mixed with the strong weed, made Louisa feel like she'd been blasted into space. Now, sitting in the back of Ashton's car as they raced out of the city with a reddish-orange sun ebbing away behind the outline of a fading, blurred London, she didn't have a care in the world.

'You won't spew up on my seats, will you?' said Ashton. He was tall, with curly hair and a lean, handsome face. He appeared much older than eighteen and she wondered if he was actually in his early twenties, not that she cared.

Louisa pointed at herself, not sure if he'd spoken to her.

Estelle leaned across the seats and grinned like a feral cat. 'Ashton said, don't puke everywhere.'

Louisa pinched her friend's cheek and said, 'Boop, boop. I won't, my little fluffy marshmallow. I feel... special. Floaty. Amazing. Where are we going?'

Estelle smiled. 'Fuck, Lou, you're trashed out of your nut.'

Louisa blinked several times. 'Is that a good thing?'

'Sure, enjoy yourself. We're just going for a spin,' said Estelle.

Louisa's phone was vibrating.

Reality hit.

Her mum?

Or worse... her dad?

Her face became hot. Had he nipped home for something? Or changed his mind about the fishing trip? He'd be furious if he'd gone back home, not only to learn that she'd gone out, but her mum had gone off on a jolly weekend adventure somewhere, too.

Perhaps he'd sussed her out. Found out they'd both gone gallivanting.

Louisa tried to keep it together as she checked the phone's screen. *Jamie.*

She took a deep breath and answered. 'What do you want?'

'You see that photo?' asked Jamie.

'No.'

'Check your phone. Where are you?'

'Estelle's place.'

'You sound odd.'

'You *are* odd. Let me check my messages. Hold up.' Louisa tried to focus on the screen as she scanned through her messages. Jamie had sent her one with an attachment. She opened what looked like a photo of some number plates. 'What am I looking at here?'

'Number plates.'

'I can see that, dummy. Why have you sent them… to… me?' She belched. 'Hello?'

'Are you drunk?'

'Just tell me.'

'Bernadette wants to play tennis on the Switch.'

'Surprised she's not too busy scoffing doughnuts.'

'You're on loudspeaker!'

Louisa sat up straight, her face burning hotter. 'Did she catch that?'

'No, I'm kidding. But can you listen to me?'

'Stop being a twat and get to the point.'

'While I was in the garage searching for those tennis racket attachments, I found a box with all those plates stashed up inside.'

'Why would there be spare plates?'

'I went online and checked them on a MOT site that confirms what make of vehicle they belong to. They must be false because they all came up with no match.'

'Maybe Dad uses different ones for work.'

'Louisa, have you spoken to Mum?'

'Why would I?'

'Something isn't right. What is she up to?'

Estelle passed Louisa a cocktail and pulled a *come on, really*, expression.

Louisa took the can and quietly said, 'My brother is being a turd.'

'I heard that,' grumbled Jamie.

Louisa took a big swig from the cocktail. 'Let Mum have a couple of nights off. Don't pester her and ruin her trip. Just go and exercise with your new girlfriend.'

'She was wearing a massive hat, and she was dressed... I don't know, differently.'

'What do you mean by that?'

'Like, not how she usually dresses. More...'

'Sexy?'

'Eew, no. I mean, more stylish.'

'No, you meant sexy.'

'Check the app and see where Dad's car is,' said Jamie.

'I thought we agreed that you'd remove that thing. Bloody hell...'

'Can you just check?'

Louisa groaned. 'You're ruining my night with this nonsense. What happened to staying out of their business? Everything is fine.'

'If Mum's up to something and Dad finds out...'

'OK, I'll check if it still has battery and message you.'

'The battery lasts for like a year. Just check,' said Jamie.

'I will. Have fun playing with Bernadette.' Louisa ended the call before he could respond, then she checked the key finder app. It was still active.

The key icon showed the car was parked up near Muswell Hill.

She updated the screen and the icon vanished. Louisa struggled to keep focus on the screen.

'Now what's up?' asked Estelle with more than a hint of frustration in her tone.

Louisa closed the app. 'Nothing, my brother is being a needy prick, as usual. Missing his mummy. Saddo.' She sent Jamie a message telling him their dad was still in North London and probably working late. Then she necked her drink.

86

HANNAH

Chloe spun her hat onto one of the single beds like a frisbee and fell backwards alongside it. 'Ah, finally I can stretch my poor legs.' She slid off her white sandals and wiggled her toes. 'My poor tootsies are free at last!' she exclaimed. 'I hate motorways so much. Don't you?'

Hannah nodded in agreement, though she was tempted to tell Chloe that if she'd accelerated above forty miles per hour, they wouldn't have spent nearly so long stuck in her car.

'Ah, that traffic was so tedious,' moaned Chloe.

'Wasn't even that bad. Now what are we going to do?'

Chloe sat up straight and gave her a sunny smile. 'Chat. Watch TV. Relax.'

'Shall we go to the bar and grab some food?'

Chloe shook her head. 'No siree, forget that idea. I can't risk being seen.'

'I think you're being a tad paranoid, don't you?'

'No. Have you not listened to anything I've told you? It's not safe. That's why I paid cash and kept a low profile,' she whispered.

'So we just stay holed up here all night and starve?'

Chloe gestured at her bag with her thumb. 'Inside my holdall is a cool box. I've got sandwiches, cakes, plenty of fizz. I'm sure we'll survive.'

Hannah sat on the edge of the other single bed and tested the mattress. 'Epic.'

'I'll get the food. You grab us some glasses and we'll crack open the plonk.' Chloe smiled and rubbed her hands together. 'This is fun, isn't it? Girly night in. I can't wait to find out all about you, Hannah. I really can't.'

'Why?'

'Because deep down, I think you're lonely. You need someone to talk to. I can be that someone. I'd like that.'

'Without wanting to sound rude, you don't know the first thing about me.'

'But I will by the night's end, won't I?'

'I doubt that,' muttered Hannah.

Chloe gave her a sympathetic grin. 'I can see it. Sense it. And now things will change for you. You don't need to be lonely any longer, sweet pea. You really don't.'

Hannah stood up and turned her back on Chloe. 'I'll find those glasses.' If she didn't get a stiff drink soon, she might just launch herself out of the window after spending another hour in this crazy woman's company.

87

ROSIE

August 1993

Rosie closed her eyes and willed sleep to claim her, even though she was certain it would elude her tonight. She wondered how Max was coping. Was he keeping a cool head? Had he said something stupid and caused Chloe to get suspicious of the situation? Rosie had told him, in no uncertain terms, that he was not to sleep with Chloe tonight. He'd agreed he wouldn't instigate sex but confirmed he'd have to go along with it if Chloe made a pass at him. It would be super suspect if he turned down a shag from her. And so, although not pleased about the situation, Rosie relented and granted him permission. But only if there was no other option. After all, what did it matter now? It wasn't like he hadn't done it with her loads of times already. What was one more quickie in the grand scheme of things? It wouldn't matter after tomorrow.

Rosie stroked the hammer pressed against her chest. The hammer she'd taken from the store shed earlier that evening. The hammer she'd used to punish herself. The hammer she would use to punish that arrogant whore when she arrived at her lake in the morning.

Chloe would be half-asleep after Max had dragged her down to the lake first thing in the morning. But she'd soon wake up when she understood her predicament. When she grasped, in sheer disbelief and utter terror, that Rosie intended to hurt her, and nobody would be around to rescue her.

Rosie held the hammer in a tight grasp and smiled in the darkness.

Tomorrow she would take control of her own destiny, and her wonderful boyfriend would be at her side, giving her all the encouragement she needed.

88

LOUISA

Ashton had cranked up the volume so much in the car, Louisa's ears were ringing from the booming, bass-heavy track. She didn't have a clue where they'd gone now. Not that she cared. She was just pleased to be out and about, and she wanted to enjoy this little taste of freedom that she never got to experience. Her mum wasn't the only one breaking the mould tonight and living dangerously.

Why was she thinking about her mum again?

Louisa drained yet another cocktail and decided they'd need to stop soon to get more supplies. The night was still young, and she was going to make the most of her newfound independence. She giggled, remembering that she'd hidden the ketamine in her phone case. She was about to blurt this out but stopped herself, deciding to check on her dad's whereabouts one last time. Just to be completely sure. Once she'd established her dad was well out of the picture, she could unwind and enjoy the rest of the fun-filled night.

When she opened the app, she immediately understood something was amiss. Her dad's location didn't look right. Why was he on the M4? She was no expert on the motorways surrounding London, but she knew enough to confirm he wasn't anywhere near the Kent coast.

Louisa poked Ashton's shoulder. 'Turn the music down!'

Ashton thumbed a switch on the steering wheel and lowered the track's volume. 'You need to stop, Lou? What's up?'

Louisa leaned in between the seats. 'This may be a stupid question, but you wouldn't travel on the M4 to go to Kent, would you? Like, if you were leaving the North London area and heading to the seaside.'

'Nah, no way, that's totally in the wrong direction,' said Ashton.

Louisa's mouth went dry. 'Right. OK. Where does the M4 go?'

'Wales,' said Ashton.

'And Bristol. My aunt lived in Bristol, and we used to visit once a month,' said Estelle.

'What about Bath? Isn't that near Bristol?' asked Louisa.

Ashton nodded. 'Yeah, you'd take the M4 for Bath, too. Why'd you ask?'

Louisa sat back and gazed at the phone in horror. The key icon was gone again. She updated the app. Still nothing. She waited. Checked again. Still no icon.

'What's in Bath?' asked Ashton.

Ignoring him, Louisa once again updated the app. The icon returned and was showing the car was definitely on the M4 near Slough. 'Oh, shit. I think my mum might be in serious trouble. He's meant to be going sea fishing.'

'What are you talking about, Lou?' asked Estelle, an intrigued frown creasing her brow.

'My dad must have sussed out what she's up to,' said Louisa, her voice matching the panic she felt. 'He's going after her. He must be going after her!'

'How do you possibly know that?' asked Ashton.

'Me and my brother stuck a key tracker in his car!'

Ashton let out a shrill laugh. 'What, you serious? Your old man is a big-time Fed and you're spying on him. That's some mad move, Lou. Respect.'

'Surely a key tracker can't be that reliable anyway,' said Estelle.

'It works on phone signals or something. From my experience, it is pretty accurate,' said Louisa, hoping that the device had glitched and her dad was actually somewhere else entirely.

'Just call your mum and warn her he's heading her way,' suggested Estelle, speaking as if this was no big deal.

Louisa shook her head, feeling sick now. 'I can't. No way. Then I'd have to tell her what we've been up to.'

Estelle laughed. 'What, and you'd rather your dad caught her in the act?'

Louisa groaned. 'No! I don't know. How did I get stuck in the middle of my parents' weird love life like this?'

'Cos you're a massive, nosy, bloody moose,' said Estelle.

'Not helping,' groaned Louisa.

'Maybe they are meeting each other for a dirty weekend,' suggested Ashton.

'Eew. No, I highly doubt that,' said Louisa.

'Yeah, Eew, Ash. Parents don't have dirty weekends with each other. They find someone else to smash,' said Estelle.

'My parents are always going off on weekend jaunts together. They even go off to big music festivals,' said Ashton.

'Nobody cares about your pretentious parents' love life, Ash,' moaned Estelle, pretending to shove her fingers down her throat and gagging.

'But now I feel like it's my responsibility to do something. I pushed her into this,' said Louisa.

'It's likely just work stuff. Could be a big coincidence and it just happens to be that he's heading that way to nab some coke dealers or something,' said Ashton.

Estelle nodded in agreement. 'Yeah, calm down, Lou. I bet Ash is right. Might not be what you think. You don't exactly have a clear head right now, babe.'

'And if he isn't?' said Louisa.

'If your mum is doing the dirty, why would she even tell you where she was going?' asked Estelle. 'She could be anywhere right now.'

Louisa considered this. Hadn't her mum been pissed on vodka when she'd told her about her trip to Bath? Was there a chance that information had slipped out by mistake? In truth, she'd most likely not intended to give her all the details.

'There is another way to play this,' said Ashton.

Louisa unclipped her seatbelt and sat forward, so she was right between the seats. 'There is? What? How? I'm all ears. Tell me? Ash?'

'I can have us on the M4 in twenty minutes from here. Less if I floor it,' said Ashton.

'You're suggesting we go after him?' asked Louisa.

Ashton tapped on his steering wheel. 'Why not? Don't know my car, does he? I don't mind taking the beast for her first proper spin. If your dad does do something, we could call the police on him.'

Louisa, in her drunken, fuzzy state, tried to consider if this was a genuinely genius idea or a downright terrible one. 'I should message my mum. That's the sensible thing to do. I should warn her. Yes, I better do that. Should I do that? Help me out here, guys!'

Estelle, clearly as drunk as she was, grinned stupidly. 'Lou, come on. This will be sick. I say we go snooping on your folks. It'll be a mad adventure. Let's do this, girl.'

Louisa shook her head. 'We can't do that. Can we?'

89

HANNAH

Hannah refilled both glass tumblers with the last of the fizzy wine. 'Nearly out of this. The bar will be open if you want me to grab us a takeout bottle of plonk.' She scanned the dreary, cramped hotel room. Off-white walls, dated furnishings, drab brown decor, two bedside lamps emitting a dull, reddish-yellow glow. 'I wouldn't mind stretching my legs, to be honest.'

Any excuse to escape this stuffy room for five minutes, she thought.

Chloe giggled and fell back on the bed. She was already drunk.

Hannah passed her a glass. 'Shall I?'

Chloe sat up and grabbed the glass. 'Don't go. You must have a cheeky bottle stashed up. You do, don't you?'

'There's a small bottle of vodka in my handbag.'

'That's afters sorted, then. Why get more wine if you're happy to share the vody? I understand if you don't want to.'

'Why wouldn't I?'

'Well… you know… because…'

'Because?'

Chloe grinned, her small, glazed eyes blinking. 'Because you're an addict… well… an…'

'An alcoholic,' Hannah finished for her.

Chloe smiled and nodded. 'Seems rude to say it out loud.'

'Yet, you still brought along wine. Thanks a bunch.'

Chloe crossed her legs and rocked back and forth. 'Would you please tell me what the sex was like, Hannah?'

'Excuse me?'

Chloe stood up and came over to her bed. 'Now, the thing is, with me and Max, things can be… mm, what's the word? Cold, I guess. We go through the motions, but it's all rather passionless.'

'I don't wish to share the details.'

'I'm not a fan of doing *that* thing. You know… that thing men are obsessed with. It's the idea of what else comes out of the same hole, I guess.'

'Jesus, are you for real?'

'Makes me quite queasy, truth be told. Although, I'm more than happy to receive.' Chloe put a hand over her mouth and chuckled. 'Listen to me, old hussy-pants.' The chuckle turned into a full-blown, horsy laugh. 'This is great, isn't it? Us, chatting about men and stuff. I never get to do this.'

Hannah knocked back the last of her wine and hoped the drink would soon send Chloe to sleep.

Chloe sat next to Hannah and shuffled up closer to her. 'Budge up. So, go on, what was it like?'

'Sorry?'

'Did you do *that* to him?'

'Oh, no. Nope. No way. We are not having this chat.'

Chloe eyed her with a sulky glower.

'You can forget it. That's too messed up.'

'Describe what it was like. Give me all the details. I need all the details. Don't you see? I *need* them.'

'Why?'

'To stop my imagination from driving me insane. I can't stand it. So just tell me. Tell me all the smutty details. Please!'

Hannah stood up and walked away from her. She heard Chloe sniffing and snivelling.

'I love him so much. I always have. Does that make me the saddest person ever?' asked Chloe.

Hannah sighed and shook her head. 'No.'

'I try to be the best wife to him. It's not easy.'

Hannah put the glass down on the bedside unit. 'I don't doubt it.'

A long minute dragged by before Chloe said, 'What about you? Were you a good wife?'

Hannah sat on Chloe's now empty bed and put her hands in her lap.

Chloe tilted her head and gave her a quizzical stare. 'Were you?'

And just like that, Hannah let it all flow out. 'Archie cheated on me. He confessed straight away. Told me it had been a quick, stupid five minutes that he could barely remember. A drunken one-night stand with a colleague. I didn't doubt him. It didn't matter what it had been. Not to me. I was furious.'

'What happened?'

'I forgave him, or at least I told him I did. Though, the thing was, I didn't. I seemed unable to forgive him. I should've left him. But instead, I stayed with him and treated him like shit. I continually punished him. Made him feel worthless. The more I pushed him away, the harder he tried and the easier I found it to hate him. About a month after he confessed, he came home late from work, and I lost it with him. Accused him of doing it again.' Hannah dug her fingers into her thighs. 'I was so angry… so wrapped up in feeling sorry for myself and focusing all my rage on Archie, that I failed my job as a mother… I completely failed my boy.'

'What do you mean by that?'

'My Ollie came to me in the night and said he was unwell. But I was in such a foul mood with my husband I ordered him to go back to bed. He'd had a sniffle and an earache that week, so I just assumed it was a cold. He said he was really hot and felt strange, yet I still did nothing.' Hannah chewed her lower lip and willed herself to stop talking, but she'd started unloading now. She wanted to say the words crashing around in her mind. 'The next day we realised how bad he was and raced him off to the hospital for treatment. But it was too late. They did every-thing they possibly could, but he died the next day. Officially, bacterial meningitis claimed my son, but I'm the one to truly blame for his death.'

Chloe took a big sip of fizz and gulped it audibly.

Hannah continued to dig her fingers into her thighs. 'Eight years old… My little boy came to his mummy for help, and I let him get worse. Instead of taking his temperature and checking him properly, I pushed him away and told him to go to sleep because I had the hump.'

'I can understand why you'd blame yourself, but how could you have possibly known?'

'I was his mother, so it was my job to know!'

'You poor little lamb,' said Chloe in a soft, doleful voice.

'After Ollie's passing, both of us lost our way. Our life together became pure misery, and rather than taking responsi-bility for my own failings, I continuously blamed Archie. For almost ten years, we coexisted in a bizarre, toxic relationship. There were glimmers of hope. Times when it almost seemed like we'd get back to what we once had. We both had it in our heads that having another child would be the answer to our problems. That another child to love would somehow pull us back together. But that never happened.'

'That's so very sad.'

'I said it was God's way of telling us we were undeserving of another baby. I mean, why would we be after what happened with Ollie?'

'You're being incredibly hard on yourself.'

'Instead of accepting that it was my fault our son died, I put it all on him, and for all those years, as my resentment and anger continued to build, his unrelenting depression grew like an unstoppable cancer. It was a burden that eventually became too heavy for him to carry. When I finally understood how sick he'd become… it was way too late. The damage had been done. He was a broken shell of a man who believed there was no way forward. No way to stop the never-ending torture. After all that time, we'd just gone round in circles and still the pain hadn't lessened at all.'

Chloe wiped her eyes with the back of her hand.

'I should have tried harder to get him the help he needed... I... I might as well have pushed him from that bridge myself. I'm to blame for both of their deaths.'

Chloe lay down on the bed and pressed her head against the pillow. Her eyes were wet with tears, and she just stared at Hannah with a forlorn frown.

'He left me a note. He told me that I was his soulmate and that he understood we'd never find happiness again. He said he couldn't bear the idea that he'd lost me and that his foolish actions had destroyed the happy existence we once shared.'

'Depression is such an awful thing. It's so heartbreaking.'

'I still pretend Ollie is alive. Silly, right? I have created a life for the boy I lost all those years back. I have invented an entire existence for him because I can't face the reality of what I did. I just can't bring myself to say what happened all those years back.'

'If it helps you cope, I can see no harm in that.' Chloe put her hand against her chest. 'You're telling *me* the truth now. I'm privileged that you have shared this with me, Hannah. Honestly, I feel this is a special moment.'

'I watched this orchestra play in London and, I swear to God, this young man playing the violin looked the spit of my son. Well, exactly how I'd always pictured he'd look in his early twenties. So... I started imagining that the boy was Ollie. That it was his life. That the orchestra was like his family. I... I have no idea why I'm even telling you this.'

Chloe just smiled sadly as she watched her with an almost innocent fascination.

'I tell people Ollie travels Europe with his wonderful pianist girlfriend. I pretend he's living the fabulous life I always wanted him to have. Quite sure that's not normal. But I see him as a young man. I actually *see* him so clearly in my head it scares me. I even write letters to him. How sad is that?'

'I think it's nice,' said Chloe.

'It's pointless. It's a stupid thing to do. I even change his bed sometimes, and I have kept all his things.'

Chloe fiddled with her wedding ring. 'It's not pointless. Not if it helps you.'

'The first violin Archie and I bought him still sits in that room. I can't bring myself to get rid of anything.'

'He could play? Even at that sweet age?'

Hannah nodded. 'He was amazing.'

'Such a beautiful instrument. It produces such poignant, heart-rendering melodies.'

Hannah thought about Max. That look on his face when he'd told her he wanted to use her spare room. He'd known about Ollie all along. She was certain of that now. He'd wanted to push her to her breaking point, and he'd worked out just how to get to her. He'd destroyed her precious memories. He'd tried to ruin her with drugs. But Ollie… he understood that Ollie was her *real* weak point. That messing with her memories of him would push her over the edge and beyond. 'I guess Max has found out about my son.'

'He would've found out, yes. He finds out everything, lovey.'

Silence fell on them.

Five long minutes passed, and Hannah thought Chloe had drifted off.

'I'm so sorry,' said Chloe in the faintest of whispers.

'Why do you think your husband preys on messed-up people like me?'

Chloe sniffed and tears streaked her face, but she offered no reply.

'I can't understand what he gets out of it. I want to, but I just can't,' said Hannah.

Chloe closed her eyes and her breathing was deep and loud.

'What makes him tick? What drives him? Did something happen to him? There must be a reason, Chloe. You must have some idea what's wrong with that man you've spent so many years with.'

'I so enjoyed our little girly natter. I really have. But I need to sleep now. Upsetting stories always drain me,' she mumbled in a sleepy whisper.

Hannah got up and retrieved the vodka from her bag.

'I wish I didn't love him so much,' whispered Chloe. 'But I can't help it. He's my man.'

Hannah sat back down and watched the other woman as she started to snore softly.

He's my man.

After hearing those words, Hannah decided to stay awake. After all, how could she trust this woman? What if she had a change of heart and contacted Max to give him their whereabouts? She wouldn't put it past this woman to do a U-turn on her.

So Hannah wouldn't risk sleep tonight. Not that she'd have slept even if she'd wanted to. 'You take my bed, then,' said Hannah and went over to the window, peering out into the dark car park below. Once again, she thought about the information Meera had sent her on the missing girls from the Gloucestershire area.

Susan Gains missing since 2002.

Michelle Wynn missing since 2005.

Bailey Lloyd missing since 2008. The same year Max transferred to the Metropolitan Police.

Three years apart.

But somehow, Hannah knew these three were just the tip of a very large iceberg and that she'd been drawn into something deadly indeed.

And deep down, his wife knew it, too. Otherwise, why else had she agreed to help her?

90

ROSIE

August 1993

Rosie made her way down the grassy bank towards her lake with a big grin on her face. She'd slept rather well the previous night and had a surprising spring in her step this morning. She'd expected to be nervous today. Yet, she wasn't. Giddy with excitement, yes. But not in the least bit anxious, which was strange considering what she and Max had planned to do on this glorious, sunny morning.

Rosie sighted the pair in the clearing by the lake. They were sitting together, chatting in hushed voices. They'd not yet noticed her, so she upped her pace and clutched her denim shoulder bag tightly until she could feel the hammer's solid, wooden handle. With a satisfied grin and a sense of empowerment, she confidently walked towards them without attempting to sneak.

Chloe turned first and flashed her a surprised frown before whispering something into Max's ear. The pair sniggered and Chloe got to her feet and brushed herself down. No crappy dress today. She was back in her shorts and signature crop top and big, matching shades. Rosie was glad about this. The floral dress didn't suit Chloe's style, so it seemed more appropriate that she wore her usual attire today. That would make this much easier.

'Rosie, you're up nice and early today. Have you come to join us for a dip?' asked Chloe with what appeared to be a cheery smile.

Rosie stopped a few paces from the other girl and offered her own charming smile. 'No, I think it's a bit too chilly this morning.' She unzipped the bag and gently removed the hammer.

The smile fell from Chloe's face, and she took two steps away from her. But then, to Rosie's complete astonishment, she lifted her chin and gave her an amused sneer.

91

LOUISA

Louisa woke up to the sound of birds singing, but she couldn't bring herself to open her eyes due to the heavy, sharp pain in her head. It was as if opening her eyes would invite even more agony.

What had happened?

The night's events flooded her groggy brain.

She'd smoked weed and drunk way, way too much. She'd gone searching for her dad with Estelle and Ashton. Vague flashbacks flickered through her mind… racing along a motorway at night and shouting for them to go even faster.

Louisa snapped her eyes open and found herself slumped in the back of Ashton's car. Estelle was asleep in the front, curled up, her head resting on Ashton's lap. He was fast asleep too, using his crossed arms as makeshift pillows.

No way. What was she still doing here? And where *was* here?

Panic surged through her body like a tidal wave. She'd be grounded indefinitely after this stunt. She'd be finished. Her parents wouldn't let her leave her room until she'd hit thirty after this utter disaster.

When she checked her phone and saw the device had run out of battery, she let out a long whimper.

92

HANNAH

Chloe's car came to a jolting stop, and Hannah's stomach bubbled with cramping pain. She'd felt woozy and tired, so she'd paid little attention to where they'd been going, though she had momentarily wondered why they hadn't seen much sign of life for the last thirty-odd minutes.

'Where are we?' Hannah asked, rubbing her dazed eyes and regretting her decision to let paranoia take over and not sleep in the hotel.

'Did you stay up all night, lovey? You drifted off just now,' said Chloe, using one finger to push up her large hat. She appeared breezy and well rested.

Hannah ignored the question about staying up and said, 'I thought this Kathy lived in Bath.'

'She does. But she asked us to meet her here.'

'Where is here?'

'Just outside of a town called Little Wick. Forty minutes from Bath. I think she's being a tad cautious, that's all. She wanted to speak to us well away from her home and any prying eyes. She understands how dangerous this situation is. If you ask me, that's a good thing.'

'What happened here?' asked Hannah, peering out of the window.

'Sorry?'

Hannah got out of the car and took in the sights. They were parked close to what appeared to be the remnants of a wooden shack or lodge, which sat on a scorched concrete base. All that remained of the building were pieces of three blackened wooden walls that were now semi-covered in lichen and wrapped in cord-like nettles. Hannah went over for a closer inspection of the charred remains. There was something incredibly eerie about the place. Something so wrong, it gave her goosebumps. Whatever had happened to the property had happened many, many moons ago.

'Come on, Hannah. We need to go this way,' said Chloe, gesturing to a line of towering oak trees in the distance.

Hannah turned back to the wrecked building. 'Why can't we wait here for Kathy?'

'She's already waiting for us. There's a path that leads to a lake. It's only a five-minute walk, apparently.'

Hannah scanned the area. Nothing but rich, sweeping fields and rolling hills as far as the eye could see. 'Where is her car? How did she get out here?'

'How should I know? Taxi, I guess. We'd better go, come on. We can't leave the poor lady waiting all morning. She's already scared out of her wits.' With that, Chloe waved her on and trudged off down an overgrown pathway.

Hannah rubbed her aching temples. Once again, she checked out the remnants of the building. This was brilliant. They were in the middle of nowhere. If this went sideways, she had no clue where she'd even run.

With a creeping sense of dread, and against her better judgement, she followed Chloe.

93

ROSIE

August 1993

Chloe's eyes moved between Rosie and Max. She was still smiling, though now she looked a little confused. But she did not appear frightened, and this worried Rosie. After all, she was brandishing a hammer and this bitch, who'd stolen her boyfriend, did not seem in the least bit worried about what she might do to her down here. Down here, where there was nobody around to help her out of this dangerous situation she'd found herself in.

Yes, her behaviour rattled Rosie's nerves, and she hesitated. She even took a step back from the pair.

Max got up and, in a languid motion, stretched his arms as if nothing untoward was going on. He directed his gaze towards Chloe. Then to Rosie. He grinned. A grin that suggested he was privy to a secret that only he knew.

Chloe positioned herself behind Max's bulky body and quietly said, 'I warned you she was off her head. I told you we needed to watch her. Do you believe me now when I say we have to do something about her?'

Max, ignoring Chloe, eyed Rosie with a vacant expression.

The hammer now felt heavy in Rosie's hands as her confidence plunged, and her desire to launch the planned attack fizzled away.

Something didn't seem right here.

Max reached behind and took hold of Chloe's hand. 'What are you going to do with that hammer?' he said to Rosie with a wily, jackal-like smile. 'Hey? You gonna beat us both to a pulp? I'd so like to see you attempt that. You don't have it in you. Especially with only one good hand, you daft bitch.'

Chloe laughed. Now she seemed emboldened by Max's support. She put her other hand on his shoulder and rubbed him seductively. Then she let go of his hand and wrapped her arms around his frame. 'She's having a silly moment.' She kissed him on the back of the neck.

Now the hammer felt like it weighed a ton and Rosie doubted she'd be able to lift the tool if her life depended on it. 'B... but... I don't understand. Max?' she stammered.

Chloe slipped out of the embrace and stepped back from Max. 'You should take that hammer out of her hand, Max. Before she drops it on her toe and makes herself shriek.' Her eyes narrowed. 'Though she *does* like to inflict pain on herself, doesn't she?'

Max came at Rosie, taking big, confident strides.

Rosie wanted to turn tail and run. Yet, she was rooted to the spot. Her legs had gone numb and wouldn't move. She wanted to protest at how unfair this all was, but the words wouldn't come out of her mouth because the turn of events had stunned her into total silence.

Max snatched the hammer from her shaking grasp and said, 'I dunno, Chloe, if she's not spying on us like a little peeping Tom, or telling horrible lies to turn us against each other, she's planning to crack our skulls to bits. What do you suggest we should do about all this?'

Rosie's legs gave way, and she fell onto her bum. She watched dumbly as Max stood over her and tossed the hammer from one hand to the other. 'So, what first, Rosie? Legs? Arms? Ribs? Surely not the head. Nah, the head would end things way too fast. What would you recommend, Chloe? Maybe I'll let you choose where we start. Unless you want to take the hammer?'

94

LOUISA

Louisa shook Estelle awake. Her friend groaned and cursed her before falling back to sleep.

'Estelle! Fuck, wake up. Where are we? What are we doing out here?'

'Go back to sleep. It's like ridiculous o'clock,' muttered Estelle.

'What happened?'

Estelle sat up and shuffled about in the seat. Ashton didn't stir.

'Estelle, please. I'm losing my shit here.'

'We followed the tracking thing you put in your dad's car. Remember?'

'Yes, but I don't remember much else. We went on the motorway. Did I pass out?'

'No, we tracked his car out here, Lou. You were in a state but defo awake.'

'Where's here?'

'Somewhere near the Wiltshire and Somerset border. I think that's what we established last night. Arse end of nowhere. Don't panic. I messaged my mum last night and said we both crashed at Ashton's place.'

'And if my mum calls her to check on me?'

'She'll say you're fast asleep. Mum's chill like that, so relax and go back to sleep.'

'What the hell is my dad doing right out here?'

'Camping.'

'He's what?'

'Geez, Lou, you must've been seriously out of it. We parked up and Ashton had a quick snoop around. He said your dad's BMW was parked off the road in a small field behind some trees. Just up the road here. About five minutes' walk.' She flapped her hand lazily. 'Up there by a metal gate. Well sus, right?'

Louisa's head pounded as she searched her memory bank. It was empty. So blank it worried her.

'Ash said he saw a tent and guessed your dad had crashed in that. He came back, and we all did a bit of ket.' Estelle let out a long yawn. 'You were talking about how you wanted to leave home and travel to Pennsylvania in search of aliens or some shit. You'd gone to another planet, girl.'

'What? You gave me bloody ket in that state? Are you for real, Estelle?'

'You had the gear, Lou. I told you not to touch the stuff cos you were in a state and it wouldn't be sensible. You wouldn't let up and kept saying something about making the most of your freedom. You dropped most of the powder over Ash's seats! He was well pissed at you.'

Louisa winced and rubbed her heavy eyes.

'Ask Ash when he wakes up. Don't get all salty with me. You kept going on about Herman Crunchy or someone. Apparently, he keeps your "drug stash" safe. You just spoke utter bollocks, to be fair.'

Louisa wanted to correct her and say, *Herbert Crunch, get it right, you dense twat*, but she instead said, 'How'd you think this was a sensible idea to stay here? With my dad literally five minutes up the road doing... doing God knows what! We should have gone home.'

'You need to ask yourself the question... I mean, why would your dad drive all the way out here to tent up on his own? That's dodgy as fuck, right?' she said groggily. Then she yawned again and put her head back on Ashton's lap. 'Or maybe he's not alone. You should sneak down there and spy on him. Now stop carping on and let me go back to sleep. I'm bored of hearing about your weird-arse parents.'

'Thanks so much for your help! Friends clearly *are* overrated!' blurted Louisa. She thought she might puke. She got out of the car and the surrounding trees seemed to spin. The birdsong sounded harsh to her fragile ears. The sound boomed around her head and amplified into a harsh trumpet-like blare. She forced herself up the lane.

This is exactly what her dad had warned her about.

She heard strange noises all around her as she walked. Echoed yells and what sounded like screaming babies. Or was this all in her head?

She quickened her pace and imagined her dad's outraged face as he scolded her. 'Have you any idea what that stuff does to your brain? Have you any idea what I go through every single day to make the streets a safer place? I risk my life to stop people selling this crap. Are you purposely rebelling against me? The first chance you got, and you did everything I warned you not to do, you stupid, stupid child.'

Louisa held her head as if trying to hold her fractured brain in place and keep it inside her skull. It felt like it might turn to jelly and pour right out of her ears. She felt so rough now she actually wanted her parents. Even her dad.

As she walked, she touched her clammy face. Her temple veins bulged and pulsated. Her stomach hurt now, and she almost tripped over her own feet.

Why had she drunk so much? The alcohol had made her lose her inhibitions. She'd never touch the stuff again.

The gate… there it was.

Louisa approached with caution. Saw her dad's BMW parked up behind some low-hanging trees in the field. She ducked behind some shrubbery and took a good nosy around. The car looked empty. So did the field. No tent and no sign of her dad.

Then something struck her. The car belonged to him; she was certain of that. Same minor bump on the front bumper and the same pineapple air freshener hanging from the interior mirror. However, the number plate was not the same as her dad's, and this made her think of the photo Jamie sent her and the stack of fake plates he'd found stashed in their garage. Did police detectives change their plates? But hadn't her dad once told her he didn't use his own car for work stuff? She'd asked him ages ago because she'd been worried that the bad guys would notice his car when they were out as a family. He'd said they had a fleet of nondescript work vehicles at their disposal, and so she didn't need to be concerned.

None of this made sense.

95

HANNAH

Hannah stumbled as she tried to keep up with Chloe, who had skipped ahead. It was almost as if she knew exactly where she was going.

'This can't be right. We should turn back,' called Hannah.

Chloe turned, waving her on. 'I've spotted the lake. It's not far. Down this hill here. Come on, I'll race you, slowcoach,' she teased.

Hannah considered turning around and heading back to the car, but as she reached the top and glimpsed the glimmering lake below, she decided she may as well keep going. 'You see her down there?'

The closer Hannah got to the water, the more sceptical she felt about the whole situation. Why did this Kathy want to bring them all the way down here just to talk?

How paranoid was this woman, and what information did she have for them that would warrant such precautions?

'Not yet,' called Chloe as she set off down the grassy hill, beckoning Hannah with an enthusiastic wave. She turned again, and the quirky little smile she flashed almost gave her a childlike appearance. Was she so credulous that she'd not even considered this meeting might not be kosher?

'Chloe. Hey, wait up,' called Hannah as she moved through

the ankle-high grass and down the slope behind her. 'I'm not sure about this.'

But Chloe had already entered the clearing by the water. A patch of dried mud with a scattering of white rocks and brownish tufts of grass. She headed to the area where the lake appeared to be at its shallowest and flicked her hat off her head with one finger.

Hannah could see the area properly now. A calm, emerald-coloured lake surrounded by high reeds that danced in the gentle morning breeze. The low banks were blanketed in soft-looking grass and dotted with bright flowers. Although it appeared unkept and wild, it was quite the spot, and Hannah decided that perhaps this lake held some significance to Kathy's life. A special childhood place where she came to for some peace and quiet. A spot which she considered safe and perhaps that's why she'd opted to come here to chat to them about Max.

As Hannah stepped into the clearing and noticed the elated expression on Chloe's face, she hesitated. Like the old burned-out building they'd parked near, something just felt strange here. She noticed a crudely made wooden sign with the words: *Strictly No Swimming* positioned down by the water's edge. It was old and wonky, with lettering poorly painted on it in a white, bold font. Near that, and out of place, sat an old music stereo. Hannah thought it looked like a big 1990s cassette player.

Chloe stood close to the shallow part of the lake where the water splashed against the earth in delicate, rippling waves. She gazed around the area with the biggest smile on her face. It appeared as if she was drinking it all in. As if she'd arrived at heaven on earth.

Then it hit Hannah. It became so abundantly clear that she didn't even need to ask Chloe to confirm her suspicion. She'd been here before. There could be no doubting that now. This place wasn't special to Kathy. It was special to Chloe. Hannah even sniggered to herself. She knew Kathy wasn't coming, yet she still said, 'Kathy isn't coming, is she?'

Still gazing at the lake, Chloe shook her head.

Hannah took a step closer to her. 'Is she even a real person?'

Another shake of the head. 'Afraid not.'

'So, come on then, what is this?'

Chloe started giggling to herself, eyes still fixed on the water.

'Answer me! Why have you led me down here? Your head-case of a husband has already threatened to have me put inside. Not to mention his threat to bury me alive. Is it your turn to intimidate me now? What's this all about, hey? Why do this?'

More giggles. Chloe even put her hand over her mouth to stifle a croaky laugh that still escaped her. 'Welcome to my quiet place.' She turned to face Hannah, her grin now wide and mischievous.

Hannah's rage was boiling now. 'Have you been screwing with me from the start? Did you ever intend to help me? Answer me. Are you that delusional that you are prepared to help that man cover up his mess?'

Chloe ceased giggling. 'He's my man, you dirty, drunk skank!' Her eyes were now fully open and no longer squinting. Eyes that were loaded with hatred. 'You think you're good enough for my Max? You really think I'd let you take him after all we've been through? He loves me.' She smacked herself on the chest. 'Me! Get that?'

It was Hannah's turn to laugh now. 'I almost pity you. He's done a real number on you; I can see that. But I was sure a tiny part of you could see him for the man that he is.'

'He's a wonderful man. The best. You had your man and you pushed him away. Pushed him over the edge. Now you want to steal mine. No chance of that.'

'Yeah, keep telling yourself that, you sad bitch.'

Chloe sneered, making her face look ugly and mean. 'You'll be in good company down there. It's nice and deep. Plenty of room for all of you and, let's face it, we'd be doing you a favour. You have a pitiful, pointless existence.'

Hannah tensed as she sucked up those words.

Good company.

We'll be doing you a favour.

'Down where?' asked Hannah cagily.

Chloe spread out her arms. 'Who wouldn't want to come here to die? Open your eyes and get a good look at this place. Just imagine it. You should thank me because you'll get to spend the rest of eternity here. Or would you rather die on some dirty railway line? I doubt that.'

Hannah's rage was fizzling out. Now panicky dread had taken over.

Chloe flicked her hair out of her face. 'Who were the ones you were searching for again? Susan Gains, Michelle Wynn, Bailey Lloyd. That's right, yes?'

Hannah's heart beat so fast she could hear the continuous thud behind her ears.

Chloe smiled and pointed to the lake. 'Congratulations. You found them. They're right here.'

Hannah's legs went weak and for a second, she thought she might collapse.

How many more were there?

'It's all some fucked up game, isn't it?' Hannah managed to whisper.

'Now she gets it,' said a loud voice from behind her.

A man's voice.

Hannah's blood ran ice cold. She didn't need to turn around to understand who'd arrived at the clearing.

96

ROSIE

August 1993

Rosie burst into tears at the injustice of it all. This wasn't right. How could any of this be fair? Why was life always so cruel to her? What had she ever done to deserve this?

Max kept tossing the hammer from his left hand to his right. 'Guess *I* get to decide where we hit first,' he said to Rosie.

Rosie sobbed. 'I don't understand.'

Max dropped his lower lip and fake cried.

'Maybe that's enough now, hey,' suggested Chloe. 'This has all got a bit much. Throw the hammer into the lake. We've made our point.'

Max continued to laugh as he stuck out his tongue and pretended to bang the hammer against his own head.

'Enough now, Max. This is way too messed up,' persisted Chloe.

Max let out a shrill, bitter laugh that made his body shake. He let the hammer drop to his side. Through the laughter he said, 'She made the effort to bring the hammer down here, so it'll be a shame not to use it to crack a few bones.' He mimicked hitting Rosie on the head now. She didn't even flinch or attempt to move.

Chloe shook her head and looked far from impressed. 'OK, enough with the psycho bullshit. Toss the fucking thing away. It's getting ridiculous and mega creepy.'

Max nodded, still grinning. His eyes held a fiery glint now. He gave Rosie a quick, sidelong glance and turned back to Chloe.

There was something in that look that made Rosie reassess the situation. Had she missed something here? Her chain of thought was disrupted when Max swung the hammer straight into Chloe's side. It struck her with a noisy, hard smack, and she doubled over, letting out a piercing yelp.

'Nobody chose, so I went ribs,' said Max. He'd spoken unflappably and with a lopsided grin spreading on his face.

Rosie gasped. She couldn't believe this. A shocked laugh even escaped her.

Chloe staggered sideways, shrieking in agony as she held both hands against her left side. Her face was a picture to behold. Pure and utter astonished torture had washed over her now.

Rosie leaped up and, with a renewed burst of energy, jumped for joy. She danced about in a little circle and became so ecstatic, she almost lost her footing and fell back down.

Max winked at her. 'Ah, almost had you there. Don't say I didn't.'

'You… you mean trickster,' giggled Rosie.

'I couldn't resist having a bit of fun.' He pulled a gormless face. 'Sorry.'

Chloe tried to waddle away. But she didn't get far before she pitched forward and dropped to her knees, coughing in pain.

'Do broken ribs really hurt?' Max asked Chloe, sounding as if he was genuinely interested in the answer. 'I bet they do.'

Chloe emitted a mewling, spluttering cry in response.

Max scratched the bottom of his chin with the hammer's claw. 'I'll take that as a solid yes, then.'

'Give me the hammer,' demanded Rosie.

Max offered her the handle, then sniggered and pulled the tool away as she made a grab for it. 'You sure you can do this?'

'Give it, give it, give it,' said Rosie, bouncing on the spot. 'Now. I want to do it now. Stop fooling around.' She laughed. 'Max. Give me it!'

Max shot her a teasing smile. 'I have never seen you so excited. Do I get something in return?'

Rosie gave him an eager nod and snatched the hammer from his grasp. As she made her way to Chloe, she caught the sound of the girl breathing erratically between deep, raspy sobs.

'I'm going to need my friendship bracelet back. Hope that's OK?' said Rosie as she clenched her right fist about the hammer. 'I find it a complete disgrace that you feel it still appropriate to wear it.' She gave a disapproving sigh. 'You made this happen. You understand that, don't you?'

Chloe screamed and wept, waving her hands and making odd snorting noises. Her face became red, twisted, hideous. Now she gazed up and whimpered with wide, pleading eyes.

'Oh dear, looks like she wants us to spare her pathetic little life, Max. Even after she betrayed me. After she tried to ruin what we had.' She glared at Chloe. 'What would they say at home if they could all see you, the great Chloe Sark, now? If they could see you snivelling at my feet like an ugly, red-faced loser.'

To Rosie's complete surprise, Chloe leaped up and came at her like a vicious cat. She hissed and screeched and gouged at her cheeks with her nails.

'I'll kill you!' boomed Chloe.

Rosie lashed out with the hammer. She swung it and heard the strike more than she felt it. Chloe continued to fight, and Rosie's hair got yanked hard. She hit out again. And again. And again. Each blow harder than the next.

'Whack her head!' shouted Max. 'Knock her down. Get her!'

Max's shouts of encouragement boosted Rosie's morale and spurred her into a fighting rage. Now the hammer was in both her hands, and she swung it in a frenzied, blurry arc, ignoring the pain spearing through her injured hand.

Chloe tried to flee the madness, but she only staggered a few paces before she fell down. Rosie, following her steps, stumbled down with her.

Chloe's body began to shudder and blood bubbled from her mouth.

Rosie rolled on top of Chloe and used her knees to pin her useless arms down. Using both hands again, she raised the hammer high. In the split second before she smashed it down, she was certain she'd caught a belligerent smirk on the girl's face. This last act of defiance drove Rosie ballistic. She screamed as she hammered down with everything she had. Kept hitting, enjoying the wet smacking sound it made. She didn't stop hammering down on that irritating face until her features became unrecognisable. Until all she'd left of Chloe's face was a vulgar, pulpy, gory work of repulsive art.

Not repulsive. Delightfully disgusting.

No face.

No Chloe.

No more vile Chloe Sark.

Panting, though elated, Rosie tossed the hammer aside and gasped in delight at the faceless corpse who'd almost destroyed her life.

'I did it... I did it,' she rasped. 'I did it!' She snapped the friendship bracelet from Chloe's limp wrist and let her arm flop back down.

'I did it,' she repeated as she stood and wiped her face that was wet with blood. 'I actually did it.' She chanted the words as she balled her fists and squeaked in joy.

The feeling was unreal. The adrenaline surged through her and made her giddy with glee. She wanted to bottle the feeling. She wanted to experience it for all time.

Mind-blowing, fabulous, life-affirming.

I don't want it to end, she told herself.

Now she wanted Max. Wanted him more than anything else in the world. No, the entire universe.

Rosie heard A-ha playing and for a second, she thought, through the excitement, she'd started imagining the music. "The Sun Always Shines on TV." It was one of her absolute favourites.

But it *was* playing. So she danced about the clearing and whooped. She thought she might explode with joy. She felt drunk on the experience. Full of euphoric bliss. 'I did it, I did it, I did it,' she sang in a loud voice.

Then she saw Max sitting nearby, watching with a devilish grin. Next to him was a boombox. The same one she'd smashed up at the lake party, she realised. It had probably been there all along, yet she'd been too preoccupied to take notice of it.

Max patted the boombox and said, 'I fixed it up. There was just a loose connection in the battery compartment. Good thing you didn't smash it as hard as you smashed her face.'

'Are you proud of me?'

He gave her a seductive stare and nodded. 'Fuck, yeah I am.'

When she spotted the family of swans in the middle of the lake, gracefully gliding past them, she smiled to herself. The head swan shot her a cursory glance, then focused back ahead. Rosie understood straight away that this was a little casual acknowledgment from the regal bird. The problem had been resolved, and so they had returned to their favourite place, now satisfied that all was well, and the troublemaker had been dealt with in a just manner. Swans were territorial and took no prisoners. They were pleased with her work here. That was now evident. Rosie smiled because the wonderful cygnets were growing bigger.

Everything had resumed to how it should be.

Rosie, buzzing with energy, slipped out of her clothes and straddled Max.

It was almost too much to take in. This was really happening.

The sex, brief, frantic, and lasting less than a minute, blew her mind.

Afterwards, she sat in his lap, a shaking, panting mess as he stroked her hair and kissed her neck.

'That was the best ever,' said Max.

The sex? Killing Chloe? A mix of both? She guessed it didn't matter.

'Do a naked dance for me, Rosie,' said Max with a lazy smile.

Rosie trembled in his arms. 'First, I want to tell you a secret...'

'What?'

'Something I've never told a living soul,' she whispered in his ear.

97

LOUISA

There was nothing around for miles. Nothing but endless hills and smelly fields full of inquisitive cows. Louisa reached the end of the lane and decided to go back to the others. She'd wake the pair up and demand to be driven home immediately. It was total madness to wander about here with every chance of bumping straight into her dad. Her life would be over if she went running to him. She was calmer now. The walk had soothed her muddled head, allowing her thoughts to become clear once more. She needed to leave this place and fast.

Louisa noticed a narrow, gravel track and craned her neck over a fence to take a peek. She spotted a blue car and headed down the track to investigate. She moved with stealth, eyes darting left to right for signs of life.

The unmade road took her to a small, fenced-in area. The vehicle turned out to be a Seat Ibiza. She stayed back but could see the car was empty. Did the person her dad had come to meet drive out here in this car? She decided there could not really be another explanation. He'd snuck down here to meet some woman and the pair of them had gone off for a romantic stroll somewhere. She couldn't rule out the fact that they may have been together in the night, snuggled up in that tent. That thought made her queasy. She imagined her dad felt so clever with all this cloak-and-dagger stuff. He'd been so careful, yet she and Jamie had unravelled his crafty plot. That's what would hurt the most. His stupid, clueless kids catching him out so easily.

But then she considered her mum. Why would he come here, to this place, when she was only forty minutes up the road? Why be so careful in one respect, yet so reckless in another?

All these questions made her brain ache. Louisa saw a pathway winding down through a line of tall, thick trees. There were no other routes in sight, and she'd not come across any footpaths or roads during her walk to this area. It was only then something else caught her eye. She crept further into the parking area for a better look, still keeping her eyes peeled for signs of life.

What was she looking at here? The remains of an old building, she decided. So, not a random parking area. No, this was once a property of some type. A wooden structure. A large outbuilding or an old cabin.

Louisa gazed at the wreckage, overcome by an odd sensation. Like she was connected to this eerie building in some inexplicable way. But that wasn't possible because, to the best of her knowledge, she'd never been out here before.

What had happened here, and why did this place fill her with such a growing, unexplainable sadness?

98

HANNAH

Hannah focused on a lily pad out on the water and the many insects hovering around it. She contemplated the idea of running, yet a voice in her head told her that would be a hopeless idea. Where would she flee to? There was nothing but vast countryside surrounding them. She had her phone, but would there be enough time to grab it and call 999 before they stopped her?

Hannah moved her eyes away from the water. She gazed at Chloe, who now really did look so very pleased with herself. Still with that childlike grin. A grin that irritated Hannah but now also chilled her to the very core. Then she turned to face Max. His expression was one of mild bemusement. Was this because Hannah hadn't panicked or broken down? She'd purposely fixed her face into a stoic mask, despite the fact that her lungs felt like they'd been filled with water, and it had become a battle to draw air into them. She eyed the claw hammer hanging at his side and swallowed in her dry, sore throat.

Max's eyes flicked between them.

Hannah couldn't work out if he was angry at her, at both of them, or even if he was angry at all.

It seemed like a long time had passed and no one had spoken.

Hannah broke the silence and said, 'It's a lovely spot. I take it this place holds some significance to one or both of you. You going to tell me what happened here?'

Max tossed the hammer between his hands. 'You don't look worried, Hannah. Quite the tough cookie, aren't you? You want to show me how tough you are?'

Hannah eyed him and opted to stay quiet.

Max held out the hammer and gestured for Hannah to take it. 'Take it. Show me how much you love me. Go on, show me.'

'Max, what are you doing?' protested Chloe in a pathetic voice. 'She doesn't love you. You know she doesn't!'

He offered the hammer's handle to Hannah and nodded. 'Go on, take it and we can set things right. You want to be with me, don't you? Take care of this mad whore so we can be together properly. Like you wanted from the start.'

Chloe waved her hands in a dramatic gesture. 'No, what are you doing? Oh, no.'

Hannah edged away from the pair of them. 'I'm guessing drama wasn't your strong suit at school, Chloe. You can drop the bullshit act. I'm not playing along with this fucked up nonsense.'

For a split second, Hannah was tempted to snatch the hammer from his grasp, yet she decided against this. As if he'd actually intended to let her take it.

Chloe chewed on her bottom lip, unable to stop a wry smile creeping onto her face. 'Aren't we being a big old spoilsport?'

Hannah took a deep breath, her mind reeling as she desperately tried to conjure up a way out of this. If she had been a stronger swimmer, she might have chanced her arm by crossing the lake. But then what? There was no obvious route to take once she reached the other side. How far would she get? Plus, she had no way of knowing how strong a swimmer Max or Chloe was.

Hannah forced out a quick, dry smile. 'I was right all along about you,' she lied.

Chloe waggled her finger. 'We both know that's not true. You were warming to me. Tell the truth.'

Hannah took a long, deep breath. 'Don't flatter yourself. That's why I told DS Kapoor what I was up to. That's why I have been updating her with details about our trip. I have been scamming you from the get-go. Same as you have me.'

The tiny grin fell from Chloe's face, and she turned to her husband. His face stayed unemotional.

Hannah stood taller and continued. 'Where do you suppose I learned about all those missing women in the first place? Susan, Michelle, Bailey. Meera's the one who's been helping me. She's been onto Max for years and had suspected you were hiding something and possibly protecting him.' She felt awful for dragging the detective back into this mess, but she'd run out of options. This was all she had. 'She has my last location. Up near the road by that old building. She stayed close by last night. She's likely mere minutes away, so I'd suggest you go before it's too late.'

Max scratched his chin with the hammer. 'Nice try.'

Hannah tried to keep her composure. She had to because her life depended on it now. 'Meera suspects there are more. She also told me about Max sending those men to threaten her daughters outside their school. That was cold.'

Though Chloe's expression didn't change, the muscles in her face twitched. 'Max, you said that interfering detective had been dealt with a long time ago. We agreed you'd deal with her.'

Max lowered the hammer. 'I did. Trust me, there is no one coming. Not Meera Kapoor. Not anybody. She's conning you.'

'It doesn't sound like you did sort it out,' scoffed Chloe.

'One call from me and Meera's life would be turned into a living nightmare. She wouldn't dare,' said Max.

Was Chloe wavering? Hannah decided to keep up the pressure. 'And come on, you really think you haven't been seen with me? Your car would've been clocked countless times. You stayed in a hotel with me, for Christ's sake.'

'The car was nicked from a long-stay car park a few days ago,' said Max.

Chloe nodded and quickly added, 'The hotel was paid in cash, and I wore a good disguise.' She kept nodding as she talked. 'That's why I didn't leave the room.' A smug grin slid across her face. 'We know what we're doing.'

Hannah glared at Max. 'You've been to my house. We've been seen in bars and restaurants together. Creeper and his gang. They all saw me with you.'

'I have to speak to my registered informers now and again. It won't be a huge surprise that someone like you has gone missing. The circles you move in,' said Max.

The cocksure smile on his face said it all. He didn't care. The egotistical bastard believed himself to be untouchable.

'No one will believe you,' said Hannah, with little conviction.

Max just gave a nonchalant shrug. 'They will. That's even if they make the connection. Which is doubtful.'

Hannah's heart was beating so fast it hurt. It was taking everything she had to keep it together. She wanted to make a run for it. The urge to sprint up the hill became agonising. Yet, she stayed put and firmly said, 'I'm not afraid. I'm not afraid of either of you.'

Chloe took the hammer from Max's hands. 'Good. That's so good to hear.'

'You don't want me to be afraid?' asked Hannah, taking a backward step away from them in the lake's direction. 'Did something happen here, Chloe? Did something important happen at this spot? What's drawing you back? This place has meaning, doesn't it?'

Max tutted and sighed. 'Here we go. She's playing the psychologist now.'

'You can't talk your way out of this. You had your fun with my man. Now you need to face up to what you've done,' said Chloe, gripping the hammer with two hands. 'You tried to destroy my marriage.'

Hannah took another step back. 'We both know that's not what happened.'

'You lost your husband, so you stole mine. I can't have that. I can't let it go,' said Chloe, eyes raging and alert as she inched closer.

Hannah's mind raced, and then a cold realisation stirred.

Had Max been given carte blanche to cheat? It all fell into place. Like a lightbulb snapping on and blinding her, everything made a sudden, awful sense. As Meera had said, she believed he targeted a certain type of individual. Widows, or women existing in a pit of grief with links to crime or addiction. Women that wouldn't be missed, were forgotten by society, or were already close to the edge.

Women like her.

Max's job was to get close to the victim. To make them feel safe and wanted before he gradually broke them down and left them lost and feeling like they had nowhere to turn. He used his power to manipulate and destroy them, leaving them fearful of what he might do next. Then Chloe steps in to befriend them. To draw them into her strange little world, offering to help them solve their issues with her corrupt husband. Offering to help them take him down. And so, they begin a complex partnership with Chloe, believing it to be the only way out of that hole they are trapped in.

But they are being led into another hole.

Into a vicious trap.

Lured into the beast's lair. A beast hungry for blood. And here stood Hannah in that very lair, but the real beast wasn't Max. He was the bait if anything.

Chloe swung the hammer at Hannah. It missed but came so close to her face she'd felt the rush of air.

'Go on! Take her down!' shouted Max. 'You can do it!'

Max's words of encouragement spurred Chloe into a wild frenzy. Hannah was forced to use her arms to defend herself, and the hammer blows smashed into her wrist. Another blow cracked against her fingers. She lost her balance and fell backwards. Chloe stood over her, swinging again, but Hannah rolled away, and the blow smacked into the dry earth so close to the side of her face that the mud showered her cheek.

Hannah jumped to her feet and pitched forward. Pain seared through her arm and fingers, causing stinging tears to cloud her eyes. Still, she refused to scream or cry out, and she turned to face Chloe once again.

'Go on. You've got this,' urged Max.

'I got this, I got this, I got this,' chanted Chloe.

'There are rules to be followed, aren't there, Chloe?' said Hannah. She clenched her teeth and fought through the pain.

'Fight back! Go on. It's better if you fight back. My friend *Chloe* fought back,' said Chloe, smiling like a lunatic. 'Most of the others didn't!'

Hannah fought down the urge to cry out as the pain in her wrist and broken fingers intensified.

Her friend Chloe…

'She's the one, isn't she? The one that started all this?' said Hannah, each word a struggle as the pain surged through her.

Chloe feigned a swipe. Hannah flinched but held her ground.

That's why she wanted all the details back at the hotel. She had wanted Hannah to provoke her, to make her jealous. So she *needed* those details. It was all part of the twisted process.

'Did Max cheat with her too? Is that what this is all about?' asked Hannah. She'd moved so far down the clearing now she was standing in the shallow water.

End of the road.

Max was sitting down now. He had his hand on the old stereo and watched them intently.

'So what, are you trying to relive the experience?' Hannah asked her. 'You keep repeating history to try to reawaken the feeling, don't you?'

Chloe's face twitched and she chewed her lip.

'But it's not the same, is it? It doesn't matter how many women you lure down here, it's just never quite the same. I'm right, aren't I, Chloe? Is that even your name, or did you take it from your friend after you murdered her?'

Max's wife stopped advancing, though the hammer was still poised and ready. 'It will be the same this time because you're like her. You have spirit. You have fight in you, just like she did. The rest cried like pathetic wrecks. Max chose well with you.' She laughed. 'He didn't even choose you like the others. You just fell right into his lap. Fate, I think. Right place, right time.'

'Did she deserve it? Your best friend?'

'Yes!'

'Because she stole Max, right?'

Chloe glowered and nodded. 'You're smarter than I thought you were.'

Hannah shook her head. 'And do I deserve it?'

'Yes,' said Chloe weakly.

'He always makes you believe, doesn't he? Makes you wonder if perhaps this time it's not part of the game.'

'That's what makes it so special. So… real.'

'I opened up to your husband. I told…' She glared at Chloe. 'I opened up to you as well. I told you about stuff I have never spoken of. I told you about my son!' Hannah shouted the words so vehemently it made the other woman flinch. 'If you want to kill me then come and try. I'm ready to die. Are you?'

'I won't die here. I can't. My kids need me. Nobody needs you. You're nothing but a wretched drunk.' Her eyes were red and watery, with a flicker of apprehension in them now.

Max got up and headed their way. 'Do you need some help? I do want breakfast at some point this century.' He spoke as if Chloe was taking too long in the shops, and he was getting bored with waiting; not someone addressing a psychopath about to butcher his lover with a claw hammer.

'I can manage,' grumbled Chloe, shooting him a scathing look that suggested he was ruining the moment. 'I've got this. Stop fretting, honey.'

Max huffed. 'Just finish what you started.'

Hannah could hardly process the absurdity of the situation.

These two had clearly been living this life for so long it probably seemed almost normal to them these days.

'This is some fucked-up role play, guys. Have you ever considered that you're maybe not quite right for each other?' said Hannah in a deliberately sarcastic tone. 'Take it from me, you've taken the term "toxic relationship" to an entirely new level.'

Max leaned forward and kissed Chloe on the neck. He flashed Hannah a baleful look as he did this. 'Ignore me. Take as long as you need. Make it last. Make it hurt.'

Hannah touched her battered fingers and tears fell from her eyes. The fight was ebbing away now. She was overcome with a sickening exhaustion.

Maybe it didn't matter. She thought of Ollie and the last time she had seen him. His milky-white skin, his shaggy, matted hair clinging to his sickly face.

He'd come to her for help. Come to his mummy, and instead of being there for him, she'd neglected him. She'd let him down.

Now this was her punishment.

She shouldn't fight it.

Just let it happen.

Switch... off.

But don't scream.

No matter how much pain they inflicted, she vowed to persevere and suck it up. Promised herself to die silently and with dignity.

Max's cold voice again. 'Make her suffer.' Then, in a softer voice, he said, 'If this is to be the last one, make it count.'

'The kids are asking too many questions. It's getting way too risky now they are getting older,' said Chloe, now sounding more like a concerned mother than a demented killer.

Max nodded and rolled his eyes. 'Tell me about it.'

They were talking like Hannah wasn't even there now.

Chloe studied the hammer with an odd, innocent smile. 'She'll sink like all the others, won't she? They'll be waiting for her.'

Max nodded. 'I'll get the music ready for when you're finished. I put the stuff we'll need in the boot of the car, so I'll fetch everything soon.'

'I'm really excited, Max. More than ever. I think this is the one,' gushed Chloe.

Hannah wanted to keep talking. Keep the battle going with more caustic comments. She wanted to tell this twisted pair that you could never recreate a special experience. It never worked. These things were only special once, and the harder you tried to repeat a past moment, the less special it felt. The hollower it became.

Whatever it was they did here had been so amazing they'd spent their entire lives trying to relive it. Trying to replicate those powerful, profound feelings.

Hannah dropped to her knees and lifted her chin as if inviting a clear shot.

'On your feet, Hannah. At least try,' said Chloe, sounding irritated.

Hannah just glared at her as she knelt in the water. She wouldn't give them the satisfaction of begging. She could hear the sad strings of her son's violin in her head. She imagined she was watching him now. A solo act. All eyes in the arena were fixed on him as he played, pure concentration etched in every line of his face.

Only, that's not your son, you delusional idiot.

The image melted away.

'Go on,' urged Max in a quiet voice.

Chloe moved closer, her expression showing a mixture of unease and eagerness. 'You've got this, you've got this,' she said to herself in a fast whisper.

Hannah closed her eyes and her tears fell. She pictured herself with Ollie and Archie many years ago. She saw them both laughing and happy. This was a genuine memory. A cherished one. She wanted that to be her last memory on earth. Yet still she could hear that mesmerising violin melody in the back of her mind.

But what *are* the rules of their game? There must be rules, thought Hannah.

The name Tara Wordsworth popped into her head. It came to Hannah like a firework exploding inside her brain.

But why?

Hannah's eyes snapped open.

Chloe, hammer at the ready, stood over her.

'Why didn't you kill PC Tara Wordsworth?' Hannah asked Max.

A brief flash of panic flicked across Max's features.

A deep frown creased Chloe's forehead. 'Who?'

Still looking past Chloe, Hannah said to Max, 'You remember her, don't you?'

Max's features darkened. 'Nice try. Again.'

'Meera said she was worried about the girl after it came out that you'd taken a shine to her,' said Hannah.

Chloe's jaw tightened. She stared at her husband. 'What's this? Who is she talking about?'

Max huffed and shook his head. 'Are you serious? She's trying to mess with your head.'

'Who is she?' hissed Chloe.

'You're playing into her hands, love,' said Max.

'I'm curious to know why she didn't end up here,' said Hannah. 'And I know she didn't because she's alive and well. Hiding in France and keeping out of your way. This happened around 2019, didn't it?'

Chloe pursed her lips. 'Who is she? I want to know who!'

Max shrugged. 'For fuck's sake. She's nobody.'

'Meera said you slept with her and then got too clingy for Tara's liking,' said Hannah.

'Lies,' said Max.

Chloe's cheeks and ears were glowing red. Her eyes were hard and full of accusation. 'Wait… 2019. No. You better not have!'

Max gritted his teeth. 'Not now.'

Chloe's cheeks turned an even brighter shade of red, and her neck veins were bulging like steel cables. 'It's not enough, is it? Has it ever been enough for you?'

Yes, there were rules to this game, Hannah now understood. Max had the licence to screw around with those women who would ultimately end up here to suffer his wife's fury.

But those were the only ones he was permitted to share a bed with.

He'd broken the rules, and it was written all over his face.

99

ROSIE

August 1993

They sat hand in hand on the grass, gazing at the cabin. Rosie, both apprehensive and jubilant, though also feeling a tad impatient, breathed in and out slowly. Max appeared relaxed. But his eyes showed signs of eagerness. They were wide and watchful.

It had been two days since they'd taken care of Chloe, and Rosie was still buzzing with exhilaration. She pictured Max now, muscles taut as he carried the empty Calor gas bottle down to the lake. She remembered the thick, blue rope wrapped around his naked torso. She'd been sitting on the lake's bank, watching him with a lazy smile. 'What if the rope rots away? Won't she float back up?'

Max had dropped the gas bottle with a donk and shook his head. 'It's strong, polypropylene rope. It'll last for years and years. By that time, she'll be nothing but bones festering on the bed.' He'd slapped the bottle and grinned. 'Help me secure her body to this.'

As Rosie had tried on Chloe's large, purple sunglasses, she'd pictured Chloe's faceless, bloated corpse. Pictured it suspended between the water's surface and the lake's bed with the heavy gas bottle tied to her ankles, preventing her hideous remains from popping up to the surface. But Max had other ideas. He'd attached the bottle to her back, tying the girl up with strong, apple-sized knots.

Rosie smiled at the recent memory. 'Will your dad remember her?' she asked.

'Nah, he only saw her twice and didn't give her a second glance.'

'He didn't question *why* you had a different girl staying over?'

'He doesn't give a toss about what I'm up to.'

Rosie rested her head on Max's shoulder. 'It sure is taking rather a long time. Maybe it's not going to work. I'm getting nervous.'

'It'll work. They're probably still asleep.'

'What if they notice it straight away? What if the smell is too strong?'

'Relax.'

'The candle might blow out when they open the bathroom door.'

'All four of them?'

She sat up and fidgeted. 'God, hurry up.'

'Can I ask you something?'

'Sure you can.'

'Why not just him? Why both of them?'

Rosie tensed and swallowed hard.

'She knew, didn't she?'

Rosie nodded. 'I tried to tell her more than once. The first time was when I was about seven.'

'She didn't believe you?'

'No. She outright refused to believe me. Said, "Don't tell horrid tales, Rosie. That's very mean, young lady." Once, she almost caught him in the act and still brushed it off as my dad just playing silly games with me.' She laughed. 'How could she not see it? It was like I was living a nightmare. Like I was…'

Max now tightened his grip on her hand. 'Shit, I'm sorry.'

'I was dying inside. I was literally dying... and she still chose him. She still chose to bury her stupid head in the sand and turn her back on me. Her own daughter. Who does that?'

'No proper mother, that's for sure.'

'When we have our children, I want to protect them. I want to shield them from the horrors of the world. I want to keep them safe. Forever.'

'We will, Rosie. I promise you that,' said Max in a gentle voice.

Rosie gazed back up at the cabin, willing something to happen. The waiting was driving her insane now. The apprehension was making the blood fizz in her veins.

'I don't want to be *her* any longer. I'd like Rosie to go away now.'

Max gave her a quick, querying glance. 'I don't follow.'

'Would it be strange if I changed my name to Chloe?'

Max shrugged. 'Not really. I don't care, it's only a name.'

'It's more than a name to me.'

'I get that.'

'Not now, obviously. In a year or so. Once I leave the care home or wherever I end up.'

'Go for it.'

'I mean, she tried to steal my life, didn't she? She tried to take away our future. Now I'm going to steal her first name. Yes, it's decided, that's what I'm going to do.'

'If you like the name, why not?'

'Yes, I do like it... I can't help feeling bad for her dad. She never even called him. He'll never know she came here. That's a little sad, isn't it?'

'From what I've learned about him, I doubt he'll give a shit. Just as well, given the fact that we... well, dealt with her.'

Rosie nodded. 'Wait... you did turn on both gas bottles, didn't you?'

'Yeah, stop flapping.'

They sat for a few minutes. A cow let out a long moo in the

distance somewhere, and she smiled at the hazy memory of being with Chloe in that meadow. Back before she'd gone and ruined everything.

'I wish it was possible to invent a time machine,' said Rosie, observing a butterfly, the colour of a tangerine, land near her trainer.

'Why?'

'So we could go back and do it again! I'd do it every year or so. It would be something to look forward to. Like when you're waiting for a holiday.'

'Better than a holiday. Way, way better than that.'

Rosie giggled. 'Yes, so much better.'

'That said, all your holidays have been here, haven't they? With me.'

'That's why I've always spent my days waiting for it.'

Max let go of her hand and stretched his arms up in the air. 'There are plenty more like her out there.' He winked at her. 'Just saying.'

The butterfly took flight, and she followed the insect's flight as it fluttered over the cabin's roof.

'Are you suggesting what I—' The immense explosion cut Rosie off mid-sentence and the pair plunged backwards.

The epic, booming blast made Rosie's ears buzz. The cabin had been completely annihilated.

The pair sat up and gazed in pure astonishment. Smoke spewed from what remained of the building. The roof was no more. Some of the cabin's walls had been blown to smithereens and bits of flaming debris lay scattered all about the field. A piece of smoking wood had even landed mere inches away from their spot.

It had been like something out of a Hollywood movie. Even better than that, because she could feel the blistering heat and smell the scorched carnage that permeated the entire area. Rosie had been worried that the blast might have been a let-down. An anticlimactic experience. It hadn't. Although, it occurred to her that had they been sitting closer, they might have been caught in the explosion themselves.

Max pulled Rosie to her feet. 'That was amazing!'

Rosie clapped her hands together and squealed in delight. 'That got them, right? That must have got them both?'

Max grinned from ear to ear. 'I'm certain nobody is walking out of that in one piece. Shall we… go closer and check?'

The choking, swirling smoke stung her eyes and got right down the back of her throat, making her expel a throaty cough. 'I'm not sure if I want to.'

Max took her by the hand and led her to the fiery mess ahead of them.

Rosie decided that today would be the start of a new life for her. She couldn't wait.

She really hoped the poor butterfly hadn't been wiped out in the ruinous blast. She'd have hated being responsible for killing that helpless little thing.

100

LOUISA

The long grass hid Louisa as she crouched on the hillside and took in the scene below her. This couldn't be right. What she was seeing had to be a figment of her imagination.

Her dad stood in a clearing that led down to a vast lake. Her mum, too.

And *her*. The other woman. The one Louisa had visited. The one who'd reeked of booze. She held her arm and appeared to be injured.

What was happening here? There was clear tension between the three of them. But her mum appeared the most enraged. Perhaps she'd caught this pair out here? Had she finally taken Louisa's advice on board and acted against him?

Had Jamie given her their dad's location? Did he even have it? She was unable to remember sending it to her brother, although she couldn't dismiss the possibility. After all, her recollection of the previous night was fuzzy.

Thick, fluffy clouds covered the sky while the sun did its best to break through. She spotted white swans on the water and a no swimming sign by the lake's edge. And was that some type of old stereo down there?

'You've let her get inside your head. Can't you see that, Chloe?' said her dad firmly.

Her mum squared up to him and Louisa sensed her mum's burning fury even from up on the hill.

Her dad sneered and said, 'She's not the first one to attempt to lie her way out of this. Why would you believe her?'

'Look me in the eye. You stare me right in the eye and swear on our children. Go on... Can't do it, can you? You can't because what she's just said is the truth.'

Louisa let out a silent gasp when she caught sight of the hammer in her mum's hands.

Her mum was going to attack her dad. She needed to do something to stop this.

101

HANNAH

Hannah edged away from the couple as their arguing intensified. She decided this would likely be the only chance she'd get. Whatever happened with this pair, she knew they'd never be prepared to let her go now. Not with everything she'd found out today.

'You can't swear it, can you? I can see it in your eyes,' said Chloe. Her face was still flushed dark red, and she quivered, consumed by intense fury. 'I let you have your way! Let you get it all out of your system. But you've still taken more!' she bellowed.

Max, keeping a straight face, said, 'Stop getting worked up. It hardly matters.'

'It matters. It matters so, so much and you are well aware it does. So don't make out it doesn't!' yelled Chloe. She sobbed, teeth gritted. 'I bet there have been others. There have, haven't there?'

Max let out a narked sigh. 'No!'

'Liar!' snapped Chloe.

Hannah took another step. Still, neither of them seemed to notice.

'Oh, so I fucked a woman, and you didn't get to smash her face in for once. Get over it.' As soon as those words came out, it was clear from his expression he'd regretted letting them spill out.

Chloe pulled a peculiar face. Her eyebrows rose impossibly high, and she sucked in her lips so hard it looked like they'd vanished inside her face. She stomped her foot like a huffy child. 'You've ruined it! Ruined everything, you selfish, selfish fool!'

'If it means that much to you, we'll find the bitch and—'

Max didn't get to finish. Chloe lashed out with a lightning-quick strike with the hammer that caught him straight against the side of the head.

Hannah froze. It had been a serious blow and she was amazed he'd stayed on his feet.

Max, eyes wide in shock and outrage, gaped at his wife for a few seconds before falling hard onto his backside.

Chloe, stunned by her actions yet still clearly raging, raised the hammer and prepared another swing.

A shrill scream echoed through the clearing.

A figure came charging out of nowhere.

A young girl.

'No, don't!' the girl screeched.

Hannah watched the scene as if it played out in slow motion.

As the girl ran at the pair waving her hands and yelling, she witnessed Chloe spin and, in a crazed, spontaneous act, smashed the girl straight across the forehead with the hammer.

The hammer hit with a brutal, echoing crack. The girl crumpled on impact and did not move.

Hannah saw that the wound was terrible. It had opened up the skin above the girl's right eye. Enough to show a few inches of bone.

Chloe froze as she viewed the girl and the awful injury she'd inflicted on her. A dreadful recollection lingered on her face. She knew the teenager.

Chloe stumbled over and let the hammer drop from her fingers.

She crouched and touched the girl's injured face. Examined

the damage with a mortified, open-mouthed expression of sheer panic and disbelief.

'No, please don't let this be happening!' screamed Chloe, placing her hand over her mouth and gagging. This action smeared blood over her face, and she seemed to comprehend what she'd done and retched.

Hannah watched on, speechless.

Chloe wiped her mouth with the back of her hand but spread the gore further and this caused her to sob. She stood, stumbled, and dropped to her knees. She pulled up handfuls of dead grass, threw the tufts aside, and screamed in violent, hysterical rage as she hammered both fists against the ground until her knuckles were split and red with bloody grazes.

Chloe's behaviour reminded Hannah of an enraged gorilla warning off an aggressor. The scene was harrowing beyond belief.

Hannah wanted to check on the girl but feared Chloe would lunge at her, so she remained motionless. She noticed Max was still alive, and he lay slumped on his side, breathing in shallow rasps, eyes reeling. Streams of blood ran down one side of his face.

Chloe pulled herself up and then stumbled backwards and fell onto her bum. 'This is your fault!' she roared. She found her feet again and snatched up the hammer. 'I'm going to hell for this. I'm going to be dragged there by the devil himself. And I'm taking you with me!'

For a moment, Hannah, so absorbed in the terrifying moment, thought Chloe had aimed those words at her, but the woman was glaring at her husband now and she was incandescent with a wild rage.

Hannah's eyes flicked back to the girl, certain she was dead or close to the end. She wanted to yell at Chloe. Tell her they needed to act. That they needed to get her to the hospital pronto, yet she could not find her voice. She set her eyes back on the couple and Chloe was hissing and screeching and giving off the impression she wanted to bash Max to a pulp.

Then Chloe finally acknowledged Hannah. She eyed her with a heart-piercing sadness that was harrowing to behold. Hannah saw how tortured and broken this woman was and, despite herself... despite everything she'd done, she felt a touch of both sorrow and anguish for her. 'Your daughter,' Hannah managed to say in a croaky whisper.

'Now I truly understand your suffering,' said Chloe, her voice barely audible, cracked and raw. Her rage appeared to be ebbing away and her lips were trembling. She started for the water, stopped and said, 'I beg you, don't leave my baby girl here. Not here. Take her far away from this place. My Louisa doesn't belong here with the rest of them.' She tugged off her wedding ring and blindly tossed it to the side. Then she stepped into the lake and waded in.

Hannah darted over to the girl and took her pulse. Could she feel it? *Yes... just about.* There was a very slight thump... thump... thump in her neck; she was sure there was. 'Stay with me. I'll take you away from here. Louisa, you stay with me!'

Hannah turned to check on Chloe and a scream escaped her when she saw Max standing over her, his face a twisted, bloodied mask of delirious fury.

Hannah scrambled up and tried to scurry away from him. She hadn't moved quickly enough, and he grabbed her about the throat with both hands. 'Get away from my... daughter,' he garbled, sounding like a livid drunk. He squeezed hard, eyes bulging with a deadly hatred. But he was struggling to hold on to her, and she could already feel his strength draining away. His legs buckled and he almost fell, and Hannah fought free of his grasp, though not before his nails dug into her flesh.

Max tried to go for her a second time, but he didn't have the legs for it, and this time she darted away from his lunge. He wobbled and groaned. Then he dropped to his knees and made a ghastly wailing noise, like an animal dying in agony. He swayed left to right and then convulsed, his eyes flicking up into his head. He went limp and fell sideways.

Hannah, breathing in deep, ragged breaths now, caught sight

of Chloe out in the lake. She'd stopped chest deep with her arms spread out wide, the hammer still clutched in her right fist.

Hannah was about to call out. To shout and tell her that her daughter was still alive, and she could not move the girl without help. Not with her own injuries. But then Chloe smashed herself on the side of the head with the hammer and, with a silent plunge, disappeared into the water.

102

HANNAH

Three days later

Hannah opened her eyes and was surprised to see DS Meera Kapoor standing in front of her. The detective looked drained and a little sheepish. 'Hello, Hannah, how are you?'

Hannah rubbed her weary face. Her eyes instinctively shot up to the monitor above Louisa's bed.

Meera stood next to the ventilator and stared at the inactive teenager with a sad smile. She touched her bandaged head. 'I heard you've been routinely checking in on the girl.'

Hannah nodded. 'I only intended to come once. Turns out she doesn't have any family. Apart from her brother, who's been taken into care. They are bringing him here to see her later, so I'll make myself scarce.'

'It's a terrible situation.'

Hannah got up out of the seat and stretched out her back. 'I should tell the nurse this catheter needs to be changed. It's almost full.'

'Hold up. I need to talk to you.'

Hannah hesitated. 'I shouldn't keep coming here. It's stupid. I don't even know her.'

'You saved her.'

Hannah eyed Louisa. The ICP monitor. The tubing in her nose. The IV fluid and various bits of intimidating-looking wires and equipment. She hated hospitals. They just made her think of her Ollie. Had she saved the girl? She didn't look like someone who'd been saved.

If anything, the teenager was the one who'd saved her.

'She might never wake up,' said Hannah.

'You still got her away from that place. She would've died there with her parents, and you know it.'

Hannah gave a self-deprecating shrug and said, 'If I hadn't found her two friends parked up, I'd have never been able to carry her away. I couldn't even get her to the top of that hill with my useless arm.'

'But you did find them. You were the one who saved her. There's no need to be modest. When she comes around… and she will, she'll be eternally grateful.'

Maybe it's best if she doesn't wake up to the circus that will be her life, Hannah thought grimly. 'She came to my house once. She must've sensed something was wrong with her parents.'

'Her brother has confirmed that he and his sister had been using a pet camera and key tracker to check on their dad. They presumed he was playing away. That's how the girl came to be there.'

'Shrewd kids.'

'How are you? I mean, really? After what you went through, you must be in bits.'

Hannah held up her cast and splinted fingers. 'I got off lightly, considering what they had planned for me.'

Meera gazed at the floor and heaved a big sigh. 'You came to me for help and I… I'm so sorry.'

'You did help me.'

'Helped lead you into their trap. I should've given you the assistance you needed. My actions were disgraceful.'

'Your main concern was your family. I get it.'

Meera touched Louisa's arm and Hannah wondered exactly why the detective had sought her out here. A cynical person might assume she'd come here to cover her tracks. To smooth things over with her in case she'd decided to tell her full story to the media. If it came out that Hannah had gone to the DS for help, and it became common knowledge that she'd given her historical case information, yet she'd refused to assist her further or report her ex-colleague, then this would likely spell disaster for her career.

'I won't mention your involvement. You don't need to worry,' said Hannah.

Meera gave her a relieved smile and nodded her thanks. She stroked Louisa's arm and said, 'Bloody hell, Louisa, how will you possibly deal with finding out that your parents have been prolific serial killers since 1993. I can't even imagine.'

A collection of newspaper headings flashed in Hannah's mind.

Quaint, quiet place holds gruesome secrets.

Women lured to their deaths by the heinous couple dubbed: The Lakeside Slayers.

Another paper showed a photo of the crooked *"Strictly No Swimming"* sign with the words: *Picture-perfect lake, now known as The Lake of Dread, unearthed as a sinister graveyard for ten missing women from the London and Gloucestershire area.*

Had the murderous couple put the sign there? The elderly landowners claimed they hadn't. The idea of someone taking a quick dip into that water made Hannah cringe. Hopefully the sign had deterred anyone who'd stumbled upon the hidden place.

Hannah sat back down and put her head in her hands.

Meera snorted. 'People are speaking out against him now he's dead. Career criminals, drug dealers, other officers. Now they all want to put the boot in and have their say. They all *knew* he was dodgy.' She grunted. 'Arseholes. What's the point now?'

Hannah frowned yet didn't voice her thoughts on the matter.

Didn't tell the detective that she might've prevented some of the deaths had she stood her ground with Max. Though she understood why she'd been too afraid to challenge the dangerous man.

Meera cleared her throat. 'It's so stuffy in here.'

'The youngest girl they found…'

'Chloe Sark.'

'His wife spoke of her when we were at the lake. The papers said she was just sixteen.'

Meera nodded. 'In August 1993, Miss Sark left her dad a note saying she was going on a trip to see a friend. Never said where. Never came back to London.'

'I believe Max cheated on her with Chloe. That's what triggered this entire thing. I'm certain of it.'

Meera nodded again. 'She was their first victim, so your theory fits. Turns out Max's wife was called Rosie Grimshaw until she changed her name to Chloe when she was seventeen. She married Max the next year. Looks like they lured a victim there every three years since killing Chloe Sark.'

'The papers have named me as "the one who got away",' said Hannah.

'You are.'

Hannah would've been the eleventh victim and, from how the murderous pair had spoken that day, perhaps the last.

'The building. Those burned remains… what was that?'

'The place was owned by Terry and Claire Grimshaw. Rosie's parents. It was their holiday cabin. The couple owned a furniture store in North Harrow and came to their little Wiltshire retreat a few times a year. What would you say if I told you historical records confirm they both died there? An internal gas explosion. The cooker in the kitchen was wired up via gas bottles and there'd been a leak. Some candles in the bathroom ignited the fumes and… boom!'

'When?'

'August 1993.'

'Jesus.'

'It's just come out, so expect to see it all over the front pages tomorrow.'

'It was them, wasn't it?'

'Well, it is looking likely. Probably never prove it now. The plot of land was passed down to their daughter, but it's been left as a neglected patch of ground ever since their deaths. Now the only people who know the truth are gone.'

What would cause a teenage girl to kill her own parents in such a way? Atrocious thoughts popped into Hannah's mind, and she shuddered. Had a young Max manipulated a damaged Rosie Grimshaw back then? No wonder she'd been so messed up.

'He got it wrong, didn't he?' said Meera, breaking Hannah from her moment of eerie contemplation.

'Sorry?'

'Max misjudged you. Saw you as easy pickings.'

Hannah pictured herself on her knees as she'd waited for the final blow to come. The blow which would've ended it all. There'd been a few seconds when she'd given up and accepted her fate. Had she even welcomed it? A frightening thought.

Would she really have been their last victim? She doubted that. She suspected the pair would never have stopped. Couldn't have. Killing was like a drug to them.

Their very own addiction.

'I should've checked her out properly. It was naïve of me not to even consider his wife might've been involved,' said Meera.

'You had your sights set on Max.'

Meera gazed at Louisa. 'You've been given a second chance, Hannah. You should take it.'

Hannah nodded. 'I'm going to try.'

And she meant it.

103

CHLOE

April 2009

She'd never in her life seen a more beautiful baby. She cradled her precious child and cried tears of happiness. She kissed her delicate head and thought she might pop with joy. 'You smell scrumptious, my angelic, adorable little pumpkin.'

'Well? You happy, Mrs Hudson?' her husband asked with a tired smile. His shirt was crumpled and his hair ruffled. He did appear rather bedraggled.

'So, so happy. I'm sure my heart is going to explode.'

'You look amazing, considering how long that took. Thirteen hours and you have a sparkle in your eye like I have never seen before. I just glimpsed myself in the mirror. I look rougher than you do.'

'Does Daddy want to hold his special little bundle?'

'Later. Not right now.'

She kissed her baby once again. 'Good, more snuggles for Mummy, my tiny squishy boo-boo. And it was almost fourteen hours, wasn't it? But every second was worth it. That's all forgotten now, right, snuggle sausage?'

'I'll be glad to get out of this ward,' he said, gazing around the white-walled room. 'You decided on a name yet?'

She smiled and let out an excited giggle. 'Yes!'

'Well?'

She brushed her fingers over the baby's shock of fluffy brown hair. 'Louisa.'

'Interesting.'

'What?'

He cracked a brief, sly grin. 'Nothing.'

'You don't like it?' She kissed the baby again and whispered, 'Well, we do, don't we?'

'No, I like it.'

'I told you Daddy would like it, didn't I, pickle pants?'

He rubbed his stubbled face and paced the room.

'Poor Daddy looks sleepy,' she whispered to the baby.

'What will happen now, Chloe? What about our... our thing? Do we stop?'

She considered this for a moment. Would Bailey Lloyd really be the last? That had been such an anticlimactic experience last year, so it was a sombre thought. She'd been hopeful Max would pick a better playmate for them next time. Someone with a bit more stoic resistance. The idea of having to wait another two years was disheartening, but she knew the rules. They both did. They had to wait. That's what made the pursuit so thrilling. God, how she enjoyed the build-up. How she revelled in that time before. As Max did his thing and got the target ready for her to swoop in and play her part. When she pretended to be their saviour and would rescue them from whatever dark hole Max was leading them into. He was very good at manipulating them and locating their weakness. A bit too good, she sometimes worried.

'Will being here solve the problems? Will it make things easier next time?' she asked.

'There'll be far more opportunities in London. It's a much bigger area for us to work with. Less prying eyes. You should know that. You grew up in North-west London, love.'

'I didn't see the side of the city that you do, Max. You sure this will work out?'

'Trust me, we'll have plenty to choose from. It'll work out perfectly.'

'She comes first, Max. *She* will always come first. Is that clear?'

'Yes.'

'Should the time ever come when our thing has an impact on our child's life, then we must stop.'

'Agreed.'

'You promise?'

He nodded and used his finger to cross his heart.

'And please… don't ever, ever break our rules. You won't, will you?'

'I swear, I won't.'

'Because I couldn't take it. I couldn't stand the thought… It can only be the way it's always been. From the start.'

'You need to rest now.' He scanned the door and raised his eyebrows. 'This isn't the place, Chloe.'

'OK. I know. Sorry.'

'I'm going to grab a sandwich. Want anything?'

'Max, do you ever question if you made the right decision that day?'

'About what?'

'About picking me?'

He let out a huff, followed by a quick, dry laugh. 'Never.'

'Do you ever imagine yourself with…' She lowered her voice and said, 'With her? With…' She almost said the *other* Chloe but hated calling her that. She was Chloe now. Not her. 'With Sark? Do you ever imagine what your life would be like now?'

'You shouldn't speak that name,' he said in an irate whisper.

She narrowed her eyes. 'That's not an answer.'

'I chose you. If we repeated history a million times, it would still be *you*.'

'There was a moment when I was certain you were somewhat conflicted about whose side you were on. Tell me I'm talking nonsense. Go on.'

'We have been through this so many times. I was testing you. I had to find out how serious you were about me. I never wanted her. She was nothing but a bitch and a user.'

She kissed her baby once again. 'Do we believe Daddy?' She placed her ear close to the child's tiny mouth and pretended to listen. 'Uh-huh. Yep. OK, me too, sweet potato.' She smiled warmly at her husband. 'We both believe you.'

Max made a clicking sound with his tongue and nodded. 'Glad that's all sorted, then. I'll catch you in a bit.' He walked to the door and pulled it open.

'There's no rush. We're fine here. We are absolutely fine.'

Max left.

She closed her eyes and saw a vivid image of Chloe Sark's body floating in the depths of the lake. The faceless corpse drifting among the long reeds as tiny fish darted to avoid the bloated alien now swaying in their watery habitat. Saw the frantic webbed feet belonging to those swans as their spindly legs worked hard to propel them across the water.

She visualised the process of the body's decomposition and saw it with perfect clarity as though watching a nature documentary on fast forward.

The girl sinking. Skin rotting away from her body at the bed of the lake. Pictured her old friend perishing until there was nothing but bones. The Calor gas bottle covered in green slime. The tatty rope fluttering about in the weeds and mud. Ragged bits of purple material from her crop top. Watched a fish swim through the right eye socket of her friend's fractured skull. It was like being inside a giant aquarium. She snapped open her eyes, panting heavily.

She'd been down there.

It felt like she'd transported herself down into the gloomy depths of the lake just then.

Taking big gulps of air, she gazed down at her daughter.

'Mummy got a little lost in her thoughts there for a terrible moment. I'm back now.'

Chloe Sark, her once best friend, wasn't alone any longer. She had five companions already. But there was plenty of room down there. Plenty of room to send her more souls to keep her company for all eternity. It was the least she could do for her. After all, she'd opened this special door for her. She'd unintentionally given a messed up teenage girl called Rosie Grimshaw, a nobody loser who inflicted pain upon herself, a purpose in life.

She thought about the paranoia they'd had to deal with in the weeks following what they did to Chloe Sark. She'd been so sure someone would've linked her to the village of Little Wick or the Deer Meadows camping park. They had been sure that the lad, Griff, or one of the partygoers, might have seen something about a missing teenage girl from London and recognised her. But they didn't. Nobody came searching for answers. Nobody from back home had even known she'd gone there for a holiday.

So they'd got away with it, but even so, they were far more careful with the next teenage girl Max lured there.

Everything had been going so well until there'd been that blip in Cheltenham and Max had received some unwanted attention with that Bailey Lloyd.

But now, it seemed, they could continue with their special three-year ritual.

She booped Louisa's nose. 'Never hurt yourself, my sweet girl. Promise me you'll never, ever, and I mean *ever*, feel the need to punish yourself. We'll have the best future together. I promise.'

104

LOUISA

She became aware of voices. She'd been aware of noises for quite a while, yet she'd been unable to open her eyes to greet the world. Had she been dreaming?

Yes, lots of dreaming. She'd been to many places, with lots of people. Had amazing adventures. She recalled zany exploits. Wild capers with her friends. Her family. But none of it made much sense. Scrambled bits and pieces. Fragments of her memories spinning about her mind like miniature planets in a black expanse.

She'd recalled seeing Herbert Crunch the dinosaur. That annoying flamingo from her room, too. Had the funny bird been talking to her at some point? No, she'd been doing the talking. She'd been telling the bird to stop watching her, even though it secretly made her feel quite safe.

I miss it all now.

She thought about her brother, and his smiley face popped into her head. He looked cheerful. No doubt he wanted something from her. He usually did. He was likely being fussy about the food he had to eat, as usual.

There'd been a lake in these dreams or memories. Yes, she remembered a massive, beautiful lake. It had been like something you'd have used as a desktop screensaver. She visualised it on a PC monitor now. A hazy yellow sun on the horizon. Big white swans. Pretty flowers and springy grass sprouting from sloping banks.

But why did her heart feel so awful? So sad and heavy.

Like nothing in the world would ever be the same again.

Suddenly the thought of this lake made her uneasy. More than uneasy. It filled her with a dreadful sensation. A gut-wrenching angst that made her wish the place had never entered her head. Now she found herself unable to shake the lake from her mind.

Strictly No Swimming.

Why did she keep seeing that crooked wooden sign?

A strange voice in her head whispered, 'This place is pure evil. Only death can be found here. Death and sadness. Don't ever come back here.'

She noticed blinding lights. A figure in front of her.

Am I dead? What's wrong with me? I want to leave this place now.

Her eyes opened. Just a crack.

A blurry face. Everything was so hard to focus on.

I'm in a hospital bed surrounded by scary equipment.

There were super bright lights that burned her fragile eyes.

'Louisa, can you hear me, sweetheart?' came a soft voice. 'Take your time. You take your time. Don't rush.'

Mum, is that you? Are you here with me? she longed to ask, but could not speak.

It had to be her mum. Her mum or an angel.

She missed her mum so much. Wherever she'd been had made her understand how much she cared about her. How lucky she was to have such a wonderful person in her life. She'd never give her a hard time ever again. She'd be the perfect daughter from now on.

'Doctor, she's awake,' the soft voice said.

This wasn't her mum, after all. A nurse. A kind nurse.

The heaviness of her eyelids made it impossible to hold them open any longer and they dropped shut.

Perhaps she wasn't ready for the world just yet. Not until her mum was here to save her. Not until then.

105

HANNAH

September 2023

Hannah took careful steps as she moved along the railway bridge. She knew this would be her last visit. She'd promised herself this many times before, yet everything was different now. She was different.

Although sleep had still been eluding her most nights, she was in a better frame of mind these days. A clearer state, at least. But sometimes, due to the endless news reports, she'd keep seeing the faces of all those victims who had died at the lake, and she thought about them often. She found herself wondering about their lives, their stories, and the dreams they never had a chance to fulfil. Especially the youngest, Chloe Sark.

Sometimes she'd picture their frightened expressions as they understood they'd been tricked by the murderous couple, and she saw their horror-struck faces as they grasped they'd been manipulated and used as pawns in their twisted game and would die at that place.

Hannah put her elbows on the railings and peered down. Now, sober and seeing things with a clearer head, she wondered why she'd experienced such a connection to this bridge. Did she really believe Archie's soul had stayed trapped here? Did she honestly think that her dead husband haunted this railway line like some imprisoned spirit, unable to pass into the next world? Of course she didn't.

He died here. That was all. He'd died and his remains were cremated. There was nothing here but a dirty track and discarded litter. Her husband didn't pick this place because it held some special meaning. He'd merely been lost, tortured and confused. He'd wanted a way out and he'd ended up here and just acted.

The end.

Yet here she was again. Drawn to this damn place like Max's wife had been drawn to that lake.

Her quiet place, she'd called it.

Was this hers?

A train shot out from under the bridge and made the walkway shudder.

Hardly quiet for very long, she mused.

Hannah shook her head. 'I wish you could hear me, Archie. I really do because I'd tell you I'm three months clean and that next week I am flying to Grenada to see Mum and Aunty Grace. Yeah, I know, I'm bricking it. Just the idea of stepping on that plane... I might even stay a while and see what happens. The pair of them have this mad idea about setting up a dating agency as a second business. Can you even imagine?' She laughed and tears pricked her eyes. 'What are you doing, Hannah?' she admonished herself. Then she took a deep breath and said, 'I found out Louisa is recovering well. It's been a slow process, and it sounds like she's got a long way to go, but she's on the right path to a full recovery. I decided to stay away from her after she came out of the coma... I'm glad she woke up. So glad, but it's best we never meet again. They say she can't remember what happened at the lake; I'd say that's a blessing.' She stood up straight. 'Anyway, I'm getting my act together and I just wanted you to hear me say it. Now it's time to move on... I'm sorry.

Sorry I wasn't there for you... Sorry I was so wrapped up in my own prolonged grief that I ignored you and your problems. You needed me and I turned my back on you. I do regret that. More than you'll ever know.' She began walking, then stopped and looked back. 'I did love you. I always will. Look after our son. Until I come and find you both.' She smiled and shook her head, feeling foolish now, yet it also seemed like a huge weight had been lifted from her. There was a real sense of relief in saying those words, and she wished she'd forced herself to say them much, much sooner.

Maybe it was being here sober for once that made it all seem so different. Without the meds and booze, her dreams had been less frequent and less deep and powerful, but she'd be lying to herself if she said that Archie didn't still haunt her slumber on occasions. She'd recently dreamed of the white horse in the snowy field again. This time, the splendid beast hadn't moved away and had allowed her to take a clear photo. She took it as a hopeful sign. After all, Ollie had once told her he loved horses. Reaching into her handbag, she pulled out the tiny horse that had once been encased in the crystal ball. She studied it, a faint smile spreading across her lips, then placed it carefully on the railing, as if setting a piece of her heart free.

Now, if Hannah was honest with herself, she wanted a drink more than anything in the world. The urge to go to the nearest pub or off licence was excruciating to endure. Leaving the silver horse behind, she took the stairs down and left the bridge.

The craving would soon pass, as it always did, leaving her a little stronger and a little more resilient.

With a deep breath and a renewed sense of determination, she pressed on, embracing the promise of a brighter, clearer tomorrow.

For the first time in a long while, she felt more than a shred of optimism for the future.

It really was time to move on and let the past go.

THANKS FOR READING

Did you enjoy reading *Her Quiet Place*? Please consider leaving a review on Amazon. Your review will help others discover the novel.

https://mybook.to/herquietplace

ALSO BY ROBERT W. KIRBY

The Breakdown

Never Forget

I Remember Now

The Visit

The Wrong Girl

Survival Weekend

The Bartell Thriller Series

Prequel: A Deception on Cold Hill

Book One: A Feud on Dead Lane

Book Two: A Lethal Encounter in Amsterdam

Book Three: A Reckoning On The Blackwater (coming November 2025)

<u>Coming soon.</u>

Where the Crows Feed

Don't Look Away

Survival Weekend: Sarek

www.robertkirbybooks.com

ABOUT THE AUTHOR

I was born in 1979 and live in Kent, England, with my wife and children. For over fifteen years, I ran a private investigation agency specialising in breach of contract claims, commercial debt recovery, process serving, and people tracing. Much of my work involved tracking down debtors, assisting with adoption cases, and finding missing persons. Along the way, I handled many unusual cases and met some fascinating and often colourful characters, which have heavily influenced my writing.

If you enjoy dark crime fiction or intense psychological thrillers, don't forget to subscribe to my newsletter. You'll be the first to hear about new releases, book deals and giveaways.

Subscribe Here
Spotify Podcast

Printed in Dunstable, United Kingdom

66370559R00214